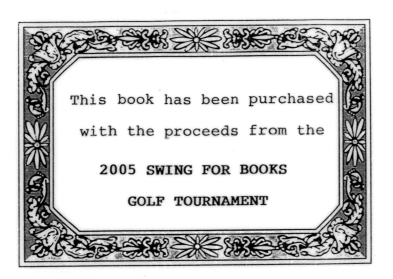

NON-COMBATANTS

NON-COMBATANTS

A novel, sequel to
WESTBOUND, WARBOUND

Alexander Fullerton

TIME WARNER
BOOKS

TIME WARNER BOOKS

First published in Great Britain in July 2005
by Time Warner Books

Copyright © Alexander Fullerton 2005

The moral right of the author has been asserted.

A CIP catalogue record for this book
is available from the British Library.

ISBN 0 316 72957 4

Typeset by Palimpsest Book Production Limited,
Polmont, Stirlingshire
Printed and bound in Great Britain by
Mackays of Chatham plc, Chatham, Kent

Time Warner Books
An imprint of
Time Warner Book Group UK
Brettenham House
Lancaster Place
London WC2E 7EN

www.twbg.co.uk

For Kate
– Ronnie's Kate, a.k.a. Katharine Gordon,
who allegedly gave up gin in Quetta.

1

'All right, Holt?'

'Aye, sir . . .' Shifting binoculars from his eyes for a moment. Dark night, tumbling sea flecked and flashing white, *Quilla* chucking herself about rather more than one might have expected in such a sea-state. An odd time for a ship's master to leave his bridge: when you could reasonably expect to be going to defence stations at any moment, were even a bit anxious on that score – and Captain Nat Beale going down for a smoke, snooze, snack, whatever. One didn't know him yet. Having signed on only two days ago as second mate of this ship – SS *Barranquilla*, tramp steamer of 7,050 tons gross, Glasgow-registered – met him then for the purpose of signing on, of course, but only a few times and briefly since; they'd not even been a whole day at sea yet. All Andy Holt could have said of his new captain at this stage was that he was a Scot, aged forty-two – might have guessed older, but that was the truth of it – and that he liked what he'd seen and heard of him this far. Would have expected to, in fact; might have been a poor outlook if one hadn't. And Harve Brown, the mate, with whom Andy had sailed before and knew well, had said he was a good man: that he watched points fairly craftily out of those seemingly easy-going, often humorous grey eyes, and reacted badly to either incompetence or bullshit; which was as it should be, in Harve Brown's and one's own view, and the expressions of approval incidentally reflected well on Harve himself, by contrast still a first officer at forty-six. A generous-spirited character, who by experience and seniority might well have had his own ship long before this, yet had been lumbered with medical problems including a dicky heart which a year ago they'd thought might kill him. It had been a pleasant surprise to find him here in the *Barranquilla* – to have him as first mate, one's own immediate superior, but in any case heartening that he should have recovered well enough to be back in a seagoing job.

Old Man growling as he started down the bridge ladder, steadying himself as *Quilla* – the diminutive by which her own people knew her – rolled harder than usual to starboard, 'I'll not be long, Second.'

Which explained it. Call of nature. Must have been up here eight or nine hours: certainly had been when Andy had taken over at midnight, probably throughout the third mate's watch before that, and the dogwatches too, a long stint during which the convoy had been getting itself through the war channel and then into shape. So, wise move, since it was odds-on that any minute now the U-boats would be raising their ugly snouts and you'd be going to defence stations; Old Man stuck up here for sure then, probably until dawn or later. The U-boats might well have embarked on their fun and games an hour or two sooner than this, in fact: during the late afternoon and evening the air-waves had been foul with chatter, according to the Marconi boys, a natural assumption being that they were preparing for a busy night. As likely as not, one of them shadowing and others homing in on him during recent hours. And for 'busy' night, read 'happy' night; there'd been a report a week ago in the *Glasgow Herald* that U-boat men were calling this summer of 1940 their 'happy time': targets galore, opposition minimal, night attacks on the surface gutting convoy after convoy.

Starting late tonight – or this morning rather, if they were going to start at all: 0130 now, 4 August, a Sunday.

2

As dark as it was going to get, the convoy in its formation as ordered, and well clear of the North Channel, having come through the mine-swept war channel in double file before having anything like room to form up. Now, four hours after completion of that nerve-racking evolution, you had Barra Head forty-five miles northeast and Bloody Foreland – appropriately named, being more or less the focal point of the bastards' depredations in recent months – seventy-five miles southwest. Which left a heck of a lot of sea-room on that side, where *Quilla* was ploughing her own broad white furrow in the port-hand column.

She was number four in column seven: three ships ahead of her and only one astern. That one – the *Harvest Queen* – even more vulnerable than *Quilla* having no sheltering neighbours either outside her or astern. The bastards did attack from astern when it suited them; on the surface they could get eighteen knots out of their diesels, whereas this convoy's ordered speed was only twelve, and *Quilla*'s best – flat-out, with her engineers sitting on all the valves – allegedly a fraction over fourteen and a half.

Convoy escorted, incidentally, by one sloop. *One.* Out there in the dark ahead somewhere. Forty-one merchantmen – four columns of five ships, and three – the central ones – of seven – escorted by a single sloop, which typically would be nine or ten years old, displace about a thousand tons, be armed with two four-inch guns and boast a top speed, when in good heart and clean-bottomed, of maybe sixteen knots. So the U-boats outpaced her as well. She'd be half a mile ahead, he guessed, crabbing to and fro across the convoy's front in the hope of maybe intercepting a surfaced U-boat on its way to penetrate the columns of plunging, blacked-out ships and let loose with torpedoes at ranges where the things could hardly miss. Even on a night like this one, with the moon and scatterings of stars showing through when breaks in the cloud permitted, a U-boat stood a

3

good chance of getting in unseen. Even when you had several escorts. A U-boat being a mere sliver to the eye, especially bow-on; and even when technically surfaced would still be low in the night-black sea, more in it in fact than on it. And while from the bridges and bridge-wings of the freighters watchkeepers could only strain their eyes downward at the shifting, heaving black confusion that hid the predators, they had their potential victims in bulky elevation against a less than totally dark sky.

Moon flushing the seascape again. Andy lowering his glasses slightly, glancing across the darkened bridge and telling the seventeen-year-old cadet who was his dogsbody on this watch – 'Check lookouts awake and on their toes, Dixon.' Ensuring he was on *his* toes, as much as chivvying the lookouts in the bridge-wings. Hearing the young Londoner's acknowledgement of the order: glasses up again, probing the port-side seascape in this flush of moonglow, taking advantage of it while it lasted. As any U-boat skipper out there would be doing too. But sweeping the port side first because attacks didn't *have* to be made from ahead or astern, or from inside the convoy's columns, and one was very conscious of the apparently empty wilderness to port – well aware it wasn't necessarily all that empty and that if one of its denizens got its sights on you, you could as well say you were done for. Simply how things *were*, when your primary defences were no more than your own binoculars and a few look-outs' sharp eyes and alertness in all the confusing vagaries of light and darkness.

Quilla rolling harder than she was pitching, meanwhile, and the quartermaster – Selby, Yorkshireman, shortish, thickset, square-jawed, eyes under his woollen cap reflecting the soft glow of the gyro repeater – shifting the wheel this way and that to hold her within a degree or two of the ordered course, 305 degrees. Being in ballast, deep-tanks filled but cargo-holds empty, *Quilla* was fully entitled to react in lively fashion to the long Atlantic swells powering in from the southwest. Westerlies, these winds were called: gentle enough at this stage, for sure, but ocean-wide in their scope, sweeping from the seaboards of North America and Canada, driving up over Iceland and the Faeroes into the Norwegian and Barents seas. One had known some very heavy weather in these latitudes, one truly had. Six months ago, as a prime example, in a ship by name of *PollyAnna*, which having sprung a leak had damn near foundered; at the height of it, in hurricane-force winds and with number two hold filled to its brimming hatch-cover, his own over-riding concern had been for Julia, survivor of another ship in which she'd been a passenger.

She was as much in his mind now as she had been then.

Having searched the port side from the quarter to the bow, he was routinely checking on *Quilla*'s next-ahead, focusing on the dimmed stern light. The MV *Daisy Oakes*. Distance still about right, near enough 600 yards, no need for adjustment of engine revs, which did tend to be necessary at frequent intervals in convoy. Six hundred yards between ships in column, 1,000 laterally between the columns, convoy thus three nautical miles wide and nearly two miles deep – quite a large area of what you might call inhabited sea, a whole community of ships and seamen shifting steadily northwestward at twelve knots. A check to starboard confirming now that station-keeping this far was unusually good: the little *Bristolian*, no more than 4,000 tons, was right there on the beam, a blossom of whitened ocean just about exactly where it should have been.

With the glasses – second-hand but good ones, Kershaws, a present from his father to mark his alleged achievements in the *PollyAnna* – he could make the *Bristolian* out better than that, too. Low funnel practically right aft, bridge superstructure amidships also low but extensive in relation to her length. She'd been anchored close to *Quilla* at Tail of the Bank in the Clyde estuary, where they'd spent some days while that section of the convoy gathered, so that her profile had become familiar – still was, even in the dark at a distance of half a mile and throwing herself around. In ballast, of course, like *Quilla*, as most of the ships in this convoy would be – barring a few who were down to their summer marks with Welsh coal. That lot would have come up from Barry, Cardiff and Newport, to rendezvous off Belfast, where those from the Mersey had been waiting for them in the Lough.

Training left now, pausing on the ship ahead of the *Bristolian:* effort of memory getting its name – memorised from the convoy diagram he'd pinned above the chart table – as SS *Cedarwood.* Somewhat ahead of station, too wide a gap between those two. *Bristolian* should crack on a bit, he thought – except then she'd be out of station on *Quilla.* So the *Cedarwood* was ahead of her station, had to be crowding her next-ahead.

He was edging his glasses slightly further left to check on that one, whatever her name might be, when the *Daisy Oakes* was hit. You heard the deep, booming *thud* of a torpedo striking, swung in that direction – left – saw the pillar of upflung black water collapsing white across her, and had an impression – all it could be, through the dark and movement and in a matter of just seconds – that she'd begun a swing away to port. Guesswork taking a hand then: that she might have seen her attacker, jammed on rudder in an attempt to ram or to save herself by 'combing the tracks'. He had a thumb on the button of the alarm that buzzed in the Old Man's cabin, then on the klaxon alarm that would send the hands to their defence stations. Glasses meanwhile one-handed and still focused on the stricken *Daisy Oakes* – who *was* sheering out to port, thus allowing *Quilla* to hold on as she was going. He told Selby, 'Steady as you go', and the Old Man as he arrived like a ton of bricks beside him in the bridge's forefront, 'Our next-ahead, sir. Hit port side. She's hauling out that way.'

6

'I'm on her.'

Quilla holding her course of 305 degrees, pitching and battering on, the *Daisy Oakes* stern-down and with a growing list to port as she swung away. *Quilla* had had all her boats turned out since dusk or earlier – davits turned out, that was to say, boats boused firmly to the griping-spars, since if they'd swung loose they'd have smashed themselves against the davits; they could be freed and lowered in a lot less time than it would have taken if the davits had had to be turned out first. All ships in convoy would have done the same – or any that hadn't would be doing so now. Old Man telling him, 'I've got her, Second. Where's—'

Crump of a second torpedo hit – fifteen or twenty seconds after the first one. To starboard somewhere. For the moment this was all one knew – except that in the hard, knocking *thud*, men would probably have died, others trapped below decks drowning at this moment – until young Dixon squawked, 'On our beam, column six, sir! *Bristolian*? Kind of a flash, then –'

'All right.'

Hadn't seen any kind of flash, but saw muck cascading – water, assorted debris, and smoke streaming. The little ship's profile less familiar now, stern half already lifting as she tipped bow-down in the boil of whiteness: instant flooding of empty holds, he guessed, perhaps more than one hold simultaneously; if a bulkhead between them had been breeched, that would mean about two-thirds of the ship filled within seconds. The inrush of ocean was the picture in mind as he trained left over the glossy black-and-white ridges, surface gloss imparted by cloud-filtered moonglow, to the *Bristolian*'s next-ahead, the *Cedarwood*. She was all right. Andy swinging slowly anti-clockwise, hearing the Old Man call down for an increase in revs that would provide about one more knot, to close up into what had been the *Daisy Oakes* station. *Quilla*'s next-ahead would now be the Pole, name of – mental effort again – oh, *Byalystok*, whatever that might mean.

7

Probing darkness out to port again. Port bow, where the attack had come from and some U-boat's crew would still be cheering. Their commander would need to get his boat down into the static depths to reload its tubes though, one might guess, if that had been a full salvo he'd fired.

Presumably it would have been. From somewhere for'ard of the beam. Salvo of four, say.

'*Bristolian*'s gone!'

Gone.

Crew of thirty, thirty-five, one might guess, gone with her in those few minutes. Vision of Julia then: her brown eyes on his, soft but urgent whisper, 'Swear you *will* come back?'

He'd sworn it. What else? Although she'd known as well as he had – having been through it herself, and then some – that any such assurance would be nothing more than whistling in the dark.

Happened, or it didn't, that was all. When it did, according to the circumstances you'd cope as well as possible. *If* possible, remain alive.

Primarily now for *her* sake. Which wasn't a thing you'd broadcast. Make any such observation to old Harve, for instance, his response would be, 'Yeah, pull the other one!'

A touch cynical, old Harve.

'Same salvo, I'd guess.' Old Man gesturing out to port. Meaning that one torpedo had put paid to the *Daisy Oakes* – who was well abaft *Quilla*'s beam now, stopped and stern-down, listing increasingly to port with the sea foaming over her already swamped afterpart – while another of the same salvo had run on and blasted the *Bristolian*. What might be called a browning shot. Second distress rocket streaking skyward – he'd heard one scorch up when he'd been focusing on the *Bristolian* just now, had been aware of the sudden streak of brilliance as it were out of the corner of his mind as well as eye – *Quilla* at that time thrashing by the *Daisy Oakes* at a distance of less than half

8

a cable, allowing a view of one boat in the water and another halfway down her side – starboard side for'ard. Others might have been lowered on her port side – *should* have been, please God: although it was the weather side it would be less hazardous than on this one, on account of the list which as it steepened could lead to boats scraping down a barnacled iron slope. Might by some miracle make it all the way down, but more likely would not – except upside-down, having spilled out its occupants. The Old Man had his glasses on the Pole, *Byalystok*, as *Quilla* closed up astern of her. And that hadn't been a second distress rocket from the *Daisy Oakes*: it was what was called a 'snowflake', hung overhead now, dazzling bright, turning – as the oft-used phrase went – night into day. Convenient for the German and his mates, Andy thought, lighting us all up, but not much bloody help to *us*, really none at all. However – this at last was Waller, third mate, beside him, the light-reflecting peak of his cap a dull shine about a foot below the level of Andy's shoulder, Waller being almost spectacularly short-arsed. He told the Old Man, 'Third's here, sir. Your permission, I'll go down.'

Since merchant ships were now armed, a second mate's responsibilities included gunnery, and his own defence station, he'd been told, was at the twelve-pounder on the poop – a steel gun-deck built above the roof of the crew's quarters right aft, that superstructure having been strengthened to support it. Merchant ships being non-combatant, crewed by civilians, were allowed such weapons only on their sterns – for defensive purposes, notably for use when running from an attacker. He went out into the port wing of the bridge – two lookouts there – turned aft and rattled down a ladder to the boat-deck, where at each boat a pair of lowerers squatted close to the out-turned davits, and further aft, abreast the funnel, were *Quilla*'s other two cadets, Merriman and Elliot. Their dark-hours' duties included the launching of distress rockets and/or snowflakes, or by day when under air

9

attack the operation of the Holman Projector – a steam-powered grenade launcher – and, in other circumstances, flag-hoists. Merriman called to ask him which ship had been the victim of the second torpedo, and Andy told him the *Bristolian*, starboard beam, adding that she'd gone down in less than three minutes: 'So put on that bloody life-jacket!'

Kapok-filled 'swimming waistcoats' in this ship, Andy had noted earlier. In the *PollyAnna* they'd had the old-fashioned kind that could break your neck if you were wearing one when you jumped. Clattering down the next ladderway now, to the main deck aft. With the amount of movement on her, especially her roll, watching his footing and making use of such handholds as were in reach – ventilators and winches, for instance. The safest route, if the motion had been much worse than this, would have been along the centre-line, over the tops of the hatch-covers of numbers four and five holds, using the lashed-down five-ton derricks as massive handrails. But it wasn't anything like that bad: there was plenty of life in her but no seas coming over, decks running wet but from no more than spray. That snowflake's light was a big help, still bright, though well astern by now and drifting seaward.

Abaft number five, another pair of ventilators and the steam warping winch, then the poop structure, with a steel weather door leading into the crew's quarters, and near-vertical outside ladders to the gun-deck port and starboard. There being two of them allowed for one of them being used for ammunition supply, leaving the other clear for access.

'Morning, Layer.' Gunlayer – Patterson, able seaman – separating himself from the knot of men around the gun and its angled shield. Identifiable by his height, which was about the same as Andy's – six-three, taller than most. Five men in the gun's crew: one wearing a telephone headset and the others acting as lookouts – or had been until the snowflake fizzled out. Couldn't see much now,

10

especially if you'd been so unwise as to look up at it. Patterson observing, 'Not *that* good sir, I'd say.'

'Well – maybe not.'

Not for those two, anyway. And doubtless others before much longer. One recent convoy had lost close on sixty percent of its ships. Admittedly that had been an HX lot, home-bound from Halifax, and laden ships were the U-boats' priority targets; but still – more than half. Cargoes the country needed, couldn't do without: food, fuel, weaponry, ammunition, medical stores, vitally needed raw materials.

Quilla's stern lifting as a swell slid under her – poop and gun-deck soaring, hanging for a moment while gradually tilting over and sliding into a swift descent. Looking for'ard you saw the dark bulk of funnel and bridge structure leaning to starboard as her forepart rose: then astern, over the great mound of fizzing wake, for a while no view of the *Harvest Queen*. No snowflake effect now, either. Andy and Patterson agreeing in an exchange of shouts that it might be getting up a bit – the sea, height of the swell – and 'Not an easy platform to shoot from, that's a fact.' Looking around at the other men's dark shapes, he was remembering their names, or trying to. There'd been only one chance of mustering for gun-drill – when they'd been at Tail of the Bank, drilling with a single dummy shell for half an hour or so before weighing anchor to file out through the boom gate. But the sight-setter, the man in headphones, was Hardy, Ordinary Seaman, and the gun trainer was AB Pettigrew. Ugly little sod – squat, toad-like. Doubtless a heart of gold: in any case a first-rate seaman, according to Harve Brown. The rest of them – well, loader and breechworker were Stone and Fox – or the other way about – but Stone was an OS and Fox was a fireman or a greaser. One of the black gang, anyway. Engine room hands being fewer than in the *PollyAnna*, since *Quilla* being oil-fired had no need of trimmers. But that one, now . . . He got it: supernumary to the gun's crew of five, the assistant cook, Bayliss, whose defence

11

station was at this sharp end of the ammunition supply team. Young, rotund and talkative – gabbling away excitedly, which was what had drawn one's attention to him – falling silent as Pettigrew bellowed at him that yon was no bloody U-boat, boy, yon was their bloody escort!

Andy beside him then. 'Where?'

'There – *there*, sir.'

Two points on the bow to port: he had his glasses on it, and it *was* the sloop – HMS *Rustington*, the escort. Coming more or less towards them – which was to say coming back along the convoy's track. She'd be passing close. On her way to pick up survivors from the *Daisy Oakes*' boats, he guessed. He told the gun's crew as much: it couldn't be bad for morale to know that rescue attempts were being made, especially as they were all aware it was contrary to convoy discipline for any merchant ship to stop for such a purpose, making an easy target of herself; might also suggest to them that there could be some benefit in having even that single escort, with her limited turn of speed and feeble armament. Or at least would be if she could *find* those boats. Time had passed, and a boat could very quickly become a needle in a haystack. And in point of fact, escort vessels were prohibited from stopping for rescue purposes either, in action conditions such as applied here and now. Although if there was a lull in the assault, she might stop. The sloop was abeam now, passing close enough and making heavy weather of it, some of these men giving her a cheer, which of course couldn't possibly have been heard. But – torpedo hit – *that* could. Out to starboard somewhere, he guessed several columns away, but you still almost felt it as well as heard it – like a kick in the gut. Then, after maybe two seconds, another. The hell, *two* more. Making five in all in the past half-hour. Distress rocket streaking up: that would be from the first of the three to have been hit. From somewhere around the centre, it looked like – where the tankers were, tankers even when in ballast invariably being placed where they were less exposed –

and the next streak searing the darkness from further over and further back. Two of the three hits could have been on one ship, he'd been about to remark to Patterson, but was saved from any such speculation as a third rocket soared up and burst. So all right, five.

Five *so far.*

The sloop, he supposed, would stick to what she was doing now – searching for *Daisy Oakes* survivors. Who could light themselves up with flares – if their boats were properly equipped, and if they had any notion they were being looked for. And the sloop itself could use its search-light and fire starshells. While for the rest of them there could be no protection, and for the time being no rescue attempts either. In mitigation of which one also knew that (a) not every torpedo hit caused a ship to sink, and (b) taking to the boats didn't *necessarily* lead to loss of life.

The thought brought to mind Julia's experience. The ship in which she'd been a passenger, guest of her uncle, its master, had fought a gun-duel with a U-boat some-where southeast of the Azores, and she'd found herself in a lifeboat with about twenty others, several of whom didn't last long, these including a seventeen-year-old cadet who'd died in her arms. He'd had a shrapnel wound in the head and a foot blown off. She'd survived that as well as later ordeals that must have been pretty well as horrible, and remained quiet-mannered, sweet-faced, in some ways you might say ultra-sensitive, and yet as far as anyone could tell, unfrightened.

As far as she'd let anyone see, or guess.

Quilla's steam-whistle stopped such thinking in its tracks. One short, mind-jarring blast, then another on its heels; pause, followed by two more. Emergency turn to port. Similar wails through the salt-wet darkness from the rest of the herd out there to starboard and astern, in differing tones and varying decibels. The convoy Commodore, at the head of column four, would have ordered the turn by switching on a red-light display on his ship's mainyard. Red for a four-point turn to port, green for the same thing to starboard. Four points meaning forty-five degrees, and ships in the seven columns seeing the lights from their bridges because they were high and there were no other lights showing – except stern lights, which were low to the sea and low-powered so as to be visible only at close range – and acknowledging the order by sound-signal – two blasts for a turn to port, single blast for one to starboard – and also alerting neighbours who might have missed it.

From all ships' bridges they'd be watching for the lights to be switched off, the executive signal to put helms over. As *now*: helms over, rudders hauling them all round. The new course would be 260 degrees, a little south of due west. Object obviously to lose the U-boats, Commodore maybe having reason to believe that the main threat was a concentration of them either on the starboard bow or keeping pace/overhauling on that side. Front-runners of the convoy now effectively the ships of this column seven – the *Catherine Bell*, then the Polish *Byalystok*, *Barranquilla*, and on *Quilla*'s quarter the *Harvest Queen*. From *Quilla*'s station-keeping point of view it meant keeping the Pole and the *Bell* on a gyro bearing of 305 degrees – four points on her starboard bow, and the SS *Cedarwood*, who had been on her beam, on 035 degrees. This simple calculation would have flashed through the brains of the Old Man and one might hope Third Mate Waller, although maintaining the new echelon formation would require close attention, especially in terms of periodic adjustment of engine revs turning the lines ragged.

Quilla pitching harder as she settled on the new course, with wind and swell nearer the bow than the beam. Less roll, for sure. The convoy now incidentally on a course to pass south of Rockall instead of to the northeast of it. With the chart in his mind – second mate's primary function being navigation – realising that depending on how long they continued on this diversion there'd need to be some adjustment of pre-established courses and turning-points. At first light, he guessed. Distance from here to

14

Rockall being something like 150 or 160 miles, on the face of it there was plenty of room for manoeuvre; and the Commodore would have been informed of the routings of other convoys either north or south of Rockall – home-bound convoys in particular, the kind that would draw the U-boats away from this one, touch wood.

Although in that respect one had to bear in mind that in a few weeks' time, after loading a full cargo of sugar at Nuevitas, Cuba, *Quilla* herself would be part of a deep-laden home-bound convoy, helping to draw the sods away from less appealing targets such as this one. At least, if she survived the next few days and nights she most likely would be. Tonight, tomorrow and tomorrow night – then you'd be passing longitude 15 degrees west, which in theory was the current limit of U-boat operations, therefore the stage at which you lost whatever escort you *had* had; the convoy dispersed and its escort or escorts transferred themselves to the nearest home-bound one.

Because they were so damn short of escorts. Hundreds of destroyers, corvettes, etc were said to be on the stocks or fitting out, but here at sea they were still few and far between. Losses in the Norwegian campaign and in the Dunkirk evacuation accounted for some of it, and the need for a substantial number of them to be deployed on anti-invasion watch and patrol was another factor. Things would get better soon, one was assured, especially when the production of corvettes came into full flood.

'That you, Holt?'

Harve Brown, the mate, on walkabout. His defence station job was to move around, checking on whatever needed checking and dealing with it as might be necessary – everything that wasn't immediately under the Old Man's eye, or in the domain of the chief engineer. Accompanied by his right-hand man, the bosun, a five-by-five tobacco-chewing Irishman, by name McGrath. Brown asking as he fetched up beside Andy between the gun and the starboard-side rail, 'How's it feel, back at sea, then?'

'Same as always, Harve. Where we belong, eh?' Except for bloody Germans and their torpedoes, which it wasn't strictly necessary to mention. He added, 'You'd know, had long enough on the beach yourself, eh?' Still sweeping with his glasses, back between the echeloned columns – which were in some disorder here and there. Telling old Harve, 'We were in Calcutta when we heard you were going to be OK. *And* missing you by that time, I can tell you!'

He'd collapsed with his heart ailment shortly before the *PollyAnna* had sailed from Cardiff with her cargo of coal for Port Said, and had been replaced as mate in a pierhead jump by a man who'd had certain personal problems and brought most of them aboard with him. Almost exactly a year ago that had been – August of '39, only a few weeks short of war, which had seemed more or less inescapable but no-one could have been 100 percent certain – efforts were still being made to avert it. In any case, owners weren't letting tonnage lie idle when it could be earning money. So it had started as an ordinary tramping voyage, and *PollyAnna* had been in the Red Sea, bound light-ship Port Said to Calcutta, when the balloon had finally gone up.

Brown observing now, 'Did yourself no harm, that voyage, eh?'

'Yeah.' He had his glasses on the *Byalystok*; either she was ahead of station, or *Quilla* was astern of hers. 'How things happened, was all.' He couldn't see the *Catherine Bell*, muttered, 'Something of a buggers' muddle developing out there.'

That remark about doing himself no harm, though – in February, on return from her voyage to Uruguay and Brazil, the *PollyAnna*'s owners – owners also of *Barranquilla* and half a dozen other tramp steamers, Messrs Dundas Gore of Glasgow, known familiarly as the Blood Line because of that name Gore – had in collusion with the Board of Trade rewarded Third Mate Andrew Holt, for what they'd considered to have been

16

exceptionally fine service, with what amounted to half a year's seniority, allowing him to sit for his first mate's certificate right away instead of after another six or eight months' sea-time. First mate's ticket leading straight to an appointment as second mate. Hence these recent months ashore – on Merseyside, at the Nautical College, living in digs and swotting himself cross-eyed, spending as little of his dwindling store of cash as possible, there being an enrolment fee at the college, and the cost of lodgings, meals, an occasional pint at the Villiers in Elliot Street – also known as Ma Shepherd's – and now and then a visit to the cinema with a girl by name of Susan, whom he'd known since she was fifteen and he'd been finishing his schooling in the training ship HMS *Conway*. Susan Shea – her father was an Aintree vet, and she was studying accountancy in Liverpool – very pretty girl, with a mass of dark red hair. Julia had been adamant at that time that he shouldn't take any more weekends off to visit her in Newcastle, because she wanted him to (a) get his ticket, and (b) not spend money he didn't have, especially when he wasn't earning – and one couldn't go forever without *any* female company, or for that matter cold-shoulder an old friend like Susan.

Harve Brown asked him – as if he was some sort of mind-reader – 'Seen much of the young lady you rescued out of the Hun steamer?'

He kept his glasses at his eyes, thinking about it for a moment before enquiring, 'How d'you know about her?'

'What a question! Whole shebang in the papers, weren't it?'

'Not about her. Not in any way that might've made you ask me that. I mean, why should I have?'

'No *should* about it. But – must've been – yeah, Don Fisher was your second in *PollyAnna,* weren't he?'

'And what did *he* know about anything?'

'All I remember he said was you were keen on her. Chasing off to visit her in Newcastle, right?' A chuckle and a heavy pat on the back. 'Leopard don't change his spots, was what I said. No offence, Andy, far from it, but –'

'That girl had been through it, Harve, really had. Passage to NZ in her uncle's ship to visit another uncle who's farming there – they'd reckoned to get her home before the war started, but – well, the *Cheviot Hills* was sunk after a gun battle with a U-boat, she and others were picked up by a German steamer, support-vessel to the *Graf Spee*, seems to've been –'

'The one you nobbled.'

'That was no picnic for her, either. Not for any of 'em, but *her* – well, imagine . . . Don signed on again in *PollyAnna*, am I right?'

'Don Fisher – yeah. South Africa bound, she was then.'

Quilla had increased revs: you could feel it, the thrumming through her frames. Since she was in ballast, her single screw was high in the water, barely covered, so that right aft here you heard that too, between whiles, the regular thrashing that had quickened to give her an extra quarter-knot or so. Andy added – about Don Fisher – 'He was third of the old *Burntisland* when I was a cadet in her.'

Twenty minutes since the emergency change of course, maybe twenty-five since the last torpedoings. Brown commenting, 'Real old deathtrap, the *Burntisland*. Should'a been took out of service long ago.' A snort: 'How it *is*, now – anything that floats . . .'

'Draw the line somewhere, you'd think.'

'Or one of our chums out there'll do it for 'em.' A gesture into the outer darkness. 'Compensation or replacement'd be more than her worth as scrap – and meanwhile there's cargoes offering everywhere they bloody look, so –'

'Owners not feeling the pinch exactly.'

'I'd say they're not. Nor neglecting their own best interests. But we got off the subject of the young lady from Newcastle somehow?'

'You may have.' Keeping the glasses at his eyes, finding

gaps astern to probe. The columns were reshaping themselves a bit, he thought. Telling the older man, 'I was never on it. Except the rotten time she'd had, and being one in a million.' Evading it again then: 'Must be half an hour since the last three copped it?'

No answer: the mate having moved away to commune with Bosun McGrath. But how many, Andy wondered, from the five gone down already – how many drowned or drowning, how many saved? Give it *another* half-hour, what'll the score be then? Or after another minute, even these next ten seconds? Torpedoes on their way *this moment?* Thoughts reverting to Julia, to his having sworn he *would* come back. He'd added, he remembered, 'Not just this time, *every* time!' His own presumption, that – that there'd be convoy after convoy, years and years of it, not what some gloom-mongers and communists had been prophesying: England starved, forced to her knees within months. But Julia accepting that assurance – Julia Carr of all people, with two cousins at sea now as second mates, babyhood memories of a father who'd drowned when his trawler had foundered off Norway – when she'd been three years old, toddling around Tyneside in the 1920s – and the uncle who'd gone down in his MV *Cheviot Hills.* As she herself might have gone down with him, might *well* have – *that* girl would take seriously any such nonsensical assurance?

But she had. At any rate had seemed to. *Needed* to. She'd sounded quietly desperate on the telephone; he'd called from Liverpool to tell her he'd got his mate's certificate and now the offer of this berth in the *Barranquilla,* following an exchange of telegrams with the owners, so that he couldn't fit in a visit to Newcastle as he'd have liked – *loved* – had to get himself to Glasgow double-quick . . .

'Back in ten weeks, maybe. Seems about the average. Twelve at most, say. See you then. I'll call as soon as we get in, and—'

'Come *now,* Andy? Please – couldn't you? Spare one

19

day? An *hour*? I can't talk over the wire, but' – voice dropping to a whisper – 'second *month*. Please, *must* talk to you. *Only* you. Couldn't tell you sooner – distracting you, and – couldn't be *certain*, see – in fact even now –'

She'd met him at the station hotel in Newcastle. Hadn't told her mother, said she simply *couldn't*, and his sudden appearance might have blown the gaff. All right, her mother would get to know, obviously, they *all* would, but by then –

'Ten weeks, say, we'll have 'em reading the banns.'

But what sort of a hole would she be in if he did *not* get back?

2

'Second mate, sir –'

He groaned.

'Seven bells, sir!'

Light on – for a moment dazzling in the small, white-painted cabin. It was supposedly a two-berth, but he had it to himself. Recollecting in his somewhat muzzy brain that there'd been no more losses, or even, so far as anyone knew, attacks. Either the U-boats had called it a day or they'd been thrown off the scent by that emergency turn, with only the five ships lost. The Commodore had turned his convoy back on course at just after 0400, by which time dawn had been a brightening orange glow in the summer sky. Now – checking his watch, seven-thirty – Andy was blinking at Cadet Merriman – lanky, cadaverous, seventeen but you'd have guessed nineteen – who'd have been sent down by officer of the watch Harve Brown to shake him, ensure he'd be up for breakfast at 0800 so as then to relieve Waller on the bridge for half an hour in order that he, Waller, could get *his* breakfast, squaring the account by spelling Andy for half an hour at lunchtime. There'd been no such routine in *PollyAnna*, but he remembered it had been the way they'd done it when he'd been a cadet in the *Burntisland*, and it made a certain amount of sense, in particular fitting in with the routines of sight-taking.

Merriman was dithering. 'All right then, sir?'

'I don't reckon to drop off again, if that's what you mean.'

'Ah. Aye, sir . . .'

'Cut along, then.'

He slid off the bunk: *might* otherwise have snoozed off. Had not enjoyed any surfeit of repose just lately. And think about Julia one minute, in the next you're dreaming of her. Reminding oneself what an absolute peach she was; but in other states of mind less than enthusiastic at the prospect of marriage. Not in any sense in relation to *her*: if one was going to be married at all – well, one *had* had it in mind as a possibility, a hope, the glimpse of a distant, post-war future that wasn't clearly definable because the war effectively blocked it out But that *was* how he'd thought of her: as something extremely valuable, long-term, and to be treated accordingly.

An intention to which he had not adhered as strictly as he should have.

But *marriage*, at twenty-one, knowing darned well that he was not and never had been a one-girl man . . .

Any more than his father had been, or expected *him* to be. Recalling, as he padded aft to the washplace with a towel round his neck, the old man's advice a year or two ago: 'Get your boozing and whoring done before you're thirty, boy!' Advice which the old man had been happy to dish out when in his forties, but which he had clearly not been guided by when, at the age of twenty-four, he'd married Andy's mother, who'd been pregnant with what had turned out to be Andy.

Not all that different from doing the same at twenty-one. The old man would make the most of it, no doubt, grind his teeth and so forth, when he heard about it, but it was near enough a case of following in father's footsteps. The two of them did get on very well, as it happened – tended to think alike, and certainly looked alike: Andy was a few inches taller, as well as twenty-five years younger, but they were both dark, with strong features which included full-sized noses. He wouldn't willingly have

22

swapped the old boy for any other father. Got on fine with his mother, too – loved her, certainly had no criticism of her for *her* early indiscretions, if that was what they'd been. She and Charlie Holt, who when they'd married had been a lieutenant-commander in the Royal Naval Air Service, had been helplessly in love, and empathising with them as one did, having gathered from their own exchanges and reminiscences how it must have been with them in those days, there was no question of taking any snooty view of the circumstances or the timing of this or that.

His father had flown naval airships in that war. Floating over east-coast convoys, spotting U-boats and mines. When his engine had begun to lose power or otherwise malfunction he'd float the blimp up another couple of thousand feet, switch off – would be 'ballooning' then, wind-driven, simply hanging on the gas-bag – climb out of the cockpit onto a landing-skid, edge up beside the engine and hang on with one hand while using the other to change plugs or the magneto, whatever. Then swing the prop to start up again. No kind of stunt – just normal practice. Entitling him to some degree of relaxation, one might think, when on the ground. He was a commander RNR now, second in command of an AMC – Armed Merchant Cruiser – on the Northern Patrol, using Reykjavik in Iceland as their forward base.

He'd had a short leave this last May, when his ship had been in dock for bottom-scraping, and Andy had taken a weekend off from his studies in order to spend a day and a half with him at home in Helensburgh. That was when the old man had presented him with the binoculars.

Quilla declining to stand still, hot water was threatening to swill over the edge of the basin. So unplug it, let some out. Visualising the scene up top: same course, near enough same engine revs, sea conditions much the same; you didn't have to go out on deck or even glance out of a port to know it. While also in mind was the fact that the two-hour emergency diversion, on course 260 degrees at twelve knots, on the face of it might have taken them twenty-four miles off track; but allowing for this, that and the other – wind, sea and propeller-slip – one might estimate it as nearer twenty. Anyway, there'd have to be an adjustment of course to pass well clear to the east of Rockall; the Commodore would most likely order it at midday, after noon positions had been hoisted. An alteration of ten or twelve degrees, maybe. Rockall would then be abeam during the dog watches, and one would be passing through position 'A' at some time during one's own middle watch – position 'A' in the convoy's routing orders being on longitude 15 degrees west, where for better or for worse the convoy would lose its escort and disperse, ships shaping courses to their own individual destinations.

Rinsing away remnants of shaving soap, reaching for his towel, washplace door opening and slamming, glancing round as Waller, third mate, came strutting in. Short, stocky, with a reddish face and curly yellow hair. Even with only a towel around him, he still had that cocky, aggressive manner.

Aggressive or defensive?

'Morning. Sir.' A space between the two words as if grudging the 'sir' – which one didn't need anyway and would be discontinued when they got to know each other slightly. Heading for the urinals. And another entrant now. Two more – Bridgeman, second engineer, and a younger man he hadn't met: skinny little guy, large eyes in a pale, narrow face. He told him, 'I'm Holt, second mate. Who're you?'

'Shaw, third sparks.' Meaning he was the junior of *Quilla*'s three wireless officers. 'How do.'

Waller was coming to take possession of one of the other basins. Andy having finished with his, backed off to let Shaw at it. Nodding to him: 'Your CRO's name's Foster, right?'

CRO standing for Chief Radio Officer. So – Foster, and

this Shaw, and the other one was – Newton. Respectively entitled RO/2 and RO/3: alternatively 2RO and 3RO. Newton was the one with the sideboards.

Bridgeman, the engineer – a large man, approximately Andy's size – had a full beard that made him look older than he was. He tapped Shaw on the shoulder: 'Telling you he's Holt, kid – he's *the* Holt. Led the *PollyAnna*'s boarding party into that Hun steamer?'

'Oh, crikey! Yeah – in the papers, wasn't it, you rescued a bunch of men and a girl, right?'

'I was third mate, did what I was told.' He touched the deeply indented, purple scar at the back of his neck: 'Got this for my pains – German with a broken bottle.'

Got that *and* the girl, he thought to himself on the way back to his cabin. Hadn't known it at the time, of course, but she'd have been worth far more serious injuries. Kicking the cabin door shut behind him, knowing this was the truth of it – that he was a very lucky man and would simply have to mend his ways, adjust to a new way of life. Having made one's bed, you might say, bloody lie in it – and thank your stars it was Julia, and none of certain others which it might have been. Circumstances *were* awkward, here and now – especially for her, or could become so quite soon. Ten weeks being two and a half months, and two gone already – bringing the total to *five* months, say. He should have insisted on her confiding in her mother – had in fact proposed it, but she'd been set on keeping her condition secret for as long as possible, and he'd been in a rush to get on a train for Glasgow and the *Barranquilla*. Should have kept his nerve on that score, he realised now, and induced her to see the sense of it: they could have spoken to Mama together, explained as much as was explainable, and he'd have put it on record that he'd every intention of marrying her – if she'd have him and Mama would go along with it, both of which were certainties – as soon as he got back from this trip.

Anyway it would all work out. And he'd spend the rest

of his life thanking God he *had* got her out of that Hun ship.

Motor vessel *Glauchau*. The Huns had had their prisoners in the 'tweendecks of number three hold, with German martial music blaring day and night to cover any noise the poor sods might make – at least while at anchor in Vitoria. His own achievement had been to spot the indications of something fishy going on, then the luck to have it confirmed by the barman in that joint where little Manuela worked. Manuela with whom he'd had a red-hot date, and tragically had had to stand her up the night of the *Glauchau* action. He still sometimes dreamt of Manuela.

He started breakfast on his own on the dot of eight. Porridge, boiled egg, toast and marmalade, served by Assistant Steward Chumley – ratty-looking, aged about twenty, deft as a card-sharp in his handling of plates and dishes. Andy asked him whether he'd learnt his trade at sea – might have started as a galley-boy, for instance – but he shook his head, said his father had an hotel, he'd waited on tables since he'd been a nipper. Roadhouse like, more than hotel. How did Andy want his egg – three minutes, four? The answer was four; and the next question, was it the truth what they was saying down aft, that he was the bloke what boarded the Germans in that port – what was it called –

'Vitoria, Brazil. Yes.' But he explained – again – that he was only one of those who'd boarded her, had no idea why the press had singled him out as they had. 'Fact is, I'd as soon we all forgot it.'

'OK, sir. No sweat . . .'

Claymore now, third engineer. Balding, with a nose that must have been broken at some stage; he came from Belfast. He dumped himself in a chair across the table from Andy, asked him how goes it and shouted for porridge. Back to Andy then: 'Disperse tonight, do we?'

'If the Commodore so decides. We'll be in position to, anyway.'

'Fifteen west.'

He nodded.

'What's to stop bloody U-boats operating further west than that?'

'*Was* mainly their range – distance from bases. Now they're working out of Lorient, on the Biscay coast – saves 'em about five hundred miles each way, so –'

'So likely we'll get the benefit.' A bark of laughter. 'Lucky us. How long'll it take us to bloody Cuba?'

The answer would have been best part of three weeks, minimum seventeen, eighteen days, but he'd had enough of the interrogation. Glancing round as others arrived: Foster, the CRO – thickset, mid-twenties, prematurely balding, came from Dundee, played a concertina – and Dixon, the cadet who for the time being was Andy's assistant, would handle his chart corrections for him, for instance – and a straggle of others. Breakfast was never a very convivial or conversational meal at sea, but Andy being a stranger came in for a certain amount of polite attention; he didn't encourage it or take any longer than he had to, was on his feet and heading for the door when the chief engineer pushed in. Name – he remembered it as they nodded good morning to each other – Frank Verity. Mid-forties, with greying hair, and according to Captain Beale a veteran of the Great War. Pausing now to ask him whether he was settling in all right. Andy told him yes, beginning to, thanks. He'd met him in the Old Man's day cabin when he'd come to sign on, *Quilla* by that time swinging round an anchor at Tail of the Bank, Old Man remarking after introducing them, 'See this feller, Chief. Second mate at twenty-one. Have his own ship before he's thirty, eh?'

Verity had said, 'Or be dead before he's twenty-two.' He'd caught himself up on that, turned back. 'Apologies, Holt. Any luck, you'll get to be *ninety*-two.'

Andy had said, 'Not sure I'd want that.'

'Me neither. You're the one got 'em out of the prison ship, right?'

'*Helped* get 'em out, sir. Captain planned it, mate was in charge of the boarding.'

'And you were near decapitated with a bottle.' A nod. 'Dare say you'll live it down, in time. See you later, Nat.' As the cabin door shut behind him, Beale had said, 'Likes to act the cynic, does Frank Verity. Never mind that, he's a top-notcher, we're lucky to have him. Sunk twice in '14–18, would you believe it?'

'*Was* he, sir . . .'

'But you're here to sign on. Cut it fine enough, didn't you?'

Dressed and with his glasses slung by their strap around his neck, he went up by the internal ladderway from main deck level to that of the Old Man's quarters – day cabin, sleeping cabin and facilities, and abaft that the 'owners' suite' that was shared by Harve Brown and the chief engineer – lower bridge deck, that was called – and then up to the bridge itself – bridge, chartroom – more accurately, chart *space* you might call it, the partitioned-off starboard after corner of the bridge – and wireless office.

Bright day, with high white clouds fast-moving in a fresh southwesterly. A lively sea and the sun well up – as it would be, in August and on 57 north. Lovely sight, he thought: ships fairly romping through and over the ranks of dark-blue swells, smashing and carving into them and flinging the white stuff away down-wind in sheets and streams sparkling in the sun. *Quilla* in her natural element and revelling in it, enjoying every moment of it – you could see it, *feel* it – and a mutter in the mind, *Please God, more days like this – more weeks – months?* Well – best not ask for *too* much. With his glasses on the SS *Byalystok*, their next-ahead, then switching to the *Cedarwood* abeam, and leading her, the *Montreal Star*. Astern of *Cedarwood*, the *Princess Judy*, and tailing *Quilla* the broad-beamed grain-carrier *Harvest Queen*.

One thing you could be sure of was that not *all* of these would enjoy another month of it.

28

Another night, even?

The *Princess Judy* was making rather a lot of smoke, he noticed. Would no doubt be in for a wigging from the Commodore when the old boy surfaced from his breakfast.

Lowering his glasses and turning inboard he saw that young Elliot – cadet, assistant officer of the watch – was at the chart table, working out a sunsight Waller must have taken since the beginning of this watch. Elliot was a Glaswegian. Skinny youth, but boxed a bit, apparently, and had scrum-halved in his training ship's rugger fifteen: info courtesy of Harve Brown over a game of cards in the saloon last evening. The boy had finished his calculations, was putting the resultant position-line on the chart. Later, Waller would run that up to noon, the meridean altitude he'd take then completing a midday EP or Estimated Position. Andy would be doing the same, and according to how it looked when it was run-on would decide whether his or Waller's was the better bet, to be adopted as the official noon position. Within a few minutes of noon, every ship in the convoy was required to hoist flags giving her own conclusions on this subject, and it was then up to the Commodore to decide which *he* liked best.

He asked Elliot, 'Mr Brown's stars on, are they?'

'Oh – yessir . . .'

Shifting out of his way, Andy moving in to check on Harve's morning starsight. Fix, not EP, as he'd be the first to point out, meaning that it was more reliable. And the night's diversion had indeed shifted them west of the pre-ordained track by about twenty miles. In fact one knew *now*, as near as dammit, where one was, but custom required a noon position to be logged and used as the starting point for the next twenty-four hours' run, noon to noon. It had often enough been argued by outsiders that Red Ensign ships tended to be overnavigated, and the answer was that every deck officer was first and foremost a navigator and expected to exercise that basic skill

29

regularly, if possible improve on it.

'OK, then ...' Checking the deck-log now, Harve's entries from the previous watch – courses, revs, weather, distance-made-good. It was all there – and as the navigator, his own responsibility to ensure that it was.

He asked the cadet, 'This your first ship?'

'No, sir. I was in the *Cromarty* a year – and *Burntisland* –'

'Yeah? Served *my* cadet's time in that old crock.' Such an old crock that she still had her crew accommodation up for'ard, in the foc'sl. Leaky, stinking, rat-infested, incredibly noisy in any sort of a blow. Shaking his head at the memory of her as he moved out into the bridge and to its forefront. Waller lowering his glasses, turning expectantly, no doubt looking forward to his breakfast. The helmsman's name was – Andy asked him, 'AB Samways, is it?'

'Got it in one, sir.' Friendly grin.

Andy said, 'Half the time can't remember my *own* name.' He nodded to Waller: 'All right, Gus, I've got her.'

Quilla's noon position – 57 degrees 12 minutes north, 11 degrees 40 west – was hoisted at a few minutes past the hour, beating most of her neighbours to it and closely matching the Commodore ship's result. Fixes would vary slightly in any case in a convoy three miles wide and two deep. Cadets Elliot and Merriman had run the flags up – two hoists each of five flags, on halyards secured at the after end of the bridge deck and rove through blocks on a wire stay linking foremasthead to funnel-top.

This was now Andy's watch, although Waller was still up here. So was the Old Man and the chief engineer, with whom he'd been conferring – yet another midday routine. And Cadet Dixon was on the monkey island, one level above the bridge, looking out for further flag signals from the Commodore, in particular for an order to alter course, adjusting for last night's excursion westward.

Andy asked Waller, 'Does Dixon know his flags?'

'Should do. We've been drilling 'em at it long enough. But I'll check.'

'Good man.' Waller went out into the bridge wing – access to the monkey island was external, iron ladders port and starboard – and Andy nodded to the helmsman. 'All right, Selby?'

'Right enough, sir. Gerry sleepin' it off like, seems.'

Meaning no indications of U-boats in the offing – yet. Mentally one crossed fingers. There'd been nothing on the air-waves that could be attributed to U-boats, according to the Marconi boys. In fact, based on convoys' experiences in recent months, one didn't expect daylight attacks. Radio exchanges were something else, customarily preceding the next dark-hours assault. Although it was quite on the cards that last night's pack could have been diverted to some home-bound convoy. Orders from U-boat headquarters in western France, maybe, if they'd received a sighting report from a boat reconnoitring further west, or from an aircraft – four-engined Focke Wulf 200s being based now in the region of Bordeaux. Based there and sinking ships too, especially any independently-routed ships they happened to come across, but ships in convoy too. It was partly to stay out of the FW's unfortunately wide range of operations that convoys were being routed this far north.

He had his glasses up, sweeping from the bow down the exposed port side, when Waller yelled down the pipe from monkey island, 'Signal from Commodore, alter course in succession to 318!'

'In succession' meant wheeling, not turning simultaneously as in an emergency turn. So the shape of the convoy would be maintained, ships in column following each other round, those on the outside of the turn needing to increase engine revs slightly, while those over to starboard came down by a few turns. Not yet – when the Commodore hauled down that hoist, wheels would be put over. Andy went to the chart and laid off the new course as from 1215, a three-mile run-on from the noon

31

position. He came back and told the Old Man, 'We'll have Rockall thirty-five miles abeam at 1730, sir.'

'Distance then to point "A"?'

'Hundred miles exactly, sir. Making it one-thirty, two am.'

After they'd turned, the Old Man had gone down to his lunch and stayed down for a couple of hours, catching up on sleep he'd missed last night, but he was back on the bridge by three-thirty when the CRO, Foster, came to report that there'd been a signal to the Commodore from C-in-C Western Approaches with the cheering news that the SS *Ellesbroek* had made it into Londonderry; *Ellesbroek* being one of the ships that had been torpedoed last night. Andy looked her up on the convoy diagram.

'She was number six in column three, sir. Belgian, I think.'

'Good for her, anyway.' Beale was filling his pipe. 'What else, Foster?'

Because the CRO was still hovering, there obviously was more. He grimaced slightly. 'U-boat-type transmissions, sir, ahead of us and northwest. Started with one call repeated several times, now there's been three or four at it.'

Old Man concentrating on the stuffing of his pipe. 'Don't have to be us the buggers are stalking.'

Foster looked doubtful. 'Across our track though, and one out on the beam to starboard.'

'Shadower. Let me know, any changes.' Flicking a storm-lighter into action, then between puffs, 'Hear that, Second?'

Andy nodded. 'Looks like another night of it.'

'Does that, all right.' Looking at him, with that creasing of what might or might not have been humour in and around the eyes. 'Arseholes up to their usual bloody tricks.' Expelling smoke, pipe going well enough now. Adding, 'God rot 'em . . .' Shake of the head. 'Thinking, Holt – your defence station – waste of you down aft there.

32

Patterson's sound enough, don't need his hand held – would you say?'

'Sure he doesn't, sir. But what about spotting and control?'

'Experience for a cadet. Whichever of 'em you reckon might do best. All done the course, eh? An' if there was problems, nothing to stop you nipping aft, eh?'

'Aye, sir.'

'I'll inform Mr Brown, you set it up, have a word with Patterson.'

This was good. You could spend all night and every night on that gun-deck and never see a U-boat; and gun-control as taught by RN personnel in dockyard sheds in all the major ports was simple enough. But why the change from previous ship's routine . . . He raised it with Harve Brown when handing over the watch to him at four, and the mate's low-voiced explanation was that the Old Man had taken an aversion to Andy's predecessor, had preferred whenever possible to keep him at a distance.

Gus Waller told them an hour later, in the saloon over mugs of tea and cigarettes, 'Seems London got it again last night. Other cities too.'

Air raids, he was talking about. Andy queried, 'Not your part of London, let's hope.'

Shake of the yellow head, red face. 'Docks, CRO said. I'm from Tottenham, as it happens. But hotting up all right – most nights now.'

'I got caught in a raid on Merseyside, six or eight weeks back.' Andy accepted a Senior Service from Bridgeman, the engineer with the beard. 'Took a girl to the flicks, had to get her back to Birkenhead, some goon in a tin hat and an armband ordered us to take shelter in the Underground. No bloody option. So I didn't get her home until sparrow-fart and her father didn't believe us, turned quite nasty.' He added, 'Piddling little raids mind you, those first ones.'

'But – end July, that week' – Bridgeman – 'supposed to've shot down more than a hundred of 'em?'

'Warming up to invade, they're saying. Soon as they can wear down the RAF.'

'Which please God they won't. Bloody Germans on British soil – give you the shivers just to think of it!'

'Shivers is fucking right!'

Bridgeman glanced at Andy. 'How they converse, in Tottenham.'

'Changing the subject' – and expelling a first cloud of smoke – 'your previous second mate, name of –'

'Shithead's *my* name for him. Gone for his Master's.' Meaning to sit for his master's certificate – which if he got it would qualify him for employment as first mate. Waller added, 'He looked like coming back here as mate, personally I'd take off.'

Like family secrets emerging, as one gradually became one of them. And the gun-control business now – all three cadets wanted the job, and he picked Merriman, who was the senior of them by a week or two, then sent for Patterson and told him.

Sleep now. Four thirty-five: might get in three hours before supper, plus another stretch during the first watch if one wanted more and the bastards stayed away that long. *If* . . . It seemed unlikely, with a shadower out there already and others closing in across the convoy's line of advance.

Three hours' caulk was a happy prospect anyway.

Write to Julia first?

Not a lot of point, he supposed, when it could only be mailed from Cuba in about three weeks' time. It was just that one had this urge to be in touch, *feel* in touch. On the other hand, if one came to grief and the ship remained afloat, a letter would exist, *might* get to her; the main thing being that then it wouldn't be only her unsupported word that they'd planned to marry.

Vital thing, really.

Write to the parents too?

When she had the child, she might want him or her to know its grandparents. Might want their help, too. But there again, with only her word for it that he was the father and would have married her – how might they react?

Just another of Andy's girls . . .

And whose fault would *that* be?

Brain-wave, then. Write not to them, but to his sister, Annabel. She was eighteen and a probationer nurse, working in a hospital in Edinburgh. Working about twenty-five hours a day, she'd told him. Write telling her everything that mattered, stipulating that the parents were to be informed only in the event of his own non-return, and if Julia OK'd it.

Two letters, then, to be mailed from Nuevitas. But sleep on it now: could be a rough night coming.

3

On the bridge a few minutes short of midnight – darkish, no moon, thickened cloud cover taking care of that – Waller told him that, according to the CRO, U-boat wireless transmissions had dried up. One could only guess at a logical progression of the situation as one had assessed it earlier when they'd been nattering to each other: closer now, fairly obviously, keeping quiet while closing in across the convoy's van – or in position, waiting for others to join them maybe, marking time, plotting the convoy's approach from data supplied by the shadower who'd been to the east or northeast some eight hours ago. Shadower silent now too, but out there still, liable to crackle into life again if he considered there was reason to. If you'd had anything like a proper escort at that time, one or two of them might have been sent out on that bearing to put the bugger down, or drive him off – *maybe* even sink him.

But you hadn't. You had one elderly sloop. Which two hours earlier, according to Waller, had thrashed doggedly up the port side and gone out of sight ahead. Would be in the northern sector now, presumably, where the shadower had last been heard from and where one might expect the rest of them – whenever . . .

That was the picture as well as one could judge, in preparing to take over the middle watch. The Commodore might have more to go on, of course, being

36

briefed by the Ops Room back in Liverpool, with whatever they had from sources such as escort commanders of other convoys, radio intercepts or patrolling aircraft – of which unfortunately there were very few, the east coast invasion watch having priority in allocation of resources, and, according to Andy's father, the RAF having their own notions of how best to use such resources, favouring wide-ranging patrols to the close defence of convoys. In memory, the old man's growl of 'Stupid sods. Blind chance of stumbling on a surfaced U-boat in a million square miles of bloody ocean, whereas convoys are where U-boats all too obviously foregather! Wouldn't you call that plain common sense?'

Course 318, still. Swell lower than it had been, though still noticeable, *Quilla* being in ballast. Wind down too, no more than force three. Coolish, for all that. The Old Man had taken a set of stars a couple of hours ago before the cloud had begun to build up, which had put them half a mile east of what would have been the estimated position as run-on from noon. Rockall now eighty-five miles south-southeast, and the distance to position 'A' twenty-two miles. Best to use that starsight fix for all practical purposes now, he thought; if for instance the Commodore ordered dispersal at position 'A', freeing one from adherence to any convoy routing.

Some freedom – if the bastards *were* already in close attendance, and seeing that ships routed independently were in any case more likely to get clobbered than those in convoy; statistically that was the truth of it, apparently. He came back to Waller: 'OK. Go get your head down.'

Derisive snort. 'How long? Ten minutes?'

'Yeah. Wouldn't bother taking your socks off.'

The helmsman was AB Samways again. Old Man propped in the port for'ard corner, binoculars at his eyes, not even grunting when Waller called, 'Goodnight, sir.' Andy put his own glasses up, checking on near neighbours first and the areas of sea between and around them. Bearings and distances seemingly about right, although on further consideration one might come up a couple of revs, if a present tendency continued – distance to the Pole having by the look of it increased somewhat in recent minutes. Although the relative bearing of the *Cedarwood* seemed spot-on. Check again in a moment. Better to take remedial action promptly than wait too long and give the Old Man reason to bawl one out. Especially since being newly-joined as well as brand-new in the role of second mate one might reasonably expect to be on trial to some extent. But checking astern – briefly out into the port wing of the bridge to do so – picking up the *Harvest Queen*'s flare of bow-wave dead astern and at about the right distance, then returning to focus again on the *Byalystok*, finding she'd wandered far enough out of column to leave the *Catherine Bell* – at least, the whiteness under her counter – clearly visible at something like 1,200 yards. *Byalystok* therefore less competently handled than she should be at this juncture?

Give it a few minutes, make certain. If you came up in revs and the Pole chose that moment to come *down* a few, you'd wish you hadn't.

Time now, 0007.

He'd written those two letters and stashed them in his boat bag or 'panic-bag', a holdall in which one kept important items like certificates and other documents and valuables, cash if one had any – which he didn't, really, having come down to his last pound by the end of the Newcastle trip. He'd been unusually well-heeled when he'd signed off from the *PollyAnna*, having a certain amount of pay due to him, also funds supplied by both parents on the occasion of his twenty-first birthday, which he'd celebrated in Vitoria at the height of the *Glauchau* business. But six months ashore at the Nautical College, with no further emoluments coming in and sundry expenses including several trips away – one to Helensburgh when his father had had that leave, and three in all to Newcastle.

'Holt!'

'Aye, sir.' And over his shoulder then, 'Dixon – steam-whistle, two short blasts, twice!' Having seen it at the same moment as the Old Man: emergency turn to port, red light signal from the Commodore – Commodore-ship not visible, but the lights on his yardarm clear enough even through a mile and a half of darkness. Whether the old boy's reason for ordering a turn might be a renewal of radio activity suggesting an attack was imminent, or a tip-off from Western Approaches, or just an attempt to lose the shadower if there was reason to think he was still with them, it made sense in terms of the broad picture in one's mind – Rockall that distance astern, U-boat pack maybe not far ahead, and that dark and empty ocean stretching away westward: why *not* dodge away into it?

Red display still there. Old Man with his glasses on it, Andy making another quick check on neighbours, a few sirens still blasting off. Neighbours all where they should have been – except for the Pole, on whom if she was clumsily handled in this manoeuvre one had better keep a sharpish eye. The new course would be 273 – near as damnit due west. He heard the Old Man's growl of 'There you go' – red lights having been switched off, the executive order to put helms over. He told Samways, who was waiting for it, 'Port fifteen.'

'Port fifteen, sir.'

Throwing the wheel around . . .

'Fifteen o' port wheel on, sir.'

'Steer 273.'

'Two seven three, sir.'

Fifteen degrees of rudder had been specified in the convoy orders, so that turning circles would at any rate approximately match each other. *Quilla*'s rudder beginning to haul her round now, *Byalystok* on the turn too – promptly enough – and *Cedarwood* falling back abaft the beam. *Quilla* would still be keeping station on the Pole, keeping him on, say, 320 degrees at the standard 600 yards – or trying to. Lumbering round through sea churned white by the *Byalystok*'s and *Catherine Bell*'s wakes; pitching more noticeably as she swung her bow into the direction of the swell.

The Old Man cleared his throat. 'Holt – we'll go to defence stations.'

Half an hour ago, that had been. The emergency turn had been logged – by Dixon, who'd since been sent to join Elliot on the boat-deck – as taking place at 0028, and it was now coming up for one am. Every passing minute maybe improving chances of getting away with this. If there'd been a shadower close enough to have spotted the red-light signal you could bet there'd have been an immediate outbreak of wireless activity – and there hadn't been. So fingers crossed. Andy still had the conning of the ship meanwhile, the Old Man having as yet shown no interest in taking over. *Quilla* this far maintaining distance and bearing on the *Byalystok*; *her* blacker-than-darkness steadily pitching image foreshortened in quarter-profile, splodgily underlined in white, stern light faint but still in the arc of visibility. Engine revs had needed to be adjusted a couple of times, the Pole presumably having had to do the same to hold her station on the *Catherine Bell*. One or both of them maybe having problems with 'critical revs', the range of engine speeds which an individual ship couldn't maintain without developing the shakes, vibration threatening damage to shafts and glands, and the only way to cope with it in convoy being to switch between slightly higher and slightly lower speeds. You needed higher revs to provide twelve knots now in any case, heading into the swell, than you had before the turn.

Pitching westward, rolling quite hard as well; empty as she was, she'd do both in anything but a flat calm. Regular ship-noise and sea-noise, rhythm of thumps, groans and shudders as her stem dug in, lifted as it butted through, white suds flying and plastering her forepart. Creak of ship's gear a familiar, unending background. Old Man in the bridge's port for'ard corner, Andy close to buzzers and voice-pipes, Waller within arm's reach of the telegraphs, all three with their glasses up and searching, shifting round, sectors getting the most constant attention being from about four points on the starboard bow to a couple abaft the beam to port, where an anticlockwise arc of search came up against the bow-wave of the *Harvest Queen*. You could leave the rest of the all-round search to her, to a group like this in *her* bridge – she being especially vulnerable to attack, with nothing but the heave of dark ocean either directly ahead of her or astern, nor to port.

Waller had muttered, having got that far for the umpteenth time and begun to edge back the other way, 'Might've given 'em the slip . . .'

Counting chickens, or wishful thinking: anyway addressing it to himself, probably unaware of having spoken out loud. Only Samways' glance and doubtful sniff had answered him. Shake of the cloth-capped head then, eyes back on the gyro repeater, its soft glow reflected in them. Andy guessing at – visualising – U-boats having been, say, six or eight miles ahead, spread across the convoy's line of advance, before the emergency turn – which rightly or wrongly *was* how one had pictured it at that stage – well, by now they'd be more or less crossing the convoy's wake, having expected to make contact sooner than this. Failing to do so, they'd – well, wouldn't continue south for long, presumably weren't dummies; they'd spread out, crack on speed, begin to hunt around. And not being morons, they'd guess that a westbound convoy would hardly have made a turn to starboard.

That might be realistic enough, he thought. And if the Commodore had anything like that picture in *his* mind, why wouldn't he order a second forty-five-degree emergency turn now? You'd be turning out of echelon into line – on course then about 235, ie southwest, directly *away* from—

Explosion – port quarter. Torpedo hit for sure – and

41

close. The brain's reaction to it – through a wave of disappointment – was that it might well have been a hit on the *Harvest Queen*. Visual confirmation following instantly, binocs having swung that way – a mound of black ocean lifting alongside the grain-carrier's substantial midships section and bridge superstructure that was noticeably larger than *Quilla*'s. Waller muttering, 'Jesus, Jesus'; Andy's own unspoken thought a grim acknowledgment, *Well, it's starting now* . . .

Grim, but not despairing. Despair was something one couldn't afford, didn't feel or contemplate. Things got bad and might go from bad to worse – you held on because you had no option.

'I'll take her, Holt.'

'Aye, sir.' Distress rocket scorching up out of a general thickening of the darkness – smoke, with the *Harvest Queen* somewhere inside it and – a second's hesitation, recalling *that* one's name, the steamer that had been number four in column six – hell, the *Princess Judy* – under helm, ploughing through the muck's nearer fringe, giving a wide berth to her former neighbour and maybe intending to come up on *Quilla*'s quarter, where she'd be welcome, since without the *Harvest Queen Quilla* was on her own, exposed to any others of them on that side. Old Man doubtless with similar thoughts in mind, telling him, 'Pass the word aft to Merriman, they see one, don't waste time telling us, bloody well let fly!'

By telephone via the sight-setter, whose name was – he got it while cranking the handle of the phone – Hardy, ordinary seaman, who'd answered with a squawk of 'Gundeck!' Andy told him, 'Captain to Mr Merriman, Hardy – see a U-boat, don't report it, shoot at it!'

'Message from the bridge, Mr Merriman –'

He'd hung up, was only just moving back into the bridge's forefront when the next bad news came – from some distance astern, well back, near the centre maybe – and another on the heels of that. Sharpening one's presentiment that this was going to be worse than the previous night. Three hits in a space of – what, five or six minutes – and widely separated. U-boats had to be all over the place, might well have infiltrated the columns.

And damn-all one could do about it except maintain station, course and speed, and plod on, say your prayers.

As bad as any other aspect, that sense of impotence. *Fact* of impotence. Last night had in fact been his first experience of convoy action, and this was a derivative he'd not foreseen – the extreme frustration, almost *shame*, of personal helplessness. It had been his first experience of convoy action because although they'd sailed from Halifax in convoy in the *PollyAnna*, the atrocious weather had split them up and left the *Anna* struggling on her own; her *good* luck had been that U-boats couldn't operate in those conditions anyway. He was at the chart now – time 0118 – noting that on this westward course they'd be crossing longitude 15 west without coming within an hour's steaming of position 'A'. Not that position 'A' had anything special to offer, other than being a cardinal point on the convoy's preplanned route and on 15 west – which had nothing magical about it either – giving rise to another depressing truth, that longitude 15 degrees west, although it *had* been seen as the westward limit of effective U-boat operations, now that the bastards were working out of Lorient couldn't be seen as anything of the sort. So tomorrow night wouldn't necessarily be any more fun than this one or the last.

Another hit – starboard side, and close. Recognition, then – just 600 yards away, the *Byalystok*. The Pole's stern engulfed in smoke and flames, burning debris flying.

'Bloody hell!' – from Waller – and 'Poor buggers!' – a groan from Samways, addressed only to themselves. The *Byalystok*'s afterpart had been shattered in an upward boil of sea and was on fire, by the look of it internally; minor explosions might have been ammunition going up. *That* gun's crew done for – instantly obliterated. Old Man snapping to Samways, 'Port ten!'

'Port ten, sir . . .'

To pass clear of the Pole as she lost way and fell back. Damage aft could have wrecked her steering: desirable therefore to pass well clear. She was still on an even keel – more or less – or looked to be. Odds were she'd be immobilised in any case: propeller shaft or shafts, he was thinking of. *Quilla* passing her now, Old Man ordering, 'Midships and meet her', and then, 'Starboard ten', and to the engine room – you buzzed for attention, then used the voice-pipe – 'Up four revolutions.' Having lost ground by steering around the Pole, needing to keep station, or rather take station on the *Catherine Bell*. Andy checking around, seeing that the *Princess Judy* had evidently had second thoughts about closing up, was back where she'd started from, in the billet that had originally been the *Bristolian*'s until that disaster twenty-four hours ago. Disaster, nothing less, every time, not just a ship but forty to fifty souls in each of them. There'd be fish exploring the *Bristolian*'s interior by this time, crabs clawing their way in. And in this column seven, where last evening there'd been five ships, there were now just two – the *Catherine Bell* and the *Barranquilla*, joint leaders of the herd; and being in echelon, a U-boat commander attacking from either the port or starboard side might so angle himself as to get them as one overlapping target – the kind he could hardly miss.

So change the subject. Tonight's score – binoculars up and searching across the bow – at this stage, four. Five last night, if one included the Belgian who'd made it into Londonderry. Running total therefore nine, and surviving ships in convoy at this moment thirty-two. While another thing in mind – had been out of it for some moments but was back now – was that Merriman and the gun's crew, having witnessed the destruction of the *Byalystok*'s stern, gun-deck and gun's crew, might themselves be feeling – say, uneasy. And Merriman only seventeen, for all his gawky length . . . Moving up beside the Old Man, on this thought: 'Captain, sir – all right if I pay 'em a visit aft?'

*   *   *

44

He'd stopped to chat briefly with the bridge-wing look-outs, and paused on the deck below for a word with Elliot and Dixon. Noting that both were wearing their life-jackets and had a distress rocket ready for launching, as well as snowflakes within reach. Dixon's opening remark was: 'Kind of asking for it on our own out here, aren't we – sir?'

The ship, he meant – presumably – overexposed, inviting U-boats to take a shot at her. Although in point of fact, in this echelon formation the *Bell* was actually the leader, might seem to a U-boat to be the one to go for. But in any case, what would the boy propose that anyone should do about it? Andy told him, for lack of any more effective reassurance, 'One thing we do have going for us – if you've noticed, Dixon – is we're still afloat.'

Elliot laughed. 'Aye. There's *that*.' Andy nodded to him, went on aft and down the ladder to the main deck, thinking that if he ever had to pick one of those two to have with him in a boat or on a raft, he'd make damn sure it was the Glaswegian.

In fact Dixon might need his arse kicked.

He was climbing the port-side ladder to the gun-deck when they scored again. He winced: involuntary reaction indicative of nerves wearing thin, to which a second mate, he told himself as he came off the ladder, was not en-titled. But – only *thirty-one* now. Put it to the tune of *Nine Green Bottles*? Humming it as he joined the huddle of men around the gun and Assistant Cook Bayliss, ammo-supply number, chose this moment to scream into the darkness, 'Bloody fucking *bastards!*'

'Feel better for that, Bayliss?'

Pettigrew explained, 'Cookie's not enjoying 'isself all that much.' Merriman, though, looming up then: 'Morning, sir.'

'OK here, are we?'

Rocket going up from somewhere in the middle. Merriman shrugging: 'Except can't see a darned thing out there. It'd have to be practically alongside – or have a blooming light on it!'

'Yeah. Lost our moon. Applies both ways, mind you, them as well as us. But dawn won't be all *that* long coming. If they're still with us then –'

'Christ.' Peering at him through the dark, braced against the ship's motion: 'Might almost say if *we* are – I mean, hour and a half, two hours –'

'Run out of torpedoes before long, I'd guess. For every one that hits you can reckon on a couple that've missed. Except when they're in the middle of us, point-blank range.'

'Only take one of 'em with our name on it, eh?'

Fox, that was, one of the black gang. Andy told him, 'Bollocks, Fox. This is a *lucky* ship, didn't you notice?'

'Can't rightly say I 'ad!'

'Saw the Polish steamer hit, I suppose?'

Merriman said, '*Didn't* we just.'

'Well – knocking 'em down all round us, haven't they? Last night the *Daisy Oakes* and the *Bristolian*, now the Pole and the *Harvest Queen*. Well' – a wave towards the *Catherine Bell* – 'if I was in *her* I'd have the wind up!'

Merriman laughed. So did Patterson – and Pettigrew. Even Fox. *Most*, if not all. Not that he was fooling any of them: they were making allowances for *him*, acknowledging the effort and its purpose. One of the things he loved about this racket – the sense of independence, individuality, which they all prized and respected in each other – allowing *him* the same licence. In this instance, freedom to make silly jokes or even non-jokes in an effort to keep spirits up, one's own as much as others'. He clapped Bayliss on the shoulder: 'A bit *more* luck, you'll get your own back, catch one on the surface at first light, eh?'

Heading for'ard ten minutes later, he was remembering his father's predictions on the subject of Atlantic convoys, of which the old man had memories from the '14–'18

46

war. Not so much personal as historical, how close the U-boats had brought Britain to starvation, especially in 1916 and 1917. He'd prophesied, 'This time it'll be worse. We haven't a fraction of what we need. Plain truth is we're going to be well and truly up against it – and your lot worse than any!'

Being both a master mariner and a lifelong member of the RNR, Royal Naval Reserve, since 1937 he'd been involved in defence planning, preparations for the arming of merchant ships, organising and running courses and so forth; despite which he'd assumed that his son would switch to the RNR, as he himself had done in 1914. But Andy, who in late 1938 had just taken his second mate's ticket and qualified as a third mate, after three years at sea as a cadet, wasn't having any. He'd trained for the merchant navy, found himself very much at home in it: this was what he *was*, and the life he wanted. In his thinking there was no question of changing over, and it led to the most fundamental difference of opinion he and his father had ever had; at the height of it virtually a stand-up row – on Armistice night of '38 when he'd challenged the old man with, 'You're saying I'd have better chances of survival in a fighting ship than in a merchantman?' The answer had been an angry rebuttal, but that *had* been a good part of his father's reasoning. While Mama's had been more the social angle – or as she'd chosen to express it, 'It's the fighting men get the respect, Andy.'

The only voice supporting him, he remembered, had been his sister's. Annabel had understood completely and naturally how he'd felt about it. And the old man had come to terms with it, finally. While as to this current Atlantic situation – well, he'd been absolutely correct in that gloomy forecast, although a memory to hang on to was his having added, 'Oh, we'll get the better of them in the end – bloody *have* to. That or starve, be starved into surrender, that'll be the buggers' aim.'

Have to. Those were the words one latched on to. Bloody *would*, given half a chance, including the luck to remain in the land of the living until they'd built, launched and manned about a thousand more destroyers, sloops, corvettes . . .

Gunfire?

First thought had been: *God, another one . . .*

But – distant, and a sharper sound, whipcracks quite different from the thudding submerged explosions. Again now – and a vision of the U-boat surfaced or half-surfaced, getting its come-uppance – please God! Rapidly up the ladder to the boat-deck now, pausing at the top and hearing it again – one single shot – from a northerly direction – from down-wind – might therefore be less far off than one had thought, sound reduced by having the breeze against it. Somewhere to starboard anyway – on which side he found a group at the rail between the boats – the two cadets, and Harve Brown, bosun and boat-lowerers. Brown yelling at him after he'd made his presence known, 'Our sloop throwing her weight about, d'you reckon?'

'Don't know what else, Harve.'

'See the snowflake, did you?'

'No – where, when –'

'Before the argie-bargie started. Well, could've been starshell, weren't there long, I suppose. I'd say either sunk it, or it could've dived. Must've got seven or eight rounds away. Quicker 'n one of us could've done, I'd say!'

'Pray God they sunk 'im.' McGrath, the bosun, drawing fervent agreement from others. Show over, though, most of them turning inboard, Andy still scouring the dark sea streaked and patched whitish in the foreground from *Quilla*'s own lunging passage through it, and a smudge of further disturbance out there around the *Catherine Bell*. Leaving her, picking up the tall-funnelled *Imperator*, and on her quarter, roughly, the *Montreal Star*. Lowering his glasses, he told Harve Brown, 'Been down aft. Merriman

48

seems OK. Heading back up now. Not too bloody marvellous, is it?'

Steam-whistle, then – above their heads an escape of steam preceding one deafening short blast: there'd been a couple from the deep field by then, and from a neighbour now the same again. Others then, astern, and *Quilla*'s repetition of the single blast, emergency turn starboard. Entire herd giving, or by this time having given tongue. Andy on his way up, pausing in the bridge-wing, his glasses finding the Commodore's green lights a few seconds before they vanished: pushing in then by way of the starboard-side weather door, leaning back on it to shut it, hearing Samways report to the Old Man, 'Fifteen of starboard wheel on, sir.'

'Steer 320.'

'Three-two-oh, sir . . .'

Commodore reckoning on the sloop's action – whatever its outcome might have been – having distracted other close attention? That might account for the briefness of the interval between the green-light signal and the turn: getting his flock round on to the northwesterly course before another of the bastards poked its head up.

'Up four turns, Waller.'

'Up four, aye aye –'

'Course 320, sir!'

Eight minutes past two am. It had been 0140 when he'd gone aft, and the last torpedoing had been just as he'd reached the gun-deck – 0145, say – so you could say no hits in the last – well, call it half an hour. Might have been another if the sloop hadn't caught one of them on its way in – and touch wood, put paid to it?

Boring thing was, you'd probably never know.

Anyway, chartwork now . . .

They'd made the emergency turn at 0030, so to all intents and purposes had spent an hour and a half steering west. At twelve knots, eighteen miles. Call that sixteen. And applying that to the 0130 EP – a new one for 0200 put you on 58 degrees 55' north, 15 degrees 10'

49

west. So you might say that any U-boats encountered from here on would in theory be out of bounds, and the convoy entitled to disperse.

He told the Old Man, '0200 EP says we're ten miles west of fifteen west, sir. And twenty miles south of position "A".'

'Dispersal at first light maybe.'

'Aye, sir.'

Glasses up again – and favouring the port side again, the unprotected side. With nothing astern now either. Although most U-boat attacks came from the flanks: which was why all convoys were given a broader front than depth, the shorter depth – very much shorter now, *this* column – presenting a narrower spread of targets to the attacker.

Not that there was any great comfort in that when the column was only two ships long and you were one of them . . .

He thought it was a good letter he'd written to Julia, but the one to Annabel might be improved upon. In much the same way as their parents, she tended to smile, as if giving him up as hopeless, incorrigible, at any mention of his girlfriends, and he thought he might have left himself open to – well, not exactly a dismissive, but a less than wholeheartedly sympathetic reaction. Tear it up and start again, he thought: explain Julia's background in greater depth, how utterly different she was from girls he'd associated with in the past, and how differently he thought of her and always would. He'd touched on this, obviously, but he thought maybe not convincingly enough; Annabel actually had to believe it, not simply reflect that it was something he *wanted* her to believe. And perhaps the most challenging aspect of it was to get across to her this essential point: that the relationship was not only different but *special* – serious, long-term, not in the least casual as others had been – to make the truth of this clear without its apparently conflicting with the fact she'd become pregnant.

* * *

50

Two forty-seven. Cloud thinner and with gaps in it, a few stars visible but no moon, sky brightening in the east and the ships to starboard – *Montreal Star* on the beam, *Imperator* on the bow and *Cedarwood* on the quarter – no longer smudges but black cut-outs with increasingly hard edges, blacker than black against the beginnings of a dark shine on the sea.

U-boats on their way back to Lorient? Leaving one destroyed for five of the convoy sunk? Five tonight, five last night – less the one that struggled home. Nine crews, each averaging forty men, say, and you might guess at about fifty percent surviving – in boats, rafts, and some no doubt rescued by the sloop: call it nine ships and 200 men, in two nights and out of one convoy. How many convoys at sea at this moment, and how many steamers on their own?

Telepathy to Julia, sleepless and fretting on her narrow bed: *Still afloat, intact, and wanting only to get back to you, my darling . . .*

Spark of light, meaningless for a split second because one's mind had been elsewhere. Expanding though, brightening swiftly, *brilliant* then, too bright to look at without being blinded – filling the overhead about five points to starboard. Roughly over the head of column four – which was the Commodore-ship *Highland Fame*. But could as easily have been launched by one of the old boy's close neighbours. Using binoculars one could see ships' silhouettes as far away as column five. He *thought*, column five. The Old Man had glanced round, growled something to himself, and Waller had muttered, possibly addressing Andy, 'Here we go again . . .'

Right, and right on the moment – *thud* of a torpedo hit. Not going – bloody *gone*. Just when one had decided one could allow oneself to believe it was over for the night. And this one having made its kill despite having been spotted – that snowflake an indication that *something* had. Stayed on the surface long enough to get its torpedo or torpedoes on their way.

51

The plural had been correct: *another* hit. Bastard inside the convoy on that side, he guessed. Tonight's score now seven. Unless—

'Holt, what course to a point three hundred miles off St John's, Newfoundland?'

Thinking of ducking out?

'Roughly 235, sir, but I'll—'

'Near enough, for now.'

With adjustments for the westerly, wind and tide, probably was. And 300 miles off that Newfoundland coast you'd be well clear of the Grand Banks, where at this time of year there tended to be fogs. If one's guess as to what was in the Old Man's mind was anything like right, he'd alter there to something more like 210, heading for the Bahamas and Cuba through waters that should be U-boat free – even if any of their larger boats did happen to possess that phenomenal range. Unless they'd risk bringing America into the war, which surely they would not.

Distress rocket, from somewhere in the convoy's rear – roughly where the first of those two victims might be by now, if when she'd been hit she'd been in the van. Commodore's neighbours there being the *Eaglescliff, Muriel Sykes, Tancred, Colombine:* unless any of those had been knocked out before, he realised. Recalling the names of a few other possibles now – *Highmoor, Brigadier, Samaritan.* But one had no way of identifying earlier casualties, other than those who'd been close neighbours.

The second rocket had burst and fizzled out, and the candelabra-like brilliance of the snowflake was fading as it floated seaward. Old Man addressing Waller: 'You handier with an Aldis than you used to be, Third?'

'I hope so, sir – at least I've—'

'Plug it in out there, make *To Commodore from seventy-four, with your consent, propose continuing from here independently.*'

'Aye, sir.' He was repeating it while getting the Aldis

lamp out of its stowage. Low-voiced to Andy then, 'Call up the *Montreal Star* or the *Eaglescliff*, d'you think?'

'Either or both.' Meaning aim in that direction, either of those two might take in the message and pass it on. *Quilla* calling herself seventy-four, despite actually being in position seventy-two, because she'd started as number four in column seven and those remained her identification numerals for all signalling purposes while in this convoy. Andy rethinking the Old Man's decision and appreciating what had to be his reasoning: remaining in convoy wasn't doing anyone else any particular good, so departure couldn't do them any harm, and with dawn in the offing it looked like a safer bet to break away under cover of four-fifths darkness than to wait for general dispersal in the first light of day. Especially being in this column and having nothing astern of her, having only to put her helm over and vamoose.

As long as there were no U-boats on this side of the convoy, of course. That was the risk the Old Man was accepting; would be why, after asking for a course to steer, he'd given himself a minute or two to think about it.

Aldis clacking away out there. Not audibly from inside here, but you could see the fall-out of light: Waller flashing 'A's, calling up whoever'd see them and give him an answering flash, the 'go ahead'. Andy had turned away from it, not wanting to have his night-vision spoil, focusing on the *Catherine Bell*'s wake and stern light and sweeping slowly left. Anything out there, this would be a good time to spot it: at least, a bad time *not* to.

Catherine Bell would be very much on her own once *Quilla* hauled out. 'Column' of one. Maybe she'd follow suit.

'Third mate's passing your signal, sir.'

Samways: his eyes were back on the compass now. Stuttering of dots and dashes from outside there, and – Andy had swung in that direction, caught an acknowledging flash from about six points on the bow. The *Eaglescliff*, he supposed: she had the Commodore on her beam, so it might not take long to get his answer. If he was still there, the *Highland Fame* still afloat, and if that *was* the *Eaglescliff*, not whoever'd been astern of her now closed up in her billet. The *Brigadier*, that would be, if *she*'d survived this far ... But if the Commodore had gone, the *Eaglescliff* (or whichever else it was) wouldn't be slow in passing back that information, he guessed. Thinking also that it was a cold-blooded as well as murderous business: just a few minutes ago two ships lost, two crews, or at least some of them gone with them, and here and now their erstwhile companions plodding on – grim, anonymous, even aloof. Until it was you it was – well, some other lot.

But what else: *how* else?

Well, maybe *this* way – a signal lamp way out to starboard sparking, calling-up with 'A's. He stayed on it as Waller gave it the go-ahead and the dots and dashes came flickering in: *Barranquilla from Commodore: Good luck and God bless.*

4

Mid-afternoon, 6 August, *Quilla* on her own, pitching southwestward through ocean blue-tinted by remnants of the Gulf Stream and white-flecked by a breeze of about force four right on her nose. Moderate swell too, to which she was reacting in her usual light-ship manner, scooping up the white stuff and tossing it back in streams. She'd been on this mean course of 238 degrees since leaving the convoy at 0300, at that time increasing from twelve to fourteen and a half knots, and at 0400 commencing zigzag number seventeen, which as it so happened gave away fifteen percent of speed-made-good, bringing her down to actually covering about twelve and a quarter nautical miles per hour. There was a book of zigzag patterns, and number seventeen was the Old Man's choice: it was open at that page in front of the helmsman, and the zigzag clock was set to buzz every twenty minutes, reminding officers of the watch to put her on the next leg of it.

The main purpose of zigzagging was to make things less easy for a U-boat making a dived torpedo attack, the man at the periscope needing to make a reasonably accurate estimate of his target's course and speed in order to aim-off by the right amount. Andy discussed this with Harve Brown, after handing over the watch to him at four pm, making the point that all recent reports of daylight attacks on independently-routed ships had been of U-boats surfacing and using their guns; indeed the Old Man's orders to officers of the watch took account of this: 'Spot the bugger coming up, press the bloody tit and turn stern-on to bring *our* gun to bear.'

'So why the zigzag, if they aren't going to attack from dived?'

The mate had shrugged. 'Always the exception, I suppose?'

'From their angle, surfacing and using the gun makes sense though, doesn't it? Saving their torpedoes for the kind of night attack we've been seeing? They must be expensive things, compared to a few shells. And they only carry about ten – one lot in the tubes, other half reloads, and when they've used them up –'

'Yeah. Dare say.'

'Of course, if one could be sure of seeing the thing surfacing, and quick enough bringing the gun to bear, since while he's actually surfacing he's blind, isn't he –'

A nod: 'Slam on wheel good and quick, and if you can shoot straight you got the sod.' A raised forefinger: '*If*, Andy!'

'Didn't go too badly this morning, I thought?'

They'd had a practice shoot during the forenoon, putting over a target composed of vegetable crates lashed together, and firing a dozen twelve-pounder shells at it, the last few of which had fallen close. He'd done the spotting and correcting himself, with Merriman standing by – careful not to look as if he was thinking he could have done it better. Maybe no such thought in the boy's head, but that expressionless look made one wonder: especially being aware that one hadn't done all that marvellously. Brown said – with his glasses up, searching for periscopes – 'The first few went wide, didn't they. Them's the ones that need to hit – especially as the swine's shooting back at you.' A shrug. 'Need more practice, lad, that's all.'

'Tomorrow forenoon, if that's OK?'

'Sure . . .'

The Old Man had come up while they'd been talking. Zigzag clock buzzing at that moment, Harve Brown glancing round as the quartermaster – Freeman, middle-aged, three-quarters bald and bat-eared – put on starboard wheel. Brown said, 'Saying we might lay on another shoot tomorrow, sir.'

'More the better.' Eyes shifting to Andy. 'It's hitting with the first shot that counts.'

Andy nodded. 'Means getting the range right – up to me, I know, sir.'

'Target was – what, thirty to fifty yards away, your first shot this morning?'

'About that, sir. But I'd say the amount of movement on her –'

'Tell Patterson try loosing off at the top of a rise or the bottom of a trough. As she hangs, like.'

'Yessir.' It wasn't all that simple, in fact, and you needed to be right for line before you could correct for range. Which the Old Man had to know at least as well as one did oneself, probably better. OK, this forenoon's effort having started at virtually point-blank range, the opening shots really *should* have hit, or at least fallen a lot closer than they had. Harve Brown opening a new subject then – the Old Man having moved to his customary port for'ard corner – 'Your young lady's uncle's ship – as fought a gun duel with some U-boat – uh?'

'Yeah?'

It wasn't his watch now, the mate had taken over, but since he was still up here he had his glasses up, out of habit, searching down the starboard side. He checked, told Brown, 'Didn't even let 'em get the boats away. Hammered the daylights out of them – smashed the bridge and set her on fire. They got Julia's boat down all right, thank God –'

'What ship, and where?'

The Old Man, showing interest . . .

'South of the Azores, sir. Motor vessel *Cheviot Hills*, A. and J. Hills of Tyneside. On her way back from New Zealand via Panama. Her survivors – one boatload – were picked up later by a Hun steamer – *Glauchau*, the one we—'

'That famous business of yours – aye, course. I'd not appreciated the young lady as just mentioned was the subject –'

'Niece of the master, sir, who went down with his ship. He'd taken her on a visit to another uncle who's farming in NZ – only one of the family who's not a seaman. Oh, he *was*, I think, when he was young. Anyway, her father had a trawler, drowned somewhere off Norway when she was little, and her two cousins – sons of the *Cheviot Hills* master – are second mates.'

'Good wife for a sailor, Holt.'

He nodded. 'Had crossed my mind, sir.'

Harve Brown smirked. 'Crossed it and continued into the wide blue yonder, eh?'

'So happens, sir' – addressing the Old Man – 'we're going to marry.'

'Going to *what*?' Harve glancing at his captain: 'Beg your pardon, sir, but – I don't believe it. Honest, simply don't.' Eyebrows hooping then: 'Unless she's in the family way? But even *then*—'

Andy cut in, asking the Old Man, 'If you'd excuse me, sir . . .'

Harve brought the subject up again that evening in the saloon over mugs of coffee, asking him, 'Pulling my leg were you, young Holt, or are you truly contemplating matrimony?'

'Concern you all that much, Harve?'

'Well – yeah.' He looked surprised. 'Known you long enough, lad – you *and* your antics. Can't get my mind round it, somehow. I mean, at twenty-one, and – well, apart from your well-known natural inclinations – not to mention there's a war on –'

58

'Ever hear of people falling in love?'

Two slow blinks. A shrug then. 'Done it meself, even. But – crikey . . . Told your folk, have you?'

'Not a soul.'

'How about her? Told *her*?'

He looked around. No-one was in easy earshot. There was a noisy game of cribbage going, one of dominoes, third engineer and CRO throwing dice. He told the mate – whose interest was benevolent, he was well aware – 'I've proposed to her and she's accepted. That's the long and short of it.'

'I'll be damned.' Round-eyed, speaking softly. Shake of the head then. 'Better tell your folk, hadn't you? What about hers – they know?'

'There's only her mother. But I'd forgotten – I've told my sister. Haven't posted the letter yet, but –'

'Don't want to seem nosy, boy, but I'm a lot older than you, known you a few years, family man myself – two grown daughters of my own, damn it –'

'Hoping I'd marry one of *them* – that it?'

'I wouldn't let you in the same room as either of 'em, not even if you were encased in plaster of bloody Paris!'

'They *must* be hot stuff. Tell you what, Harve –'

'Seriously, now. What about the young cadet – apprentice – she was so close to? Your chum Fisher told me –'

'Him again.' Don Fisher, who'd been second mate in the *PollyAnna*. 'Really bent your ear, didn't he?'

'Well – just him and me having time to kill, and an interest in your various carryings-on –'

'You're talking about an A. and J. Hills' apprentice name of Mark Finney – formerly of the *Cheviot Hills*. He and another one who died of wounds in the boat with Julia – died in Julia's arms. Head wound and – other injury. Anyway, Mark Finney – age seventeen, and Julia by the way is twenty-one, same age as me – he and Julia were what you might call inseparable. It was a trio, when we first had 'em aboard, the *Cheviot*'s chief engineer playing daddy and young Mark as little brother.

59

They'd gone through all that together, d'you see, sort of hand-in-hand: he'd looked after her all through – time of the sinking, and in the boat, then prisoners in the Hun steamer, and later in the *Anna* when it was a toss-up whether she'd stay afloat another night – another bloody *hour* . . . But how it was between those two – listen, a way I can describe it, in her own words, near enough. She'd said something about me being kind to her – dare say I had been, I was dead scared for her at some of the really bad times, and I said something like, "It's not just blooming *kindness*" – yeah, all right, wanting to let her know how I felt about her – and she warned me off, saying Mark Finney was "quite a sensitive soul". Believe me though, I'd given it a lot of thought, and whether you'd believe it or not I may say I was being as good as gold: that remark was the first what you might call *approach* of any kind I'd made – and I said then, about Finney, something about she and him being close like a sister and young brother might be, and her answer was, "He may *think* it's become more than that. I'm very fond of him, and he's been marvellous, there've been times I couldn't have done without him. What I'm saying is I wouldn't want him hurt."'

Brown's eyes were thoughtful. 'Won't he be, though?'

Andy hesitated. Having the answer, but no reason to let Harve in on every damned aspect of the business, one thing constantly leading to another as it seemed to. He shook his head. 'No. But that's how it was. She wasn't only telling me to lay off, she was saying that what was between her and Mark was *not* "any more than that" – d'you see? I was standing well back anyway, I truly was. Thinking how bloody marvellous she was, but leaving the pair of them to hold hands and whisper in each other's ears, all that. Because that was best for *her*. My way of looking after her was to make sure he was with her every damn minute. What kind of bull did Fisher come up with?'

'His only reference to it – that I recall – was when you went off to Newcastle, he wondered about her and the youngster and you maybe barging in on love's young dream.'

Chief Engineer Frank Verity had just entered the saloon, stood for a moment looking around, saw them and started in their direction. Andy told Brown quickly, 'After we docked I was sent ashore on a job the chairman wanted done, and when I got back she'd gone. The old sod had given her a lift in his bloody Daimler. But she'd left me a note – which Fisher knew about, told me where to find – saying "Please come visit – *please* – ring and say you're coming". Best thing I ever read in all my life. That sound like I was horning in on anything, Harve?'

Andy moved, making way for the engineer. 'Evening, sir.'

'Evening to you, Holt.' To the mate then: 'Wind's up a bit, did you notice?'

It had freshened to about force five and also veered due west by sundown, soon after which they'd ceased zigzagging – no point in it during the dark hours, when any U-boat you encountered would be on the surface. With the wind up by this amount and three points on the bow she'd be losing a couple of knots in any case. Also, soon after sundown the Old Man had got a good set of stars through gaps in the low, fast-moving cloud, and from the resulting fix had altered course from 238 to 241. None of which was any different when Andy took over the watch at midnight: wind the same, sea-state, say, four, and visibility not bad, judging it by the distance at which one could clearly make out the oncoming streaming crests. Stars still visible here and there, moon wouldn't be up for a couple of hours.

Waller had gone down, having expressed the hope that he might get some bloody sleep tonight for a change. Elliot followed him below, and Dixon, with the glasses he'd taken from him – bridge binoculars, cadets weren't expected to provide their own – took up his usual position in the starboard fore corner. Selby was on the wheel.

Quilla wasn't as good a sea-boat as the *PollyAnna*, Andy thought. Even allowing for her empty holds, she was making a bit much of it.

Old Man had his pipe going, generating a stink that was a reminder of *PollyAnna*, of old Josh Thornhill and *his* foul old burners. Josh now sixty years of age and with an OBE after his name, letters for once *not* standing for Other Buggers' Efforts.

Captain Nat Beale was on the move now, though. Telling Andy, 'I'll be below, Second. Call me for anything at all.'

'Aye, sir. But not likely they'll bother us tonight?'

'Such a thing as speaking too soon, lad.'

A nod, and he'd gone. With luck, *might* get a whole night in. Andy sent Dixon to check that the lookouts were on their toes, then asked the helmsman, 'You happy, Selby?'

'Happy enough, sir. Subs don't like it rough, do they?'

'Well. Guess they might cope with this, at a pinch.'

Putting his glasses up then, unsure whether they would or wouldn't, but remembering those truly gigantic seas with which, thank God, they definitely had *not* been able to cope. Would have been about all you'd have needed, if they had. Recalling one night in particular, second or third day and night of fighting hurricane-force winds, waves that came at you like white-topped sheer black walls shutting out the sky then smashing down – deafening, stunning, *drowning* – and the ship driving on with that weight on top of her, dragging herself on out of it, time after time, and all of you knowing next time maybe *not* . . . And in the saloon, Julia, white-faced but keeping her voice more or less steady, telling him and Finney, 'Think I'll see if I can't get some shut-eye.'

Shut-eye. Might have laughed, if it hadn't been so terrifying.

Moving around below decks hadn't been easy. You
moved when you could from one solid object to the next,
hung on to that through the next thundering impact,
which each time could have been the one that would
finish it, drive her under: truly *could*, and they'd all known
it, that any minute could have been the old ship's last –
there was a snapshot memory of Finney asking him after
Julia's departure for her shut-eye, 'Isn't she really something?'

After the *Anna*'d docked in Glasgow, Finney – who'd
never see his eighteenth birthday – had gone on a week's
leave to his home in or near London. A week had been
all he was getting since A. and J. Hills had offered him
a berth in a ship due to leave Liverpool in ten days. Mid-
February, that meant, and the ship had been the SS
Scotswood. Not all the A. and J. Hills vessels had names
ending with 'Hills'. But talking with Julia and her cousin
Dick in Newcastle at about that time, Julia having
commented that it seemed a bit rough on young Mark
after his recent experiences to be shipped out again quite
this soon, Dick had compared it to a rider being thrown
off a horse. 'Getting right back up again's the thing. Don't
want to sit and think about it.' An arm round his cousin's
shoulders then: 'Not as I'd wish that on *you*, girl. Bloody
marvel, I'd say you've turned out.' To Andy then: 'Aren't
I right?'

Dick Carr was twenty-four or twenty-five, not especially
tall, but solid, dark-haired and grey-eyed, with a strong
jaw that turned blue-black by mid-afternoon. There'd
been a memorial service for his father Harry, late master
of the *Cheviot Hills*, in the small church at South Shields
where he'd lived, during the few days that Andy had spent
with them on that first visit. The family group had
comprised Dick and his mother Alice, and Julia and her
mother Jean; unfortunately not Dick's brother Garry,
who'd been away at sea. But maybe forty or fifty other

Merchant Navy men, mostly in navy-blue serge suits and including half a dozen ships' masters, had packed in, also A. and J. Hills people – directors, and their marine superintendent and office staff. Andy had been put at the end of the family pew, beside Dick, and afterwards, trooping out, had felt the man's hand on his arm, heard him growl, 'We'd 'a lost her too, hadn't been for you. We're beholden.'

Her mother had said much the same thing the day before, only more emotionally, within minutes of his arrival by train from Glasgow. Little sparrow of a woman. Andy had told Dick Carr – or begun to – in the churchyard, 'But it was Mark Finney who *really*—'

'—helped her along, yeah. Hadn't been for you though, they'd've gone together, more 'n likely. You saved the lot of 'em – and as *she* rates it – tell you this gratis an' for nothing, in *her* little eyes –'

'What you gassing on about, then?' Dick's mother – grey-headed, fifty-ish, rather noticeable moustache also greying – telling Andy, 'Spitting image of his dad, is this one. Well, so's Garry, mind . . .'

Dixon was back from his tour of the lookouts, had found them all awake and on the job. Not that one would have expected otherwise, but it was as well for them to know they weren't forgotten, and that their job was important enough to be checked on.

0045 now. *Quilla* still throwing herself about, no noticeable change in the weather, visibility still fairly good, but that wasn't to say you'd spot a U-boat bow-on – which it would be within seconds if it spotted *you*. So although one wasn't *expecting* trouble, with things as they were tonight, one still concentrated totally and full-time on the business of looking out.

At about 0230, Dixon broke the silence from his corner – something about the CRO. Andy looked round – glasses removed from his eyes by an inch or two – saw Foster coming from the ladder, stopping and grabbing at the handrail as she made one of her more sudden and violent rolls. She really had no business making such a lot of it, he thought. Turning back to where he had been in his search – port bow and inching left, while waiting for whatever news the Marconi man might have brought; he had a clipboard with him, no doubt a signal the Old Man might want to see.

News of U-boats?

'Morning, Second. Captain turned in?'

'Got any sense, he has. What's up?'

'Distress call – SS *Princess Judy*. Torpedoed, filling, abandoning ship, 57 25 north, 23 40 west.'

'Put that on the chart, Dixon.' He told Foster, 'Better shake the Old Man anyway.' Dixon had taken the clipboard to the chart, was jerking the canvas screen across before switching on the light. Andy added to Foster, glasses back at his eyes again and searching, 'When we can give him a bearing and distance. Not that he'll want to divert.' Adding to that, 'I imagine', since he still didn't know this captain all that well, as yet – not well enough to read his mind with any certainty – and the *Princess Judy* had been in their convoy – in column six, in fact, a near neighbour. Poor devils. This wasn't much of a sea, but it wasn't ideal for launching boats in either.

Dixon's shout then: 'Near enough due north, seventy-five miles!'

Foster recovered his clipboard and went down. Andy telling himself that the Old Man would certainly expect to be informed of it, but would not divert. Seventy-five miles would take them six hours – at *least*, with wind and sea on the beam she'd be really wallowing. And in six hours' time – broad daylight by then, but odds heavily against finding any boats, whereas there'd surely be other ships nearer to her – others from the same convoy, some maybe close enough to see the distress rocket or rockets she'd have launched.

He thought again, poor buggers.

Then: 'Dixon.'

'Yessir?'

'Your report should have been seventy-five miles due north, *sir.*'

'Oh – I –'

'If you were a third mate and you had a report from a lookout, wouldn't you expect that "sir"?'

'Yessir. I'm sorry, I –'

'If you have hopes of ever becoming a third mate, I'd advise you to keep it in mind.'

'Sir . . .'

He didn't have too good an opinion of young Dixon, he realised. Didn't feel that on his present showing he was suitable material for cadet, let alone third mate.

Might not get that far anyway. One way or another . . .

'Second?'

Foster telling him, 'Captain says maintain course and speed.'

'All right. Thanks.'

First hint of pre-dawn radiance back there in the eastern sky, and as if that wasn't enough, a sliver of moon in the southwest. The Old Man, who'd come up a few minutes ago and had been out in the port wing getting some ozone into his lungs, came back inside now.

'See, Holt? U-boats *were* at it.'

He nodded. 'Yessir.'

'The *Princess Judy* was in column six, low funnel growing right out of her bridge structure, right?'

He nodded. 'Looked a bit like one of the Lamport and Holts, I thought.'

'Come to think of it – she did, after a fashion . . . Name of Holt's all over the damn place, eh?'

'Do see it here and there, sir.'

'You're not related to Blue Funnel, though?'

'Regrettably not. Nor to J. Holt of Liverpool.'

'Well. Can't have *all* the luck.'

This concluded the social break. Which in itself was

66

to be appreciated. A lot of masters – in years past, *most* – barely addressed their officers on any subject at all except ship's business. Anyway, that was it: Old Man moving into his usual corner, putting his glasses up.

Sky lightening all right, sea with a shine of polish on it. Not light enough to call for the resumption of the zigzag yet, he thought. It would be a decision for the Old Man, anyway, now he was up here.

'Relieve helmsman, sir?'

AB Freeman, up to take over from Samways: 0345. Quartermasters did two-hour tricks, and changed over at a quarter to the hour so the bridge wouldn't be cluttered with too many change-overs taking place at one time. He nodded to him: 'Go ahead.' And to Dixon, 'Better shake the mate and Merriman.'

Turning in, thinking sadly about the *Princess Judy* and the luck of the draw: to have been in her, or in *Quilla* – safe, at any rate for the moment, and warm, about to enjoy the luxury of sleep in this small but adequate so-called 'double' cabin, for the moment sitting rather than standing, the way she was still lurching and hammering around. Reaching to his boat bag for a quick look at the snapshot of Julia which he kept in it: snap of Julia wearing that quirky little smile of hers. He'd taken it with her mother's box camera on the last day of that February visit to Newcastle, and had asked her to send him a copy if it came out all right, since he wasn't then expecting to see her again until he'd completed his studies and won his first mate's ticket. Julia had persuaded him that he shouldn't interrupt his work or waste money on further visits – just get down to it and make sure of it. Then – OK, high jinks, when he could afford it, and why not? High jinks such as they'd enjoyed at the Assembly Rooms in Newcastle, for instance, where they'd attended the Saturday night dance and he'd taken her behind the heavy curtains screening the recesses of the first-floor ballroom's tall bow windows. Not that he'd any doubt there'd eventually be other, *higher* jinks, so to speak: he'd begun to realise she did have propensities in such directions. Under tight control, but there all right.

Anyway, he'd agreed with her about hard work and no weekends off, and stuck to it – really had put his back into it, treating himself to an occasional pint and even more occasional evening out with Susan Shea. And writing to Julia every weekend, right through to the beginning of June – Dunkirk time, and a couple of days after Belgium and Holland had surrendered to the Nazis – first week in June, when he'd had the telephone message from her: please call back, urgent, soon as possible. Which he had done, from Ma Shepherds that same evening, but was answered neither by Julia nor her mother, but by the woman – Hilda, surname Simpson or Simkins – who was Mrs Carr's partner in the dress business in which Julia also worked. Hilda told him they'd gone to church – she'd have gone too only Julia had asked her to wait in case Andy telephoned.

'Church – on a Thursday?'

'It's the young lad, Mark. Him as was with her on the *Cheviot Hills*?'

'Mark Finney?'

'Aye, him. In the steamer *Scotswood* this time – as you may have heard? The poor sweetheart's desperate – as she would be, that poor young feller –'

'The *Scotswood* lost?'

'Off Freetown, West Africa. Gentleman from Hills called round here, spoke to Mrs Carr, then –'

'All right. Tell them I'll come. Tomorrow evening, spend Saturday with them if they'd put me up Friday night –'

'Oh, not a doubt they will!'

Snapshot back into its envelope and the boat bag. Thinking back to that Friday night when he'd taken what must have been the last bus from the station to a stop within a few hundred yards of the Carr house, and covering that final stretch at a fair canter through the blacked-out suburban streets. There'd been air-raids on the docks and shipping in the river in recent weeks – as there had been on the Clyde, Mersey, Portsmouth, Plymouth – and of course London worst of all. But as Julia had assured him, not a single bomb in any residential area; certainly on this Friday night the only sound apart from his own heavy footfalls and hard breathing was the hiss and drip of rain in the whitebeams that lined the pavements. Then at the house he'd been hesitant about knocking or ringing the bell at such an hour, and had remembered that on the night they'd attended the Assembly Rooms thrash, back in February, Mrs Carr, who liked to get her head down early, had simply left the door unlocked for them.

Turning its brass handle very carefully, therefore – and sure enough, door opening to light pressure on it. Slight squeak as it did so, and pretty well instantly Julia's murmur from across the hall where a lamp glowed in the sitting-room: 'Andy?'

Looking more like sixteen than twenty-one. Pale-faced, big eyes amber in the half-light, soft brown hair loose on her shoulders, little navy-blue dressing-gown that could have been a schoolgirl's. Except it wasn't. In his arms: he'd clicked the door shut, turned back, and there she'd been.

'You're all wet. Bless you for coming.'

'Wettish place, Newcastle.' He disengaged enough to get his raincoat off, dropped it and re-engaged, hugging her now. Her voice in his ear, 'Sweet to have come so quick, Andy pet. I feel so dreadful for him, so – not *lost*, but – as if he should be here, suddenly just *isn't* . . . Rambling – sorry. But on the happier side – you, how marvellous you were to us both –'

'Don't know how you'd have expected . . .'

Calming her then, stemming the flow, nerves as well as sadness. Getting round to reminding her of things

69

she knew as well as he did, facts of life such as that even in peacetime those who lived on the sea stood fair chances of ending their lives on it – which Mark had been clearly aware of, had seen with his own eyes, as indeed she had herself: one was in it, that was all, took the chances. Stating the obvious for sure, also broadening the subject: 'Three of my own friends been sunk this far, training-ship friends I mean – two picked up, one not.' That word 'not' being gentler, he thought, than 'drowned'. 'All three on the east coast, ships sunk by mines – U-boats laying 'em, sinking more that way than they are by torpedo, so one hears.' Back to basics then: 'The *Scotswood* was off Freetown, Hilda said.'

'On her way home *from* Freetown. Independently routed, was to have called for bunkers at Las Palmas.'

'No chance he'd have been in a boat, could still be picked up? Thousands of miles and coast and ocean –'

'No.' Jerk of the head. 'Because—'

'Survivors have been adrift for weeks, you know, before –'

'There *were* survivors. How the folk at Hills know all about it. He was killed when she was torpedoed, they *know* it.'

'Then he might not have known anything much about it.'

'Pray God he didn't. Andy, that's sopping wet.' The coat, she'd touched it with her bare foot. 'I'll put it on the rack over the stove. And anything else.' That smile, then: 'Same cabin trunk, I see.'

The haversack which he'd dropped in the doorway, that also being wet. Explaining, 'Even less in it than last time, what's more. Have to go back Sunday, so – one clean shirt, razor, couple of pairs of socks?'

'Should do you, I suppose. Once it's dry. Better come on up. Oh – if you'd like some tea, or –'

'Don't want to clatter around, do we. Heavens, I've messed you up –'

'I'm not objecting. In fact, after waiting up half the night –'

'*That* long?'

'No. Suppose not, really. Seems – seemed so, but . . .' Nervous? Tongue-tied? Shake of her head, the cloud of hair: he loved the scent of it. 'See, instead of putting lights on . . .'

She had a torch. His room would be the attic one he'd used in February – second floor, passing her own and her mother's, and the boards up there covered with linoleum, as they were down here, except that there were carpets too, carpet also on this first flight of stairs, but not on the upper one. Thinking of which he stopped, sat on the lower stairs to take his boots off while she focused the torchbeam on him. Her whisper: 'Sodden, are they?'

'Used to it. Just don't want to wake your mum.'

'Best not, if we can help it.'

Climbing again, torchbeam lighting the way, then on the landing, the sound of her tiny mother's loud, whistling snores. Julia turning to look at him, a hand over her mouth as if to suppress giggles, then on up narrow attic stairs, the door of his room standing open, the other being a space they kept junk in. She lit the way into his, then followed him in, shut the door with great care and switched on the light.

'Give me your wet things, I'll take them down.'

'Well.' Looking at her uncertainly. The legs of his trousers were pretty well soaked. It was a very small room: iron bedstead, chest of drawers, hooks on the door for whatever needed to be hung up. You couldn't have got a wardrobe in, the slopes of the ceiling barely gave standing room except in the middle. He muttered, 'Can't just – undress.'

'I'll turn my back.'

Turning away. Lovely little figure, the cotton gown a bit small for her. Probably *had* had it in her schooldays. Bottoms of striped pyjama legs below it. Figure almost

71

as hour-glass as that Brazilian girl's. Although you could bet *she* hadn't worn striped pyjamas. Hand-downs from the cousins, maybe? He'd thrown off his jacket, was sitting on the bed to peel off rain-darkened flannel trousers.

'Here you are. Thanks. Keeping you up all night . . .'

'Not *all* night.' Gaze still averted. 'Want to use the bathroom?'

'Might wake your mother. And even if *you* don't mind me wandering around bare-arsed . . .'

'Once she's out it takes a lot to wake her. But – no dressing-gown, or –'

'I'd have used the raincoat.'

'You'll be half-frozen. Look, wrap this towel –'

'Oh, *yes* –'

'Have enough light from here, will you? Leaving the door open?'

'Perfect.'

She'd gone, taking the torch. He waited a moment, then crept down into the sound of snoring, which mercifully continued while he did what he needed to and then crept back up, hesitating first as to whether to shut the door – which he did – then whether to strip off and turn in or wait in case she was coming back up to say goodnight.

He discarded the towel, turned off the light, groped his way into bed.

Surprising she *hadn't* said goodnight.

Then he saw the torchbeam and heard the door shutting, although he hadn't heard it open. Hardly believing this: not daring to. Mind and body rising to the occasion none the less, accepting with surprisingly little hesitation a situation that was totally new, unthought of even in any passive sense, let alone pre-meditated or even hoped for.

New thought then, virtual body blow. *Damn* . . .

No. It was OK. Huge relief, after that flare of panic. In his wallet, which was in the jacket, which thank God she hadn't taken downstairs with her. He had two in there, their ring-shapes visible through the wallet's fabric; if he'd thought of it before departure from Liverpool he'd have left them behind, as indeed he had last time.

'Julia?'

'Sh . . .'

Sounds of the removal of navy-blue wrap and striped pyjamas. Incredibly alluring sound. Making way for her, flipping the bedclothes back, and then as she slithered in enfolding them around her, and one ultra-thrilling second later her warm breath in his ear: 'Couldn't have stood leaving you up here alone. *Couldn't . . .*'

Dozing. Remembering again – he'd had time and good reason to think about it, recently – that two hadn't been anywhere near enough. There'd been Saturday to follow, after all. He suspected that the ones he bought in Newcastle that morning, on the face of it getting aspirins for Julia's alleged headache, might have included a dud.

It had been a weekend of contrasting sadness and excitement. Sadness genuine enough, certainly on her part, and he'd liked young Finney well enough to reflect it. Also, when on their own, her insistence that how things had changed between them shouldn't be allowed to interrupt his work. No more weekends until he'd finished the course and won his ticket. While he'd wondered, on and off – and since then, too – what Mark Finney might actually have meant to her. There'd been nothing physical between them, he felt sure of that, but if only in her dreams – daydreams, he supposed he meant – well, whether she might have had notions of waiting, giving the lad time to grow up?

In which case his own aspirations mightn't have come to much.

But you couldn't blame anyone for their dreams. Or probably ever know the answer. Anyway, he'd been back at work in Liverpool on Monday 10 June, the day the Italians decided it was in their best interests to become allies of the Germans, and Churchill commented, 'Only fair – *we* had them last time.'

5

August 7th. *Quilla*'s noon position of 54 degrees 52 north, 26 degrees 48 west was based on Waller's morning sunsight and Andy's meridean altitude, worked out by Elliot and found to be compatible with a run-on EP from the Old Man's early fix from stars. Very much a joint effort, due to the fact that Waller had had a clearish sky for his morning sun soon after eight, whereas by the time Andy had been ready to take his an hour later the cloud cover had been total. It hadn't broken up until shortly before noon. But based on this, speed-made-good over the past twenty-four hours had averaged a fraction under twelve knots, which seeing that the zigzag had been resumed at first light wasn't bad.

He came back from the chart, told Waller, 'OK. Enjoy your lunch.'

'Wasn't a bad shoot this morning.'

'Wasn't, was it, all things considered.'

Referring to the amount of movement on her. Andy had wanted to go ahead with it, Harve Brown had been opposed to it on grounds of danger to life and limb, but the Old Man had insisted that in anything but much rougher conditions than these, they had to be capable of manning and using the gun effectively – which meant they needed practice. As it turned out they'd hit their target with the second shot and dropped the third so close to it that on anything larger it would have been another hit; which was enough, Andy had thought – that the lads knew they could handle it, even from a highly mobile platform. He'd called the bridge over the sight-setter's telephone and received the Old Man's permission to pack up, secure the gun, by which time the target had in any case disintegrated.

Waller came back up to relieve him for his lunch just short of one pm. Lunch was corned beef, mashed spuds and cabbage followed by stewed prunes with custard; Harve Brown's comment: 'Not exactly your regular *gourmet*'s choice, but OK if you're famished.'

'I've known worse.'

'Well, sure . . .'

'In the old *Burntisland* for instance.'

'Christ, don't remind me.'

He'd pushed his chair back. To return to the bridge, take over the watch again. 'Head down now, Harve?'

'*Had* crossed my mind . . .'

Had crossed the Old Man's, too: what was known as a 'one to three', the afternoon kip or caulk. So Andy with Dixon and Quartermasters Samways and then Selby had the bridge to themselves for the next few hours, *Quilla* thudding and rollicking along on mean course 240, zigzagging twenty degrees each side of that, under a sky that was virtually clear now, had only tatters of white cloud against brilliant blue. Idyllic, worth guineas per minute just to be here, if you didn't have in mind that it could terminate very, very suddenly in the splitting crack of an explosion, upheaval of ocean and – whatever then, what-ever . . .

Newton, though, Marconi man with the ginger side-boards, arriving from the wireless office complete with clipboard and anxious look. After one glance, Andy continuing his binocular search for a periscope you wouldn't have a hope in hell of spotting in this expanse of broken sea. Hearing the man's yell then: 'Captain below, is he?' and turning, lowering the glasses.

76

'Another poor sod bought it?'

A nod. 'Kids on board, what's more.'

'What?'

He read it out: 'SS *Sarawak* – bombed by Focke-Wulf, fires out of control, one hundred and thirty-one children on board, abandoning in position . . .'

'Dixon –'

'Aye, sir!'

Children. Evacuees presumably, US-bound, being transported for their own safety from the Luftwaffe's assault on Britain's towns, ports, cities. But Christ, what a *hell* of a –

Well. Hope – pray – this one might be in reach. Dixon meanwhile breaking all known records for putting positions on charts and taking off range and bearing: a yell of 'Sixty miles on 153, sir!'

Prayer answered, then. Surely. He told Newton, 'Hang on', and pressed the Old Man's alarm buzzer. Thinking, *Sixty miles, say five hours.* Checking the time and gesturing to Dixon to resume his looking out. Old Man pounding up, seeing Newton and snatching the clipboard from him, Andy giving him time to scan it before telling him the bearing and distance-off.

Grim-faced, swiftly rescanning: eyes narrowed and lips compressed, muttering while moving to the chart, 'Sixty miles . . .' This time one did know what his reaction would be, although he was making certain of it, checking it out somewhat less rapidly than Dixon had done before returning to the bridge's forefront, telling himself, 'Sixty-five, call it', and telling Selby, 'Cease zigzag.' Watching the ship's head by gyro, as Selby brought her back to 240, then 'Port fifteen, steer 155.' Two-degree allowance for the fact she'd have wind and sea abaft her starboard beam. Andy thinking also that without the zigzag she ought to do better than twelve knots, and telling Dixon to switch off the zigzag clock.

Sarawak, though. Pacific origins, obviously. And carrying that number of passengers, an intermediate liner, most likely. Blue Funnel? Bibby? Wouldn't have thought so from the name, but –

'Dixon.' The Old Man cleared his throat. 'Ask Mr Brown and Chief Engineer Verity to come up, please.'

So they'd had their one-to-threes. Just gone three anyway.

On the turn, for a while with wind and sea directly on her beam, she'd *really* rolled. But it had been an alteration of eighty-five degrees, and now on a course of 155 – SSE, roughly – she was steadier than she'd been when heading into it.

To get there with a decent margin of time before sundown was important. Get there *fast*, anyway. The chief had consented to winding on a few more revs – notionally for a flat-out fourteen and a half knots, which in these bouncy conditions might boil down to, say, thirteen. Visions of a blazing hulk, 131 frightened children packed into open boats, and an hour or so at most between the soonest one could hope to get there and the onset of darkness. One wondered about the decision to send them – in an independently-routed, maybe somewhat antequated passenger and cargo steamer, as like as not still crawling with cockroaches of Far Eastern origin. Decision presumably the Ministry of War Transport's, basic requirement being for a ship with a good number of passenger berths – and if she could make fifteen knots or more she *would* be sailed independently.

But on a track southerly enough to be inside the range of long-range bombers from western France?

Where *Quilla* was now, in fact – and heading deeper into it. In U-boat waters still, with no time to waste on zigzags. The Focke-Wulfs' primary function, one had gathered, being reconnaissance, locating convoys and reporting their positions, then acting as radio beacons for U-boats to home in on. But they also attacked and sank ships, especially solitaries – ships having as yet no effective defence against the bastards. That twelve-pounder on the poop for instance had no high-angle capability; all you had was the Holman Projector – grenade-launcher – next to useless, *completely* useless except against an aircraft passing directly overhead at something like masthead height.

Lookouts had been stationed, and boats were still turned out on their davits. All hands had been informed of the reason for the diversion, and Andy had stayed on watch an extra hour, relieved then by Waller, sharing the first dogwatch and part of the second between them while Harve Brown looked into alternative rearrangements of accommodation and victualling, provision from stores of such things as blankets and donkeys' breakfasts – straw mattresses – and scope for the treatment of injuries, especially burns; he was mugging this up from the *Ship Captain's Medical Guide*.

Brown asked Andy – in the saloon, over mugs of tea – 'Know what it recommends here for toothache?'

'Not off-hand.'

He quoted: '"Piece of cotton wool dipped in creosote and pressed into the cavity often brings relief."'

'What if there's no cavity?'

'Might as well ask what if there's no creosote. Is your St John's certificate up to date?'

Every deck officer was required to have a St John's Ambulance Corps certificate of competence in First Aid. Andy nodded, adding, 'Not in dentistry, though. What's the cabin situation?'

'You'll lose yours and share Waller's. Chief and I'll share yours. That guest suite's an obvious place for an unspecified number of kids – two good-sized cabins and a bath and wc. Cadets'll lose theirs, caulk in here, junior engineers as well. It's all provisional, obviously, numbers could be anything from – well, from zero to – what, hundred or more?'

'A *lot* more, could be.'

'If they were all out of her and in boats and we found 'em and were able to pick 'em up. Yeah, could be.'

'A hundred crew, say?'

'In crew's quarters. Bosun and donkeyman are working that out.'

'Well – a hundred and thirty-one kids anyway, plus, say, a dozen adults looking after them; and the ship's officers –'

'Bugger *them*!'

You laughed or smiled, but nothing about this was at all light-hearted. A big hope was that there might be other ships assisting. Might even be one or more there already: oh, pray for *that*. Nothing further had come in over the air-waves, and the Old Man had vetoed any call from *Quilla*. She was in U-boat waters, the Focke-Wulf would have radioed a report of its attack on the *Sarawak*, and that on its own could have brought a U-boat in to finish the job off; in which case its commander might jump at the notion of adding a rescuer to his bag. In any case, you didn't transmit if you could avoid doing so. Didn't receive, either, except on certain essential maritime wave-lengths on which the Marconi boys listened out round the clock; while private radio sets were disallowed, since apparently the act of tuning in caused oscillations on which direction-finding apparatus could get bearings. If sets were hidden on board and found, they could either be confiscated or 'given the old hammer test' – ie got rid of. But another angle on whether or not to let the *Sarawak* know help was coming was that since she'd said her fires were out of control, abandoning, who'd be likely to receive your message?

Wouldn't make it in five hours anyway. At just after six pm Chief Verity came up to the bridge to tell the Old Man that a reduction in speed was essential. Bearings were running hot; he wanted to come down to revs for ten knots – which would leave her making-good no more than eight.

'Sorry, but there it is.'

'Essential, you say.'

'To avoid breakdown, yes.'

'For how long?'

'Probably until morning. She's no chicken, you know. We've been driving her flat out, and being in ballast there's a tendency to race. Frankly, Nat, sooner the better – uh?'

'All right.'

Since turning south three hours earlier she'd covered thirty-six miles by log, leaving her about thirty short of the position given by the *Sarawak*. So making-good eight knots now meant another three and a half, four hours. ETA in that vicinity therefore nine-thirty pm earliest.

Dusk. Darkness.

Harve Brown, on his way up at seven pm to stand the last hour of his watch, to give Waller a break for a 'seven bells' supper before the start of his own at eight, said 'If what's left of her's still afloat and burning, maybe . . .'

He put his gear together, so if he did have to move out of this cabin he could do so quickly, or it could be done for him if things were happening during his middle watch.

Seven-twenty now. Brief kip maybe, before supper, in preparation for at least seven hours on the bridge. Aiming to be up there by about nine pm, then on watch from midnight. Might still be searching then: in fact almost surely would be, and as like as not through the dark hours into morning. For one thing, boats would have drifted eastward, both wind and the mid-Atlantic current contributing to this. Six hours of drift, say, by the time one was on the spot, and drifting at just one knot would put them six miles east of the position given in the distress call. Between six and ten miles from it, say, and the current would be setting not due east but east-by-north or east-northeast. Gave one a biggish area to scour, for God's sake, looking for lightless boats in a dark and lively sea. The sea *had* come up a little. At the lower revs she was rolling more, pitching less. Should have rigged the bunk-board, to jam a knee against; had thought of it earlier in the day but – hell, couldn't be bothered to turn out now and fix it.

Supper was pilchards and baked beans, washed down as always by tea or coffee, which came out of different jugs but were otherwise not easy to distinguish from each other. Andy was on the bridge by eight-forty, wearing old flannel bags and a sweater, over that a duffel-coat that had been a birthday present from sister Annabel, and his cap, mainly for identification purposes. Clearish sky, but only a few stars visible as yet. A good fix would be useful at this stage, as distinct from dead reckoning – distance as recorded by log, courses as steered, influence of wind and current largely guessed at. Given a decent fix, at least you'd know the starting point of the search with certainty, whereas one couldn't be *as* sure of the *Sarawak* position.

Except they'd put that out at about three, and it would have been based on their noon EP, only three hours earlier, so it shouldn't be far out.

Light turning milky but visibility still OK, stars showing up more generally. Patchy cloud driving eastward flushed with pink, sea steeper than it had been during the afternoon, and *Quilla*'s motion reflecting this. He went in from the bridge-wing to find Waller in the forefront amidships, the Old Man in his corner and Elliot in the other, all with glasses up. Freeman was on the wheel.

'Captain, sir?'

'Uh?'

'Intending to take stars, sir?'

A grunt. Binoculars out of the way for a moment as he glanced skyward. 'I'll leave it to you, Second.'

'Aye, sir.' He told Waller, 'I'll borrow Elliot, OK?'

'You're welcome.'

For noting down times and sextant altitudes: but first setting the star globe and picking the trio he'd use. Had to change his mind on one of these, on account of a bank of cloud that was obscuring it, but the substitution was no problem, and fifteen minutes later he'd established *Quilla*'s position at 2056 – call it 2100 – as twelve miles northwest of that given by the *Sarawak*.

The Old Man joined him at the chart, after he'd suggested altering a few degrees to port.

'I'd have said we're about right.'

'But if they abandoned at 1500, sir –'

'Damn.' Slight smile, wag of the head. Admitting, 'Easterly drift, six or seven hours.' A nod. 'We'd do better on 150.'

'Long as her position was a good one, sir.'

'No reason not.' Returning to the forefront then, telling Waller, 'Come to port to 150.' A glance round: 'Holt!'

'Sir?'

'Good thinking.'

'Oh.' Embarrassed, slightly, but liking the man for his honesty, lack of bullshit. 'Thank you, sir.'

There was still a huge element of luck involved; the distance they might have drifted for instance was really no more than guesswork. And small boats in a vast black ocean – not that the boats would be all that small, those of a passenger liner would normally be certified as holding fifty people, he thought, so how many children – seventy-five or so, at a pinch? Fact remained, in the dark and conditions like these it would be all too easy to pass within a few hundred yards of one and not see it.

Ten o'clock, and dark. He'd spent the past hour on the bridge-wings, one side then the other, assisting in the looking out while leaving the wheelhouse uncrowded. Harve Brown had been up for a while, in conversation with the Old Man, no doubt outlining his plans for the accommodation, feeding and care of 131 children – plus adults, number unknown. They'd be getting close by now, approaching at least the general area of the *Sarawak*'s abandonment. If she'd been still afloat and on fire you'd surely have seen at least a glow on the horizon. The distance from that nine o'clock position being twelve miles; making good about eight now, you'd only have four to go – well within visibility range in the context of flames by night. Might have seen a glow even at twelve, he thought. And four miles was no distance at all for boats adrift at the mercy of wind and sea, although for *Quilla* it would be another half-hour's steaming.

One was looking out not only for boats, but also for darkened ships – other would-be rescue ships which might be searching around while showing no lights, and if so would pose a considerable hazard. He'd passed this thought on to the lookouts on the wings: McAllistair port side, Smith starboard. Down aft, members of the gun's crew were stationed as lookouts, and there were two hands, O'Donnell and Farr, on monkey island. Also cadets Merriman and Dixon on the boat-deck with the snowflake launcher ready for use, keeping busy meanwhile as extra lookouts.

A lot of eyes. And Harve Brown on tour from time to time, ensuring they stayed open.

You could be sure they would. One hundred and thirty-one children, for God's sake. As Bosun McGrath had grated an hour or so ago, 'What'd they be after sending the little beggars to sea for, any bloody how?'

Minutes dragging slowly. *Quilla* wallowing southeastward seeing nothing but the surrounding dark and the rolling, white-toppling sea. Not showing any lights, she'd pass within a cable's length of a boatload of kids and not even trained seamen with them would see her. While if the *Sarawak*'s hulk was still afloat and burning, he reckoned the men on monkey island would have seen something of her at even fifteen or twenty miles.

He'd intended leaving it to half-ten before going inside to check the distance-run by log and put on a DR, but at about twenty past the hour Harve Brown came up via the boat-deck and starboard bridge-wing, and he trailed in after him. Harve by then conferring with the Old Man again, the latter not desisting meanwhile from his own looking out. Andy went to the chart table, or rather to the Chernikeeff dials on the bulkhead above it, to read off the data he needed.

Since altering course to 150 she'd covered ten and a half miles. That was in an hour and twenty minutes. So she'd been making just under eight knots. Surely had to be in the area where the *Sarawak*'s boats might be.

Old Man, as it so happened, asking Harve Brown at this moment, 'Standing by the contraption now, are they?'

'Yessir. All set.'

'Best go down yourself, see they don't blow their heads off.'

Talking about snowflakes, Andy realised. Harve confirming that the cadets were standing by the launcher. 'But you mean at the half-hour, sir, or –'

'Bugger the half-hour, Mister, just loose off.'

Swooping rush of sound back there, audible over the roar of weather noise like ripping sailcloth, then after about fifteen seconds the multiple *cracks* of high flares bursting. He was outside by then, in the starboard bridge-wing to see sky and sea lighting up – *lit* up – a square mile or so of ocean floodlit. Searching it with naked eyes at first, wanting that wider coverage: finding damn-all at any rate in easy range either ahead or down this starboard side, so – glasses up and sweeping fairly swiftly . . .

Nothing. Then nothing port side either. Having hoped for not just one boat but several, guessing they might have linked themselves together in order to remain together. As he'd have been inclined to do himself, if he'd been in charge of boats with children in them.

Children's wide eyes staring up at those drifting, slowly falling stars?

Brilliance fading soon enough, though. Snowflakes longer-lasting than any other kind of flare or starshell, but in present circumstances you'd have liked them to last longer. Foam still glittering where *Quilla*'s stem smashed through the black rollers and sent explosions of phosphorescence flying, but beyond a cable's distance not only fading but leaving one blinder than before. Glasses sea-misted anyway. He was mopping the front lenses with cotton-waste when he heard a shout – Elliot yelling down to the boat-deck: 'Captain says one more, sir!'

Yelling to the mate, evidently. Andy wondering whether they wouldn't more usefully have pressed on a mile or so before sending up another, lighting a different acreage of sea. It was on its way though, and within seconds illuminating the same considerable but still limited area. If you'd had half a dozen ships in line abreast and half a mile apart, he thought, *then* you'd have a decent chance. *Quilla* on her own could only light up maybe a square mile at a time, whereas to make an effective search you'd need to floodlight fifty.

Still trying – searching – with glasses that were dryish, unfogged, for the moment. Leaving naked-eye stuff to the lookouts who didn't have any. And the illuminations again beginning to fade all too soon. *Quilla* thrashing on, shrouded in a halo of the spray she was kicking up. Andy thinking that if it had been up to him he'd have given it ten minutes before trying again. Ten minutes at eight knots – one and a third miles. Well – Old Man might have some such calculation in mind, he guessed.

Front lenses already remisting, damn it . . .

Faint yell – high and penetrating as a gull's screech.

From monkey island?

Yelling into their voice-pipe, he supposed – on his way to the weather door and inside. Waller at that moment taking his face from the pipe – not straightening from it, not having had to bend to it, might even have been up on his toes to reach it . . . Shouting, 'Red light, port beam, sir. Hung a moment then fell.'

'Who's up there?'

'Sounded like Farr, sir.'

Welshman, Ordinary Seaman. Reliable enough. The Old Man was acting on it anyway, telling Waller, 'I'll take her, Third', and Selby, 'Port ten.'

'Port ten, sir.' Easing the wheel over.

'Steer oh-six-oh.'

Ninety-degree turn to port. Old Man growling, 'Very's light, could 'a been.' Noticing Andy then: 'Second – nip up there, see what you make of it.'

'Aye, sir.' Leaving his cap on the chart table, since up there it wouldn't stand a chance. *Quilla* already responding to her rudder as he went back out into the wing and to the ladder – there was one each side, near-vertical – that led up to monkey island, which was the roof of the wheelhouse, itself roofless but surrounded by guard-rails. By no means weatherproof. The standard magnetic compass was up there – so as to be as far away as possible from other magnetic influences – also OS Farr and AB O'Donnell. Andy identifying himself in the darkness as he came off the ladder: 'Second mate. Both of you see the flare?'

'Taff here seen it first, then –'

'Nice work, Farr. Right on the beam, was it?'

'I'd say so – near as makes no—'

'We're turning towards it now. Hang on, uh?'

Pitch and roll very clearly necessitating that as she swung, transferring impact of wind and sea from her starboard quarter to the other. Stern directly into it at one stage, Farr commenting in his high, lilting tones, 'Bucking bronco she must think she is!'

Through the worst of it soon enough though, settling on the new course of northeast by east. Andy on his knees, glasses up, elbows on the top rail.

'There, now! But green, this one!'

Green, but otherwise just as Farr had described the first one, lifting for a few seconds and then falling. A flare, all right. A long way off, and very small: if he hadn't been pointing just about right at it, might well have missed it. The colour change made sense in the context of the Old Man's guess that it might be a Very's pistol they were using: Very's cartridges came in red, white or green; they'd use whichever they had handy. He was crouching at the voice-pipe, which had a hinged copper lid on it and a reek of stale tobacco smoke in the tube. He yelled, 'Bridge!', and when Waller answered told him, 'Flare – right ahead, two or three miles at least. Green this time, guess it *is* a Very's!'

Waller, sounding like Donald Duck through the tin pipe and surrounding din, was shouting that to the Old Man. Andy guessing how it might be in that boat. They'd have seen the snowflakes, maybe fired a Very's which no-one had seen after the first one, repeated it after the second, and now the green one. They'd be frantic – with no idea whether they'd been seen or not. And the children in what sort of shape, after seven hours of it, let alone what they'd gone through earlier?

He told Farr and O'Donnell, 'One of you keep all-round watch, other stay on that bearing, OK?'

There'd be more than one boat, and they didn't *have* to be together. Would almost certainly be under oars. You'd try to keep head to wind, while still drifting east or northeast, and performances would vary. Off the ladder, he hung on for a moment waiting for her to come back from a heavy roll, then let go and moved fast to the wheelhouse door: wind was definitely up a notch or two, it wouldn't be anything like comfortable in those boats. Ramming the door shut with his shoulder, shutting out a little of the noise, hearing the Old Man telling Harve Brown to rig both scrambling nets starboard side aft. 'Have McGrath pick a team to go down on 'em.'

'Aye, sir . . .'

He wouldn't want to lower any of his own boats if he could avoid it. Obviously he'd put *Quilla* across the wind to provide a lee on her starboard side. At present there was a scrambling net each side, stopped-up to the guard-rails, and they'd be moving the port side one over. Each net was about twelve feet square and made of three-inch sisal. They'd lob heaving-lines out down-wind to haul boats in alongside, and the bosun's party would climb down on the nets to grab survivors and haul them up. *Carry* kids up, he supposed. None of it would be easy.

Might join in. Having long limbs and being reasonably fit.

'Second?'

'Sir?'

'We'll have the Aldis in the starboard wing. That flare about three miles off, you said?'

'At a guess, sir. Two – three . . .'

Ten minutes had gone since then, so deduct one mile, call it one or two. In which case, another ten to twenty minutes. No point plugging in the Aldis out there yet. Its purpose wouldn't be for signalling, only to light up the boat or boats, *Quilla*'s side and the scrambling nets.

'Captain, sir. Might Elliot handle the Aldis? I'd as soon lend a hand on the nets.'

'See Mr Brown about that. Elliot see to the Aldis, yes.'

'Aye, sir – thank you.' He asked Elliot, 'Know where the plug is in the starboard wing?'

He did. So that was all right. For want of any more useful occupation he went to the chart table to make diary notes for the log. Time of firing the snowflakes, sighting the flares and altering course. It was surprising in a way that there'd been no more flares. Unless they'd only had a few: or in the absence of visible response were saving the rest for some later encounter, if this one came to nothing.

Knowing it could be *days* before the next.

How might it feel, Christ's sake, with boats full of little kids?

'Third.' Old Man stirring again. 'Or Elliot. Tell 'em to put up another snowflake.'

'Elliot –'

'Sir.' The boy shot out. Andy put a DR on the chart, marking it 2300 – exact time now being 2304 – and went out into the bridge-wing, weather side. Snowflake scorching up. Important not to look at the thing itself, wreck one's night vision by watching the separate brilliances open and expand. Eyes down while that was happening: then up – at the seascape, not the sky – glasses ready, but a survey first by naked eye. *Quilla*'s forepart deep in foam that seemed actually to glow in this intensity of light and the leaping periphery of gleaming ocean: and a howl from McAllistair, bridge-wing lookout on this side – 'Ship's boat two points on the bow, sir!' A smart-enough naked-eye sighting, but also simultaneously or right on its heels a Very's light curving at the apex of its rise, green again but less so, watery-green in surrounding brilliance. Farr or O'Donnell screeching from monkey island, Old Man telling Waller as Andy crashed in there again, 'Two thousand yards, I'd say', and then to Selby, 'Port wheel, bring her to 040.'

'Oh-four-oh, sir . . .'

Two thousand yards: ten cables, one nautical mile.

One boat only?

He had his glasses up but couldn't even see that one now. Old Man calling, 'Elliot – tell 'em as one snowflake fades, put up another and keep on.' And to Waller, 'I'll want you on the telegraphs, Third.'

'Aye, sir.'

'Course 040, sir.'

The boat would now be right ahead again. When he was a lot closer to it he'd come round a few more degrees to port, inserting *Quilla* between boat and weather, doubtless reducing at the same time from half ahead to slow ahead, then from slow to dead slow and stop.

Looking back on it afterwards one would find it incongruous that in the course of that fairly hectic rescue operation, all of one's thinking had been determinedly but quite cheerfully centred on those few children – twenty-seven of them, aged between six and ten – white-faced, wild-eyed, clinging to the boat's thwarts, the smaller ones in adults' arms, boat standing practically on one end and then the other while also hurling itself from beam to beam as if doing its best to ditch them. Kids dressed in

90

a variety of clothes, but all soaked of course, and frightened half to death – the incongruity looking back on it being that it had seemed like a great achievement, getting these twenty-seven out of 131 up into the ship, up a dozen feet of soaking wet rope-netting thumping and slithering on the ship's iron side – but as if saving this handful of lives was the be-all and end-all of the hours of effort, only afterwards facing the dreadful truth that the vast majority had drowned or been burnt to death.

Because one would have had in the back of one's mind, unquestioned at that stage, that other boats would have got away, that this was only the start of it. And in any case, there and then this was what you had – lives you actually *were* fighting for.

Anyway, by the time he'd gone over the rail on to the net, McGrath and Patterson had sent their heaving-lines soaring across the boat's bow and stern, and with others helping were dragging the load in alongside, seamen in the boat having secured the lines for'ard and aft. *Quilla* meanwhile by no means standing still. The Old Man would in fact have been using her screw and rudder to hold her in position relative to the boat while wind and sea flung both around. Harve Brown had yelled in Andy's ear to hold on until they had the boat right in alongside, and he'd stayed where he was for a minute or two, on the net but not at that stage climbing down into the highly dangerous gap of alternatively sucking-away and up-gushing sea – which was something the kids were going to have to face, run the gauntlet of – but on the net anyway so they could see they were going to get this kind of help and be ready to accept it.

Transfer from boat to net was going to be the most difficult part – one took account of this before it started: not all that difficult for grown men, at any rate for seamen, but for children, lacking much strength or understanding of the dynamics of it – for instance, that you needed to be on the net and climbing as the ship rolled away to port, not hanging there to be dunked

91

under and maybe crushed between boat and ship's side as she rolled to starboard – well, not easy, and hazardous in the extreme. One's own job being to receive them from the arms of adults, of whom it seemed there were ten or twelve, release those capable of it on to the net to climb, or carry them up: as it turned out, carry *most* of them, passing them to men waiting higher up. Most frequently to the carpenter, Fellaby, ABs Patterson and Morton, or a fireman by name of McPhaill, but there were others at the rail who'd at times come over to help when things were difficult. Climbing one-armed with the weight of a child in the other did have its moments, especially when the child was struggling.

Then the adults, giving them as much help as they might need – mainly getting them on to the net, then staying close to assist as needed. The first, pushed up from the boat by a ship's officer with some quantity of braid on his sleeves, this one helping another younger one who turned out to be strikingly athletic, needing no help once on the net, fairly racing up; followed more slowly but steadily by an elderly civilian in a donkey jacket, grey-headed, even longer-limbed than the young one who'd preceded him – he'd shouted upwards, 'All right, Sam?', and the answer as that one reached the top was a yell of, 'Don't worry about me, Doc!' *Girl's* voice, for God's sake: girl in soaked trousers and sweater, wool cap as worn often enough by sailors, and with a knapsack on her back – at the ship's rail already and helped over whether she needed it or not by Harve Brown. Others swarming up under their own power were the mate – a chief officer's three gold stripes on each sodden sleeve, who'd offered assistance to the elderly one, 'Doc', who'd declined the offer, waved him off – had a Gladstone bag slung from a belt, one saw as he climbed on up – and then the rest. Half a dozen maybe, *Sarawak* crew.

Leaving the boat half full of water crashing around down there. Had served its purpose, saved thirty-seven lives. Heaving-lines still attached to it for'ard and aft, to be cut now at the rail, new ones to be made in due course by young seamen under McGrath's eagle eye and tutelage. Snowflake light still brilliant, but Elliot in the bridge-wing keeping the Aldis beam on the boat drifting away downwind.

6

In the light of day, thinking about Julia and her situation, inevitable delay now to its resolution, since they were heading for New York to land the children before pushing on down to Cuba. Mightn't necessarily be held up more than a day or two – he was trying to convince himself of that but still worrying. Exhaustion might have been part of it: he'd slept fitfully instead of going out like a light as he might have done, a part of *that* being nightmare images of drowned children.

Which still lingered. On the bridge again now, relieving Gus Waller; Waller with shock in his round, red face, muttering, 'Bloody nightmare – honest to God. More than a hundred drowned?'

'More than *two* hundred.'

Some not drowned but burnt. Or killed by the exploding bombs. Waller had added, 'I meant the kids. God almighty . . .'

'Yeah.' Hardly credible, thinkable. Adding as an afterthought, 'Anyway, twenty-seven fewer than there might have been.' Putting his glasses up, starting a sweep from beam to beam, telling Waller, 'Off you go, I've got her.'

Sea and wind well down, surface ruffled white and *Quilla* still corkscrewing – enough of a swell still running to warrant that – but compared to how it had been at the time of the rescue or during his own middle watch, the midnight to 0400 – well, summer days were here again. Sky a pale blue except for scraps of flying white, and sun well up: 0830 now. He'd come up as usual to relieve Waller for his breakfast, and while up here would take his morning sunsight. Routine – except for awareness of the thirty-seven survivors on board, some of them with burns or other injuries, and – having the figures now – 214 men, women and children drowned or killed in the bombing or its aftermath.

Not long after midnight the Old Man had broken wireless silence to report the rescue, SS *Sarawak* having been bombed and set on fire, only one boat having got away, thirty-seven survivors, including twenty-seven children, now on board SS *Barranquilla* and no possibility of other passengers or crew having survived. Names of those rescued as followed, first name on the list being that of Chief Officer Raymond Barclay, who'd made it clear that there could be no other survivors. He'd described to the Old Man, with CRO Foster making notes, how at least one bomb had penetrated to explode deep inside the ship, blasted a hole in her side at the waterline somewhere between engine room and boiler room and releasing bunker oil which had ignited. The bridge itself and the for'ard part – initially only the fore part – of what had been a very long central superstructure already blasted and in flames by then, some of the boats smashed, others unreachable on account of fires which, driven by that brisk wind, were rapidly taking charge, that whole central part of the ship, boatdeck and promenade-deck below it, 'A' deck below that, becoming an inferno. The children had been in their cabins, mainly on 'A' deck, but some, who'd seen themselves as the lucky ones, on the higher level, promenade. It had been their afternoon rest period, on which the lady in charge of them, a former hospital matron, had insisted. There'd been two other children's nannies, including Miss Vaughan, who'd been wonderful with the twenty-seven in the boat.

Barclay had told the Old Man that within minutes of the attack the midships section of the old liner had been ablaze at all levels. Foster quoted him as saying, 'If you was for'ard you couldn't get aft, and abaft it couldn't get for'ard. Well, she'd been hit for'ard too. And the bridge – bridge structure, captain's and officers' cabins, forward end of it at lower level, all of that was done for in the first minutes. I'd been aft, seeing to one thing and another, then – well, started for'ard at the double when the first bomb hit us. Hun circling then but coming back, wasn't finished with us, not by any means – however many bombs it carried he didn't reckon on taking any home with him: did three runs over us in all, masthead-height like. I got knocked off that external ladder, not sure how, got myself up it then any road – on the boat-deck then, sort of dazed and guessing I'd not get much further – did have a go, but that was after I'd mustered this lot abreast the boat. Tell you, though – one boat – I never seen this, steward by name of Price did – would've had its quota of kids and crew, in charge of the third mate if he'd got himself to it – should've, but I never saw him . . . Price says they had it started down and it got caught in a gust of flames from inboard, the falls must've caught alight and burnt through – that was that. There was oil-spill afire on the surface by this time, so – well, Christ, *horrible* . . .'

He'd begun to shake, Foster said. Crouched over on the chair, face in his hands. The Old Man had put a hand on his shoulder. 'Nothing you could've done you didn't do, was there?'

'No, but –'

'Crew's quarters aft, in your *Sarawak*?'

'For'ard, foc'sl itself and two lower decks. Been hit there too – gone on fire in the foc'sl-head. But with the fires amidships, see, bridge structure *and* below –'

'Then the boat you came away in –'

'Mine. Starboard side, the aftermost. My boat's what it *was*, them I brought away with me was allocated to me, had the luck or savvy to get aft to it quick. Miss Vaughan had rounded some up right at the start, ones she could get to, them as was missing she'd reckoned had gone already – gone the right way, she hoped to God. We'd given 'em boat drills enough. Well, a couple of 'em *had*, must've run like rabbits. Then when we'd mustered, seen which we'd got and – well, how few like – she'd've gone chasing off into the worst of it again, but I held her back, told her the ones we already had there needed her with 'em, state they was in, poor little sods; we'd try for others as might be wandering or trapped like, but – see, *did* try, far as we could get, trying different ways, that's to say levels – me and the doctor and Searle – third wireless officer – and an AB name of Houghton, but, like I said, not a hope, just bloody *wasn't*. Not much time for us neither, by the time we knew it, so – give up, nothing else you could do, I swear to God, so –'

'Mister –'

Nodding, swallowing, getting his voice back under control.

'Got back to the boat, put the doc on board, and RO Searle for want of a deck officer to take charge if I came to grief. I kept four seamen with me as lowerers – saw to that all right, wouldn't have five minutes later, I tell you *that* – and we slid down the falls and joined 'em – cast off, searched the water up for'ard and around her stem to search port side too, but – Christ, the *sight* of her from sea-level, flame stem to stern, smoke pouring away downwind, oil-fires on the sea that side . . .'

CRO Foster had given Andy all this verbatim and with a surprising amount of sympathetic mimicry when they'd met in the washplace before early breakfast. He, Andy, having been on watch last night when the interview had taken place in the Old Man's cabin, and by the end of that four-hour stint fairly groggy when Harve Brown had been taking over, hadn't really put much of it together, main thought in mind being to get his head down. Whereas earlier, immediately after the rescue operation, he'd had to move fast to shift into dry gear – in Waller's cabin – before taking over the watch a few minutes after midnight. Foster, anyway, had wound up his performance with: 'Old Man had a job calming Barclay down, telling him more than once no-one was going to blame him for having been where he had been and thus surviving and getting at least these few away, God's sake. Decent fellow, looked and sounded as if he'd been through hell – still *was*, know what I mean. But you can imagine – like some massacre you walked away from?'

'What's the doctor like?'

'Haven't met him, but Steward Hastings says he's sixty-seven and six-foot-four.'

'And the girl?'

'Haven't had *that* pleasure, either. She's with the kids in the suite, have her hands full too, I'd guess.'

Orders to divert to New York had come in during Harve Brown's morning watch, the diversion necessitating an alteration of course of no more than three degrees. *Quilla* was on course 245 now, and Chief Verity had grudgingly consented to an increase in revs that should be giving her about ten knots, which under present conditions would get her to New York in about nine days.

Delay of up to a week, say, in terms of getting back to Julia? Having told her ten weeks, or twelve at the most. Nothing to be done about it, obviously. Except post letters to her and to Annabel – should get there quickly enough from New York, he thought.

Nine and a half days to New York maybe. Two or three days' steaming closer to the US seaboard, you'd be safe enough without the zigzag, thereafter make better progress. At this stage though, on longitude 27 west, realistically speaking one was still in U-boat territory. At least, where any longer-range U-boats *might* be. In reach of marauding Focke-Wulfs too – all too obviously – and with no more defence against them than the *Sarawak* had had. *And* having last night kept the sky alight for the best part of an hour, then broken wireless silence with a report that had necessarily included one's position.

Couldn't cross fingers – except mentally – with glasses up, sweeping steadily, continuously; with Dixon, who'd temporarily relieved Elliot, similarly engaged eight or ten feet to his right. Just as yesterday, it had to be about a thousand to one against spotting any periscope cutting that choppy, whitened surface, but one was paying attention also to the horizon, where any FW would be likely to make its first appearance.

Evil bloody thing. On board the *Sarawak*, Barclay had said, no lookout had seen it until it had been practically on top of them.

A buzz from the zigzag clock. Didn't need to interrupt one's search to know that Selby would be easing on port rudder.

Anyway, as far as it went the rescue had been something of an achievement, from *Quilla*'s point of view. That number of kids alive and kicking who otherwise might not have been, and their families at home spared the misery of those of the other hundred. Absolutely crippling misery, you could imagine. While here, from the point of view of one's own state of mind, it was certainly a lot more comfortable to concentrate on being glad for those saved than to think about the rest of them.

Although one did. So how might that wretched girl be feeling, who'd known them all?

He didn't meet her until supper that evening. Hadn't expected to then, either, since Harve Brown had told him at some time during the forenoon that she was going to mess with the children in the owners' suite. They were to have all their meals up there, cafeteria-style, using some folding card tables borrowed from the saloon and the crew's mess room. Harve also mentioned that the Old Man had given the doctor the use of his sleeping cabin, which he – Dr Creagh – would also use as a dispensary. Injuries amongst his patients were in fact surprisingly few – one broken arm, a few cuts, sprains and bruises, inevitably some burns, but thank heavens all quite minor.

One of the *Sarawak*'s seamen had the worst burns, actually quite severe, the doc had admitted. He'd been given a berth down aft, of course, and the doc was spending quite a bit of time down there with him.

'Pretty lucky kids on the whole, eh?'

Harve had nodded. 'Say that again. Anyway, I've given Creagh the medicine locker. In return he'll deal with any problems our own people may have. But he'll be helping out generally as well as medically with the nippers. Physical injuries apart, most of 'em are to some degree in shock, he says. Absolutely natural – they'd need to be made of cast-iron not to be. But you can see they all like him, and he and Miss Vaughan get on as if they'd known each other all their lives. What the kids *need*, of course, is their mothers.'

'Is Miss Vaughan a nurse?'

'No she's not. She's *nursing* 'em all right, but not qualified, just hired as a nanny, so I gather.'

'As well she's got the doc's help, then.'

'And two of the other survivors are stewards, who'll do the donkey work, meals and so on.'

'Unpaid?'

'Up to the *Sarawak*'s owners, isn't it.'

When a man lost his ship he lost entitlement to pay. Ancient tradition of the Merchant Navy which still applied, but wouldn't for much longer, so it was said. The British Shipping Federation were setting up what was to be called the Seamen's Pool, which would control appointments to ships and the pay to which all registered seafarers would be entitled, even when ashore between voyages, not only between formally signing on and signing off, or the signing on and then being sunk. It was expected to come into force within a few months, apparently.

Harve Brown was talking about the *Sarawak* now. Intermediate passenger and cargo liner, 14,000 tons and seventeen knots. Re-engined quite recently, switching from coal to oil, with bunkers in her double-bottoms and so forth, but otherwise a bit of an antique. Hence her readiness to burst into flames, maybe. Had had Chinese owners at one time. There'd been a high proportion of Lascars among her crew apparently – Indians mostly from Bombay, stewards from Goa, Chinese seamen, as well as laundrymen, greasers and firemen from all over. He'd got all this from Barclay, he said.

'What cabin have you given him?'

'Cadets'. They'll doss in here. And the wireless officer – Searle – is using one of our Marconi boys' berths, so they'll work hot bunks with the other two.'

Hot bunks meant the man coming off watch taking the bunk of the one who'd just gone *on* watch.

'Owners' suite, though – twenty-seven kids and the girl – day and night *and* meals –'

'Once she and the doc have got 'em settled in, we'll see to some entertainment for them. Boat-deck as a recreation area, for instance. Weather permitting, of course. Off-watch cadets supervising and organising games, I thought. And tours of the ship – in small groups, of course.' He shrugged. 'I'm working on it. Any ideas, let me hear 'em.'

'How about employing them as lookouts?'

'You serious?'

'I mean *pretend* lookouts. Pretend tricks at the helm, even?'

At supper that evening – pilchards and beans again – he'd just been served with his, by Chumley the rat-faced assistant steward, when Harve Brown arrived with the girl in tow. Like a stroke of magic – one minute the sporadic talk mainly of 'shop', this extremely unexciting canned fish and the same old boringly male faces – second and fourth engineers, cadets Dixon and Merriman, Newton with his awful sideboards. One *new* face was that of Searle, the *Sarawak*'s somewhat podgy second wireless officer – for as much as *that* was worth – then suddenly this vision: quite tall – five-nine or ten, he guessed – slim, with dark-brown hair, straight nose, wide-apart eyes over high cheekbones, noticeably elegant, slim neck. Eyes light blue, in pleasing contrast to her dark hair. He'd made this much of an appraisal in the few seconds while pushing his chair back and standing up, observing then that she was wearing dark-coloured slacks, white shirt, yellow pullover. Either she'd had those items in the knapsack or there'd been a very swift job done of drying-out and ironing. Ironing anyway: she actually looked quite smart. Last night, one had heard, the engine room gratings had been fairly laden with clothes drying-out. *Quilla*'s officers all on their feet now, Harve announcing rather pompously that he had the honour to introduce Miss Vaughan, children's nanny, who was joining them for dinner and he hoped would make a habit of it, since the kids had their high tea much earlier and were now either asleep or having stories read to them by Dr Creagh, who'd be down for his supper later.

She was looking around at them, smiling slightly. 'Hello . . .'

Not shy, exactly. Lonely, maybe. Sad . . . One's own age, or a year or two older, he guessed. Getting a chorus of hellos and good evenings, and smiling more positively; Harve pulling out a chair between the bearded Charlie Bridgeman, second engineer, and the *Sarawak* radio man. Bridgeman telling her she was very welcome indeed, and Harve putting in, 'This fellow of course you know' – meaning Searle – who agreed in his rather high voice, '*Old* mates, we are!' The girl showing faint surprise and looking across at Andy. 'I know *you*. You were on the net last night. Absolutely marvellous you were too!'

'Pretty good yourself, I thought. All I did was give you a hand up out of the boat and you went up like a rocket!'

She sat down. 'I'd seen how you did it. And unlike you *I* wasn't carrying any children, had my hands free. No, I mean it, all of you were splendid, but you actually were *terrific!*'

Bridgeman advised her, 'You'll be giving him a swollen head, Miss Vaughan. Actually he's not a bad fellow, but—'

'Thanks for the kind words anyway.' He'd interrupted Bridgeman easily enough because she was still looking at *him*, had ignored the interruption. He added, 'Fact is, it was the children really *were* terrific. How's the lad with the broken arm?'

'Oh, William.' Quick, happy smile. 'He's doing well. He broke it two days ago – fell down a companionway outside the children's playroom. Yes, I remember you taking him from Doctor Creagh . . .'

The doctor had passed him over, bawling over the surrounding racket, 'Broken arm, this chap!' Small, wild-eyed toddler with one arm strapped to him in bandaging almost like a miniature Egyptian mummy – a virtual parcel that had squeaked into his ear on the way up, 'Mind my *good* arm!', and he'd panted at him, 'We'll mind 'em both, old lad!' He'd taken him all the way up, not handing him over until they were at the rail. Thinking at the time that it was probably the most perilous journey the boy would ever make: one slip, fumble it and drop him – with only one arm he couldn't have saved himself or clung on. Or, down there between boat and ship's side, lived very long.

Best of reasons to make damn sure of *not* fumbling it. The basic technique had been to lean in hard against the net and the ship's side, climbing as fast as possible when she was listing away to port, then stop and just hang on, wait, during the starboard roll. He said now, 'Heck of an experience for a little kid. Bet he'll remember it all his life.'

'I know *I* will.'

She dropped her eyes as she said it. He read the strain in them, the reality behind her pleasant, friendly manner. Eyes on his again: he nodded slightly, registering his sympathy, at least partial understanding, the background horror she couldn't *not* have in mind most of the time, if not all. But how could one broach the subject without inflicting pain, maybe provoking tears . . .

To what point anyway: what had happened had happened, you all knew it, and the last thing she'd want was to talk about it. In any case, Harve broke in at that point with, 'Should have made introductions all round – sorry. The man you're speaking to, Miss Vaughan, is our second mate, name of Holt. Believe it or not, a married man, as near as makes no difference.'

'Oh?'

'He's right. Getting spliced soon as we're home. Name's *Andy* Holt, though.'

'I'm Samantha Vaughan, Andy. Usually called Sam.'

'*Great* name for a girl!'

'Not exactly girly, would you say?'

Harve had cleared his throat, by way of interrupting this. 'Continuing with introductions, if I may – the man on your right is Second Engineer Charlie Bridgeman, and opposite him Fourth Engineer Hobbs.'

'*Dan* Hobbs.'

'Howdy, Dan!'

'While this one is our second wireless officer. Newton. *Tommy* Newton, isn't it?'

A nod, mouth full of pilchard.

'Then we have two of the ship's three cadets.' Nodding towards them. 'Dixon and Merriman. And at last, but perhaps not least, your pilchards.' Steward Chumley smirking, murmuring, 'Miss . . .' and Samantha looking down at them: 'What are *their* names?'

Andy laughed, joined by a few others. She was lovely, he thought. Incredible, after that ordeal. Bridgeman asking her, 'D'you do this job as a regular thing, Sam? Looking after kids on –'

'Certainly not. Well – looking after children, yes. I help out in a nursery school in London, off and on. But nothing of this kind.' Meeting Andy's eyes again. 'Actually I don't think it's all that sensible, shipping them out like this.'

He agreed: 'I'm with you there.'

'Certainly' – Harve Brown, pompously – 'in the light of *this* terrible experience –'

General discussion then, all in agreement: if whoever had set it up had had any idea of the danger, the number of ships that were being lost, whether in convoy or sailing independently – and how could they be that ignorant, wouldn't you think someone at the Admiralty or Ministry of this or that might have put up an argument against it? Samantha saying quietly, 'Despite the bombing getting so much worse – which it really *is*, you know. It's become quite frightening. You can understand parents jumping at the chance to have their children out of it. Especially – well, father in the Forces, mother in some kind of war work, grandparents if still around maybe beyond coping?'

Chief Engineer Verity arrived at that stage, bringing with him the gloomy-looking Chief Officer Barclay; they'd been communing with the Old Man apparently, would probably have had a tot or two of gin or rum with him. Verity was introduced to Miss Vaughan before moving to his usual chair at the other end of the table, with Barclay beside him and facing Harve Brown down the length of it, remarking that they might have found something more interesting than pilchards to lay on for their guests' first meal in the saloon. Asking Samantha, 'No doubt Mr Brown will already have apologised?'

'Haven't, though.' Harve looked up with his eyebrows raised. 'Happen to *like* canned pilchards.'

'So do I.' Samantha nodded. 'Baked beans too. And look at what's coming next – delicious peaches and cream, do I spy?'

'Tinned fruit of some inferior kind and condensed milk, Miss Vaughan.' Verity shrugged. 'Never mind. Ten days' time – New York, bright lights, and the fat of the land!'

'For a day or two.' Andy querying this with Harve Brown, 'Or maybe only a few hours – land our passengers – including Sam, unfortunately – and scoot on out again?' He asked her, 'D'you plan to stay in America?'

'Oh, no. Return passage guaranteed by the Ministry.'

Bridgeman suggested, 'Stay on board with us, then?'

'Hardly.' Harve Brown was answering Andy's supposition. 'Day or two in New York, I imagine. Land the children, take in fresh water and bunkers, store ship. Fresh US produce for the trip down to Nuevitas, Cuban then for the long haul up to Halifax, stock up there with Canadian. But' – turning to Samantha – 'I should think you'd get a berth home in one of the big liners. A lot more comfortable than in this old tramp, also quicker and much safer. Liners taking Canadian troops over, of course, but you'd be in first-class, *cordon bleu* and champagne, the lot!'

Chief Verity sighed. 'Take me with you?'

She told him, 'Love to. As it is I'll have Dr Creagh with me, but join the party.' Asking Barclay then, 'You too, perhaps?'

'Take what I can get.' A shrug of the heavy shoulders. 'Could be a mate's berth going.' Dull-voiced, dull-eyed, dispirited.

Andy asked the girl, breaking an ensuing silence, 'The doc won't be tempted to stay this side of the pond then?'

'Not on your life. He has a wife and daughter in Colchester and two sons in the army . . . I mustn't stay down here too long, incidentally, he'll be starving and the children will be exhausting him.'

'But I was going to say' – Chief Verity to Harve Brown – 'changing the subject slightly, while in New York I hope we'll get ourselves some dockyard assistance. Dry dock, get the stern gland and shaft bearings bang to rights. I've raised it with the Old Man, he agrees.'

Meaning, Andy thought, *at least* a week's delay. Depending on how long they might have to wait for a dry dock, maybe longer. Thinking about that and the effect of it on Julia, her predicament, while Harve Brown waffled on to Samantha about the children – what might be the best time or times of day for exercise periods on the boat-deck; for how long, for instance, did they rest after lunch? She told him, however long they liked, or maybe not at all: they could rest if they wanted to, but she wasn't insisting on it, for fear it would remind them of what had happened the last time they'd been sent for what Mrs Thompson had called 'a nice lie-down'. Telling Andy, 'Actually Tommy was an old darling. A bit starchy on the surface, but – sweet woman, truly *adored* the children.' To Harve then, voice a little shaky, 'I think, if you'd excuse me –'

'I'll see you up.'

'Oh, but –'

'It's no trouble.' Harve on his feet, looking concerned, and Bridgeman easing her chair back as she moved to get up. Andy also standing: Julia and the unwelcome prospect of delay still very much in his mind, as well as recognition of the degree of strain there had to be in Sam's, and how well she was coping with it. A lot better than Barclay, despite the loss of 104 children who'd been at least partially in her care, and her two colleagues, the shock of the whole business. He'd mumbled – dimly enough, but for want of anything better, in the slight confusion, embarrassment even, of that moment – 'See you tomorrow I hope', and caught her surprisingly bright smile and assurance, 'Oh, you *will!*' Asking himself then how would they *not* see each other, since neither could exactly get out and walk ... Chief Verity remarking as the door closed behind her and Harve, 'A lot of young women in that one's shoes would be having nervous breakdowns.' Looking at Barclay then: 'Pretty damn special, wouldn't you say?'

7

So much for 8 August – a Thursday, which he was aware of because between enjoying half an hour of the old doctor's company and getting his head down for some rest before his middle watch, he'd written a second letter to Julia and rewritten the one to Annabel, and in dating them had checked in his diary for the day of the week. Weekdays and weekends being very much the same as each other at sea, at any rate on a longish voyage such as this, one tended to forget which day of the week it was, thinking only of the date, as of course was necessary for navigational purposes. Sunday forenoons admittedly, ships' masters usually read a few prayers and encouraged the singing of a hymn or two, either on deck or in the crew's mess room, but in U-boat waters Nat Beale had preferred not to wander that far from the bridge, nor to concentrate so many off-watch officers and men in one part of the ship. Sundays therefore were no different from other days now, and you stood the same watches seven days a week.

Anyway – Friday the 9th now, two-thirty pm. *Quilla*'s noon position had been near enough 51 and a half degrees north, 34 west. Any U-boat encountered this far west really would be chancing its arm, but she was still zigzagging, either side of mean course 245; Andy and Dixon – Dixon absent at this moment – still intently searching a much less jumpy surface. You *might* spot the feather of a periscope in these conditions, if there should happen to be one, and with the swell so much lower there was a lot less motion on the ship. A slow waltz in place of a quickstep, as Dr Creagh had put it, hence the shrill cries of children at play on the boat-deck under the supervision of Samantha and cadets Merriman and Elliot.

He'd sent Dixon to make the routine tour of lookouts' positions, asked him now on his return whether his fellow cadets looked as if they were enjoying themselves down there. Dixon's answer was, 'Seem happy enough, sir. Third mate too.'

'*He* there?'

A grin. 'Seems mostly Elliot and Merriman organising the sprogs, Mr Waller going strong with Miss Vaughan, sir.'

Imagining it. Waller would come up to Sam's waist, roughly. Unless she was sitting on the deck, allowing him to tower over her. Andy turning a laugh into a cough and glancing to his right, seeing that Dixon was still grinning as he put his glasses up. Dixon had been improving, he thought, in the last couple of days: his general attitude seemed a lot healthier. Ever since he'd torn him off a strip, in fact. Which was fine, justified one's having done so.

Or maybe the rescue operation had had an effect on him. A sense of having done something to justify his existence, finally?

Waller, though. Hadn't been asked to help with the children, and at this time of day would routinely have had his head down.

Well – why not. In fact, best of luck to him. Sawn-off little sod . . .

He'd told Julia in this second letter that there'd been a change which might mean his not getting back as soon as he'd anticipated; also that he begged her to forgive him, but he'd written to his sister Annabel explaining the situation and asking her in the very

110

unlikely event of his *not* getting back (a) to get in touch with Julia, and (b) if she agreed to it, to inform the parents – hers and Andy's. *Only* if she, Julia, agreed to this; Annabel could be relied upon to keep her mouth shut otherwise. But knowing they were the child's grandparents and that he'd intended marrying her, they'd surely want to *act* like grandparents and help in any way they could.

And if initially they didn't, Annabel was perfectly capable of jockeying them into a better frame of mind. No need to mention this to Julia, but if there was any sort of battle to be fought, Annabel was the girl to fight it.

My darling, this is only a precaution. I say 'if I don't get back', but actually we're a lucky ship, and don't worry, she'll stay the course. We're a good team, tell you the truth, and the crew's as sound as any I've known. I'm only taking this precaution – telling Annabel – because one has to face the fact that in war-time all things, including frightful ones, are possible – as you know so well – and I have an absolute horror of the thought of leaving you in the lurch, people having only your word for it that we would have married, and not just because of the circumstances being as they are, but because there's nothing I'd have wanted more in any case. I love you desperately, think of you every day and night and pray to God not just to get me back to you but to make it SOON.

I still think it would have been best to have told your mother. Please, if you begin to feel the need of her support – which she'd give you, I'm certain, as soon as she was over the first shock – darling, don't hesitate, please don't. Just square up to it, get it over, and you'll be glad you did. If you haven't by the time you get this letter, why not show it to her? Use it as it were to break the ice, sort of a preface to what you have to tell her – might make the telling easier? It must be an awful strain to be carrying on alone; and your mother's a kind, understanding person, I'm sure it would be better to tell her than wait until she begins to suspect the truth?

111

He asked Samantha at supper whether when she got home to England she'd be going back to work in the nursery school, and she said, 'Probably. If they'll have me. It's in London of course, at least has been up to now, but whether it'll carry on or simply close down – because of the bombing, I mean – who knows. If they're carrying on they might have taken on some permanent replacement by the time I'm back. In fact I should think they might well have to. In which case' – she shrugged – 'just have to see what else.'

'Wouldn't take on another job like this one, I imagine.'

'Definitely not.'

'How did it come about?'

'It was offered, that's all. A friend of mine was lined up for it, then had the offer of a part in a play just going into rehearsals – for the West End, which she'd been hoping for for ages. And sooner than just back out and let Tommy down – Tommy Thompson, who'd offered her the job – *cruise*, she called it –'

'Asked you to take her place, and you did.'

'Since no-one was offering *me* any parts – West End or anywhere else. And it was something new, bit of an adventure, I thought. Free trip to America, heaven's sake!'

'So you're an actress too.'

'Had a few parts. Always hoping. The nursery school was something to keep the pennies trickling in while waiting for the great break. Anyhow, I have an agent, of sorts, so . . .'

Crossed fingers. He said, 'I'm sure you'll make it. Bound to. Henceforth I'll scour the billboards and press notices for the name of Samantha Vaughan. And when it's up in lights, one night you may find me waiting at the stage door with a bouquet of – roses, right?'

'And your fiancée?'

'Ah. *Could* be a snag . . .'

'I'd have thought it could. Very few lights in London these days, anyway.'

Charlie Bridgeman tapped her arm. 'I have no fiancée, and I'd love to see you act. In London, would it be?'

'Or Doncaster, John o' Groats, Aberystwyth –'

'Where's home?' Andy again, mopping up the remains of bully-beef stew. 'Parents, so forth?'

'One parent only. Intrepid birdman. Well – Group Captain RAF.'

'And where's home?'

'Real one's in Kent, but it's let to other people. Too big for us. Well, I'll tell you, get this over. My mother died ten years ago, giving birth to twins, my baby sisters. I was twelve then, and I sort of helped bring them up. Now they're at boarding school – summer hols right now so they're staying with an aunt, my father's sister, near Exeter. Her husband's in the army, she has bags of room and loves having them, has me too whenever I want. And that's more than enough about the Vaughans.' She asked Bridgeman, 'Where are you from?'

'Barrow. Barrow-in-Furness? Where they build ships?'

'Build more than ships.' Andy once more intervening. 'My father was based there just after the last war. He was still in the navy but teamed up with Vickers, building airships – naval airships. During that war he'd piloted them, in the RN Air Service. By golly, *that* lot were intrepid . . .'

August 10th, noon position 49 and a half north and just on 40 west. Course unchanged, ditto revs, still the same zigzag throughout daylight hours. In view of that westerly longitude, which surely had to be about the limit of U-boat operations, he'd asked the Old Man, when up top at midday to get his meridean altitude and take over the afternoon watch from Waller, whether the zigzag might not be discontinued, increasing the day's run by fifteen percent and saving pretty well a whole day in passage-time to New York.

After spending a few minutes at the chart the Old Man agreed they'd steer a straight course as from sunset that evening, would not resume zigzagging at first light on the 11th.

Quilla had made-good 230 miles in the past twenty-four hours. In the next twenty-four, with improving sea-state and no zigzag, might reckon on 250. And better than that thereafter. Every little helped, and the sooner one got to New York the sooner one might get into dry dock and out of it again. Chief Verity had said that if the shoreside engineers were on the ball, one full day's work should see it fixed: so a couple of days' wait, maybe, then say another three for docking, pumping down, doing the job and getting out again, two more for bunkering, watering and taking on stores – a week in all mightn't be far out. Then 1,200 miles to Cuba – say five days for that transit, and with ETA New York 16th, call it eighteen days from here to Nuevitas. Then the loading of 10,000 tons of bagged sugar: a lot would depend on the Cubans, but say another five days, which would bring one up to twenty-three. (All mental arithmetic, this, with glasses up and searching, while Waller tidied up his entries in the deck-log.) So, after Nuevitas, now deep-laden, you'd have the long haul up to Halifax to join a home-bound convoy – 1,500 miles approximately, making-good, say, twelve knots – looked like six days. Might call the running total thirty days: one over the odds to allow for the possibility of bad weather slowing one down.

A few days at Halifax then, awaiting convoy assembly and departure. Could be a week or even more, but call it a week, bringing the total to thirty-seven days. A rough enough estimate, sure, but call it that. Then the crossing – in an HX convoy, meaning the sort that was categorised as 'fast', comprising ships capable of maintaining between 9 and 14.9 knots, anything faster than that being sailed independently. Estimates necessarily on the wild side now, home-bound convoys being subject to various influences

114

such as major rerouting in avoidance of U-boat packs, but guess at twelve or fourteen days?

Depending on U-boats. And weather. *Mostly* on the U-boats. And a fourteen-day crossing would bring the notional total to fifty-one. Call it fifty. August 10th now, so – seven weeks, which would see *Quilla* back in home waters at the end of September.

He'd told her ten or twelve weeks from the start of this month, and in point of fact – believe it or not – it looked more like eight weeks that they'd have been away. If that figuring had been right, which he was pretty sure it had been. Even if one had to wait a fortnight or three weeks at Halifax, you'd still be inside the limit. From Julia's point of view maybe not exactly *splendid*, but a hell of a lot better than it had begun to look in the last day or so.

So scrap the second letter. Write a new one, tell her things were running pretty well as forecast, and leave it at that – leave room to give her a nice surprise.

Really, *huge* relief. And Waller hovering, awaiting his release.

'All right, Gus, I have the weight. Enjoy your shepherd's pie.'

A grimace. '*That* again.'

'Don't like shepherd's pie?' Glancing at him in surprise. 'One of the best things Loomis does, in my view.'

Loomis being the cook. Waller shrugging as he turned away. 'Not saying all that much, is it.'

'You have higher culinary standards than I do, maybe. Compared to what I remember of cadet days, we eat like kings. And looking *further* back, well, ask Mr Brown how it was in *his* apprentice days. Damn near starved, *and* worked like slaves. For three-and-ninepence a week, what's more – and deck officers carried whistles for summoning them when they thought of some other filthy job that needed doing. Going to help with the nippers again this afternoon, are you?'

'Oh.' A cautious look . . . Dixon smirking as he put

115

his glasses up; Elliot had gone down. Waller nodding to himself as if in recognition of a surprising but quite good idea. 'Perhaps I will. If they're going to be out there.'

'Bound to be. This calm – just right for them.'

By her own in-ballast standards *Quilla* was virtually rock-steady. There was still a swell but it was even lower than yesterday's, and the surface was barely ruffled, the westerly down practically to light airs. The CRO had circulated a transcript of a BBC news bulletin to the effect that the *Luftwaffe* were now concentrating on southern England, and particularly on the airfields, in an all-out attempt to break the back of the RAF.

He'd asked Dr Creagh last night, over coffee after supper, how he thought Samantha was taking the shock of the *Sarawak* disaster and the unspeakably dreadful fate of so many children whom she'd known, been caring for.

The doc's eyes held his. Grey eyes in a seamed, tanned face. Long-fingered hands opening questioningly. 'Not easy to be sure. The last thing she's going to allow at this stage is to have it show. In fact I only see her when she has children around her, and she's certainly not going to bare her soul in their sight or hearing. Especially as she's deeply concerned for *them* – four or five of them especially, including a pair who're barely capable of speech. Nods and headshakes are the best one gets. Not a hint of a smile, sobs at night and tear-stained faces first thing. You might say to be expected, at least not entirely surprising, but . . .' A sigh.

'Bloody tragic.'

'As of now it is. Except that it can only be a temporary affliction, and coping with it I think helps to keep her mind off her own distress. She's at pains to be seen as weathering it, you know?'

'Seen that way by the children, you mean?'

116

'Yes – mainly. And very much contributing to their own recovery, you see.'

'She's terrific, isn't she?'

'Well – yes ... Anyway, thanks be to God most of the kids barely seem to realise what's gone on – infantile water-off-the-duck's-back syndrome, might call it. Although there again, there could well be delayed reactions.'

'And – if you don't mind me asking – how about yourself?'

A silence: slow blink. 'I'm old. Case-hardened, you might say.' Deep breath, then. 'Not to the incineration or drowning of small children, I admit, but – in more general terms ...' Checking the time. 'And right now, better be getting back up there, bid them all goodnight.' Pausing then, asking quietly, 'Taken with Sam, are you?'

'Oh.' He was surprised at the question: wondering then whether something *she*'d said might have provoked it. But in any case, straight question, straight answer: '*Taken* – yes. Meaning attracted. Admire her, too. But as she knows, I'm engaged to be married – soon as we get back from this trip, as it happens – so that's it.'

'Quite.' Moving. 'Quite. And good luck to you – the getting back, to start with.'

'Thanks. One trifling question though, Doc. She mentioned you read to the children at their bedtime, and I was wondering, read *what?*'

'Brer Rabbit.' Wide smile. Huge teeth, the man had. Yellowish, like tusks. 'Know him?'

'Well – heard of him – it – I think –'

'It's a book of stories I'd been reading to some of them on board the *Sarawak*. Brought it with me in my bag.'

'Gladstone bag slung from your belt, I remember.'

'I'd an idea some reading matter might come in handy, stuffed it in at the last minute along with more obvious items. They love it – same stories over and over, must know 'em almost by heart. Look, must go ...'

*   *   *

117

August 11th: course 246, no zigzag, clear sky for the morning sunsight. Was going to let Dixon put the position-line on the chart and run it up to noon, then thought better of it, told him to get out the ship's slightly battered old sextant and take his own sight. The cadets' sight-taking was a regular exercise, but for some reason had been neglected in the past few days – at any rate Dixon's had. But one never lent one's own sextant. No more than you'd lend anyone your toothbrush. Andy had learnt this way back, in the old *Burntisland,* when as a cadet he'd asked to borrow the third mate's and been bawled out for his bloody cheek.

Today in fact there couldn't be the least doubt of the ship's position. The Old Man had taken a set of stars last night, and Harve Brown had done so this morning during his four to eight watch, and both fixes confirmed that by noon *Quilla* would be as near as damnit 290 miles due east of St John's, Newfoundland. And making-good eleven knots, say 265 nautical miles a day, she'd make New York now in five days.

He found himself explaining some of this to Samantha in the afternoon. The children were on the boat-deck as usual, with Waller as well as cadets Merriman and Elliot in attendance, and Harve Brown had asked her whether she'd like to see the bridge – the Old Man having authorised this, apparently. It was about three pm, the Old Man had come up and had his pipe going, hadn't said anything about expecting visitors, and the first Andy knew of it was Harve's 'Miss Vaughan, sir . . .'

'Ah, Miss Vaughan. How's your little lot?'

'Mostly very well, Captain, thank you. As I dare say you can hear?'

'Can indeed. They *all* on deck?'

'A few still aren't up to it. Dr Creagh's with those. It's kind of you to allow me up here in your holy of holies.'

'Ah, you're more than welcome.'

'Afternoon, Miss Vaughan.' Andy had taken the glasses from his eyes for long enough to exchange smiles with her. Back to the ever-continuing search then, leaving her to the Old Man. Dixon had murmured politely, 'Miss Vaughan . . .' and had *his* glasses up again, and Harve was excusing himself, to keep an eye on proceedings on the boat-deck. Andy feeling annoyed with himself for having addressed her as Miss Vaughan rather than as Samantha, as if that small degree of familiarity wasn't to be aired in the presence of the Master. Master meanwhile showing her the telegraphs and now the helm, so forth, and introducing Able Seaman Samways, quartermaster of this watch. 'Gyro compass, this – in fact gyro repeater, what we call a pelorus. The gyro itself's two decks down, out of harm's way as you might say. While the standard compass – magnetic – is up *there*' – pointing at the deckhead – 'on what's called monkey island. There's ladders up both sides, out there in the wings, see. But I'd not recommend that you – ah –'

'Disturb the monkey?'

'Well.' A laugh, of sorts: Old Man explaining that the ladders were narrow and vertical, and she'd find nothing up there to interest her.

Samantha accepting this advice and changing the subject. 'Captain, hasn't been a chance to until now – may I thank you for saving our lives? I know it was a terrific effort finding us – Mr Brown's explained to me, the odds *against* it –'

'We were lucky, Miss, that's the long and short of it. Only wish to God we'd been closer and could've got there quicker. Although from as much as I've come to know of it, from Chief Officer Barclay, seems however close we might've been –'

'I'm afraid you're right. But might I see it on the chart – where we were, and where you were, and –'

'Why, by all means.' A moment's hesitation, then: 'Holt. Show Miss Vaughan . . .' To her then, 'Second Officer Holt is our navigator – you're acquainted, I'm sure.'

'He pulled me out of the lifeboat, after all!'

'Oh, aye . . .' The Old Man nodded to him, gestured towards the chart corner, turned for'ard then, raising his own binoculars.

Samantha looking at him – Andy – expectantly. He told her, 'This way . . .' Passing around Samways, and aft to the chart table. 'Here we are – the chart we've been on for some time. About to change to *this* one, now we're approaching the US seaboard. Ever see a chart before?'

'D'you know, I haven't?'

'Well. Here's where we were at noon. Land features here, see – Newfoundland, Gulf of St Lawrence, Nova Scotia. This pencil line's our route down to New York. New York *here*.'

'How far is that?'

'You take the scale from the side here. Latitude scale, that is. One minute of latitude is one sea mile – on the equator, that is; it varies slightly with the curvature of the earth as you go north or south. So to check, say, *this* distance, you measure it on the scale at about the same level. Get it? Here, see – when we pass Cape Race around noon tomorrow, the distance-off will be' – measuring it with brass dividers – '*that*. Seventy miles. OK?'

'If you say so.'

'It's very simple. But you're looking absolutely marvellous, Sam.' He'd dropped his voice to tell her that: knew he should not have said it, but – well, the sight of her in such close-up, and the proximity itself. Had never been so close to her. Her eyes on his now, and not smiling, quite disturbingly serious. He moved the chart slightly, ran his finger northeastward up what had been *Quilla*'s track. 'This is the way we've come. And back here – on the seventh, that was the noon estimated position, and we were here – at 1500, three pm – when we took in the distress call. Turned here ten minutes later, estimating sixty miles to this point here, which was the position given in that message. Would have taken five hours at the twelve knots we *were*

120

doing, and we increased to our maximum – on which basis we'd have had a decent chance of getting to you in daylight, but partly because of the increased revs she developed a mechanical problem and we had to come down by several knots. Not the best time for it, eh?'

'You're really very happy in all this, aren't you? The way you look and sound, when you talk about it?'

'Sam, the way *you* look and sound –'

'Hush. *Hush.*'

'Yes. All right. But –'

'You were saying you had to slow down – engine trouble?'

'Shaft trouble: propeller-shaft. Definitely *wasn't* the best time for it, I can tell you. Down to low revs then, and the weather not helping much, visions in mind of – of how actually it must have been, pretty well, and – conscious of losing hours. And – well, looking for boats then, because if the ship had still been afloat the flames would have been visible a long way off, and with wind and sea as they were, boats would have been drifting down-wind – *this* way – all that time. So approaching the position given in that signal we sort of aimed-off – guesswork mostly – and eventually started letting off snowflakes, as they're called.'

'Which we saw, and thought, "Oh thank God!", but it faded away, and Mr Barclay didn't want to use up all his Very lights –'

'Might have been the second or third of those that our lookouts spotted, and we turned towards it. Hadn't aimed-off enough, you see. But another snowflake or two then, and there you were.' A hand on one of hers – it had moved of its own accord. 'At that stage we were thinking yours was just the first boat, there'd be others, but . . .' A pause. 'I'm so sorry, Sam. We all think the world of you for the way you're standing up to it. Sorry if I'm speaking out of turn, but –'

'Children to think about, and keeping busy's the great

121

thing.' She retrieved her hand. Voice up again. 'New York *when?*'

'Sixteenth. Probably early.'

'Friday . . . What's the little blue flashing light?'

'The log. Type known as a Chernikeef. Distance run's shown on the dial, and that table printed on the switch-box converts the time for twenty-one flashes into knots. See – "Time in Seconds" in this column, "Speed in Knots" here? The log itself sticks out about eighteen inches below the hull, little impeller inside it buzzes round and the results come up here electrically.'

'Marvels of modern science.'

'As long as it doesn't get bunged up with mud or seaweed, it's all right.' He turned back to her: she'd edged away a little but they were still eye to eye. 'Anything else I can tell you?'

'There is, actually. Keep meaning to ask – what's "Barranquilla" mean when it's at home?'

'It's a seaport in Colombia, in the Caribbean. Our company, Dundas Gore of Glasgow, bought her not long ago from owners who mostly traded out that way. And if they wanted to change it now they couldn't: changing ships' names in wartime isn't allowed, for some reason. Love *your* name, Sam.'

That evening in the saloon she was distant both in manner and location, sitting between Harve Brown and Chief Officer Barclay and chatting mostly with the second engineer – Bridgeman – who was facing her across the table, with the *Sarawak*'s radio man on his left and CRO Foster on his right, Andy thus effectively excluded. In fact a lot of her conversation was with Harve – about the children, how most of them seemed to be as right as rain but just a few – older ones, oddly enough – still subject to nightmares and crying fits and largely unresponsive to efforts by herself and Dr Creagh to cheer them up. Andy chipped in at that stage, asking whether they listened with the others to the doctor's Brer Rabbit stories, and she replied with a laugh, 'Oh, they're all crazy about old Brer. Rather keen on him myself, tell you the truth.' Explaining to the others then, 'Book of stories the doc reads to them. *He's* worth his weight in gold. Honestly don't know where we'd be without him.'

But even while answering that question, she'd barely glanced Andy's way. His own fault, he supposed: he'd pushed it a little too hard on the bridge this afternoon.

Grabbing her hand, and so on.

Stupid – and quite pointless. Liked her, that was all, sympathised with her and wanted her to know it. What it actually came down to was wanting to help. Certainly had no other motive. Especially as she knew of the existence of Julia – which he'd made no bones about, would have told her about at some stage, even if Harve Brown hadn't taken it upon himself to do so. Which was another thing entirely, old Harve's rather annoying preconceptions.

She was trying hard with Barclay, he noticed. So was Harve. Barclay near-silent however, giving short answers and never opening any new topic of conversation. Smiled a few times, but only a perfunctory contortion of the features, no warmth or humour in it. Sam and Harve both making the most of anything the man did say, but still not getting him to loosen up.

Andy asked Creagh about him later on, after Sam had gone up to the children and Barclay had retired to his cabin. The doctor glanced round, making sure of not being overheard, then confided, 'Broadly, survivors' guilt. Not an unusual phenomenon. I saw it a few times in '14–'18, as a matter of fact. I was doctoring in the army in that lot. Periods of action resulting in heavy casualties, you'd get individuals who'd come out of it unharmed reacting as if they shouldn't have, were ashamed of it. No rhyme or reason – faced the same odds, just had the luck to survive. But' – another glance around – 'in that man's case I believe there's a more specific explanation. When our group got together he mentioned several times that

123

he'd been knocked off some ladder, and my guess is he'd stunned himself. He was – you know, slightly groggy. Well, we set off in search of children who might have been trapped or lost, didn't find any, had to clear out of it prontissimo what's more. Well, we'd left Sam at the boat with these other children, and Barclay's recollection is that it was on his insistence she'd stayed with them. It wasn't, it was on mine. Point I'm making is that he was suffering from at least that one delusion and probably still is, and I'd *guess* what he's most aware of is the fact that he, Chief Officer, came out of it on his feet and over a hundred children didn't.'

'He took charge of lowering the boat, I heard.'

'He did. But he could do that pretty well as an automaton, couldn't he. Second nature – as it would be with you.'

'The others are all right, are they, the crewmen?'

A nod. 'Few problems there. One quite nasty case of burns, otherwise – well, nothing, really ... I hear you gave Sam some navigational instruction during the afternoon.'

'Oh, she wanted to see the chart, where we were when it happened, so forth.'

'*I'd* be interested to have that explained. Any chance?'

'I'll mention it to the Old Man. I'm sure he'll be only too willing. You've met him, I suppose?'

'When he so kindly offered me the use of his little cabin. "Old Man", though – I'd say he's half my age?'

'It's the term we use, that's all.'

'Wouldn't "skipper" be more appropriate?'

'Never. That'd be derogatory. Skipper of a trawler, drifter, dredger, so forth, but not of an ocean-going ship of the Merchant Navy. Old Man, Captain, Master, or sometimes Commander.'

'If I'm invited to the bridge I'll bear that in mind.'

'"Captain" would be your best bet.'

'Right.' He put down his knife and fork. 'That was really very good.'

'Suet pudding smeared with treacle next.'

'Oh, crikey . . .'

At the Old Man's invitation, Dr Creagh paid his visit to the bridge during the forenoon of the 12th, escorted by Harve Brown, who with the aid of the deck-log explained the chart workings to him. Noon position that day being eighty miles southeast of Cape Race, the lower promontory of Newfoundland. Several ships on northeasterly courses had passed during the night – showing lights, *Quilla* too, for the first time since leaving the Clyde – and during the forenoon they met and spoke several others. During Andy's afternoon watch they spoke two Americans, one British, a Frenchman and a Pole, all of whom were steering west or southwest – for Sydney Nova Scotia, the Gulf of St Lawrence or Halifax. *Quilla* on each occasion hoisting her four-letter identification, cadets Elliot and Merriman being responsible for this, making it easy for themselves by leaving the four flags bent on and ready for hoisting, taking it in turns to run the hoist up above the bridge while the other stayed with Sam, Waller and the children.

Waller making a bit of an idiot of himself, Andy thought.

Being now in safe waters, the Old Man had radioed to the sea transport officer in New York giving ETA as 0800/16th, telling him that he had thirty-seven survivors of the SS *Sarawak*, including twenty-seven children on board, British consul please to be informed, and requesting dry dock facilities in order to refit the stern gland. The request had been acknowledged. A shaft bearing was still overheating, Chief Verity had said – though not dangerously so, or at this stage getting any hotter – while as for the stern gland, there had been vibration in it, seemingly wasn't now, but clearly both did have to be attended to, otherwise a spell of dirty weather could see old *Quilla* in bad trouble.

Over the past twenty-four hours, noon to noon, she'd made-good 270 miles.

The STO and consulate in New York would probably have been notified already about the survivors, as a consequence of *Quilla*'s signal in the early hours of the 8th, but it had as well to make sure of it, so that the US immigration service and the families receiving the children would be geared up for their arrival. The consulate would presumably have been in touch with everyone concerned.

At supper in the saloon that evening, Samantha had put herself between Andy and Searle, the *Sarawak*'s former RO/3. She'd chosen that chair herself, having had a choice: evidently he'd been forgiven, or was supposed to have learnt his lesson. He'd written another letter to Julia during the dogwatches, had told her that this and earlier ones would be posted in just a few days' time and he hoped might not take too long getting to her. He'd number the backs of the envelopes so she could open them in the right order. All was going well, they were up to schedule, might even be back with her a little sooner than anticipated.

Touch wood. Or as they say in certain other parts, knock on wood. In other words, don't count on it; delays can crop up suddenly and quite unexpectedly. Julia darling, there's a newish moon up there, just a sliver, I was looking at it last night and thinking only one more moon after this one, and we should be together!

Should be: but not counting chickens. Some way to go yet, and not all of it by any means plain sailing. HX convoys were in fact battlegrounds; you all knew it, only by and large chose not to talk about it.

Small-talk instead: like asking Sam, 'Doc enjoy his visit to the bridge?'

'Very much. The chart stuff especially. Unlike me, he's seen charts before and even worked with them, used to sail quite a bit, apparently.'

'He's a great chap.'

126

'Isn't he just.'

'And you're a great girl.' She glanced at him sharply, and he defused it with: 'Doc and I agreed on that last evening.'

8

Heavy mist as *Quilla* nosed her way in towards New York. Flat calm too, the lack of motion on her contributing to the eerie quiet which so often accompanies a curtaining of fog. The sun wouldn't take long to burn it off, but meanwhile it had her down to about five knots, and the St Ambrose lightship moaning as if in pain; closer sounds were the swish of sea washing along the ship's sides and the regular thrashing of her barely submerged propeller. The Old Man was in his usual corner with his glasses on a small passenger steamer, American, that had overhauled them in recent minutes and seemed to be altering now to starboard. Andy checking all round for any other ships or potential hazards, having already checked ship's head, engine room telegraph at slow ahead and the distance-off from Sandy Hook and the Ambrose.

He lowered his glasses, nodded to Waller. 'OK.'

Half an hour to go at these revs. Waller would be up to take over again before they got there. Earlier than usual start to this 16 August, Waller having relieved Harve Brown at 0700 instead of 0800, Andy breakfasting at that time too in order to allow Waller this breakfast break. Seven-thirty now, and ETA off Sandy Hook, where *Quilla* would be stopping to embark the pilot, 0800 New York time, Zone +5, ship's clocks having been adjusted in easy stages during the past few days so as to even out the hours on watch. Keeping the right time for Cuba now as well.

Ship right ahead. Smack on the bow, red and green navigation lights pinpoints in the haze, masthead lights above them even less distinct – fog thicker of course at that level. He told Selby, 'Come ten degrees to starboard.'

A tanker: she too altering to starboard. *Quilla* amazingly steady on this mill-pond – as if she'd forgotten she was in ballast and supposed to cavort around.

'Course 285, sir.'

The tanker's starboard light no longer visible. She – the tanker – was probably what that passenger steamer had been altering for. They'd pass well clear, in any case.

On his way out of the saloon after early breakfast, Andy had bumped into Harve Brown on his way in, had asked him, 'Paperwork done with?', because it was what he'd been relieved early for. There was always paperwork on arrival anywhere, but this time there'd be more than usual on account of the passengers, the unusual nature of this unscheduled visit. Harve, Barclay and Samantha had all been at it, the mate having a lot of routine stuff to attend to anyway.

He'd nodded. 'If Port Health want to know which of the kids have had mumps, measles, chicken-pox or scarlet fever, etcetera, it's there for them.'

That sort of question, one imagined, might be asked either at the Quarantine Station or by Immigration after berthing. One could assume the children would be spared any Ellis Island immigration procedures, arrangements for their coming here having been made months ago, Sam had said. For 131 of them, not just twenty-seven. She'd also listed the names and addresses of the people who ought to be here to meet them: had had the documentation in her boat bag – that satchel – for all 131. She'd said last night, 'Dare say some of those others will be meeting us too. Either on the off-chance of having been misinformed, or simply not believing in anything so awful.'

'In which case –'

'Have to convince them, that's all. Preferably without hysteria in the sight or hearing of *these* children. But thank heavens Tommy insisted each of us should have a copy of the register, as she called it. Without it we'd *really* have had problems.'

'Think she foresaw some such possibility?'

'Must have. Can't say I caught on to it.'

'I doubt there's much you don't catch on to.'

The light blue eyes on his, speculatively. Small smile. 'You're an unusual man, I think. Say nice things but actually mean them.'

'Well.' Cocking an eyebrow at her. 'I don't say things I *don't* mean. Do speak out of turn, on occasion. As you've noticed, a couple of times. Get carried away, just sort of blurt.'

Smiling again: 'Tell your fiancée I think she's a lucky girl.'

They'd been on their way up to the lower bridge-deck at that stage, Andy escorting her because this was her last evening on board and Harve for once hadn't claimed the privilege. She'd neither objected nor commented when he'd left the saloon with her.

But Julia *lucky*?

He'd told Sam, 'As a matter of honest truth, I've serious doubts of that. Not sure I'm doing her any favours at all.'

She'd stopped at the top of that section of the companionway. 'What *are* you saying?'

'Well.' He'd started now – blurting again. Hadn't meant to, but having started, could hardly just leave it in the air. Realising, or semi-realising, that the reason he'd burst out with it was that it was something that had been building up inside him, despite efforts to suppress it, and Sam was someone he could share it with – or burden with it . . . 'For one thing, one's away at sea four-fifths of the time. Another is that a second officer doesn't get paid much. As in fact Julia knows very well – she has two cousins who're both second officers, her family background's all Merchant Navy.'

'The cousins not married?'

'Neither of 'em. But right now, you see, she's content enough, works in her mother's dress business – they're diversifying into uniforms and working clothes, overalls, whatever – and OK, for reasons best known to herself she'd sooner I didn't drown, but if I did – well, her life wouldn't be stood on its head exactly, as it would – up to a point – if we were married. And facing facts, the odds on living for ever aren't all that good, you know. We've been losing a heck of a lot of ships lately.'

Looking at him steadily. 'You'll come through, Andy.'

'Do my best to, naturally, but –'

'You *will.* Some are bound to, and you'll be one of them.' On her toes, she'd kissed his cheek. '*Will*, Andy. I'll say praycrs for you. And listen, I'll give you an address – my aunt's, in Devon?'

'I'd certainly like to have that.'

'When you get back, send me a postcard, admit I was right?'

'*Right.* And I'll give you my address at Helensburgh in Dunbartonshire so you can let me know when you get some terrific part.'

'It's a deal!'

'Also Christmas cards?'

'Why not?'

'And when you get yourself engaged or married.'

That steady look again, then almost to his surprise, a nod: 'When, or if.'

He kissed *her*, this time. 'Night, Sam.'

They'd passed the tanker – French flag, and a wave from some frog in the bridge-wing – and he brought *Quilla* back to 275, then on second thoughts 273. There was a clutter of small ships on the bow to port: might be trawlers, but well clear in any case. Visibility was improving. He was searching for the Ambrose light vessel now, and thinking again about that exchange with Sam: that if he'd said Julia's life *would* be stood on its head if he drowned, it would have been the understatement of the year, but of course had not been sayable.

Another that hadn't was in a way an extension of the point he *had* made about being away at sea for something like four-fifths of every year: the fact that one was perhaps more than usually susceptible to the attractions of the opposite sex, and in foreign ports couldn't help coming across them now and then. All right, Sam was in a class of her own – one wasn't likely to meet others of her stamp – but none the less, after weeks and months at sea, especially in bloody convoy – and being one's father's son –

That especially.

There were also the Manuelas of this world. Likely to be one or two in Nuevitas, for instance.

Liking them, was most of it, and finding it difficult not to *show* one's liking.

Scent of porridge, though: and Waller down there at his side. 'All right, then?'

'Can see a few yards, anyway.' At that same moment spotting the Ambrose: realising it had ceased its bleating in recent minutes, although it was still showing its light. Mist thinning, of course, which was how one had spotted it so suddenly, and could also discern a greyish low-lying hump to port, which had to be the coastline running about north-by-west to Sandy Hook. He pointed it out to Waller. 'And there's the Ambrose. Some little widgers out there on the bow – see 'em? Fog's breaking up anyway, and we're on 273.'

'Right.'

He told the Old Man, 'Third mate has her, sir. Might do without lights now, d'you think?'

'Yes. Switch off.' Then: 'Know this city, Holt?'

'Not really, sir. Here only once, as a cadet in the *Burntisland,* short visit and I didn't get ashore.'

Hadn't gone ashore on that occasion, largely on account of having been stony broke. And for a similar but not identical reason, might not land this time either. Had funds, of sorts, but needed to conserve them – having

Julia in mind, and not wanting to arrive back home without a bob or two.

Off Sandy Hook the Old Man turned her to stem the flood tide with the telegraph at 'dead slow', while the pilot boat flying its red and white flag came creaming out to run alongside, where the bosun had put a jumping-ladder over abreast number three hatch. There was no sign of Harve Brown, who'd normally have been there to receive a pilot, so Andy, who'd been on the boat-deck keeping an eye out for Samantha, went down for'ard and did the honours.

'Morning, pilot!'

'Morning to you.' Climbing through the rail, breathing hard from the climb: elderly, small, three-quarters bald, face like a walnut; white trousers, reefer with a master's four stripes on its sleeves, naval cap of sorts, bony hand out to shake. 'Jake Large.'

Andy told him, 'Andy Holt, second mate. Captain Beale said to welcome you aboard, sir.'

'Crowd o' kids you bringin' us, outa some ship got sunk?'

He nodded. 'There've been a few lost, these last few weeks.' Better than admitting that British and Allied ships were being sunk in droves. Ushering the pilot to the starboard side door, adding, 'Kids have come through it well, though.'

'Shipping 'em out safe from the bombing, that it?'

'The intention, sure. Frying pan into fire, you're thinking. Safe enough now, though, *this* lot . . .' He secured the weather door behind them. 'Care to lead on up?' Vibration increasing as engine revs mounted, the Old Man turning her upstream again, gnarled old pilot shouting as he started climbing, 'Germans ain't gettin' it all their way. News on radio this morning, your boys downed close on two hun'ed yesterday.'

'German aircraft – two hundred?'

'Close on. Hun'ed an' eighty some'n. If it's the truth, we can believe it?'

'Don't see why we shouldn't. Lower bridge-deck, this – one to go.'

'Keeps a guy fit, leastways.'

'Well . . .'

'Whether he wants it or fucking don't.' Climbing on, repeating, 'Hun'ed an' eighty some'n, in one day. But what I heard, squareheads is still beating the living shit outa dear old England. You seen much o' that?'

'Can't say I have. In fact I'd say might be putting it a bit strong. Anyway, if we're shooting 'em down at that rate –'

'If you can believe it . . .'

The CRO's transcript of some recent bulletin had said the battle in the skies was now centred over the south of England, the fighter airfields in particular, but the news earlier had made mention of night bombing attacks on London, Portsmouth, Harwich, Humberside, the Clyde, Liverpool, Manchester and Tyneside. He'd crossed his fingers, thinking not all on the same night, they'd surely not have that many bombers. Please God, they didn't. And please God, while you're at it, have them lay off Tyneside and Clydeside anyway: the Tyne for Julia's sake – although she was a good distance from the river and any dock area – and the Clyde for his mother's. Mama working full-time now for the WVS, Women's Voluntary Service, her lot dealing exclusively with convoy and other naval survivors – feeding, clothing, accommodating, arranging medical treatment, cash advances and railway warrants home.

Plain truth of it was, *everyone* was in this thing, one way or another. And incidentally, if a Merchant Navy man whose ship had been sunk didn't go back and sign on in another within two or three weeks, he stood to lose his registered seafarer classification and be called up, find himself square-bashing, then God only knew what. Well – *fighting*, being shot at . . .

He'd written to his mother and to his father in the course of the past few days, having belatedly caught on

134

to the fact he wouldn't hear from either of them – or more importantly from Julia – for a while yet, since *Quilla*'s mail would obviously have been sent to Nuevitas. Fortnight or so, he guessed – if one got out of here in a week, say.

At the Quarantine Station off Staten Island, where *Quilla* anchored, Port Health didn't take as long as the Old Man had expected. Sam and the doctor had the children mustered on the boat-deck in more or less orderly fashion, and the Old Man had asked the officials when they'd boarded to go easy with the kids, and if possible make it snappy: they'd had a rough time, and the sooner they could be transferred into the hands of their new guardians, the better for all concerned. He had all his own documentation ready for them – crew lists and so forth – and Sam had hers. There was no question of any infectious disease on board, and that was that – clean bill of health, rubber-stamped and autographed. Harve Brown sent Merriman to haul down the yellow flag Q, and went for'ard to prepare for weighing anchor, while Andy escorted their visitors to the jumping-ladder, starboard side for'ard, at the foot of which their boat was waiting.

There was another boat in the offing, though: had come from shore and was lying off, stemming the tide, waiting to take the Port Health boat's place. One of the Health men told Andy, 'Customs. They'll take passage with you to your berth. Press, too, looks like.'

Civilians in trilby hats: half a dozen of those, and three Customs officers in uniforms. He asked the Port Health trio, 'Do us a favour, hang on here a minute?', and shot up to the bridge, told the Old Man, 'Customs launch lying-off has reporters in it, sir. I've got Port Health stalling for a minute, but – press might be badgering the children?'

'*Mightn't* they just.' He gave it about one second's thought. 'Elliot – tell the bosun, shift the foc'sl hose to that ladder.'

135

'Aye, sir!'

Andy went down at a slower pace than the cadet's, while the Old Man took a megaphone with him into the bridge-wing, aimed it at the Customs launch and bawled, 'Customs, ahoy there. You're welcome, but I'll have no press aboard. Any try it, they'll be washed off the ladder. Rigging a hose this minute. Don't try it, fellers, you been warned now!'

There was some angry shouting and gesticulating, and the launch began edging closer, poised to shoot in along-side as soon as the other shoved off. Down on the main deck the first of the Port Health people was clambering over the rail: Andy told him and the other two, 'Please don't hurry.' Bosun McGrath was coming in a hurry, all right, a charge not unlike a rhino's, with ABs Morton and O'Donnell in close support and the business end of a canvas fire-hose. The last of the Port Health team growled, 'Guys only tryin' to do their job?'

Andy told him, 'Happens the captain doesn't want 'em upsetting the kids, it's his ship and she's not open to the public, he *has* given 'em fair warning.'

'Yeah . . .'

Unconvinced. Jamming his cap down so as not to lose it while climbing down; over the rail then, looking glum.

McGrath had the hose's long brass nozzle on the top rail, aimed down at the water: he yelled back over his shoulder, 'Stand by. I'll sing out when.'

One Port Health man was off the ladder: now the second, third with only a rung or two to go. He'd stumbled into the launch's bow, one of the others had cast off and the boat was surging away. Sounds meanwhile from *Quilla*'s foc'sl of the steam capstan beginning to clank around, taking up some of the cable's slack: they'd heard it in the launch, one uniformed man pointing, alerting the pressmen to what was happening. Andy suggested to McGrath, 'Best get it running, let 'em see it's for real.'

Drenching Customs officers might *not* be seen as a

136

friendly act. Boat approaching now: all faces including that of the man at the helm gazing up. A shout from McGrath – 'Here we go, then!' – and the hose convulsing as it filled then gushed. Morton was with McGrath at this end of it: it was a powerful hose, a good pressure of steam driving the pump that fed it, a heavy stream of salt water plunging into the bay's calm surface not all that far from the ladder's foot. Launch still coming – having to pass only a few yards from that cataract. Slowing: engine chugging astern to take the way off, Customs men crouching ready to jump for the chain ladder with its wooden rungs. And the Old Man up there using the megaphone again: 'Bosun – let the Customs up, but any press try it, wash 'em off!'

'Aye aye, Cap'n!'

'Customs – save us all a load of trouble, tell your cox'n to let you off then clear off quick?'

The man at the helm had raised a thumb. One reporter shaking a fist, and a shout of, 'You'll be sorry, Limey bastards!' There'd been a couple of camera flashes. Launch thumping alongside, first of the uniformed men on the ladder, civilians wisely staying put, gesturing and arguing amongst themselves. Andy gave the Customs a hand over the rail, telling the front-runner, 'Captain doesn't want 'em badgering the kids, is all.'

'No skin off my nose, Mister.'

Second and third men over, and the launch already clear, gathering way. From the foc'sl-head then – perfect timing – Harve Brown's yell of 'Anchor away!' telling the Old Man he'd seen the swing of the cable as the hook itself broke out of the mud. McGrath had shouted for the hose to be shut off, remarking to Andy, 'Be needin' us up there now.' Hose needed up for'ard for washing mud off the cable as it rose. You didn't want stinking mud going down with it into the cable-locker. As a cadet in the *Burntisland* he'd been stationed in her cable-locker often enough during the weighing to see the cable flaked down properly, didn't pile and jam. Stinking as well as

137

dangerous, those great links rumbling down. He nodded to McGrath, 'Did the trick all right, Bo.' From the moment of Harve's report that the anchor was out of the ground, *Quilla*'s steel had been humming to the vibration of her shallowly churning screw – at slow speed, then revs increasing to turn her across the flood tide and take her on over to the Coney Island side for safe entry to the Narrows.

From the Narrows, following around the bulge of the Brooklyn shoreline, something like five miles into the middle of Upper Bay, then passing Liberty Island with the statue on it, Governor's Island off to starboard in the approaches to East River, and Ellis way over to port, inshore; she had the Hudson's mile-wide entrance ahead then, a few more miles of continuing flood tide to her allocated berth, Pier 59.

Opposite West 18th Street, the old pilot had said.

The children were going to be returned to the owners' suite before she berthed. Having seen the sights and other shipping on the move, and finally treated to a view of the Manhattan skyline, getting them back inside was aimed at making their transfer into the hands of foster parents less chaotic than it might otherwise have been. Sam's task, of course, assisted by Dr Creagh and backed up by cadets Elliot and Merriman and the two former *Sarawak* stewards, who'd be laying on a meal of soup and sandwiches. Some pressmen might manage to sneak aboard – although efforts would be made to keep them off – and they might be in a hostile as well as inquisitive frame of mind; they weren't on any account to be allowed access to the children, and Harve Brown had put the word around that the less said about the *Sarawak* disaster, the better.

Andy had given Sam a note of his home address at Helensburgh, and she'd had her aunt's ready for him on a postcard. He'd also added a PS to the latest of his letters to Julia, telling her that as a result of a change of route, although these letters to her would be on their way within hours, any that she'd written to him would be waiting for him elsewhere, and he couldn't hope to get them in less than ten or fourteen days' time. When he did, he'd answer them at once.

William, whose arm the doctor had said was mending nicely, slipped away from the others when Sam was herding them below, and asked Andy whether he might be allowed to stay on deck to see the ship tie up. He and Andy had had several chats during the past week, after the doctor had introduced him as 'the man who carried you up from the boat, young Bill'. Andy answered this request with a regretful, 'Better not, old son. I'll be too busy to keep an eye on you, there's sure to be a big crowd milling around soon as we get in there, and your friend Samantha'll have her work cut out – really does *need* to have you all in one spot. So just for her sake, eh?'

A shrug. 'OK.'

'That's the boy. But also they're giving you a meal of some kind, you don't want to miss that.' He was crouching, to hear and be heard in the surrounding racket. 'You'll have a whale of a time here, I expect. Least, I hope you will. That arm's nearly mended, uh?'

'Andy.' Samantha had come looking for William. 'Fond farewells?'

He straightened up. 'About as fond as a farewell could be.' She caught his meaning and took William's hand. 'Reciprocated. Just don't forget to write.'

'Not a chance. But saying goodbye this soon?'

'Might as well, don't you think, before hell breaks loose?'

'All right. In case there isn't another chance.' Taking her free hand in both of his. 'Good luck, Sam. Be happy.' Borrowing one hand back to ruffle the boy's hair: 'So long, William.'

His job when the ship was berthing was to take charge of things on her stern, the passing of ropes and wires, so forth. There was a tug up for'ard pushing her bow in – flood tide if still running making such assistance more or less essential for a ship with only a single screw.

Stern-line over now, anyway: Patterson and Pettigrew taking it to the winch on the centre-line abaft number five, Stone and Walker backing it up while Pettigrew put steam on the winch to warp her in. The double-decker pier looming over them was thronged with people, a lot of whom would no doubt be swarming over – or trying to – as soon as a gangway was rigged. Sightseers and reporters probably (who'd be barred, initially at any rate, by Harve Brown and the bosun plus quartermasters) as well as those who'd be welcomed – recipient families, consular staff, immigration officials, maybe the Sea Transport Officer with news of the dry docking programme.

For Sam, the next hour or so was likely to be hectic. Her priority and anxiety would be to get the right children safely into the right hands, and with the doctor's help ensure that those in need of specialist attention were set to get it. Consular officials might be expected to play a part in this, especially in the case of children who were being removed to distant parts of this huge country.

Quilla was now alongside and the tug was backing off: hemp breasts secured for'ard and aft, wire springs being passed. Tide slackening, by the look of it, a comparative stillness around the timber piles, arrival alongside seemingly having coincided with the height of the flood. In any case, *Quilla*'s screw was now at rest, Patterson and co. taking in the slack on the after backspring, Andy at the ship's side signalling OK, make it fast, while up for'ard longshoremen were swinging a gangway into place.

Now for bedlam . . .

First off the ship, before the gangway was properly secured, were the Customs officers and the pilot, the latter seen off by Harve Brown, and yelling at a large, florid man in a sky-blue suit, 'Parker, what's your goddam hurry?'

About the pilot's own age but twice his size, fringe of thick grey hair showing under a two-tone grey fedora. Late fifties probably, and might have known better than to encumber the gangway so these others had to squeeze around him, also inconveniencing a docker who was still setting up wire handrails, but enquiring genially of the Customs men, 'Find enough contraband to make it worth your while, boys?', and ignoring the crabby little pilot's question. Stepping aboard then, telling Harve Brown, 'Parker Lloyd, sea transport officer, to see Captain Beale.'

English, apparently: Yorkshire accent overlaid with American. Droopy, spaniel-like brown eyes. Harve Brown had introduced himself and at the same time seen Andy, who'd come by for a word on his way up to the bridge to see to the safe stowage under lock and key of binoculars, sextants and other navigational gear. Harve telling the STO, having to shout to do it, 'Second Officer Holt'll take you up. Listen – might one of that lot be our consul?'

'Vice-consul.' Pointing at a youngish, narrow-headed man in a noticeably well-cut, grey-checked suit. 'He can come up with me if he wants.'

The big man was wearing an RNR tie, Andy noticed. Which figured: most STOs were former merchant navy masters. Shaking hands with him and waiting near the port-side weather door for the vice-consul – a very different sort, in pebble glasses and clutching an attaché case, could have been a slightly self-conscious schoolmaster, who on arrival through the gathering crowd gave his name as Wilkinson, adding, 'And my colleagues . . .' They were behind him, a red-haired woman in a hat and flowered summer dress, with a friendly, forthright manner, and a young man in a flannel suit, brown trilby, sunglasses: overweight, could have done with some fresh air and exercise. Parker Lloyd had pushed on inside and was on the ladderway, bawling down, 'On the bridge still, is he?'

'Or his day cabin, for'ard end of the lower bridge-deck. Try there first?' Andy stood back to let the vice-consul go

141

ahead of him, and told the woman, 'Children are on the lower bridge-deck too, waiting for you in what we call the owners' suite. Miss Vaughan and Dr Creagh have been looking after them, they'll be delighted to see you. Follow me?'

Sam was up there looking anxious; the doctor was in the doorway of his, or rather the Old Man's, sleeping cabin, in conversation with two small girls. Parker Lloyd had banged on the day cabin door, pushed it open and looked inside, called to the vice-consul, 'Must be up top.' Andy meanwhile telling Sam, 'Consulate staff. Didn't get their names, but –'

'Ursula Wainwright, and this is Martin Hyams. Miss Vaughan?'

'Call me Sam. Saves time.' Shaking hands, then straight to it: 'Look – only four of the twenty-seven have any sort of problem, but they're going to need special care and I imagine psychiatric help. Dr Creagh'll tell you –'

Andy went on up to the bridge, where the Old Man was telling the vice-consul he could use the day cabin for interviewing foster parents, so they'd have the whole of that deck, a bit more elbow room, and if they needed it some degree of privacy.

'More than kind, captain. May I congratulate you on the rescue? Although so few survived – *terribly* sad –'

'It is that.' Looking towards the STO, who as well as the RNR tie wore a merchant navy badge in the button-hole of his lapel, and was in conversation with Chief Engineer Frank Verity. Old Man looking meaningfully at Andy then, who put a hand on Wilkinson's arm: 'I'll show you the day cabin and introduce you to Dr Creagh and Miss Vaughan.' Turning him back towards the ladder. The Old Man had nodded goodbye to him, now called to Parker Lloyd, 'What about dry dock, then?' Andy asking the vice-consul as they started down, 'One thing, if you can tell me – Miss Vaughan and the doctor, once the children are taken care of, what happens to them?'

'All set up, I'm glad to say. Accommodation at the Barbizon Plaza, and early return passages to the UK. Same with the others incidentally – Chief Officer Barclay, and –'

'Well, that's splendid!'

'What we're for, you know. Amongst a few other things, of course.' Smiling as they reached the lower bridge-deck. Below them, starting upward from main deck level, was Gus Waller with what looked like several sets of fosterers. Andy telling Wilkinson, 'Captain's day cabin's here. But if you'd come *this* way –'

'That's all right, thank you, I'll –'

'Anyway, here's Dr Creagh.'

Also, a sallow individual in a dark suit and light-coloured fedora, whom Andy took for press and stopped, but was actually from the Blood Line's New York agency, carried a bulging briefcase and was looking for Captain Beale: who was going to need him for sure, but probably not in the next few minutes. From above them, on their way down ten seconds ago, he'd heard the Old Man shout, 'You say *this evening*?', and it had sunk in now: dry docking within hours was all it *could* mean. No wait at all. Too good to be true, almost. If they worked Saturdays, and as Chief Verity had hoped could do the work in one day – undock Sunday, bunkers etc Monday, sail for Cuba Tuesday?

Maybe wouldn't work a full day Saturday, though. Even then . . .

Dr Creagh and the vice-consul were shaking hands. Andy called to Sam, who was on her way to join them, 'Customers on the way up. And you have reservations at the Barbizon Plaza. Sounds pretty grand.'

He wasn't sure she'd heard him: she'd looked at him, but by then the doctor had been introducing her and the vice-consul to each other, and he, Andy, was heading back up to where Parker Lloyd was telling the Old Man, 'Pilot'll board you five pm, 1700. No more 'n a stone's throw across the river to Hoboken, the McLellan yard, they'll start pumping down soon as you're in, start work first thing in the morning. OK?'

'I'd say it would be, Mr Lloyd.' Telling the Dundas Gore agent then, 'Be with you shortly, Mister.'

'See, Captain, it's kind of urgent –'

'*Commander* Lloyd, for the record.' The big man – Andy's height, more or less, and about twice his bulk – showed a lot of teeth when he smiled. As now, telling them, 'Don't spend much time watching the grass grow, this side of the old pond.'

'But you're from *our* side?'

Verity had asked that, and Lloyd nodded. 'Been here a while, however. Master Mariner, chief officer when I first come. Home port New York, five-month voyages outbound via Panama, homeward round the Cape, ports of call after LA – hell, China, Japan, Philippines, Dutch East Indies. Saw Blighty once in a dozen years.'

'And how come you're STO here now?'

'Oh – wife here, coupla kids. Might've gone back, for all that – war and all, and masters in short supply, I know, but – see, this is where they wanted me. Ministry of Supply, that is. They have a local director here, I'm sort of teamed with him, see to stowage plans, so forth. Speaking of which –'

Verity had been taking a look at whatever was happening on deck, cut in as he returned, 'Pump down in the dock tonight, work a full day tomorrow, bunkers and fresh water Monday?'

'Something like that.' Rubbing his jaw. 'Tell you for sure in the morning. But tell *me* – ever hear of a steam-ejector system for lower holds and bilges, Chief?'

'May or may not have heard of it, who'd want it?'

'Well.' Lloyd switched to the Old Man: 'You were bound Nuevitas, Cuba – right?'

A nod: suspicion replacing his usual amiability. 'Far as I know, still am.'

'And that may be the case. We'll know better in the morning.' Offering a crumpled pack of Lucky Strikes:

the Old Man declined, Verity took one and flicked a lighter into flame; Andy, at the chart table with Dixon, out of range and taking no part in this, hadn't been included in the offer. Parker continuing, through a cloud of the first lungful of his own smoke, 'When we've had a look below. See, there was a cargo dumped here the Ministry'd like to be shot of, and *Barranquilla* could be the answer to our prayers. It's not a cargo you'd exactly jump at, but if your lower-hold layout's adaptable to steam-ejection –'

'Noxious, or what?'

The agent had asked that. The name on the card he'd given Andy was MacPherson. The thought in Andy's mind meanwhile being that however noxious this cargo might be, if it was one for the UK – and Parker Lloyd's 'that may be the case' suggested a possibility of cutting out Cuba – therefore, saving *weeks* – well, grab it and run . . . There was an interruption, though, at this point, Steward Hastings and his assistant Chumley arriving with corned-beef sandwiches and coffee, Lloyd taking advantage of this to avoid a straight answer to that question, talking instead about the dry docking and McLellan's yard. Andy barely listening: interested in both sandwiches and coffee, also wondering about the cargo. The only truly noxious ones in his seagoing experience having been wet hides and fishmeal, both of which stank, but neither of which one would expect to load on *this* coast.

Any case, if it meant an early trip home, saving Julia about a month of her ordeal . . .

Lloyd was saying that the guy to see if they had any problem or special requirement when they got into McLellan's was Hank Smith, general manager and vice-president. He was the guts of the business, McLellan himself no engineer but a shrewd businessman who'd seen the writing on the wall and bought in when it had been not exactly a steal but certainly an investment of very high potential.

'He's counting on the US getting into this war before

145

we're any of us much older, the yard then coining it in in a big way with the repairing and refitting of minor warships – destroyers, sub-chasers and so forth, never-ending stream of 'em, as there will be. US Navy an unstinting paymaster – and Gil McLellan incidentally a buddy of all the top brass – any case, they'll have no option, or damn few –'

Verity commented, interrupting, 'How it's done. Like the fortunes that were made last time.'

The stewards had gone down. Old Man coming in on Verity's heels with, 'This cargo now – as you were saying?'

'Yeah. Was about to. It's just you won't like the sound of it. Any case, we can't know till morning, and it's not *my* decision but the Ministry's.'

'So?'

He took a breath. Told them quietly, 'Hundred octane gas – aviation spirit – in forty-gallon drums that leak a little.'

'*Leak . . .*'

'Had some rough handling. Came out of a Greek that had been through a hurricane, damn near foundered, got in here under tow. They took the gas out of her, other stuff as well, also in lower holds. Drums'd be stowed on end, see, except maybe at the sides – and a heck of a lot of dunnage – more'n you'd have on board, so we'd supply . . . All right?'

Old Man looking at Verity. 'Christ.'

Slow shake of the engineer's grey-streaked head. 'Not April Fools' Day, is it?'

'Thing is' – Parker Lloyd's spaniel eyes shifting to and fro between them – 'with the steam-ejection, nothing like it sounds. Basics of it is – well, petroleum vapour heavier than air, left to itself it's going to lie in the bilges, accumulate. Which OK, you wouldn't want. Steam-ejection, however – see, you'd have pipes connecting your main deck steam-line to the after bilge bay both sides of each hold, other pipes open-ended, leading outboard, so flooding steam into the bilges drives the vapour up and out via these outlets. Hot air rises, huh, taking the stink up with it?' Toothy, friendly smile: 'Chief – I'm a plain seaman, could be technical aspects you'd see and I may not have. All I can tell you is we do know it works – OK?'

The Old Man was thinking about it, watching him. Andy remembering Harve Brown telling him that Nat Beale detested bullshit; he guessed from his expression – or lack of one – that he was suspecting its presence here.

Glancing at his engineer. 'Huh?'

A shrug. '*Might* work.'

'Does work. Has worked. Documentary evidence of that, and blueprints of the installation.'

'What else you offering us, Commander?'

'Come again?'

'Leaking drums in the bottom of lower holds, stowed on end, then dunnage – all five holds, would this be?'

'Say that for sure when we measure up, but the estimate's three holds, leaving two lower holds and all five 'tweendecks for other cargo. We'd fit steam-ejection only to the holds that are to have high-octane in 'em.'

'Other cargo such as what?'

'Likely thing's timber from St John, New Brunswick. But there again –'

'In the two empty holds and five upper and lower 'tweendecks. What else in there with the high-octane, on your dunnage?'

'Well, in the Greek's case – that is, if they want you to take the whole parcel –'

'They will, won't they? Meaning *you* will? Wouldn't sail us with half-empty lower holds, would you?'

'No. No.' A pause. Old Man and Chief Verity silent, watching him. A shrug, then. 'What the Greek was carrying was boxed ammunition. Entirely stable, I might say. The high-octane's safe on account of the steam-ejection arrangements, and the ammo's boxed, heavy timber boxes as sound as you could want 'em. Shells, 5.25-inch – that's a Royal Navy calibre, no use to anyone this side of the pond, main armament of just one class of British cruisers. The Greek took it on from – oh, Grenada or Bahamas, someplace, must've had a ship or ships of that class based there, and now we don't.'

The Lucky Strikes were out again: Old Man and Verity ignoring them, just looking at him. Lloyd gesturing as if he thought they were making too much of this: 'All right – mention aviation spirit and ammo in one breath as it were, sounds sorta –'

'Damn right it does!'

'Shells wouldn't be in any way susceptible to petrol vapour, as some other cargoes might. So you're maximising space left available for – oh, sawn timber, say? Look, it's how they had it in the Greek, and you're near enough the size of her –'

'Captain, sir?'

Waller – getting a nod from the Old Man, telling him, 'Last of the children are on their way ashore, sir. Doctor and Miss Vaughan'd like to say goodbye.'

9

The Old Man would no doubt have gone down to say goodbye to them in any case, but he'd jumped at it as a way of seeing Parker Lloyd on his way too. Not that the commander could rightly have been blamed for foisting the high-octane on them, in Andy's view: STOs in foreign and neutral ports were responsible for loading plans and cargo-handling in British and Allied ships, and if the Ministry of Supply had a local representative who wanted a certain cargo sent on its way, the STO would have no option but to take any chance of doing so. Just as the Old Man had no option but to accept it, if he was so instructed.

Probably what was annoying him. As Harve Brown put it later, having his ship converted into a floating bomb, whether he liked it or not.

Anyway, the Old Man had elected to go down and say goodbye to Samantha and old Creagh, growling at Lloyd, 'No further business, have we?'

Verity had gone down too, but Andy had stayed put. Having already said goodbye to Sam, not especially wanting to do so again more publicly; also he'd been toying with the notion of paying a visit to the Barbizon Plaza – probably not tonight, but tomorrow maybe, depending on how all of this turned out, on the off-chance of finding her still there and at a loose end, as it were.

149

Better not though, he'd decided at this stage. *Definitely* better not. For reasons including an earlier resolve not to spend money he was going to need when he got home; also that there'd really be no point. Samantha being no Manuela was the nucleus of *that* thought. Another factor in not going down to say goodbye for a second time was that when the others had left the wheelhouse his priority had been to check distances and timings in relation to what really mattered – the hope of getting home to Julia a lot sooner than expected, if they *were* to cut out the Cuban jaunt.

He'd told Dixon, when the others had gone down, 'Time being, may as well forget the Caribbean charts.'

Acting on earlier instructions – Andy's – Dixon had begun sorting out chart corrections, a wad of Notices to Mariners pulled out of a box-file of them; he'd been somewhat morosely setting aside those applicable to charts they'd have used on the Cuban leg, and being told he could put it all away again obviously brightened him up a lot. Rather to his credit, Andy thought: one might have expected anyone who was not actually desperate to get home double-quick to have been happier with the prospect of five holds full of sugar to that of three floored with a mix of petrol and high-explosive.

'Reckon we *will* be loading high-octane, sir?'

'I've a hunch we will.'

Had in fact begun counting on it, on saving the five days it would have taken to get down to Nuevitas, plus say a week loading the sugar, and another five days returning to this latitude. About seventeen days saved, he'd been thinking while listening to Parker Lloyd, and after those three had left the wheelhouse he got out the North Atlantic, Northern Portion chart and a pair of dividers, measured the distance from New York to St John, New Brunswick: 180 miles to pass outside Nantucket Island, plus another 300 into the Bay of Fundy – 480 nautical miles, at twelve knots, forty hours' steaming. Calling that thirty-six hours, a day and a half, and guessing at needing two full days here to load this other stuff – or three, say, to include storing ship, bunkering and taking on fresh water, and this next day a Sunday, presumably not a working day.

Sliding that chart back into the drawer, he'd concluded that the net result of cutting out Cuba would be to save sixteen or seventeen days. Be knocking on Julia's door, therefore, in –

No. Hang on . . . Allow for at least a day's wait for a timber-loading berth at St John, then two or three days' loading, and one more steaming around the bulge to Halifax. Saving therefore not seventeen days but twelve, but still getting home – God willing – nearer the middle of September than the end of it.

So, write and tell her this was now on the cards. Should be quite a fillip to her morale. Mention also that owing to the changes that were making this earlier return really quite probable, he mightn't have any of her letters before getting home – might have all the news from her own sweet lips before getting any of them. This in fact was virtually certain – if Cuba *was* being cut out, mail awaiting them at Nuevista was very unlikely to be forwarded to Halifax in time to catch them before they sailed east in convoy.

Quilla with her explosive contents likely to be put in the middle of it, as tankers were?

He went below, moved his gear back to his own cabin from Waller's, wrote the letter and then visited the saloon for a mug of tea: finding Harve Brown there for the same purpose, having just said goodbye to the Dundas Gore agent, who'd brought the usual paperwork – Customs entry forms, etc – and dollars for the Old Man to dish out to those in credit who wanted any, and had also taken Harve's and Steward Hastings' lists of stores to be ordered from chandlers. Some of the paperwork had been more involved than usual, since although ships' owners were still responsible for pay and victualling, feeding survivors from other ships was a recoverable cost.

Harve had talked gloomily about the high-octane cargo: he was praying for the shape or dimensions of the bilges and bilge bays to be found unsuitable for steam-ejection gear. Andy hadn't expressed his own contrary hopes, largely because they'd have been difficult to explain – to Harve, of all people. In any case, it had been getting towards five pm by then, time to get ready for the move over to Hoboken. The pilot, a swarthy character with an Italian-sounding name, had come over the gangway exactly on the hour, *Quilla* casting off shortly afterwards, crossing to the New Jersey side of the river, nosing into the McLellan graving-dock and its gates then closing astern of her well before six pm. Visual memory of a gangway swinging over, suspended from a dockside crane, and of other McLellan workers standing by the baulks of timber that would support her as the water drained away. Andy on the ship's stern meanwhile – having seen to the putting out of wires on both sides to hold her middled until the props would be floated into place to hold her upright – seeing a somewhat outsize, brown-suited figure come stumping over the gangway as soon as it was in place, Harve Brown hurrying from for'ard to meet him, and a second gangway being lowered on the port side.

But in the vicinity of where they'd dumped the first one, as well as the timber lying around there'd been stacks of some other material. He left Patterson and Pettigrew to look after the stern wires, went for'ard and up to the boat-deck for a bird's-eye view of it.

Pipes, different lengths, in separate stacks, greyish-white. Asbestos piping, something like four-inch diameter. Heck of a lot of it: might be on the other side too? He crossed over, and found he'd guessed right – similar stacks of piping. And the second gangway thumping down.

Piping for the steam-ejector system, one might assume. Two conclusions then – one, they didn't waste much time in this yard, and two, they had to be counting on *Quilla*'s interior being suitable for the treatment – a lot more sure of it than Commander Parker Lloyd had claimed to be.

The commander hadn't necessarily been dissimulating, he thought, only trying to break the news gently, knowing it wasn't likely to be welcomed and that Merchant Navy masters tended not to be the most persuadable of customers. And in fact that bit about the ammo being stable might be seen as something of an overstatement. Shells *would* be 'stable' enough, in normal circumstances, but not if you happened to ignite a few thousand gallons of aviation spirit right under them. OK, no reason that should happen: it was only the way one's imagination reacted when thinking of the crossing that lay ahead. These and other reflections being then intruded upon by loud conversation from the bridge-wing: he'd gone up there and found the Old Man, Chief Verity and Harve Brown in conversation with the big man in the brown suit, who turned out to be Hank Smith, the yard's general manager whom Lloyd had mentioned. Heavyweight, balding, middle forties to maybe fifty, yet for all his bulk as quick-eyed as a ferret: glancing round to see who this was, giving him a friendly nod then turning back to the Old Man, 'Might have hatch-covers off so the boys can start six am, Captain, that feasible?'

Old Man cocking an eyebrow at Harve Brown, who nodded. 'Get it done right away might be best.'

A nod. 'What I was hoping.'

Verity put *the* question then: 'Are you so sure we're right for it?'

A jerk of one rather short, thick arm: 'Find it's no go, too bad. Can't be dead certain until we get in there, is all.' Glancing down at the nearer stacks of piping. 'Jobs on hand, however – *wham*, one day, finish the one or both, Sunday we have the dock clear, uh?'

Hatch-covers were removed from all five holds that evening; by the time it was done, *Quilla*'s keel was about

153

settling on the blocks along the dock's centre-line, props in place and wedged all down her length and men wanting to draw dollars against their pay mustering outside the Old Man's cabin.

Saturday 17th: by 0700 the sun was up and work had started on the puddled dock-bottom around *Quilla*'s screw and shaft, as well as internally, in the shaft tunnel – that would be going on all day. At the same time, McLellan fitters accompanied by *Quilla*'s third engineer, Claymore, and with Harve Brown clucking around up top, were checking measurements and alignments in the lower holds, until close on 0800 when the man Hank Smith had put in charge of the steam-ejector project emerged from number five to tell Harve there'd be no problem fitting the system to any or all of the bilges. As it happened, Parker Lloyd, wearing the same electric-blue suit, arrived on board within minutes of this pronouncement, raised a thumb towards Harve and called, 'That's it, then. Load here, not Cuba.'

'But – *your* decision – sir?'

'Ministry of Supply's.' He patted his breast pocket. 'In writing, and a copy for your captain. Sooner we start, sooner finish.'

'How many holds?'

'Three. I'd guess one, three and five.'

Harve's business, this, cargo distribution being very much the mate's department, although as *Quilla* would be sailing from here to St John with two holds completely empty and all five half-empty, spreading the load over numbers one, three and five obviously made sense. He'd nodded. 'I'll check with Captain Beale. Come on up?'

Andy got a résumé of all this from Harve a quarter of an hour later, when he'd just finished his breakfast and Harve had come down for his. The fitting of those holds with piping for steam-ejection had been agreed to by the Old Man, and they'd already started on it. Harve shaking

154

his head, muttering, 'High-octane and bloody ammo – in an HX convoy. I ask you, just bloody *ask* you . . .'

According to the *New York Times*, the Battle of Britain was growing in intensity with every passing day, its outcome far from predictable. Airfields and ports had been the enemy's prime targets, but there were bombers over London now most nights. On the 15th, as that pilot had said, 180 German planes had been shot down, but the RAF too was suffering heavy losses, military analysts predicting that Nazi success would inevitably be followed by seaborne invasion.

None of which was exactly new. Only that it was mounting in ferocity, maybe approaching climax. You crossed your fingers, said your prayers. Were doing that more and more frequently, in fact. *Most* would be. You didn't talk about it much because you didn't want to admit the possibility of ultimate defeat, not even to yourself. Andy had gone back to reread an item higher on the same page, to which Foster, the CRO, had drawn his attention, to the effect that a British freighter had docked in New York yesterday, 16 August, to land a number of children saved from a passenger vessel in which they had been evacuees in transit from Britain to the US for safety from the German air assault. Their ship had been torpedoed in mid-Atlantic and it was understood, although not officially confirmed, that a considerable number of crew and passengers, including children, had been lost.

'Torpedoed, this is saying. And no names, no numbers. Better than it might have been.'

'A lot better. Just hope our blokes don't get blabbering ashore when they've a few beers inside 'em. You thinking of going ashore, Holt?'

He nodded. 'Thought I might stretch my legs. You?'

'Don't see why not.'

They landed after lunch, Waller and Merriman with them – in civvies, of course, this being a neutral port –

155

walking briskly northward along the New Jersey foreshore, eyes mainly on the Manhattan skyline across the river. Andy had in fact drawn the sum of ten dollars – at four to the pound, two pounds ten shillings – and used only about a quarter of that on a round of beers and bacon sandwiches in a waterfront bar called Quinns. Work was of course still in progress all over the ship when they returned on board at about seven pm, and it continued under arc-lights until close on midnight.

Sunday 18th: cloudy, for a change, with a threat of rain, although the natives were saying it wouldn't. The main deck, with its new clutter of piping in the vicinity of those three holds, was swept and hosed down to clear it of asbestos dust and other litter, while the dock gradually filled. Parker Lloyd arrived on board early, as did Hank Smith with a few other McLellan people, the steam-ejector system was inspected and a little steam passed through it from the main deck line – the steam-line that powered winches and the windlass up for'ard – work sheets then being signed by Chief Verity and the Old Man. The McLellan team went ashore, a pilot boarded, the one remaining gangway was removed, and *Quilla*, with Parker Lloyd on board, undocked at eleven am – destination the Bayonne fuelling wharf, where she was to top up bunkers first thing next morning and then shift to a berth alongside in Brooklyn to start loading the high-octane, also take on fresh water and ship's stores. All as arranged by the flamboyant but unquestionably effective STO, who from the fuelling wharf took the Old Man to lunch at the Master Mariners' Club – wherever that might have been, but he wasn't back from it until some time in the dogwatches.

Monday 19th: fuelling was completed early forenoon, and *Quilla* secured in the Brooklyn berth before midday. Holds one, three and five had been made-ready before this, and teams of longshoremen were standing by, lighters being brought alongside one and five to start

156

with, dockside cranes with jibs that reached to them across *Quilla* from the jetty soon at it, bringing the drums aboard in rope slings – rope, not wire, since friction between steel-wire rope and metal had been known to spark-off fires.

You could smell the stuff, all right. Drums weren't visibly dripping as they were swung down into the lower holds, but there undoubtedly was leakage. Akin to sweating, Andy wondered, if that was possible, through the drums' steel – which it was not, according to the donkeyman, Passmore, who'd served in tankers and reckoned he knew all about it: more likely seams that had been 'started', he thought, during the rough handling in that Greek.

In the holds the stink worsened as the day wore on, the three deck officers including Andy supervising the loading, essentials being tight stowage with dunnage mats wherever they were needed, and ensuring that loads were set down gently, drums then rolled carefully into place and stood on end in close support of each other: that way they'd stand the weight that was going to be put on top of them. Please God, they would. Stand it a lot better than they would on their sides, anyhow. Meanwhile, the carpenter, Fellaby, and Hobbs, fourth engineer, saw to the taking-in of fresh water by pipeline from shore, and around midday a truckload of chandler's stores drew up alongside. No-one had an easy day of it. Numbers one and five being finished an hour or so before knocking-off time, *Quilla*'s own people were turned-to to tidy those off, topping the drums with a layer of dunnage mats and timber, while the dockers worked on number three. By six pm, when the foreman's whistle blew, it was about a third done, one lighter load remaining alongside, work to be resumed at eight am.

Steam-ejection now, though, in accordance with Parker Lloyd's advice to run it for an hour each night and morning. With steam on the main deck line, valves had to be opened on the new connections, port and starboard inlets to each bilge, and within a few minutes it was first seeping and then gushing from the outlets, *Quilla* soon shrouded in petrol-scented steam, which on the southerly breeze drifted away only slowly. It would be a lot better at sea, of course – wind or no wind – when she was making her twelve knots or more; although she'd look peculiar enough to other ships in convoy, Harve Brown pointed out, regularly spouting-out steam from three points on each side.

One was sensitive to one's own ship's appearance to others in company.

'Dusk and dawn, maybe. But they'll still smell us . . .'

Hatches were being left uncovered overnight, with a quartermaster and two other watchkeepers on the gangway and patrolling, and No Smoking signs on deck and on the quayside. Harve was staying on board, having paperwork to attend to, so Andy, after showering and shifting out of dungarees, went ashore with Waller and Charlie Bridgeman for a beer or two.

Bridgeman said glumly at one point, 'Kicking myself. Meant to get that girl's address, just clean forgot.'

Andy smiled at him. 'Do recall you angling for it.'

'Forgot I *hadn't* got it. Remembered sort of last minute, went up and they'd gone. Bloody daft . . .' Long swallow of beer, and slight shudder. 'Christ, but that's cold . . . Didn't give it to you, did she?'

'Her address? Think she would have, knowing I'm engaged? Or I'd bloody ask for it, even?' Touching his glass: 'Yanks only like it frozen. If we asked for it at room temperature, they might have some at the back, so to speak unprocessed. Try, next round.' He asked Waller, the red face down there at elbow height, 'Sam give *you* her address, by any chance?'

'Me?'

Bridgeman chuckled. 'Yeah. *Likely* . . . Look, my round, I'll see if they do have warm ones.'

Waller watched him head for the bar, then told Andy,

'Near Exeter, in Devon, her aunt's place.' He looked smug about it. 'Told her be nice to swap Christmas cards.' Shrugging. 'There on, see how it goes.'

Tuesday 20th: steam-ejection was run from 0700 to 0800, when work recommenced on number three. Ammunition lighters were arriving then, and after they'd been secured alongside, a start was made on one and five. It was a more complicated operation than it had been the day before, using ship's gear, one of the after five-ton derricks, as well as the cranes, and three shore-side gangs being employed instead of only two, all of which called for close co-ordination and control. Work on five in fact continued for about an hour and a half after the other two gangs had finished and gone, steam-ejection procedure being initiated only after that. Hatch-beams and boards had been replaced by then on numbers one and three; five to be left uncovered until morning.

Claymore, third engineer, commented in the saloon that evening, 'Must get decent pay and overtime, those blokes.'

'I believe they do.' Harve Brown nodding over bread and cheese. 'STO was telling me they've had no end of trouble with the union or unions in recent years, but now it's been sorted, things go smoother. Left to themselves in other respects – gang bosses only allocating men who toe *their* line, so forth. Mafia's involved, he said.'

'Certainly keen enough to rush *us* out.'

'Hidden hand of the STO. What *he* wants out is the high-octane.'

'Hardly surprising. Still smell it, can't you?'

'Bloody *taste* it!'

'Be better at sea.' Andy touched wood. 'With a blow around us.'

'Unless we get into real dirt like the Greek's supposed to've done.'

'The steam-ejection'll take care of it. What's more, the

drums are well stowed now, and maybe in the Greek they weren't.'

'Greeks being Greek.'

'Well. Do tend to be.'

Waller asked Harve Brown, 'Out of Halifax, think they'll put us in the middle, with the tankers?'

'Let's hope not.' Claymore. 'Seeing as it's tankers the buggers go for.'

Wednesday 21st: with all hatches battened down and deep-tanks ballasted to trim her as well as compensate for the empty holds, *Quilla* left her berth at eleven am with about two hours of ebb tide to help her on her way. Estimated time of arrival at St John New Brunswick first light Friday, which might mean a couple of wasted days, if there wasn't a loading berth available in that allegedly very busy port – and if the naval authorities weren't in any rush to have her join an imminently departing home-bound convoy, which might otherwise justify the extra cost of weekend work, ie the Saturday afternoon and Sunday.

Might be a lengthy wait at Halifax in any case. Recalling that in the *PollyAnna*, January last, they'd swung around an anchor in the Bedford Basin for the best part of a week, with Julia on board, Julia and young Finney . . .

Poor sod. Rough start, rough finish. Decent kid, at that.

Over the ten miles between the Narrows and Sandy Hook they worked-up from six to ten knots without any untoward propeller vibration or heating in shaft bearings, and Chief Verity was beginning to relax a bit. Andy's watch now, although the Old Man was still conning her when they stopped off Sandy Hook to drop the pilot. Tide slackening, weather fine, clear skies and good visibility; several other ships in sight, the pilot boat not returning shoreward after taking its man out of *Quilla* but awaiting the arrival of an Argentinian freighter.

'Course from here, Holt?'

'075, sir.'

160

Old Man stooping at the gyro repeater, checking that 075 would leave the Argie well clear to starboard. He was his old cheerful self, seemed to have reconciled himself to the cargo he'd been lumbered with. That long lunch session at the Master Mariners' Club might have helped. But another thing, which Harve had stumbled on, probably heard from the Old Man, was that the high-octane and the ammo constituted a war cargo, war materials, and this was a neutral port. So they'd want to be rid of it, first chance they got, you could take that as read, but as Harve had pointed out, 'Even so, if we were Huns, think we'd get away with it?'

Old Man nodding as he straightened from the pelorus. 'Half ahead.' And to Freeman, as Andy jangled the telegraph over, 'Port wheel, bring her to 075.'

'Port wheel, sir . . .'

A lot of wheel: she had no steerage way on her as yet. Soon would have, and he'd take some of it off once she began to swing. Old Man buzzing the engine room, getting Verity on the tube and telling him, 'You can work up to revs for twelve knots, Chief.'

Bomb-vessel on her way.

10

Friday morning, the 23rd, when handing over the watch at 0400 to Harve Brown, *Quilla* was down to eight knots and had been since last evening, in order not to arrive off St John before sunrise. Some ship that had completed loading at dusk was sailing at 0600 and *Quilla* was to take over her berth; the information had come by signal from the St John harbour master some time during the first dogwatch, when as it happened Andy had had his head down and only realised on waking that revs had been cut, guessed at new trouble having developed with the shaft, which could have meant serious delay – dry docking in Halifax, for instance. However, false alarm – although a message that came in later was not so good. *Quilla* was to load not just timber, but grain, bulk wheat, in the lower holds of two and four, and this meant the fitting of shifting-boards, fore-and-aft barriers shored-up to the ship's sides with heavy timbers to prevent a bulk cargo shifting laterally in foul weather. Essential, obviously, shifting cargoes being potentially extremely dangerous, but rigging the barriers was a biggish job and needed to be done right away, so that loading could start as soon as they got in – which was the reason they'd been warned, of course.

It had been completed well before midnight, anyway, when he took over the middle watch as always, but he'd been two hours on his feet in number two hold, and knew

162

it – knew it even better after another four. Showing Harve their position on the chart, with only two hours to go before arrival and the sky already lightening over Nova Scotia. Sea calm, light westerly breeze. They'd been passing the island of Grand Manam when he'd come on watch, now had Point Lepreau abaft the beam to port and the entrance to Musquash Bay coming up on that beam at a distance of about six miles. Course a few degrees east of north, and AB Samways on the wheel. The charted position was as good as it could have been, since Canadian lights, like US ones, were all showing.

'All right then, I've got her.' Harve, with his many years at sea, *had* been here a few times before. Only thing was, the Old Man had said he wanted a shake at 0400, and had had one – Dixon having been down to bang on his door, and obtained some sort of answer – but he hadn't yet shown up, might have gone back to sleep. So maybe on the way down . . .

No need. Here he was, clumping up. Scent of tobacco indicating that he'd taken the time to get his pipe going. Extraordinary – straight out of one's bunk . . . Pipe out of mouth for a moment as he moved towards his corner, telling Harve, 'Best run some steam through the bilges, Mister.'

'Aye, sir . . .'

Andy offered, 'See to it, shall I – with Dixon and Merriman here?' Asking Harve, hence the omission of a 'sir', but the Old Man gruffly approving the suggestion anyway. 'Do that, Holt.' It saved getting spare hands up. Andy took a torch down with him, let the cadets do the work while he shone it on the right valves, two to each of the three holds. Within a few minutes of finishing the job, warmed-up petrol vapour was gushing out of her, rolling away into the dark like ectoplasm.

An hour or so's kip now. Fairly whacked, but things looking very good, he thought: the loading berth available to them immediately, possibility therefore of completing by noon tomorrow – or evening, maybe,

163

working overtime – and making it to Halifax on Sunday. Then, if an HX convoy *was* leaving within the next few days . . .

Really surprise her.

He was on the stern when they entered, enjoying the panorama of the harbour and its surroundings in the hazy early morning light, the sun's hardening glow dispersing layers of mist, gilding the waterfront and shipping and the swirl of tide. The ship whose berth they'd be taking now and with whose master the Old Man had exchanged greetings by megaphone while the pilot had been transferring from her to *Quilla* was one of the 'Barons' – Hogarth Line, out of Glasgow – her master an old friend of his. Would as like as not be seeing each other again in the Bedford Basin, they'd agreed, and then in convoy homeward. Timber was a good cargo, everyone said, tending to keep a ship afloat when she was torpedoed; unlike ore, for instance, which sank you like a stone in a matter of seconds. In *PollyAnna* they'd been carrying iron ore – had been very much aware of it too, and in the circumstances applying then, exceptionally lucky to have got away with it.

But what about timber and grain in some holds and a mix of explosives and highly flammable liquid in the others?

With any luck, he told himself, we won't find out. Gazing up at the Martello Tower that Harve Brown had pointed out to him, on high ground named on the chart as Lancaster Heights, and built, according to Harve, during the war of 1812. Actually, Harve had been less airing his general knowledge than recommending the tower as a useful navigational mark visible from a long way out. *Quilla* inside now, anyway, forging dead-slow past moored ships and stone quays stacked predominantly with timber: Andy rehearing in memory, in the context of what one might or might not find out, Samantha's fierce assurance: *You'll come through, Andy.*

164

Wishful thinking, of course. Which as it happened was more or less what one lived on anyway, but still kind of her to have expessed it, and so fervently.

Crossed fingers, Sam . . .

There was a vacant berth beyond this next ship, and what looked like grain elevators at the back of the quay. Where *Quilla*'s grain would be coming from, no doubt. And on the other bow a small, battered-looking tug puffing smoke rings out of its tall funnel, standing-off at the moment but ready to nudge one in when so requested. To starboard meanwhile this cargo carrier similar to *Quilla* but maybe slightly larger, probably more like 8,000 tons gross than *Quilla*'s 7,500. Very little difference in their profiles. He had his glasses with him, and focusing them on her waterline saw she wasn't far off her North Atlantic summer marks; would probably be finishing today. Another convoy mate, he guessed. Red ensign aft, and house flag at the mainmast-head. Yellow and black – yellow background and two linked black cones – or hills, representationally: he woke up to the fact that this was one of A. and J. Hills' ships, Hills being the Tyneside owners Julia's cousins worked for.

In just a moment would have a view of the name painted on her bow, angle of sight broadening as *Quilla* came up abeam.

Blackheddon Hills.

Dick Carr's ship – extraordinarily enough: and the thought immediately that he might have news of Julia.

An hour later, the man himself: average height, square-built, bullet-headed, middle twenties, either growing a beard or just hadn't shaved for a day or two. Questioning stare – Andy having hailed him as he came over the gangway, Dick obviously wondering who the hell this was. They'd only met once, at the memorial service for Dick's father earlier in the year, when he'd expressed gratitude for the saving of Julia's life.

Reaching him, he put out his hand. 'Holt. Andy Holt.' Shouting over the racket of cranes and sawn timber crashing around: this was deck cargo, planks of varying lengths being slung over in huge bundles and deposited where they'd then be stacked neatly and the stacks lashed down. Andy pointing – 'Come from next-door, SS *Barranquilla*. Remember me? Visiting with your cousin Julia when –'

'Andy Holt.' You'd hardly call it a smile – more a grimace, but might have been an attempt at one. 'Be damned.' More surprise than pleasure – even startled for the moment. Well – busy: that was plain enough. Looking around distractedly, then summoning a cadaverous-looking crewman wearing a marlin-spike as well as a knife on his belt, indicative of his being the ship's bosun, which was confirmed by Carr's yell of, 'Five minutes, Bo – in the saloon if you need me!' Then to Andy, 'Come on down.'

In at the weather door, down a short companionway, noise from above and outside fading slightly, a shout over his shoulder of 'Just got in, did you?'

'Hour ago. Looks like you're off soon?'

'Midday, finish. And the mate's ashore, so' – thrusting into the saloon – 'not a lot of time.' Andy had noticed up there that the foremost holds had already been covered and battened down, with battening currently in progress on number three, while at the same time timber was being craned over both for'ard and aft – all this activity well inside the radius of *Quilla*'s dust.

Grain-dust – rising from her numbers two and four holds, which were being fed with wheat from those elevators.

'Tea do you?'

'Thanks. If you've time. But listen – have you heard from Julia lately?'

A quick, hard look, either as if the question had surprised him, or he'd been expecting it and it told him something. He was at the pantry hatch by then, shouting for two teas, Andy waiting close to a porthole, looking out at the dust-haze emanating from *Quilla*, a fog of it darkening the air and powdering the harbour's surface. Nothing you could do about it: grain poured in through the chutes and the dust rose like smoke: on deck around those holds you couldn't breathe except through a filtering cloth of some kind.

The hands of an unseen steward or cook were passing tea mugs through the hatch. Dick Carr asking him, 'Come light-ship from Glasgow, then?'

'Light-ship to Cuba for sugar was how it started, but we picked up a boatload of kids, evacuees – ship had been holed and set on fire by bombs from a Focke-Wulfe, poor little buggers. Ours were the only survivors. We diverted to land 'em in New York, took on cargo there instead of Cuba, getting the rest here now. How about you?'

The *Blackheddon* had come in an OA convoy – outbound from UK east coast ports – with Tyne coal to Sydney, Cape Breton. Coal for ship's bunkers, that would be: the 'slow' SC convoys were assembled at Sydney, just as the 'fast' HX ones were mustered at Halifax, around the corner. Andy nodded, not having had his question answered yet, and beginning to wonder whether Dick – well, the Carrs – might know of Julia's condition. If she'd got round to telling her mother, Mama then confiding in Dick's and Garry's mother. Alternatively, if one of them had caught on – eagle eyes and female acuity, family whispers then?

Whispers, or shrieks. Poor Julia. They weren't exactly sensitive or subtle people, the cousins. In fact compared to Julia herself – well, *and* her mother – they were noticeably rough diamonds, Dick in particular having a distinctly bovine look about him. But if Dick *had* heard of Julia's predicament – from his gaunt, somewhat forbidding mother was the only way he could have – he might well be at a loss as to how to deal with her seducer now.

Wanting neither confrontation nor appearance of

167

collusion, or, say, acceptance. You could understand that, seeing it from his angle, *their* angle.

Especially knowing it couldn't have been anyone but Andy Holt. Knowing Julia well enough for that, as surely he must, even if he *wasn't* the brightest in the land.

Saying now – stone-walling – 'Filling you up with grain, then.'

'Two lower holds grain. 'Tweendecks all through, pit-props. All we were told before this was timber. Dick – heard from Julia at all?'

He'd been gulping tea, now put his mug down.

'Can't say I have. Good while since ever I wrote *her.*' A shrug. 'Year or more, may've been some Christmas time.' A nod towards the pair of stripes on Andy's sleeve. 'You got your Mate's, then.'

'Julia, though –'

'Keen on you, as I remember.'

'It's mutual. Reason I ask is we've had no mail, and I know she'll have written. I sent letters from New York, but our mail will have gone to Cuba, they'll forward it here and we'll be gone again.'

'Happens . . .'

'Dick, listen. Julia and I are going to marry. I've asked her and she's accepted. Don't know whether she's told her mother yet . . .'

No comment. His eyes had shifted away. Definitely ill at ease. No smile, let alone congratulations: might have taken advantage of that opening, and hadn't. Andy continuing, 'Only had a couple of days between finishing at nautical college and signing on in *Quilla.* I'd had my nose down to it, hadn't seen her in weeks, she'd insisted I didn't take time off to see her. Then I managed a flying visit – proposed to her – and as I say –'

Still no smile. You'd think, no interest. Or just plain bloody awkward, the guarded manner his way of signalling that he knew what he knew, including the fact this marriage talk was only a smokescreen to the fact one had knocked her up.

168

He put his mug down. 'Dick, d'you have some objection to me and Julia marrying?'

'Mr Carr, sir –' The door had crashed open: a cadet with a serious acne problem skidding to a halt inside. 'Sorry sir, but the Old Man –'

'Yeah. On my way.' A hand closed on Andy's elbow: reassuring, apologetic? Shake of the head then: 'No. Course not. Have to get along, though – mate's ashore see, and –'

'You said.'

'Sorry.' Was on his way. 'All right, Carter . . .'

A few hours later, watching the *Blackheddon Hills* leave her berth, he was wondering whether there might be another, very different explanation of Dick Carr's behaviour: whether he might have a yen for his cousin Julia.

Thing was, it might explain the almost tortured nature of his reactions – which was how it seemed now, in retrospect. If he'd really got it badly, might explain *him*? A simple man, with little if any sophistication, virtually tongue-tied in that really hopeless and obviously unmentionable situation?

Although the other interpretation was more plausible. They'd have had mail from home either when they'd docked at Sydney NS, or on arrival here, and as likely as not he'd have heard from home. Then, out of the blue, faced with the man responsible and too embarrassed or confused to make an issue of it – and maybe seeing that as cowardly, therefore shaming?

The *Blackheddon* had been lying bow-on to *Quilla*, and when she pushed off, Dick as second officer would have been right aft, so Andy didn't see him. Didn't look for him all that hard either: saw the same tug drag the ship's stern out, so she could then manoeuvre herself out stern-first and continue the clockwise turn-around well out in the clear, with the tug's aid as long as it was needed; but before that stage was reached he'd had to return his attention to matters closer at hand.

Numbers two and four lower holds were filled by early afternoon, and within half an hour railway trucks of pit-props were clanking to a halt alongside, the two motorised cranes that had been working on the *Blackheddon* being already there, waiting to start work on one and five, then two and four. For'ard holds under Andy's eye and after ones under Waller's, all of it under Harve's. The pit-props, each one a fairly substantial piece of timber, were slung aboard in bundles in wire slings, which inside the holds were released and the props manhandled with cargo-hooks to fill every cubic foot of space; working inside, you needed to be fast on your feet and watch out for the heavy loads swinging down. The stevedores knocked off at six pm, Harve reckoning that (a) less than a full day's work next day should finish it, (b) she'd then be down to her marks without taking on deck cargo, and (c) they certainly knew their business in this port.

They didn't want high-octane vapour drifting around ships, warehouses and even the town itself, however, so *Quilla* was required to shove off and anchor outside the port at about eight pm for her hour of steam-ejection, the STO arranging for a harbour launch to land and later bring off any of the crew who wanted a run ashore. This was also in the interests of local businesses, especially bars. There were a few drunks brought off, but no serious trouble. Steam-ejection was run again from 0600 to 0700, during some arrivals and departures of other vessels, and the Old Man bumped *Quilla* back alongside for the resumption of work on numbers two and four at 0800, completing on these in mid-forenoon and shifting to number three, which was finished by 1400; with only that one hatch then remaining to be covered, clearance was obtained to depart at 1530. ETA Halifax – at twelve knots, say, twenty-two hours' steaming – early pm next day, Sunday 25th. In fact she was there after an uneventful passage shortly before two pm, embarking a pilot outside the harbour, then passing in at slow speed through the boom gate – the anchorage being protected in the usual way by a floating boom and suspended anti-submarine net, with a gate in it which the trawler-sized boom-gate vessel dragged open and shut again when the newcomer and the pilot boat were in. *Quilla* had spent most of the dark hours at fourteen knots, then after the dawn steam-ejector exercise had reduced to eight in order to have the midday meal out of the way before arrival.

Halifax, capital of Nova Scotia, stands on a peninsula which splits the harbour into two basins, inner and outer, Bedford being the inner and larger and the assembly point for HX convoys, the other containing the harbour and dockyard. There was a big crowd of deep-laden ships in here already: no question at all that a convoy had to be leaving soon. Not easy to guess how many, though, as *Quilla* threaded her way through them, tailed by the boat with its red and white flag. As many as seventy or eighty? It was a very extensive deep-water anchorage, and occupied to pretty near capacity; the pilot – grey-headed, sixty-ish – conning her through the thick of it mainly by means of hand gestures and grunts to Selby on the wheel. Even at low speed it was an impressive performance: at anything but low speed, might have been hair-raising. Old Man watching points but leaving it to them, Andy also in the bridge, since he'd have had nothing to do down aft. Harve Brown was on the foc's'l-head with McGrath and his anchor party, Waller standing by at the telegraph, Dixon and Elliot in the bridge-wings from where either of them might be required to pass orders to the foc's'l – or run errands, or use the Aldis – and Merriman at the halyards abaft the bridge, from which *Quilla*'s four-flag identification hoist was flying.

From thinking how smoothly things had gone in both New York and St John, Andy was beginning to wonder whether this might be where the run of luck stalled, as far as getting home to Julia in something like record time was concerned. One convoy doubtless was on the point of departure, but *Quilla* might be too late for it, destined

171

to wait and join the next one. There surely did have to be some limit on the size of any convoy. She'd been one of forty-one ships in the outbound ON from the Clyde and Mersey three weeks ago, and the *PollyAnna's* HX last January had started out with nearer sixty. Seventy or eighty would be a hell of a great armada for its commodore to control or escorts to protect, as well as a mouth-watering target for the U-boats. While the nucleus of a follow-up convoy might be here already, ships along-side in the harbour still loading, for instance. If one did have to wait for the next one – how long, ten days or a fortnight?

Might not be left in doubt for long, he thought: the Old Man most likely had the answer already in his pocket – in a brown envelope with a red seal on it which the pilot had handed to him when he'd boarded, about forty minutes ago, Old Man only glancing at it before stuffing it away inside his reefer jacket.

Hadn't spotted the *Blackheddon Hills*, as yet. Had just passed around the stern of a freighter that might have been her, but wasn't. Name on her stern in fact had been *Faraday James*, port of registry London. Nine thousand GRT, he'd guessed. And now – wheel over the other way to pass the other side of her – *Belle Isle*, a rather smart little frog originally out of Cherbourg, no more than 4,000 tons. Of course, speed more than size was what counted most in acceptability or otherwise for this or that type of convoy: a ship that couldn't make nine knots wouldn't qualify for an HX, she'd be relegated to an SC with assembly-point Sydney, Cape Breton; whereas if she could make fifteen knots or more she'd be expected to take her chances solo.

As the *Sarawak* had been doing.

The pilot was pointing, calling to the Old Man, 'There's your billet, Captain. Let's have her dead slow?'

'Third –'

'Aye, sir!'

Waller jerking the telegraph over: within seconds you

felt the difference, and within a minute saw her new sluggishness through the water. Andy checking the charted depth: they were to anchor in fourteen fathoms, which meant just under three shackles of cable – fifteen fathoms to a shackle, and three times the depth of water being a safe norm, for the cable to have some 'spring' in it. Harve Brown had been apprised of this already – after initial consultation with the pilot, told in the vernacular 'three on deck': necessarily, since once he let go the anchor he couldn't be told anything at all, he'd be deafened by the cable's rush. Andy nearer the bridge's forefront now, with his glasses up, *Quilla* about to pass between a tanker and a freighter both flying the Norwegian flag – freighter about 10,000 tons, name on her counter *Nordaust Kapp*. Tanker probably more like 15,000 tons. Beyond her then – name faded but just decypherable as *Norsk Bensin* – out on her bow to port was another tanker, British-flagged, and according to the pilot's indication likely to become *Quilla*'s nearest neighbour when she dropped her hook. Any moment now – Elliot in the starboard wing getting the Old Man's order and raising his megaphone to yell down at the foc'sl to stand by, and Harve lifting a hand in acknowledgement. His team would already have used the windlass to walk-back the anchor, have it hanging clear of the hawse – windlass declutched, cable held only on the screwed down brake.

She was clear of the Norwegians. Pilot narrow-eyed, judging distances, *Quilla* down to a snail's pace and steady as a rock. That tanker's name was *British Destiny*. To starboard at about the same distance, a steamer with two funnels and midships structure substantial enough to have passenger cabins in it. Name – no, couldn't read it . . .

'Let go, Captain?'

'Let go!'

Elliot had howled it almost simultaneously: on the foc'sl McGrath flung off the brake and the cable began roaring out. Old Man gesturing to Waller, who'd been waiting for it, to put her slow astern, stop her in her tracks.

After the pilot had left them, the Old Man had summoned Harve Brown and Chief Verity to his day cabin, presumably to divulge the contents of the sealed envelope, and shortly afterwards Harve announced that there'd be no shore leave on the grounds that the ship was under sailing orders. As an exception to this, an HDML – Harbour Defence Motor Launch – would be alongside within about the next half-hour to take the Old Man ashore, to a meeting in Admiralty House.

Andy asked him, 'Convoy conference?'

'That's in the morning. Ten am. MLs collecting masters between eight and nine. Masters and navigators, including you.'

'Sailing Tuesday, then?'

'They'll tell you at the conference, I imagine.'

'Meaning you don't know?'

'Doubt even the Old Man does. Or he's been told to keep it to himself.'

'Walls having ears, all that?'

'Have been known to, haven't they.'

'Spies ashore here, is that it?'

A shrug. 'Who knows? But if it was you carrying the can, would you take a chance on it?'

He supposed not. Remembering warnings of shifty characters in bars insisting on buying drinks and asking questions without seeming to. This would pre-suppose that they had means of getting information out by radio: a sailing date and the number of ships in convoy, say – which here there'd be no need to ask, all they'd have to do was perch up there somewhere with binoculars and a view across this basin. Maybe a scouting U-boat in range of any such transmission, relaying it back to U-boat headquarters or to its brethren in mid-ocean.

But if the convoy conference was taking place tomorrow, Monday, probably *would* be filing out of that

174

boom gate on Tuesday 27th; and banking on a fourteen-day crossing, home before the middle of the month.

The motor launch for the Old Man chugged alongside within half an hour of that conversation with Harve, and Chief Verity was going along for the ride. Both in civvy suits and soft hats, although this was most certainly not a neutral port and it was the naval authorities they were visiting. How they preferred to be dressed when ashore, was the answer to it. Merchant Navy style – MN philosophy even. How they'd turn out for the conference tomorrow too, he guessed. Crowd of non-combatants getting together to cross an ocean.

The Old Man told Harve before jamming his hat down so it wouldn't get knocked off on the ladder, 'Back before sundown, likely.'

'Sneakin' ashore for a smoke, eh?'

Quiet voice from an onlooker on the after well-deck, as the boat sheered off. Smoking was banned in all parts of the ship except crew's quarters, saloon and owners' suite – and the Old Man's quarters, obviously – forbidden altogether during steam-ejection intervals, and might be further restricted if for any reason that seemed necessary. There'd been very little grousing about it. Nor for that matter had anyone been talking much about the high-octane, not since departure from New York. You had the stuff down there, and you knew that in certain circumstances it had the potential to explode, but there was no point going on about it.

At one point towards the end of the convoy conference next day, Andy thought it might usefully have been mentioned, but the Old Man had kept his mouth shut, and it wasn't a second mate's business to speak out. He was only there to take notes, mainly on navigational matters, for which purpose he'd brought along a note-book and a few pencil-stubs. And in fact a lot of it was already known and on record, the Old Man having returned on board last evening with a file of documentation, much of which was probably standard, common to all HXs, on such subjects as communications, zone times – alterations of ships' clocks – zigzag plans and navigational routines, domestic routines even, such as approved times for the ditching of gash, and so forth; as well as the convoy plan itself – eight columns of ships, columns 1,000 yards apart and ships in column 600 yards – the pattern as before, in fact, with six ships in each column except for the two centre ones, numbers four and five, in which there were to be only five. This was to leave *Quilla*, as rearmost ship in column six – her convoy number therefore sixty-six, ie sixth rank from the van and sixth ship from the right – with two empty billets on her starboard side, consequently a gap of 3,000 yards between her and her nearest neighbour on that side, which was to be a cargo-liner by name of *Aurelia*, number sixty-three.

It was a big conference hall – had to be, with the shore staff of British and Canadian naval officers as well as two Merchant Navy men from each of forty-six ships. Not in fact as many ships as one had anticipated, but this was still a crowd: RN and RCN officers moving around, Merchant Navy personnel crowded at long tables, and the big white chief – Commodore Westerwood RNR, formerly Rear-Admiral Westerwood RN (Retired) – together with an RN four-stripe captain who was chairman of the conference, British chief of staff presumably, and like the Commodore wearing WW1 medal ribbons – those two on a raised platform with chairs available to them but a lot of the time on their feet. They had two blackboard easels up there, one with the convoy plan on it – ships' names in columns – and the other displaying a chart of the North Atlantic.

What they were getting into now was mostly secret stuff that would not have been duplicated on paper for general distribution and possibly careless handling: the intended route, emergency diversions from it which might be anticipated, and known or suspected dispositions of the enemy – recent sightings by patrolling aircraft, intercep-

176

tions of German radio, and Intelligence interpretations of all these.

Escorts: initially, one Canadian AMC – armed merchant cruiser – and one destroyer – Canadian, formerly American, very recently acquired. In point of fact, the Commodore admitted, these would do little more than see the convoy on its way; a close escort would rendezvous with it in the region of longitude 20 west, would consist most probably of sloops or the new corvettes, which would be transferring from a westbound convoy.

A hand had been put up; the Commodore paused, waiting for whatever this might amount to, Andy meanwhile catching on to the probability that the interrupter was the master of the *Blackheddon Hills*, since he had Dick Carr beside him. Carr grim-faced, dour as ever, and his captain red-headed, tall on his chair, challenging: 'Sloops or corvettes, ye say – may we know how many?'

'Probably two. *Possibly* three.' There was a general murmur: not exactly protests, more like gloomy repetitions of those words. The Commodore – a small man with thinning grey hair, aged about sixty – adding, 'That's the probability. May I add, this is not an ordeal that I'm inflicting on you, as one might put it, as usual I'll be one *of* you.' Turning to point at the convoy diagram, its upper centre: 'In the motor vessel *Yorkdale*, by courtesy of Captain Nichol. But let me explain – at risk of boring you with what many of you must appreciate already. The air battle over Britain is at a crucial stage, the enemy have invasion forces concentrated in and around French, Belgian and Dutch ports, and our need of minor warships, destroyers in particular, for anti-invasion purposes far outstrips the number available to us. I know, you *have* heard this before, but the plain truth is we're in a state of crisis – invasion threat at its height, own forces available at their lowest. The best I can tell you is that this situation may not continue for much longer. The RAF has been performing wonders, despite incurring frightful losses, and we may hope that what our Prime Minister has dubbed the Battle of Britain will soon be decided in our favour. We also do have an extensive building programme – of destroyers and corvettes – and when that really comes on stream, as they put it nowadays, well, different kettle of fish entirely. Meanwhile, once the *Luftwaffe* can be seen to have been defeated –'

'Won't happen in the next two, three weeks, uh?'

'Not quite that soon, no, probably not. But you must know it's not for want of effort. Might even say *heroic* effort. And what I was about to say, gentlemen – once the RAF has won the Battle of Britain for us, we can get down to winning the battle of the Atlantic – in which *your* efforts, I may say, even though most of you'd probably sooner I didn't, have been and still are no less heroic. Let's get on with this, now . . .'

First of all, with what he knew would come as a surprise to them, a departure from what had become standard practice, and had hitherto been rigorously insisted on. Taking a radically new look at it now would, he realised, be all the more controversial. It was the matter of rescue ships in convoy. Plans were afoot, had been agreed and were being implemented, to convert a goodish number of small, handy ships for this purpose: they'd need a good turn of speed and manoeuvrability and would be specially equipped for the rescue of survivors, with built-in hospital facilities and small operating theatres, each of them carrying a doctor and ancillary medical staff. Adapting and fitting-out even the first of them was likely to take several months, and in the meantime it had been proposed that unconverted but otherwise suitable ships might serve a similar purpose, saving at least some lives while also providing insight into special needs that might otherwise not be foreseen.

'It's a radical departure, certainly. As you know very well, stopping to help ships that have been hit, or to rescue their men from boats, has been seen to put the rescuer in considerable danger. Can indeed amount simply to throwing away *another* ship. And it is not proposed that during an assault by U-boats any ship should break formation, stop engines or drop back for any such purpose. In the course of action, even escorts are not permitted to do so – and that remains the case. Only *after* such a night's activity – to turn back then, when there have been casualties, take men out of boats and off rafts or foundering ships, whatever's possible, and then – a vital point, this – catch up, regain station in convoy before dark. Which obviously means having the speed to do that. We don't want stragglers – ever. Stragglers, as we've learnt to our cost in the past year, are at greater risk than any. Well – I'd like to go into some details of these proposals later, with the masters concerned. Specifically –' turning to the convoy plan again, but then pausing. 'Understand me, please, these are suggestions only. If a master has reason to think his ship's unsuitable for the task, all he need do is say so, and no-one'll think any the worse of him. So – as much as anything on account of their designated positions on this plan, I'd suggest numbers sixty-six and sixty-three. That's to say, SS *Barranquilla* and MV *Aurelia*. Both claim speeds of over fourteen knots – and convoy speed's unlikely to be more than eleven, so they'd have that margin when they need it – for the essential purpose of regaining station, as I've explained. And the *Barranquilla*, I understand, performed a notable rescue in mid-Atlantic very recently, managing to accommodate a good number of survivors, while *Aurelia* being a twelve-passenger cargo-liner has cabins galore –'

'Galore, he says!'

A big man, rotund and bearded, Westcountryman by the sound of him, halfway to his feet and then subsiding. 'Squeeze in a few, but – see, I got naval gunners –'

'Then they may have to crowd up a bit.' The Commodore joined in a rumble of amusement. 'Squeeze in a few's as much as any of us could do. May I count you in, Captain?'

Gesture of acceptance. 'Suppose you might, sir.'

'And *Barranquilla?*'

The Old Man raised an arm. 'Aye.'

While the Commodore was thanking them both and asking them to spare him a few minutes when the conference broke up, the Old Man was looking down at his folded hands: glancing under his eyebrows at Andy then, growling, 'Makes no odds what we got inside us, Mister.'

11

Quilla, following the *Aurelia*, was one of the last ships out, the very last of them following at slow speed in her swirling wake being the refrigerated motor vessel *Sir George* and the much smaller French *Belle Isle*. Evacuation of the basin had begun at first light – Wednesday, this was, the 28th – and as *Quilla* passed through the boom gate it was still a few minutes short of seven am. Not bad, an hour and a half to get such a great herd of ships off their moorings and out to sea, in the prescribed order and with no collisions or other snarl-ups in the process. Roughly two minutes per ship, with two motor-launches as ring-masters, getting the right ones on the move rank by rank – ranks according to the convoy plan – with the second rank weighing anchor in time to follow the rear ship of the first one without much of a pause between them, and so forth – second rank, third, fourth, fifth, and now sixth, *Quilla* and company. By this time the front rank of eight ships would be a couple of miles outside and have formed itself into line-abreast on course due east at five knots, while the others came up into station astern of them, reducing to the same five knots. When the six ships of this rear rank were in station and the Commodore was satisfied with the formation as a whole, he'd order eleven knots by hauling down the speed signal he was flying now – numeral five under flag K – and hoist numerals eleven under K;

thereafter hold on eastward for four hours before altering course ten degrees to port, to 080. It would then be as near as damnit midday: exactly as programmed at the conference on Monday.

Quilla was out now: Old Man in the bridge's forefront with his glasses up, seeing the *Aurelia* beginning to draw away ahead, telling Waller to come up to full ahead. Clash of the telegraph: Old Man on the voice-tube then telling whoever was down there at the other end of it to put on the revs he wanted.

All concerned were making a better job of this, Andy thought, than they had when he'd sailed from here in the *PollyAnna*. There'd been a certain amount of blundering around at that time, as he remembered it. Early days then, of course, the war only a few months old; in the long interim the staff here had obviously improved their *modus operandi*. Just as ships' masters and deck officers had become more adept at convoy work – including this kind of evolution. But in the old *PollyAnna*, he remembered, when leaving Halifax he'd spent an hour or two with Julia and Finney on monkey island, Julia huddled in a duffel coat and heavy oiled-wool sweater she'd bought in the town, but still occasionally shivering with cold. Midwinter then, of course, and up on that exposed platform with the *Anna* wallowing and thumping into a northeaster; Julia had been anxious about seasickness, preferring to shiver than to go below, and worrying even more about how she'd stand up to it in the much rougher stuff which they'd been told was waiting out there for them. Seaman's daughter and niece averse to letting the side down, naturally, and Andy doing his best to convince her that seasickness, to which even Nelson had been prone, wouldn't last more than a few days, after which she'd be as right as rain; also that foul weather was if anything to be welcomed, since U-boats couldn't function in it.

Which was nothing but the truth. In that sense regrettable that it looked like staying reasonably fine this trip. But in *PollyAnna*, when things had got really bad, really

182

exceptionally bad, Julia had been absolutely bloody marvellous.

Might be a little anxious now, he thought. Guessing he'd be on his way, and knowing what it could be like out here. Counting days . . .

Ten days, minimum. In earlier reckonings he'd allowed fourteen, but in putting the convoy's planned route on the chart and giving it eleven knots he'd concluded that it might conceivably be done in ten or eleven days. That allowed for a diversion northward when about four days out, which most likely would be implemented, since unless this particular HX had the luck of the devil, U-boats *would* be lying in wait across its route somewhere on the other side of 30 degrees west. The diversion as envisaged would be triggered or modified in the light of intelligence received by the Commodore between now and then, but that was the probability. While another variable in the general outlook was that not every ship in the convoy might find it possible to maintain eleven knots: several of them were pretty ancient. By and large, and with the luck of the devil being as always a scarce commodity, you did have to allow for setbacks.

Settle for twelve days, he thought, rather than ten, having in the last few minutes walked dividers set at 250 miles *per diem* clear across the chart from Halifax to Barra Head. Acknowledging to himself that twelve might well be extended to fourteen. And that even then you wouldn't actually be with Julia: would be reasonably sure by then of getting to her eventually, but – well, rounding the Butt of Lewis into North Minch, say, or Kintyre Head into the Firth of Clyde.

That wouldn't be *so* bad.

He went out into the starboard wing to watch the final stages of the convoy's forming-up. It did already have a shape: first four ranks pretty well in station on each other, the fifth still getting there, leader and three or four others in their places, numbers five, six, seven and eight crossing diagonally from right to left to take up their positions astern of the same column numbers in rank four. The *Blackheddon Hills* was in her billet, all right. She was number fifty-three – fifth rank, third from the right. All ships flying their convoy numbers, also as they approached their stations, speed flags – flag K and numeral five, as flown by the Commodore ship *Yorkdale*. At this stage, with the block of ships between here and there, one couldn't see her, but she'd also be flying her own convoy number, fourteen – first rank, fourth column – and at her mainmast head the Commodorial blue St George's Cross.

Andy hadn't spoken to Dick Carr at the conference. Would have, in an effort to clear the air between them, but by the time the Old Man and the *Aurelia*'s master and navigator had finished their private rescue ship session with the Commodore, Dick and his wild-looking captain had cleared off. In fact most of them had dispersed.

Sort it out eventually in Newcastle, he supposed.

Quilla was leading the *Sir George* and the Frenchman further away to port now. Number one of this rear rank – sixty-one, the *Nordaust Kapp*, Norwegian, who'd been a near-neighbour in the Bedford Basin – was cutting her speed as she closed up astern of the Dutch *Zuid-Holland*, and the second – *William Herschel*, number sixty-two – was falling-in behind fifty-two, which bore the name *Maglemosian*. Then the *Aurelia* pushing up into her billet astern of the *Blackheddon Hills*. *Quilla* by now well separated from the *Aurelia*, having to cut across the two unoccupied billets – which would have been sixty-four and sixty-five if there'd been ships in them – and nose up astern of number fifty-six, the *Mount Ararat*, another refrigerated motor vessel, ie food carrier; reducing to revs for five knots as she arrived, and with the *Sir George* and *Belle Isle* slanting up on her port quarter to their billets astern of the *Faraday James* and *Tancred* respectively.

The Commodore might wait a while before he increased to eleven knots, give them time to settle down.

184

Time now 0727, convoy to all intents and purposes formed: two Dutch, two French, one Belgian, two Norwegian, thirty-nine Red Ensigns. Four tankers in the centre, three of them British and one Norwegian. *Quilla*'s own explosive contents unknown to anyone but herself, the steam-ejection display having been queried only once so far, one of their neighbours asking by Aldis yesterday morning whether she required assistance; the Old Man had replied that it was a routine steam-ventilation of bilges on account of some noxious cargo. Not saying whether it was a cargo they were carrying now, or one they *had* carried. Bilges could and frequently did become foul with odorous substances – rotting vestiges of bulk cargoes for instance, dead rats and so forth – so the explanation couldn't have been dismissed out of hand, although it didn't explain the multiple jets of steam, and the neighbour would have smelt the high-octane all right. Everyone within half a mile would have. Anyway, there'd been no further enquiries. The Old Man seemed determined to keep it dark – as if it might have been some infectious disease they'd picked up. Even when the Chief of Staff, checking through some notes, had murmured, 'Grain and pit-props, you're carrying', he'd only nodded and turned a warning glare at Andy. And later, back on board, when Harve Brown had shown surprise at their having been offered and accepted the role of rescue ship, his comment had been, 'Gotta be done, why not by us?'

Quilla now had rafts as well as boats. One of the naval staff who'd been present at that meeting with the Commodore and who'd raised various practical suggestions, had asked both captains whether they had space enough in boats and/or rafts for survivors of other ships if they had a crowd of them on board and were themselves torpedoed. The Old Man had told him not for a whole crowd, no, and they weren't carrying any rafts at all: with the result that she now had four, each capable of supporting about a dozen men – 'at a pinch' – and

185

currently lashed to her foremast and mainmast shrouds. On the outboard side of the shrouds, so that launching them might be effected simply by cutting them loose. They'd been delivered yesterday forenoon by a dockyard tug, as had two additional scrambling nets and a consignment of the latest kind of swimming waistcoats, life-jackets that were fitted with lights and whistles, enough for all hands plus a dozen spares.

At midday, when Andy was ready to take over the watch from Waller, a flag signal ran up on the Commodore ship ordering course to be altered to 080. An hour earlier he'd increased speed to eleven knots, the first general signal he'd made, and compliance had been pretty good – or about as good as it ever could be, in an assembly of close on fifty ships, all with different responses through variations in hull shapes, propeller sizes and degree of 'slip', etc. None of the foreigners had seemed to be at any disadvantage either: they had their own-language signal manuals, of course, as well as lists of the flag-signals most likely to be used – course and speed alterations, both ordinary and emergency, and such orders as 'Make less smoke' and 'Keep closed up.' But a course alteration was slightly more complicated than a simple alteration of speed, as ships had to keep station on each other while making the turn, in this instance the port-side columns cutting revs slightly and starboard-side increasing: all of it commencing when that signal was hauled down.

As now. *Quilla* following astern of the *Mount Ararat*: Waller at the voice-tube ordering, 'Down two' – which might need to be increased to four, if you found you were closing up too much, and not actually putting on wheel any more than might be necessary to tail your next-ahead while keeping an eye on the ships on your beams – in *Quilla*'s position, only on the *Sir George*, a thousand yards to port.

Going nicely – almost unnoticeably. No helm on, at this early stage: Waller had only told Samways to keep her in the centre of the *Mount Ararat*'s wake. With 3,000 yards, a mile and a half, to be covered before the convoy should be in its correct formation on 080 instead of due east as it had been all forenoon.

Andy told Waller, 'I'll take her when you're ready.'

A nod, and a glance at the Old Man, who might have insisted on the turn being completed before the control of it changed hands, but who in fact showed no great interest in the matter. So having completed the handover, Waller could go down to an early lunch and come back up in half an hour's time to relieve Andy while he had his.

Back into routine. You'd be on 080 for the next four days.

On the 29th there was news from London of a deal by which America would give Britain fifty old destroyers in return for the use of several British-owned bases in the Caribbean. In the saloon that evening it was hailed as definitely *good* news: not only would fifty destroyers come in handy in protecting convoys like this one, but the deal and the public announcement of it seemed to indicate a hardening of American pro-British inclinations.

Foster, the CRO, had suggested, 'Take that a step further, might even have 'em as allies!'

Chief Verity had been cautious. Whatever the basis of his knowledge, he'd said he guessed the destroyers must be what the Yanks called four-pipers – pipes meaning funnels. Adding, 'Flush decks and four thin stacks. Came to sea at about the end of the last war, as I recall.'

Foster said, 'Better than a poke in the eye with a sharp stick, then.'

'Oh, anything that floats is that.'

Harve put in, 'Flush deck, if *I* recall correctly, includes a rather short, low foc'sl. Not what you'd cheer about in Atlantic winters.'

Claymore had shrugged. 'Not *our* concern.'

'Except if they're rotten sea-boats –'

'Plug the gap, anyhow. While the yards are churning out these so-called corvettes.' Andy explained, 'Commodore was on about them at the conference. A handful at sea already – in fact we might have a couple for our close escort after twenty west, he said – but coming soon in large numbers.'

The Armed Merchant Cruiser the Commodore had promised them was not in evidence, this far. The Old Man had said earlier that he guessed it might be a distant escort – as distinct from close – might be keeping pace with them a few miles seaward. The destroyer *had* shown up, however: during the forenoon had circled the convoy a couple of times, presumably to let them all have a sight of it and feel reassured.

In fact you didn't need any escort in these Canadian home waters. That evening Cape Race and its light were no more than thirty miles abeam to port, and by 0200, when it was well abaft the beam, you were in fog-drifts which thickened steadily, soon became solid enough to totally obscure it. Eyes skinned and steam-whistle shrieking, extra lookouts posted on bridge-wings and gun-deck. The *Mount Ararat*'s blue stern light was at times difficult to find: stern lights in convoy *had* been half-power white ones, but there'd been some new edict on the subject, and blue bulbs had been distributed in Halifax. In these conditions and less than total confidence in how one's neighbours might handle themselves while practically stone blind, watchkeeping was hard work, and Andy wasn't sorry to have the Old Man with him in the wheelhouse. He thought the Commodore would almost certainly have ordered a speed reduction, guessed the only reason he hadn't already done so would be a fear of some of them failing to realise what was happening and running up each others' sterns – with resulting chaos, whole damn lot out of station – but also that they should have streamed fog-buoys, even without being told to. A fog-buoy being a sort of floating kite or paravane which you towed on a long line astern to scoop up a six-foot waterspout for the guidance of your next-astern. And as it happened – thought-transference, maybe – just minutes later the *Mount Ararat* streamed hers. It *was* a help – a lot easier to see than that faint blue glimmer. Then, searching for it, he found one astern of the *Baron Delamore* as well. She was the somewhat antique Hogarth Line steamer whose master was a chum of the Old Man's: they'd exchanged greetings outside St John NS a few days ago, and again at the conference. Then the *Faraday James* streamed hers, to the relief no doubt of the *Sir George*.

'Relieving at the wheel, sir . . .'

Selby, taking over from Freeman. Time to send Dixon down to shake Harve Brown.

Speed was reduced to six knots at steam-ejection time – first light on the 30th. That revs had been reduced had been obvious from the feel of things when he'd woken, and while shaving and showering prior to his usual early breakfast, Dan Hobbs, fourth engineer, fresh up from the engine room, gave him the detail. Six knots, though. All dreary day. Losing about 120 miles a day. And in view of the drastically reduced visibility having to postpone a practice shoot for which he'd obtained the Old Man's sanction, expenditure of half a dozen rounds on a target of the kind they'd used before, a couple of vegetable crates lashed together and chucked over the stern. The gun's crew had had no practice since before the *Sarawak* rescue, were therefore overdue for some; and having the advantage of being at the convoy's rear, might just as well make use of it.

By noon on 1 September, in position (estimated, no sights having been possible) 200 miles east of St Johns Newfoundland, it was thinning rapidly: at any rate the convoy having been through it was steaming out of it. Eleven knots was ordered, the convoy's station-keeping going to pot for half an hour or so, with ships increasing

189

engine revs at varying rates, and the Commodore then gave notice that he'd be exercising them from 1400 onward in emergency turns. This continued almost to sundown and the evening steam-ejection as well as stars, and *Quilla*'s shoot was therefore postponed to the following morning, when Andy took charge for the first three rounds, at an opening range estimated as fifty yards, second shot splashing in close enough to be considered a hit, the third going well over, and Cadet Merriman directing the last three, two of which fell close enough to be counted as would-have-hits if the target had been anything like as tall out of the water as a bow-on U-boat; and the six rounds had been fired in less than a minute and a half.

Not bad, he thought, although it hadn't been much of a practice from the spotting point of view. In fact the only skill displayed had been Gunlayer Patterson's and Trainer Pettigrew's. But they'd worked well enough as a team – if ever they were in action he thought they'd make a passable job of it.

Noon position 2 September, 48 degrees 40' north, 40 degrees 40' west. With this established after the customary flag-hoists, course was altered to 050, which accorded with the route as promulgated at the convoy conference and scribbled in Andy's notebook. Laying the new course off on the chart now he noted that at this course and speed, in two days' time, noon on the 4th, they'd be as close as made no difference to longitude 30 degrees west, which was generally accepted as the current western boundary of U-boat operations. There'd been some discussion of this at the conference, the Chief of Staff telling them that while most of the nocturnal wolfpack attacks had been closer to 20 or 25 west, every precaution such as zigzagging, manning of guns and posting extra lookouts should be taken well before that.

And with any of the simpler zigzag patterns reducing the daily distance-made-good by fifteen percent, days' runs would come down from about 250 to, say, 210. *If* uninterrupted . . . Laying this off on the chart now, this course and speed maintained until, say, the 6th – four days from now would see you about one day's steaming west of Rockall. What you might call the heart of U-boat territory.

He mentioned it to Harve Brown, when Harve was taking over the watch from him at four am on the 3rd. Harve putting a brave face on it – grey as it was, under the thinning grey thatch: 'With luck, won't see hide nor hair of 'em!'

'So how many HXs have got through unscathed this summer?'

'Run of bad luck – or what they see as their *good* luck –'

'Their Happy Time, don't they see it as?'

'Have to return to base, don't they, time to time. Can't be unlimited numbers of the vermin either, eh?'

'I don't know. We're building escorts, won't they be building U-boats?'

'Dare say. New boys, though, second and third eleven. It's the first eleven do the damage. Anyway – I got her . . .'

Harve was showing strain, Andy thought: almost desperately looking on the bright side – or less bad side – as if to reassure himself at least as much as others. Thinking this again when they ran into each other down aft next forenoon – the 4th – Harve making his daily inspection of crew's quarters and Andy in conclave with the carpenter, Fellaby, on the subject of ammunition supply to the gun – which had gone well enough in yesterday's shoot, certainly, but could hardly have not done so, seeing as they'd had only six shells to pass up. Needn't even have passed up that many, there being eight rounds in two ready-use lockers on the gun-deck which they could have used, if Andy hadn't wanted to exercise the whole team, Fellaby in the locker-sized magazine passing out shells to Galley-boys Stephens and McIver and Assistant Steward Chumley, who delivered them to

Assistant Cook Bayliss on the gun-deck using the port-side ladder. It had looked like a bit of a free-for-all between the weather door and the ladder, and Andy's thought now was to station Chumley permanently on the ladder while the other two did the leg-work between that point and the magazine. Chumley could have a rope's end around himself and the ladder, a bowline in it so he could lean into it if he wanted and still have both hands free.

Fellaby agreed. Might improve things, especially in bad weather. 'Don't want him hanging hisself, mind.'

'No. Best to avoid that, if possible . . . Hello, Harve.'

'Avoid what if possible?'

'Well – hanging Steward Chumley, as it happens.'

'Thumbs in the soup again?'

'Wouldn't mind that so much if he didn't lick 'em before handing out the next one.'

'Hanging *might* be the answer, come to think of it. But all else apart, Andy' – Fellaby had gone inside – 'wedding bells coming closer day by day, eh?'

He nodded. 'Almost hear 'em, can't you.'

Starting for'ard together, stepping over the asbestos exhausts from number five. No high-octane stink at the moment, the breeze was taking care of that. 'Subject of getting spliced, though, d'you happen to know how many Sundays the banns need to be read out in church?'

'I think it's three Sundays running. Not certain, but –'

'*I* thought three. Probably is, then. But whether one has to apply to the vicar in person, or if when we get ashore I could just phone Julia and she'd set it going. But then again, I'm not sure she's told her mother yet. And not having had a single item of bloody mail –'

'Not told her mother that she's accepted you?' Harve was astonished.

Andy shrugged. 'It was all last-minute – as I think I told you. And she didn't want to make a song and dance about it – especially not knowing how long, or even *whether* –'

'Bollocks to *that*, lad!'

'May have told her by now. I sent five or six letters from New York urging her to. Should've insisted in the first place, told the old girl myself – see that now, but it was a bit of a pierhead jump for me, as you may remember.'

They'd stopped abreast the mainmast, port side, moved on to be clear of that raft and look out towards the *Sir George*'s dark silhouette in its constantly expanding and contracting surround of white, a thousand yards away. The wind was from that direction – about force three, a lively sea imparting more roll than pitch to *Quilla*'s motion. Harve saying, 'You've a problem with your banns, haven't you? I see that. Wouldn't normally expect to get as much as three weeks ashore, would you – and you'd need more than that, eh? Four at least?'

'Have to fit it into however long I get.'

'Alternatively, set it up and then make an honest woman of her after your *next* trip, eh?'

He didn't look at him. Knowing he'd be grinning, under the impression that he'd made a joke. Watching the *Sir George* butting through it, sending the white sheets streaming. Sky lighter now, sea sparkling; earlier there'd been cloud gathering from windward, but that had all gone over, should be fine for meridean altitudes at noon. Andy recalling that he'd heard of something called a Special Licence, which he'd an idea might be a way of bypassing the routine with banns. But maybe they charged you for it?

On the bridge at midday, having run-on the morning sunsights and got his meridean altitude now, deciding to use his own rather than Waller's – for no particular reason, nothing much between them – and seeing the cadets run up the two five-flag hoists, one for latitude and one longitude, *Quilla*'s contribution to the whole convoy's brightly-coloured bunting. It was OK, matching the Commodore's near enough, both this one and Waller's having in any case come within spitting-distance of the run-on EP from Harve's first-light fix by stars.

Noon position logged therefore as 52 degrees 20' north, 31 degrees 41' west. Distance to the point of crossing longitude 30 west, seventy-five miles. Seven hours' steaming, say.

Dixon was with him at the chart as he was checking this, and muttered, 'In the zone by steam-ejection time, then.'

'What zone?'

'The could-run-into-Huns zone?'

He shrugged. 'Could do at any stage. More likely at twenty west than thirty, but maybe not even then.'

Gospel according to Harve. Dixon murmuring, 'Nice thought, sir . . .'

'Couple of points worth bearing in mind, Dixon, in case they haven't occurred to you. One, a convoy can be attacked without any but a few ships getting clobbered; two, not by any means all of *those* actually go for a Burton; three, a heck of a lot of guys – well, ditto, end up in boats and then on survivors' leave, everything hunky-dory.'

'I'll try to memorise that, sir.'

'Another thing, you cheeky sod, is that whether you know it or not, *Quilla*'s a lucky ship.' He moved into the forefront, nodding to Selby and telling Waller, 'OK, I've got her.' Glasses up, checking their distance astern of the *Mount Ararat* – which seemed about right – that the *Sir George* was nicely on the beam, and a mile and a half to starboard, the *Aurelia*. A very orderly convoy – and making very little smoke, he noted. A lot of them, like *Quilla*, would be oil-fired, and some of the coal-burners would still be on the Welsh or Newcastle variety; Canadian coal was something else, could make problems for engineers and provoke rude signals from commodores.

With good reason. This armada – three and a half miles

wide and one and a half deep – could pass unseen within a few miles of a patrolling U-boat, but a leak or two of smoke could really blow its chances. Recalling a warning given by the Chief of Staff in Halifax in a speech he'd made – that while 20 degrees west was about the crucial longitude, you could run into trouble – 'stir up the hornet's nest' was the expression he'd used – more or less anywhere. It had become known, for instance, from radio intelligence, that following a wolfpack action a month or so back, one boat that had expended all its torpedoes was ordered to proceed westward to the limit of its oil-fuel endurance in order to send back a mid-Atlantic weather report, and in the event had by pure chance run into a follow-up HX, radioed therefore not only the weather state but that convoy's size, course and speed, guaranteeing it a warm welcome in the region of 25 west.

Waller came up after about half an hour to give Andy his lunch-break – corned beef and mashed Canadian spuds – and on his return he found the Old Man there too, sucking at a post-luncheon pipe.

'Afternoon, sir.'

'Holt.' A nod, then putting his glasses back up – to starboard, examining the empty, dancing sea between themselves and the *Aurelia* and no doubt beyond her. Trickle of funnel smoke from the ship ahead of *her*, at that moment. *Blackheddon Hills*, that was. But from this position in the convoy's rear, the sector to watch was the huge expanse astern – for which purpose there was a lookout in each bridge-wing and another on the gun-deck.

Routine: day after day very much the same. Watch-keeping, station-keeping, sunsights and starsights and steam-ejection, and when the light went, ditching gash. You did that at dusk to give it time to disperse or sink during the dark hours, rather than mark the convoy's broad trail for any shadower to find and follow. Forty-six ships dumped a hell of a lot every twenty-four hours: as long as the passage lasted – long as *you* lasted and they hadn't found you – day after day and night after night the same.

Ploughing on: sky virtually clear, wind still west-northwest, cooler than it had been of late, on account of the approach of autumn. Thinking of home – leaves turning gold, etc – Helensburgh initially, all the changing colours and the beauty of that estuary and its hinterland, especially Loch Long and Arrochar, Loch Lomond . . . Which reminded him of a girl named Liza. Liza Sharp. Best not thought about too much, perhaps, at this juncture. In particular, though, remembering an outing he'd made with her to Arrochar. In mid-summer, that had been – summer of '39, before departure eastward as third mate in the *PollyAnna*. They'd climbed the Cobbler, on a blazingly hot day, picnicked on it.

Sort of picnicked. Some girl, old Liza.

At 1345 Selby surrendered the wheel to Samways; and shortly after that McGrath, down on the main deck for'ard, was putting half a dozen hands to work applying red lead to areas they'd chipped and scraped bare of paint the day before. Wanting to get it covered, but taking a bit of a chance, Andy thought. Could have been on the bosun's own judgement or on Harve's, but if the wind came up at all – well, salt spray had never mixed well with red lead, as McGrath would know very well. You could be left with a real mess that wouldn't dry for a long time but would need to be left until it did, so it could then be scraped off and the job started all over again.

Back home even, that might be, if the wind did get up. They were taking an awful chance, he thought.

'Captain, sir . . .'

Foster, the CRO. Old Man staring at him with something like defiance; Andy glancing round too, having in mind that a CRO's unscheduled appearance on the bridge wasn't always good news.

Same thought in the Old Man's mind, judging by his expression.

'Well?'

'Been picking up Hun transmissions, sir. Same call repeated several times now. I'd say from somewhere astern – and no great distance.'

12

The Old Man had drafted a signal to the Commodore reporting enemy radio transmissions astern which might have been sighting reports of this convoy. Andy had passed it by light and had it acknowledged, then after a few minutes took in an answer reading: *Thank you, we have been listening to him too, will probably take evasive action later this evening. Meanwhile a sharp lookout astern is essential, please.*

Most of the ships would have read both signals, would therefore be on their toes and expecting a deviation to be ordered, probably at dusk. It was getting on for three pm now. Andy concluding an exchange with the Old Man with: 'Was just thinking, sir – situation as described at the conference, just about?'

The Old Man had nodded. 'Not so different, maybe.'

Situation as described by the Chief of Staff, could be a carbon copy of that. U-boat astern calling others further east who'd be gathering across the convoy's track – or what they'd have been told would be the convoy's track. Happened more than once before, maybe? Or had happened that once, from their point of view fortuitously, and they or their U-boat command ashore had latched on to it now as a rewarding tactic?

Except that a long-range scouting U-boat could hardly count on finding itself so surely on an HX track. There was no obvious or prescribed transatlantic route. This lot

198

had started by steaming on what might have seemed a *direct* route, then after four days turned northeast, but it could as easily have turned north after rounding Cape Race, steamed most of the way to Greenland before turning east: there'd be hundreds of such alternatives.

Chance, was all.

And you plodded on, trying to guess at what might be happening around you.

Harve said, when he was taking over at four pm, 'Suppose he'll turn us after dark, give the bugger the slip that way.' Reaching surreptitiously to touch wood. 'Wouldn't you say, sir?'

'Wouldn't think he'd have us in sight. Got a look at us, some stage, but I'd say he's dived. Could come up now an' then – periscope stuck right up, say.'

Andy thinking it was a pity they didn't have an escort that could nip back there and make things difficult for the bastard, at least induce him to keep his head down. But they hadn't seen that destroyer for a couple of days now; general opinion was that it wouldn't have had the range to stay with them. Harve was saying, 'He'd need to have been on the surface when he was using his radio, surely.'

A shrug from the Old Man. 'Been quiet the last hour or more, no matter what. CRO'll sing out if he pipes up again.'

'I see.' Harve nodding. 'I see.'

'Another thing, Mister – when he's dived, he can hear us, hear our screws. Can't say at what range, but listening on hydrophones – the heck, damn near fifty of us . . .'

How Andy envisaged it was that the German would have had to have been on the surface when transmitting, calling to his friends. That had been about two hours ago, and as the Old Man had said, nothing since. Then again, he'd made the same call several times, would have been surfaced throughout that period and would then need to catch up, in order to continue shadowing; and while on the surface a U-boat could run rings around an eleven-knot convoy – having diesels that gave him seventeen knots, by all accounts – he certainly couldn't when submerged, dived speed being no more than five or six knots, according to the pundits. So logically, the bloody thing would be tailing them on the surface. Needing to stop from time to time and maybe put his 'scope up? Would need to stop its engines before doing that, he guessed, rather than risk damage to the periscope through vibration. One would imagine ... Especially having magnification in the periscope lenses: you wouldn't waste a facility of that kind. Getting what kind of a view, though? Smoke-haze, and under it this rear rank's masts and funnel-tops?

Dixon had gone down, and the Old Man looked like doing so. Harve before coming up here had seen to the davits being turned out: boats still secured against the griping spars, of course, but only two slips to knock off to release a boat for lowering, a couple of seconds' instead of several minutes' work. Now he was sending Merriman up to see how it was on monkey island, looking out astern. Not from the point of view of Merriman's personal comfort, but the exent to which the funnel's bulk and haze immediately down-wind of it might obscure his binocular view of the horizon. Merriman had gone out into the leeward bridge-wing. Andy asked Harve, 'All right, then?'

A nod. 'Away you go. Be getting your head down, I suppose.'

'Yep. Mug of tea first, then crash.' Thinking, but not saying, that bunk-time might be somewhat limited, henceforth; and Harve adding, 'Swimming waistcoats from here on, remember.'

The dream he woke from had featured Julia and his parents in the house at Helensburgh, his mother's smile freezing as his father snarled, 'Left it a bit late, ask me, why bloody bother?' Julia looking about eight and a half months gone – little face as pretty and appealing as ever, but hurt, and scared.

Rolling more briskly than she had been. *Quilla*, not Julia. Still sickened by the dream, his father's oafish behaviour and his mother's uselessness, both of them completely out of character but acting their parts so convincingly, and the shock in Julia's eyes as she turned to him for help, which for some reason he was incapable of giving. Wrenching himself out of that lingering, humiliating sense of paralysis to the reality that by the bunkhead light it was seven-twenty – 1920, in fact – and either the weather had changed dramatically or the convoy had altered course.

Remembering the Commodore's expressed intention of doing so, then. Hadn't waited for dark either. It was dark in here because it always was, in this little box of a cabin with the deadlight screwed down over its porthole. Maybe the old boy had decided to get them round while daylight lasted and he could be reasonably sure of their remaining more or less in station. Andy off the bunk, putting on shoes, sweater and reefer jacket, then draping his brand-new swimming waistcoat over one shoulder; reflecting that the Commodore's decision re evasive action would have been influenced not only by those transmissions astern, but by whatever coded information he may have been getting from home.

Presence of U-boats ahead being the obvious thing. Transmissions which *Quilla*'s fairly primitive radio equipment had not been able to pick up; answers or reactions to those repeated calls. Well – reactions: the answers would only have been brief acknowledgements – or *an* acknowledgement, singular; reactions would be a pack leader whistling-up his gang, individuals then reporting their positions and estimated times of arrival on some new patrol-line.

Seven-thirty now. He looked into the saloon, saw Waller who was waiting to be served a 'seven-bells' supper in order then to relieve Harve Brown at 2000. He'd had his head down too, he said, didn't know which way they'd turned. Newton, RO/2, called from the far end of the table where he was playing a game of patience, that they'd made a fairly large follow-my-leader turn to port, but what course they were on now he'd no idea; adding to Waller, 'Interesting that our navigating officer hasn't either.'

In fact the turn had been of fifty degrees, from 050 to due north, and Harve had made a note that it had been ordered at 1800 and completed by 1812; he'd also noted the log reading at that time. Andy entered all this in the deck-log and laid off the new course on the chart, deciding then that while he was up here he might as well get a set of stars; being into nautical twilight now, and with a clear sky, able to take one's pick. As it was, dead reckoning told one that at the point of turning *Quilla* had been on latitude 53 and a half north, and so close to 30 west that with wind and sea on her beam now she'd be on that longitude or a couple of miles over it by first light.

On the edge of wolfpack territory, therefore. Wolves somewhere inside it but – please God – expecting you still to be steering 050.

In the wheelhouse again at midnight to take over his middle watch, and as a preliminary checking over earlier chartwork, he wondered about the 'close escort' of sloops or corvettes which the Commodore had said would be transferring to them somewhere around 20 west, where an outbound convoy would be dispersing. Wondering how that rendezvous would be made. Because the Commodore would not have broken radio silence to tell the Admiralty or own forces at sea where he was or that he thought he was being shadowed and therefore about to turn north. That was the very last thing he'd have done – risk having U-boats as well as distant shore-stations intercept, decode *and* home-in on his transmissions.

So how could those escorts have any better notion of the convoy's position, course and speed than the U-boats had?

Couldn't, surely. So it was difficult to see how you'd have any escort until after you were attacked. *Then* you'd break radio silence, because once the bastards found you – well, they'd *found* you, there'd be no reason *not* to tell them back home where you were and what you were up against, so that whatever escort units were available could be directed to you.

Maybe from some distance. From the convoy's present position, for instance, the shortest distance to or from longitude 20 west would be approximately 350 nautical miles. For a sloop making, say, fifteen knots, about twenty-four hours' steaming. Depending on where they were starting from therefore, could be only a couple of hours, but might take a whole day and night.

With a wolfpack around you and no escort, you could lose enough ships and lives in a couple of hours, let alone twenty-four.

New idea dawning now, though. If the convoy's initial route as planned in Halifax had been known to Admiralty – as surely it would have been – and the alteration to due north ordered by them, in consequence of their own knowledge of present U-boat dispositions? Such signal passed to the Commodore in unbreakable code, presumably. Unbreakable not only by U-boats at sea but by U-boat command in western France – and the Commodore not having to emit a single peep.

Touch wood . . .

Could be the answer, though. Even if those escorts might still have the outbound convoy on their hands. *That* might complicate things a little.

Anyway – taking over the watch now. Course due north, revs for eleven knots – unchanged since leaving Halifax and miraculously maintained by all ships, including the old crocks, this far . . . Wind west force four, sea moderate, visibility good. The *Mount Ararat*'s blue stern light visible (to binoculars) right ahead, and on the port and starboard bows respectively, the *Faraday James*'s and the *Baron Delamore*'s from time to time; and the *Sir George* a smearywhite disturbance alternately flaring and subsiding as she kept her thousand-yard distance on the beam to port. The Old Man was in his cabin, Waller had mentioned, snatching forty winks and having left the usual instructions – to be shaken without hesitation at the first sign of any trouble.

Andy patted Waller on the shoulder. 'Sweet dreams, Gus. Give her my love.'

Waller had said he dreamed of Sam quite often.

The Old Man came back up at about 0130, hung around the chart for a while, at the same time getting his pipe going, then moved to his usual corner and told Andy, '*Might*'ve lost him.'

Lost *him*, singular. Assumption being that they'd had this shadower at least until the turn nearly eight hours earlier. Andy said with his glasses up and searching to starboard, 'Hope so, sir.' Though why one should assume that such a turn by a whole mass of ships in broad daylight would have 'lost' anyone or anything . . .

He began: 'If he was still out there shadowing –'

'Wouldn't be far out.'

'You mean – not to lose us –'

'Makin' use of the dark, when we can't see him – him on the surface, got the legs of us, sneak around seeing what's what – like how many of us, and no destroyers, and where the tankers might be hid – all that.' Coughing to clear pipe-smoke from his throat. Then: 'My guess is the turn would'a lost him.'

Why he'd felt he could safely leave the bridge for a couple of hours, Andy supposed. Fair enough as far as *that* went – even when it had meant leaving young Waller on his own. Well, Gus Waller was competent enough, and in emergency the alarm buzzer'd get the Old Man up here in just seconds anyway.

Next question – taking advantage of the Old Man being in a conversational mood, which usually he was not – 'If a Hun was shadowing, on his own, sir – waiting for chums to join him – think he'd wait indefinitely, mightn't be tempted to have a go?'

'Depending on his orders, I'd say. Square-heads do what they're bloody told. Might be in for a bollocking if he didn't.'

What it came down to was – again – that guesswork was all one had to go on. That and experimentation, like this business with rescue ships. And it would all change, maybe when there were enough escorts to go round and tactics became more fluid. Searching the half-mile gap between the *Baron Delamore* and the *Mount Ararat*, and thinking that in the case of a ship in convoy there were no such things as tactics, only the essential of holding on. *Quilla* creaking as she rolled; pitching too – accounting for the thumps as her stem smashed through waves four or five feet high – but more roll than pitch. A lot of the creaking would be cargo-creak, he thought. Pit-prop creak.

Not high-octane creak. High-octane *slosh*. Fortunately inaudible.

Thinking then – escaping the realms of fantasy – if the shadower was still with them, following in the convoy's combined and seething wake, would one have any hope at all of spotting him, end-on?

Well – once the moon got up, maybe . . .

'Tell you what, though, Holt.' Old Man again – surprisingly. 'First light or soon after we'll be on zigzag. Being where we are.'

On 30 west. Might have started a zigzag after the turn last evening, Andy had thought, kept it up until the light went; but – guesswork again – as like as not the Commodore's priority would have been to shift his convoy northward a certain distance before accepting a reduction in its speed of advance. And there was a possible solution in that to an earlier puzzle: Commodore making his turn not to throw off any close shadower astern – not convinced maybe of any such close presence – but in response to intelligence of U-boats gathering somewhere ahead.

Which was what one dreaded. Silently, in one's heart of hearts. Although if he was being kept informed, and was taking avoiding action . . .

Getting colder. He wasn't surprised when Dixon came in from the bridge-wing, pulling on an oilskin over his other gear before returning to the looking-out.

By 0400 this 5 September there'd been no more U-boat chatter, or none that *Quilla*'s Marconi team had heard, and Andy remarked to Harve Brown when handing over to him that it could have been a false alarm. 'We're not the only convoy at sea they could've been talking about. This one *might*'ve given 'em the slip.' Seeing the sardonic look developing, adding, 'Could be you were right, is what I'm saying. Might get away with it, for once.'

Not actually believing in this: only more whistling in the dark. And Harve in fact denied having made any such optimistic forecast.

'Mentioned it as a possibility, was all. Obviously *could* happen, but . . .'

Pigs could fly.

Faint lightness in the southwest, where the moon would be rising soon. And wind down a little, sea less boisterous: sea-change on the way, general weather-change maybe. Commenting on this, Harve had growled, 'A calm would suit those sods better than it would us. Myself, I'd settle for a force eight.' Then: 'All right, Andy, I've got her.'

Zigzag was commenced at 0700, diagram number fifteen, the Commodore having timed it with daylight and the convoy's ability to read his flag signal. And three quarters of an hour later, the SS *Brechonswold* – number twenty-three, third from the right in the second rank – signalled to him by light that she had machinery trouble which obliged her to fall out in order to stop her engine for about four hours. The Commodore replied, also by Aldis, telling the master that he intended altering course early in the afternoon to 075 degrees, so that if by chance his repairs took longer than he was expecting he should allow for this, cut the corner, in order to rejoin as soon as possible. Only snatches of this exchange had been picked up on *Quilla*'s bridge, mostly by Merriman in the wing – there'd been a zigzag alteration in the middle of it, which hadn't helped – but that was the gist of it as relayed to Andy when he arrived back in the bridge at eight-thirty.

The *Brechonswold* was several miles astern by then, a black smudge halfway to the horizon. Waller told him she'd dropped back between columns three and four – the near-side of the *Aurelia* – and that she was distinctly long in the tooth, a three-island steamer with a tall, thin funnel and a raised foc'sl for the accommodation of her crew, a feature not only of antiquity but also of discomfort for that crew. Her machinery would no doubt be fairly ancient, too. It wasn't a good time for a breakdown, but having come this far without any – well, you'd been lucky. One could only hope her repairs could be completed in as little as four hours.

Wind and sea *were* down. Light breeze, sea classifiable as slight, patchy cloud: about as much cloud as there was clear sky. Zigzag clock ringing every twenty minutes, Samways following the set pattern and using fifteen degrees of rudder; there was a slight loss of station in the columns here and there, but by and large they were getting it about right. Andy got a morning sunsight while it was still possible to do so, although chances of pairing it with a meridean altitude later looked pretty slim.

Waller came back up, smelling of bacon; Andy asked him whether he'd seen her in his dreams again and he said no, regrettably he hadn't. As he took over, Andy spent a few minutes tidying up the deck-log and the chart, and while he was doing it, Shaw – RO/3, looked a bit like a tadpole – came with a message from CRO Foster to the effect that they were hearing German transmissions now 'from all over'. When the Old Man asked him angrily what that meant – on the principle, one recognised, of shooting the messenger who brings bad news – he stammered that the calls had been coming from virtually all directions except north.

It was bad news, all right. Didn't in fact bear thinking about. Any case, one didn't have to – the Commodore was there to do the thinking. This time the Old Man didn't bother reporting it. He'd be listening to the same stuff anyway – or his signal staff would.

How might it be for the poor bloody *Brechonswold* – lying stopped back there, listening to it?

Andy went below. He had an inclination to write to Julia, was also aware that doing so would be pointless. Would be the nearest he could get to talking to her, was the origin of the urge.

Like reaching for a hand to hold?

Instead he went through the contents of his panic-bag, discarding a few items in order to cram in a wool hat and a second sweater. Despite the wind being down, it was definitely colder than it had been. Checking through paperwork – his mates' certificates and so forth, odds and ends – he came across Samantha's aunt's address in Devonshire. With Julia in mind he was on the point of ditching it, then reminded himself of his promise to send her a postcard when he got back, the fact she'd be expecting one.

Wouldn't be right to let her down, he thought, or have her thinking he might have come to grief. She was a friend, and a man didn't ditch his friends just because he was getting married.

By midday the overcast was solid, no question of getting a meridean altitude, and the convoy's noon position by dead reckoning was established as 55 degrees 50' north, 29 degrees 15' west. Andy had marked the *Brechonswold*'s position, where she'd been about four hours earlier, thirty-five miles to the south of that. Four hours was the time she'd expected her repairs to take: touch wood, by now she might be on her way.

Steering northeast, although the convoy was still on due north?

Waller, relieving Andy for his lunch, muttered over the chart, 'Wouldn't give a lot for her chances. Least, if she doesn't rejoin by dusk.'

Stragglers weren't good news. He remembered the Commodore's remarks on that subject at the conference. Although there'd been nothing anyone could have done about the *Brechonswold:* a ship that had to drop out, dropped out. He said, 'No reason to think she won't.'

Except that being the old crock she was, she wouldn't have the speed to do much catching up. One had thought that from the start.

He went on down. Lunch was toad-in-the-hole – Canadian or American sausages in batter – with baked beans. The only way the *Brechonswold* might get away with it, he guessed, would be if all the U-boats currently in this part of the Atlantic knew of this convoy, and in concentrating on intercepting it somehow managed to pass the old crock by.

Pray for *that?*

In the saloon, Harve Brown asked him, 'So what's new?'

'All's quiet all round, I gather.'

Frank Verity said, 'A few hours ago, I'm told, seemed like the tribes were gathering.'

'Dare say they were. Are.'

'In other words' – Harve, finishing his coffee – 'we may be in for it.'

Andy saw his toad-in-the-hole coming, Steward Chumley's thumbs as usual well inside the plate. He said, 'One thing certain is we're better off than the poor old *Brechonswold.*'

'I know her well, as it happens.' Verity had pushed his chair back, was lighting a cigarette. 'Know her chief engineer and her master. Knew her master in the last schemozzle.'

'Be damned.'

'Good blokes. Good as any. She should've gone to the

209

breakers' yard long ago, but if anyone could bring her through, they will.'

'Given the luck.'

'Well, sure . . .'

The Commodore hoisted *Cease zigzag* at two-fifteen pm. Easy order to comply with, since a minute earlier they'd turned back on to the mean course. The Old Man had been below, enjoying a 'one to three', which Andy had been obliged to interrupt, cessation of zigzag at 2.20 when the signal was hauled down almost certainly presaging the alteration of course about which he'd warned the *Brechonswold*. And sure enough, a minute later a new hoist ran up ordering *Alter course 075*.

The Old Man muttered, 'Taking us clear of 'em, let's hope.'

Smoke was issuing from the *Blackheddon Hills* and a couple of others in the starboard columns: due perhaps to their having reduced by a knot or so in order to remain in station during the turn, but with so little wind now the smoke was rising more steeply than any had before this, would be visible for miles.

All forty-five of them were round on the new easterly course within about ten minutes. And sure enough one of them was being hauled over the coals by Aldis from the Commodore ship. Not the *Blackheddon*, whose funnel-top was now clear. *Anglian Prince*, he thought, or the *Orcadian* – consulting the convoy plan – or maybe the *Ezekiel White*. He'd buzzed the engine room, told Charlie Bridgemen who'd answered, 'Down four.' Having come up four revs for the turn and evidently not reduced again quickly enough, finding himself too close now to the *Mount Ararat*. Old Man refraining from comment, only demanding suddenly, 'Where'll this course take us if we hold to it?'

'Dixon –'

'Sir.' He went to the chart. Andy was watching out for the next commodorial edict, which would be *Resume zigzag*. Dixon called, 'North of Rockall, sir', adding after a few seconds, 'Three days' steaming.'

Three days. Three *nights*, the bits that counted most. But before that – in about two days maybe, vicinity of 20 west – *might* be joined by escorts. And then from Rockall onward, say, another two days. September 5th today: maybe the 10th?

He was on the bridge at 1900, to be ready for stars if gaps in the cloud-cover made it possible. There were clear spaces here and there, and from time to time, although no general clearance seemed likely, especially with so little wind; but if there was a fleeting chance he'd grab it, preferring not to go too long without a fix. He set the star-globe and listed suitable stars and planets well spread around the compass, went out in the wing with his sextant, watching for useable combinations as twilight deepened, Merriman standing by to note down times and altitudes.

Steam-ejection had been running, was in the course of being shut down. As they were steering now the *Mount Ararat* would no doubt have been getting a good whiff of the high-octane vapour. But the overcast was if anything solidifying again, he realised. There'd be no stars shot this evening. Try again at morning twilight, maybe: or suggest to old Harve Brown *he* might have a stab at it, if he had the chance.

He went back inside, and *en route* to restow his sextant in its cupboard told Harve, 'No luck. Thicker again, if anything.'

Zigzag bell: Freeman putting on port wheel. Forty-five ships under helm on the darkening seascape. Old Man with his glasses up, Merriman on his way out into the other wing. Harve had mumbled something that had sounded like, 'At it again, astern and to the south.'

He'd stopped, looking round at him, realising that might have been *exactly* what he'd said.

'U-boats?'

A nod. 'CRO was here a minute ago. Nothing much

211

else it could have been, he said. One outburst to the west of us and two replies – acknowledgements, whatever.'

'Well. There we are, then.'

Carefully replacing the sextant in its box: thinking that one might as well face up to it, it could only be a matter of when, how soon.

13

The *Brechonswold* was torpedoed soon after nine pm, and news of it was brought to the saloon by RO/2 Newton at about half-past. Foster had taken in her distress signal – SSSS, signifying *Have been torpedoed*, with her identifying four-letter group – at 0907, and a few minutes later *Torpedoed amidships, filling rapidly, abandoning in position 55 20' north, 29 00' west.*

Andy and Harve went up to the bridge, Harve to consult with the Old Man and Andy to check that position on the chart – which showed that the *Brechonswold* hadn't moved, must have lain stopped all day, easy meat for some Hun who'd happened to come across her. Now her boats, with an unguessable number of survivors in them, had to be about eighty miles southwest of *Quilla*'s present position; *Quilla* and the rest of them on course 075 and, the zigzag having been discontinued after sunset, making eleven knots again.

'What would be of interest' – Harve, joining him at the chart table – 'would be to know which way the U-boat might've been going. Whether they might have thought we were still steering north.'

'Might . . .'

'Which case, we might be lucky.'

Referring to earlier speculation, of course, and Andy thinking *for the time being*, might be lucky. Get through this night without an assault developing, maybe. That would be something. Every night that one survived was *something*. On the cards for tonight simply because one of the bastards had sunk the poor old *Brechonswold* half an hour ago and as much as eighty miles away?

If that wasn't clutching at straws, he didn't know what was. Old Harve and his ups and downs ... The fact there'd been a U-boat in that position at that time didn't lessen the chances there might be another half-dozen an hour or two ahead. What was more – if the one which had sunk the *Brechonswold* had reason to think she was a dropout from this convoy – well, he'd surely know the bearings of Rockall, Bloody Foreland, Barra Head, etc, the *general* direction in which the convoy'd have to be steering?

He'd had another hour and a half's sleep: dreamt of docking in Glasgow and being welcomed not by Julia but by Susan Shea, the vet's daughter, and asking her if by chance she'd seen Samantha lately. Crazy. Better than dreaming about U-boats, but for God's sake, why not Julia?

Anyway – on the bridge then before midnight, realising as he checked the DR position that before the end of this watch they'd be crossing longitude 25 west. All serene, this far: wind about force two, near enough astern to give one acrid whiffs of *Quilla*'s own funnel-fumes, but still very little motion on her, the sea's black surface ruffled but not even choppy, and the overhead as dark as pitch. Course unchanged, engine revs within the same range, ie had been up or down between two and four throughout the previous watch. Selby on the wheel, Old Man in his corner.

'All right, Gus. Got her.'

'Closer we get to bonny Scotland, cooler it gets, you noticed?'

'Closer the better, all the same.'

'Oh, no argument ...'

Only a month ago, Andy remembered, when he'd

joined this ship, he'd seen young Waller as rather a stroppy little cuss. Actually he was a perfectly likeable one. It could have been his size – or lack of it – causing him to behave in a cocky manner towards new acquaintances: and perhaps especially to one out-ranking him as well as being twice his size. Odd, that – seeing that being knee-high to a dachsund hadn't discouraged him in the least in his pursuit of Sam.

A case of needs must, perhaps. If one woke to find that one had effectively been cut off at the knees, would one's ardour be much dampened?

Not for long, he thought. Not when you'd got used to it.

'Morning, sir.'

A grunt: 'Holt.'

'Be on twenty-five west by 0300, sir. Might get an escort soon, d'you think?'

Further grunt. And the *Sir George* was noticeably abaft the beam; Andy checking ahead, deciding that *Quilla* was maybe getting too close to the *Ararat*. Buzzer to the engine room therefore, and 'Down two.'

'Down two . . .'

Claymore, the Ulsterman, on watch down there. Wasn't quite the awkward sod *he'd* seemed to be a month ago. Watching this now: maybe should have come down four rather than two. Thing was, if you overcorrected you could end up with a sort of concertina effect, making life harder all round.

A little before 0300, one of the tankers in the centre went up in a sheet of flame.

He saw the flash of ignition a split second before the sound arrived, a deep *crack* followed by rolling thunder, by which time his thumb was on the alarm button to send all hands to their defence stations and bring the Old Man up at a run. Night had savagely, instantaneously, become day, or rather a lurid inferno, a column of multi-coloured flame reaching up from the Norwegian tanker who'd been in column three, next astern as it happened of

215

where the *Brechonswold* had been; the *Norsk Bensin* a furnace swinging away to starboard, visible from here between other ships, stark black silhouettes, what one might see as the foot of the column of fire still on the turn, seemingly now between what had been her next-astern and the steamer on her quarter – starboard quarter – with unspecifiable disruption there as they cleared out of her way. Looking straight at it in fact was blinding, so one desisted. The Old Man bawling something, but it coincided with another explosion – on or in the tanker's afterpart, it looked like. She was aflame from stem to stern now, the glare of it lighting the underside of cloud. The U-boat must have been inside the convoy, actually between columns – as one had heard had become a favoured tactic; could have penetrated from the van or the starboard side – or even from the rear, sneaking up between the *Aurelia* and the *William Herschel*, for instance.

The Old Man had repeated, 'All right, Holt.' Meaning he had the weight. Waller was there too, reflection of the burning Norwegian in all their faces – from a mile and a half away, floating inferno passing between the *Blackheddon Hills* and the one with the peculiar name – *Maglemosian* – then on the far side of the *Aurelia*'s blocky silhouette, at that range toylike, miniature, but still clear, straight-edged, with the brilliance behind her, leaving her or she leaving *it* – the tanker not so plainly ship-shaped now, more a bonfire on what could have been black sewage, the flames so much lower than they had been that in the circle of his glasses it looked more like an acre or two of the ocean itself on fire.

Could be, too. Convoy pushing on, ships in the columns that had been disrupted no doubt making efforts to regain station, but in the course of it all over the place, at any rate in that quarter. U-boat or boats still in amongst them somewhere, or out of it for the moment while deciding on their next line or lines of attack? All initiative entirely in *their* bloody hands. He was at the chart table with its canvas surround pulled together to allow for a light over the chart itself: pencilling on a DR position for the Norwegian. Come dawn, one might be sent back: not that there could have been survivors in that inferno. Couldn't have launched boats: wouldn't have been time, even if any of them could have lived long enough to do it or the boats not gone up in flames right at the start – as they would have, the way that had been. Smashed into kindling. Marking the time of it, 0255, and checking again on the convoy plan, wondering about the direction of the attack, where the bastard might have sprung from. Toss-up, though, especially as one hadn't seen the actual hit, impact of the torpedo either port or starboard side, only the flash and explosion then vertical leap of fire. Most likely, though, it would have come in from that starboard side and close to the van – looking for a tanker, and that one the first he'd come across. There were two others in the third rank, and if the German had come in the other way he'd more likely have picked on one of them, the *San Marino* or the *Anglo Crescent*, or coming up from astern might have gone for the *British Destiny* in rank four astern the *San Marino*.

Imagining it. Moving at any speed, in the prevailing near-calm sea-state an attacker's wake or bow-wave would surely catch *some* lookout's eye? Even with the boat trimmed down so that not much more than the conning-tower would be visible, it would still be carving that white trail. Except that from ahead it might more or less just *drift* in?

Alternatively, coming up from astern, have the nerve and skill to pass so close to ships in column that the submarine would be virtually in water already whitened?

Explosion – torpedo hit. Same underwater *tonk* you'd heard a few times in the outward convoy. Not close, but still unmistakable. So this was *it* now – what you'd hoped might be avoidable, pretending you knew better than to entertain such hopes but still nursing them in your heart of hearts. As likely as not, every man on board doing that. In his case, less on his own account than Julia's, his own *desperation* on her account: seeing this now as the plain and total truth which as long as she lived he'd never let on about – his own damn business in every sense, no-one else's. He was in the forefront of the bridge now – there'd been a bark from the Old Man of 'Port column there!' – looking in that direction for either a distress rocket or a red light at a masthead. Red lights had been discussed at the conference as an alternative to rockets, of which the primary purpose was to alert escorting destroyers, sloops, corvettes, etc, which could be at more or less any distance around the convoy, to the fact there'd been a casualty; so when you had no escort, a red light at the masthead would be as much as you'd need, letting your neighbours know so they'd steer clear of you as you dropped astern or swung off course, whatever.

Distress rocket streaking up – closer than he'd expected. The ship ahead of *Quilla* was the *Mount Ararat*, on her port beam was the *Faraday James*, and outside the *Faraday* the *Kelvin* something-or-other. *Kelvin Drummond*. As in Bulldog, Sapper's hero. She was in the outer column, and was the victim this time. There was a haze around her image in the lenses of his glasses that would be the falling saltwater rain from the spout of the torpedo hit, and she seemed to have turned out to port. Which figured: the French *Belle Isle* astern of her would have starboard wheel on, one might guess, would be closing in on the *Sir George* – for whom one needed to keep an eye out now in case she put *her* helm over.

Old Man doing that, for sure. And Waller had gone out into the port wing for some reason. Old Man having taken over, of course, one wasn't much more than a spectator here. But thinking of the *Belle Isle* and outer columns and general vulnerability, *Quilla*'s stern and starboard quarter – starboard side, even – were very much open to infiltration from astern. There were lookouts in the bridge-wings, of course, and down aft on the gun-deck quite a few pairs of eyes that should be well and truly peeled – if Merriman and Patterson were keeping them up to it.

'All right if I pay a visit aft, sir?'

'Uh?' Then a similarly loud grunt signifying 'yes'.

The *Kelvin Drummond* was away back on the quarter, down by the bows – one might hope getting boats away, but at the distance couldn't make out that much detail. Pausing for a binocular sweep of this whole sector, and drawing blank. Another few seconds' study of the *Drummond* then: she didn't seem any lower in the water than she'd been two minutes ago. Maybe she'd float, would *surely* have had time to lower her boats. Candidates for rescue in the morning, maybe – if other factors permitted any such attempt. If she did remain afloat and a U-boat with a torpedo to spare came across her, for instance. But there'd still be men in boats to rescue. If the rescue ship herself made it, of course. He went down the port-side ladder to the boat-deck, had a word with Dixon and Elliot who were standing by the snowflake rocket apparatus, and with lowerers at the boats who were doubling as lookouts, then on down to the main deck aft. The gun's crew deserved a visit, he thought, were his own responsibility in any case. Merriman was to all intents and purposes in charge back there, as had been arranged a few weeks ago, although Andy had warned him recently – after that last practice shoot – 'Don't feel obliged to throw your weight about. We're putting you here for spotting fall of shot, mostly – if ever we're into that kind of action – but Patterson's a good hand, knows his stuff, and the same goes for Pettigrew. OK?'

Merriman had a head on his shoulders – he'd handle it all right. Was aware that a cadet was not an officer, even if in some circumstances he might be called upon to function like one, and therefore needed to watch his step.

On the gun-deck now: wondering if the wind might be coming up a little. Patterson had greeted him with a shout of, 'Buggers turning nasty again, sir', to which he'd replied, 'Never did think they were *nice*.' Merriman had somehow equipped himself with binoculars, he noticed. Pettigrew remarking – shouting, as was necessary to be heard: even in comparatively calm conditions *Quilla*'s progress wasn't quiet, exactly – 'Takes you back, don't it – four weeks, darned near, could'a been like yesterday.' Another of them – either Fox or Stone – commented that this was a slow start compared to what *that* little lot had been. 'What was the score this far – three, was it? In what – forty-five minutes, a bloody hour, even? *Five* got their packets in the hour that night, uh?' He wasn't addressing Andy particularly, only like his mates adopting strange ways of keeping spirits up. Andy agreeing with him anyway, 'Five the first night, wasn't it, seven the night after.'

'Us being a lucky ship, an'all.'

Pettigrew again, raising an easy laugh – obviously at Andy's expense, that theory he'd aired. And let them laugh – good that they'd remembered it, might even believe in it, or half-believe. Especially as it might prove true, he thought. He asked Merriman, 'Where'd you get the binocs?'

'Fourth engineer, Dan Hobbs, sir. Paid five bob for 'em in a pub in Birkenhead, he said.'

'Do they work? Lenses in 'em, and everything?'

More amusement – in the course of which the *Sir George* was hit. Familiar *thump* of a semi-drowned explosion, black plume of salt water lifting like Nelson's Column – well, seemingly, at a distance of 900 or 1,000 yards – this side of her, abreast about four or five hold. You gritted your teeth: knowing *some* would have died in that warhead's explosion, others be drowning in these ensuing moments. Both Andy and Merriman initially with their glasses on her, then shifting to search the sea astern and on that quarter. The *Sir George*, a smartly modern refrigerated motor vessel crammed with food for the British populace, had lost all her way and tilted stern-down so steeply and fast that one guessed the hit might have ruptured both numbers four and five, flooding both, in which case she was a gonner for sure.

And *Quilla* now pretty well on her own. Really, very much exposed, had *better* be a lucky ship. Although the little frog, the *Belle Isle*, now *Quilla*'s nearest companion on that side, was just as much on *her* own. All this without a glimpse of any bloody U-boat: although this one could only have fired from somewhere not far from *Quilla*'s stern – on which at the time this crew had been exchanging pleasantries, pretending they weren't wondering how long before *they* got it. Pettigrew in fact as a change from joking, now cursing foully and luridly for about half a minute, Patterson advising him, 'Save it, 'Arry, there'll be more ...'

You could bet there would be. Andy and Merriman searching the slightly broken sea astern and on the quarters and starboard beam, others doing the same all round – bare-eyed, no glasses, which since any U-boats infiltrating could show up between columns at virtually point-blank range could well be as good or better than the narrower searching with binoculars. Resting his own effort for a moment on what he knew to be as much as was left of the *Sir George*, now barely visible even with the glasses' aid – well back astern, the size of a squashed fly, blacker than the surrounding dark and as far as one could interpret its shape – well, vertical – final move imminent, namely to slide under. Binocular search resuming – having seen a few do that and knowing how it felt to watch it, visualising even though one tried not to the subsequent descent through – oh, a thousand fathoms maybe, hereabouts – above all, hoping to God they'd have got boats away, and men into them ...

On which subject, with the *Aurelia* in his glasses now, another small dark-grey shape all of 3,000 yards on the beam but oddly distinct at this moment, with the intervening mile and a half of ocean surely livelier than it had been half an hour ago – wind coming up a little, but still seemingly empty. Thoughts on the *Sir George*'s and other ships' boats, and that come first light – well, he'd marked on the chart where the *Brechonswold* had been when she'd got hers, and if *Quilla* or *Aurelia* were sent back on a rescue mission at first light or soon after, the Old Man would only have to set a course for that position, searching for survivors along the way. But also – an issue one had meant to work out earlier, a question of distances and the time available – the *Brechonswold* had been torpedoed at nine pm, and if you started back at, say, six am, you'd have come around ninety miles and have maybe twelve hours of daylight to get there and back: so, wouldn't cover even half that distance, with stops for rescue operations included and being bound to rejoin by dusk. That was the answer – training his glasses slowly and steadily clockwise around *Quilla*'s stern and up her port quarter – the best you could hope for would be to scour through about *half* the night's trail of wreckage. And that, only if—

Belle Isle. He had the glasses on her when she went up. Flame, this time, an upward streak of brilliance simultaneous with the sound – brilliance expanding and growing skyward, thunderous explosion *in* it, through it. She was engulfed in fire, end to end and way above masthead-height, internal explosions then with her hatch-covers soaring, blazing, blown off by the eruptions in her guts.

Greenish tinge to the flames now. Chemicals? Ammunition? Cased petrol in *her*?

'Holy cow!'

'God bloody help us . . .'

'Help *them* more like!'

'There's no bugger alive in *that*, mate!'

'Yeah, well – no. Christ almighty . . .'

You could almost have read a newspaper by the light of her. Or the Book of Common Prayer, he thought. Meanwhile ploughing on because there wasn't a damn thing else you had to do or *could* do. Plodding on, might say, because that was how it felt – donkey-fashion, beast of burden stuff – and actually what you were bloody well *for.*

With *whatever* you had inside you.

Merriman asked him, 'Emergency turn might help, would you say, sir?'

'Hardly lose 'em when they're in such close touch, would it.'

'Suppose not. No.' Then: 'Fired from her other side, I suppose.'

'Not sure. Blinding . . .'

Still was, if you put your glasses on it – burning hulk *still* burning, back on the quarter. Not as fiercely as she had been, but still burning. Those explosions – you'd have thought she'd have blown her sides out, but she looked to be still highish in the water. There'd be no boats, no halyards or rigging, no paint on her anywhere above the waterline – and no frogs, at least not live ones. Floating hulk, was all, wouldn't board *her* if you came across her in the morning; the Royal Navy'd punch a few holes in her waterline, was all.

If they happened to turn up at some stage. Or came across her later.

Meanwhile, *Quilla* was on her own: must have the *Mount Ararat* ahead of her but nothing on either side. She'd have been well illuminated to any happily watching U-boat too, at the height of that, the newspaper-reading stage. He'd had his glasses up again for several minutes now – searching, almost *expecting* the damn thing to come for *Quilla* next. Merriman searching, too. *And* the gun's crew . . . But the three ships who'd comprised what you might call the bottom-left corner of this convoy were all gone. Gun's crew still discussing the situation, agreeing that it was worse than last time, *much* worse: Bayliss almost screaming, in that plaintive tone of his, 'Don't stand a fuckin' *chance*, do we?', and Patterson growling, 'Course we do, you stupid ullage!'

'Well, Jesus, *look* –'

'Shut up, Bayliss.' Andy told him, 'Patterson's right, we

223

stand as good a chance as anyone, maybe better. Captain'll shift us over, is my guess – to column four. Shut your face now, *keep* it shut!'

He thought the Old Man would be bound to do that, rather than stay here isolated and really extremely vulnerable, an obvious, easy target. He'd edge her over – steer five or ten degrees to starboard and come up a few revs to pass through the wake of the *Baron Delamore* and end up astern of the *Delagoa Bay*, with the *Aurelia* then on the beam to starboard.

And Bayliss could swap jobs with one of the galley-boys, Stephens or McIver, in the ammo chain below. Not now, at the height of things, but when this little lot was over.

Merriman interrupted his looking-out a few minutes later: 'Believe we've altered to starboard, couple of points . . .'

He'd seen the bend in her wake, apparently. Spoken a bit soon, though, the turn was still in progress – more like four points now, forty-five degrees: Old Man not only shifting station but moving to get there quickly, would need to increase by more than a few turns, more likely by a couple of knots, to maintain the set distance astern while shifting some twelve or fifteen hundred yards to starboard. Which was fine: not only great minds thinking alike, but would feel a lot more comfortable when you got there. Having a neighbour half a mile on your beam was no guarantee of safety, but being completely on one's own as she was now might almost guarantee being picked off. Glasses up again now, searching to starboard where the bastard very well might be, and remembering the high-octane.

There was a stippling of white on the moving surface now, the beginnings of a chop that could only be to the enemy's advantage.

Making for even *happier* Huns.

And screeching suddenly from Bayliss: 'U-boat! Christ – truly *is*, bloody *U-boat*!'

Being Bayliss, one didn't immediately take him

seriously. He was on the port side of this raised steel deck, well clear of the gun, outside and for'ard of its shield's outer edge. Andy joining him there and by luck getting his glasses straight on to it – glittering black object in a surround of broken white, wouldn't have been in sight from here if it hadn't been for *Quilla*'s four-point turn to starboard. Not in the least helpful from the point of view of gunnery – the gun being trainable only on after bearings – but there all the same, *the* enemy, the killer. He yelled to Hardy – sight-setter, in the telephone headset – 'Tell the bridge U-boat two points on the port bow, three or four hundred yards!'

Hardy had to buzz them first, get someone on the line. Waller probably. Andy keeping it centred in his glasses: stern-on, foam streaming back, going flat out he guessed, as much like a motor torpedo-boat as a submarine – which was how Bayliss had happened to spot it, had his eye caught by the disturbance. Flat out, up between columns four and five . . .

'U-boat two points on the port bow, sir, it's—'

He'd been interrupted. 'Aye, sir. Aye.' Voice up then, looking towards Andy. 'They're on it. Mr Waller said they're—'

Gunshot-like departure of a rocket. Snowflake: the scorching sound of its ascent. To light up the U-boat, obviously, which – also obviously – they would have seen first, from the bridge or bridge-wing, bloody *should* have. Snowflake opening now way up ahead, brilliant great chandelier-like thing high above and beyond the sudden black silhouette of mainmast, funnel and bridge upper-works, and lighting a wide acreage of sea and ships and the U-boat's conning-tower and – oh, periscope standards, he supposed – shining *glassy*-black under the flood of light, pretty well central to the lit-up area – much more by chance than skill, since it would have been Elliot and Dixon who'd fired it off, simply aiming the thing slightly forward and jerking the lanyard that fired it. But there it was, one brilliantly illuminated U-boat, with the *Baron*

Delamore to the left and the *Delagoa Bay* right, in sight from this point solely because of the course currently being steered. Might be going for the tankers again, he guessed: with a choice of three, nearest being the *Delagoa Bay*'s next-ahead; it would be coming up on that one's port quarter, and she – the tanker – would have a gun on her stern, twelve-pounder like this one, or a four-inch, surely to God in that snowflake's light, which from here was actually blinding, you had to shield your eyes.

Gun-flash to the left, beyond it. Sound then, a little pop-gun *crack*. Had come from the steamer on that tanker's beam – next-ahead of the *Baron Delamore*, must be. Couldn't see the U-boat now, though. Submerged? Even part-submerged you'd lose it at this range, especially if it had slowed, which maybe it would have. Second gun-flash, though: *they* must still have it in sight. The snowflake's circle of radiance closing-in as it drifted lower, and two gunshots then – so close together, had to be two ships at it now. Maybe the tanker: but he'd seen no flashes. *Could* have been from the tanker. From whichever, please God might one of them have hit the sod. Darkening, though, and – a strange lighting effect quite suddenly: kind of subdued but general lighting up, seascape upwards. And – Christ, *thunderous* percussion, with damn-all to see, account for it. The lighting phenomenon seemed then to be a result of the snowflake still being airborne, and some layer of obscurity rising until you were looking at the remnants of that light through either smoke or low cloud. Hardly made sense. What *did* – seconds later – was a surge of fire rising swiftly through it, cloud now like a mushroom with a burning centre, solution to this being that the tanker – or *a* tanker – had been hit, torpedoed, and those flames now spreading outward and upward were lighting up a couple of square miles of convoy.

Although the core of it was now being shut off behind *Quilla*'s forepart.

Glasses down for a moment, checking round, eyes

resting from that dazzle. Realising *Quilla* had now to be back on course in her new station. To starboard – yes, the *Aurelia*. With the blaze up ahead – unknown tanker – it was getting to be prayer-book reading time again: with a U-boat probably still inside the convoy's spread? Maybe more than one? Having a good light to see by, ships in silhouette or simply floodlit, just about all over, whichever way a carefree Hun might choose to look? *Thump* of a torpedo hit at that moment – as if in confirmation. Sickening – and the gun's crew shocked into silence. He'd called to Merriman to keep looking out astern and port side, port quarter. Trying to make out what might be happening ahead, as he himself had been doing in recent minutes; was (a) impossible now the ship was back on course – except broadly on the bows where in that patchwork of radiance one could identify the *Blackheddon Hills* out to starboard and the *Baron Delamore* to port, and (b) pointless, since this gun in any case couldn't be brought to bear on any target for'ard of the beam. (By international law was not permitted to, being only for purposes of defence, ie for use when running away, the non-combatant's only lawful reaction to assault.)

But – close to the *Delamore* now, another – very close, *too* close, surely out of proper control. Might have been the victim of that last hit – to the left of the *Delamore*, the gap between them widening, *Delamore* maybe under helm to achieve that: had passed each other, therefore, the newcomer *was* another casualty falling back between the columns. A steamer about *Quilla*'s size, down by the bows and with a red light at her mainmast head. And – *starboard* bow – shifting again to improve his view of it – gradual reappearance of the burning tanker, out to starboard of the *Delagoa Bay*. Beyond the *Blackheddon*: biblical phrase in mind *Column of fire by night*, though doubtful she'd survive to become a column of smoke by day. The *Blackheddon* blacker than black in silhouette against it, and even the steamer on her beam – *Maglemosian*, supposedly in column two, probably therefore more than a mile distant, lit up now, might have been visible even to the naked eye. Out of station, he guessed: surprising any of them were anywhere near *in* station . . . Shifting again, focusing on the unidentified bow-down casualty still just for'ard of the beam to port. Bow-down to the extent that her screw and rudder would be high and dry; couldn't see that, but her angle in the water made it inevitable. They'd abandon, surely . . .

Meanwhile – starting again, torpedo hit up ahead, probably in column seven or eight. And a second, on that one's heels. Two hits on one ship maybe: almost certainly in one salvo, one U-boat's spread of the bloody things. And *another*. Again, in the van and a port-side column: guesswork, but that direction, and some distance. One salvo, torpedoes running on and finding other targets? Must happen, probably quite often. From the port side of the gun-deck, swivelling left, glasses back on the nameless, bow-down steamer now well abaft the beam; conscious that the lighting generally was being – had been – much reduced. First thought being of the tanker on her way down or having gone down, drowning her fires: hard to be sure of anything much – except seemingly all smoke, and an oily reek of it even against the wind, smoke like heavy cloud with occasional flare-ups in it, low on the sea, glowing here and there at its base – seeing that now. Well – oil burning on the surface there: the *Blackheddon Hills* and the *Aurelia* would have to either alter course or plough straight through it. Drive a load of high-octane through sea that happened to be on fire? Fanciful as that thought might have been, a word in and out of one's mind at this stage was *massacre*. Rejecting it – trying to – as a concept because it implied total or near-total disaster, defeat, destruction, and this wasn't, was probably not even all that exceptional, only that was how it *felt*, about as bad as it could be. He'd lost count, thought maybe they'd lost up to about a dozen ships, and a dozen out of forty-six was roughly twenty-five per cent, whereas one had heard of an HX losing fifty percent or more.

Linking in memory to a phrase he'd overheard in a conversation at Ma Shepherd's in Liverpool: 'Convoy torn to bloody ribbons'; he remembered dismissing it as line-shooting by some chancer wanting to impress, but actually that was *exactly* how this felt.

Partly because all you could do was see it through, to whatever form its logical conclusion might take. Like *Quilla* joining those twelve. As far as *you* were concerned, that might conclude it.

Yet another recollection – one that came to mind quite often – that one of his father telling him before the war began that it was going to be bloody awful before it got to be any better. For the *Merchant* Navy especially, he'd been saying – grinding an axe of his own, admittedly, but not far wrong in his predictions generally. Admit *that* much, he thought, next time I see him.

If I do.

'Weathering the storm then?'

Harve Brown. Getting Merriman's 'More or less, sir', and a general growl of similar response from others. Pettigrew, with his apparently one-track mind, coming up with, 'Seeing as we're a lucky ship – accordin' to Mr 'Olt, that is –'

'We are, too.' Andy was close enough to clap the little runt on his shoulder. 'Afloat – alive – pointing the right way – and thanks to Bayliss here, spotted one of the buggers that was subsequently engaged –'

'Bayliss, was it?' Harve peered at him. 'Yeah, when we were shifting billet. And we'd spotted it – Old Man did.' Speaking as if he might be having difficulty remembering it, as if it was something that had happened weeks or months ago, not just minutes. Old Harve, with his grey face and dicky heart – for which his doctor would *not* have recommended many nights like this one. The tanker in its cloud of wreathing, jet-black smoke was a fair distance on the quarter now, surroundings consequently darker again than they had been for a while. Harve observing, 'Must have been scoffing raw carrots, Bayliss.'

Meaning, to have such good eyesight, and Andy cutting in – the cook having had more than his due now, in the way of limelight – 'Several hits, last few minutes, three up front somewhere?'

'Three in a row, you mean.' A wave eastward. 'Leaders of columns six and seven – or thereabouts.'

'There was a Belgian there, small motor-vessel –'

'If you say so. Gone, anyway. Two of 'em went down like bloody ninepins – carrying ore, I'd guess – and t'other hauled out to port, big list on her. Might've got boats away – for rescue in the morning, who knows. Won't be all that long now, daylight. Gone four, so –'

'That *all?*'

He'd have guessed five – except you'd have had early signs of dawn: at least some lightening of the overhead. Four-thirty though, surely. That, or it had been the longest hour in history. Couldn't read his watch's dial . . .

Torpedo hit, close by. To starboard somewhere.

Blackheddon Hills. The spout of the hit, white-topped, streak of fire like a match sparking but failing to ignite – failing initially, then flame spreading aft and all that deck-cargo of sawn timber flying around like leaves blowing off a bonfire. She'd been hit on this near side and amidships, just for'ard of her midships superstructure. She might float, on the timber that was in her. Unless she had ore or somesuch in her lower holds. Dick hadn't said. Or if he had, one hadn't taken notice. Telling Harve, 'She was berthed astern of us in St John, remember?'

Had been, at that far-off time. Was now losing way and by the look of her filling, foundering. A moaning sound – air being forced out through her ventilators as she filled. Could be . . . *Was,* he thought, settling. Might do so to a certain extent, though, and then still float waterlogged on her timber. The *Aurelia* was under helm to pass clear of her. Casualties fell out, sunk or sinking, or struggling to keep going, and the rest of you pressed on across the littered ocean wondering how long before *we* get it?

Harve saying, 'Do remember, yeah. Timber deck-cargo, and a chum you went to visit.'

'Second mate.'

'Well. Good luck to him. I'm going back up – you staying?'

'No, I'll—'

'Reckon we'll see our escorts soon, sir?'

Patterson putting the question, Andy guessed, as much as anything for the others' morale as his own interest or anxiety. Harve telling them, well, he'd have hoped to have seen them before this, but if they had an outbound convoy to look after at this stage – floundering, rather. Andy cutting in with, 'They're supposed to switch to us when we're on twenty degrees west longitude. Right now we're on about twenty-four west. If we stay on this course, be about – oh, hundred and fifty miles. Fifteen hours, say, be there around dusk this evening. So – touch wood, *tomorrow* night –'

Thump of a hit – ahead again. Harve having begun to say, 'But who knows, *could* meet us at first light', and Andy thinking, *Or next bloody week*. Glasses up, lines of sight either side of the bridge structure – dark seascape to starboard now lacking the *Blackheddon*: not even looking for her, counting on her having dropped astern by now. If she'd sunk he didn't want to know it. Immediate concern anyway being to identify the victim of this latest—

Explosion up ahead, big one, and brightness once more outlining *Quilla*'s forepart against a spreading glow. Another of the tankers, for sure. You shrank from it as from a kick in the belly or elsewhere, but inescapable – more dead and crippled, incinerated in yet another floating blaze building skyward to floodlight the killing-ground. *Quilla* afloat, intact, *for the time being*, killing-ground still shifting eastward at something approaching eleven knots, *Quilla* and others concerned only to stay with it, in it, well aware that if you dropped out you'd have no chance at all, didn't have all that great a chance in any case. Harve had grasped his arm, yelled some-

231

thing, but it was lost in an absolute roar of flames from
– what, a mile, mile and a half away . . .

That had been the *San Marino*, and she'd been followed
over the ensuing fifteen minutes by the *Zuid-Holland*, the
Ezekiel White and the *Glen Rannoch*, all from column one,
and the *Casterbridge*, who'd been in the front rank, close
neighbour of the Commodore's *Yorkdale*. There'd been
considerable confusion in the ranks and columns by that
time, but no further torpedoings, and he'd got back up
to the bridge just after five am, with the U-boats' score
sixteen and the *San Marino*, who for what had seemed an
eternity had been a gradually dwindling blaze astern, was
no more than a reddish pinpoint visible only through
binoculars.

Hull as like as not still smouldering, he thought, plates
red-hot, sizzling in the oil surrounding her.

Leaving just one tanker in convoy out of the four who'd
started. But for the past half-hour now, still no more torpedoings. He'd studied the convoy diagram and updated it
as far as possible, from memory of ships that had been
hit – *Blackheddon*, for instance, the *Sir George*, *Belle Isle*,
Kelvin Drummond, the three tankers and the three recently
out of column one – and the *Casterbridge*, *St Luc* – so forth
– but the convoy wasn't in a shape now that made it easy
to tell one survivor from another. There'd been a lot of
closing-up and shifting-over: any ship that had others on
her beams at half-mile distances and/or was tailing
another at roughly 600 yards could consider herself as
being in *some* kind of station.

Fact was, in two hours you'd lost sixteen ships.

But light *was* coming, finally. Marking close of play?

'Emergency turn starboard, sir!'

Waller, up front with his glasses up. Andy noting the
time and log-reading, jotting both down on the chart's
margin. You wouldn't turn until the green lights were
switched off, and the Commodore might leave it longer
than usual, allowing for slow reactions in some of his

remaining thirty ships; so this note was an approximation, to be corrected when helms were actually put over, steam-whistles blasting. An emergency turn was always of forty-five degrees, four points, so one to starboard now would put this mob on a course of 120 degrees, which – running his ruler from the compass rose to *Quilla*'s present DR position – would if extended have taken them to pile up on Mizen Head, southwest corner of bloody Ireland. So it was a dodge, no more, a side-step that he was taking, while there was still half an hour of dark to cover it. Come daylight or not long after, you could guess he'd turn them out of echelon into columns, doubtless reform them to some extent before altering to – well, some other course, easterly or northeasterly.

With another night ahead – actually *two* more, for those who survived the next one – having made this side-step, steer for the top of Ireland or thereabouts. Hoping that if the sods were reforming – which they would be if they had torpedoes and fuel remaining – they'd put themselves astride the course one *had* been steering.

A fairly slim hope, he thought. But the closer you came to your destination, the fewer your options. And meanwhile, if with full daylight *Quilla* was to be sent back to look for ships' boats, it was essential to have emergency turns and so on plotted accurately; also to know the Commodore's intentions from that point on, so you could (a) steam back precisely on the convoy's former track, and (b) rejoin before dark.

'Execute, sir!'

'Starboard fifteen.'

Old Man glancing round as Samways span the wheel and then confirmed she had that much rudder on. Then: 'Steer 120.' Sirens out there shrieking their single short blasts. Time, 0518; and ahead, diffused beginnings of the dawn that you were turning into. Andy marking the point of turn and appending essential data, then extending the track as it might be – not marking it on, only using the rule and dividers: guessing at two hours on this side-step,

233

then an alteration – to a course for Malin Head, say – and assuming a twenty-four-hourly distance-made-good of 240 miles. All right – early morning September 8th, could theoretically be off Malin Head, and that afternoon, entering the Firth of Clyde.

Theoretically. And please God, touch wood, etc. Meanwhile, though – *bloody* tired . . .

14

Gone seven now. Since 0600, when she'd left the convoy, *Quilla* had been on mean course 255 at revs for fourteen knots, but zigzagging – using zigzag seventeen, the Old Man's choice when he had one – so making-good about twelve. This was still Harve Brown's watch, but Andy had gulped down an early breakfast half an hour ago and come back up to relieve him so Harve could get his and then return. The Old Man was also below, Waller too. Merriman was present, with his borrowed glasses, and Dixon who'd breakfasted at the same time as Andy was on monkey island, assisting in the search for boats, rafts or floating wrecks.

Or periscopes.

The ship was no longer at defence stations. Had been for the first hour, but relaxed from that state at seven, primarily so men could eat and sleep. Lookouts were still doubled however, on bridge-wings and gun-deck, plus young Dixon on the roof here.

Wind NW force three, sea moderate, visibility now good. Cooler than in recent days. The overhead was still about two-thirds cloud, but it seemed to be thinning and one had hopes of getting a sunsight later.

The *Aurelia* was three or four miles to port, making her own zigzag. They'd agreed (back in Halifax) to stay within sight of each other, if that proved possible, in case either of them ran into trouble or needed to communicate. But the basis of this rescue ship business, as the Commodore had explained it at the conference, was that following a night battle the U-boat pack could be expected to withdraw eastward at first light in order to regroup, maybe reload torpedo tubes and catch up on sleep, whatever, in preparation for a second dark-hours assault by those that had torpedoes and sufficient oil-fuel remaining, joined maybe by new arrivals, replacements for those who hadn't. This would conform with their tactics as demonstrated in recent months – as developed in fact in the latter part of the '14–'18 war, according to the Halifax Chief of Staff – and since they'd be redeploying *ahead* of the convoy, you could be reasonably sure the waters astern of it would be clear of them.

Unless, the same individual had pointed out, one of them had been left to shadow the convoy. This had been discussed as a possibility, and the consensus of opinion had been that any such shadower would be (a) submerged, having seen or heard the rescue ships' approach, and (b) within a few miles of the convoy's rear or flank, since at any greater distance it couldn't very well be shadowing. So after an hour's steaming one could feel safe enough even in stopping to embark survivors.

Although you'd still be a *little* wary. In discussing potential hazards surrounding this experiment, there'd been mention of a trick also dating from '14–'18: U-boats hanging around in the vicinity of a torpedoed ship or ship's boats, waiting for a Good Samaritan to stop, making an easy target of herself. It was a risk one had been aware of in the case of the *Sarawak*, although in the dark and foul weather it hadn't seemed all that serious a threat. Some element of risk in any case had to be accepted.

Like going to sea in wartime. Or stuffing your holds with high-octane.

Zigzag bell: Freeman stooping to wind on starboard wheel. Time, 0710. With this plan seventeen you altered course every twenty minutes, and they'd started it at 0610. Andy with his glasses up, searching across the bow. So far,

236

nothing, except that at one point they'd passed through several acres of sawn timber and pit-props. He'd been having his breakfast at that time – Harve had told him about it when he came back up – and his first thought had been of the *Blackheddon Hills*. But a fair number of the convoy must have been carrying timber.

Not that one had any particularly deep anxieties for Dick Carr. Only that he *was* Julia's cousin, and she'd always spoken of him and his brother affectionately.

Anyway – getting on for two hours ago, when still in convoy and semi-darkness, *Quilla* actually in the process of steam-ejection, the Commodore had signalled in Morse from his masthead light that an escort of one sloop and three corvettes would be joining at noon in position 56 30' N, 23 10' W, and at that same time course would be altered to 095; and secondly that MV *Aurelia* and SS *Barranquilla* might now proceed as previously arranged, rejoining no later than 1900, at which time the convoy's position by DR would be 56 20' N, 21 30' W.

The only way this differed from Andy's earlier guesswork was that the old boy was keeping them on that 'side-step' course of 120 until noon, instead of just for an hour or two. And having plotted it on the chart, it did seem to make good sense. Had been encouraging news anyway about the escort, a fillip to tired brains and anticipation of worse to come, visions of those bastards flushed with success and expecting within the next two nights to sweep the board. *Total* destruction of a convoy, as far as one knew, was something they'd not as yet achieved, but they'd surely have it in mind as the *ultimate* in happiness. While now, factors that seemed to lessen their chances were (a) imminent provision of an escort, (b) that the 1900 position was sixty miles south of where the convoy would have been if they'd held on as they *had* been going, and (c) that that previous course, 075, would have been a perfectly reasonable one to have stuck to, in that it would have taken you to the north of Rockall, a route which HXs had been known to use as often as not.

Discussing this over the chart after Andy had plotted it, the Old Man had commented, 'Good for the admiral. Might *well* fool 'em.'

Old Man coming off the ladderway now. He'd only been down there ten minutes.

'Nothing?'

'Nothing, sir.'

A yell from the monkey island voice-pipe then: '*Aurelia*'s calling, sir!'

Andy moved towards the port bridge-wing, where the Aldis was already plugged in. Old Man nodding – go ahead, he'd take over. Outside, Andy pulled the Aldis out of its stowage, sighted on the *Aurelia* and gave her a flash, getting then, 'Boats in sight port beam three miles, investigating. See you later.'

She was already turning away. He came back inside and told the Old Man, adding, 'Could have been more of a southerly drift than we reckoned on, sir?'

Meaning, if that was where *some* boats were, why not others too? Wind was northwest all right; one might have underestimated the northerly component in it.

Old Man evidently in agreement.

'Cease zigzag. Port fifteen.'

'Port fifteen, sir.'

'Steer 240.'

'Two four oh, sir . . .'

If one was justified in assuming that there could be no U-boats around, didn't need zigzag anyway. And one did have to make that assumption if one was going to stop and take men out of boats when one found any. The Old Man wouldn't remain stopped for any longer than he had to, anyway. He marked-on the new course and log reading and the time – 0728. The Old Man was apparently in no hurry to hand over the con, so he started on another job that might as well be disposed of now as later: to work out the time by which they'd need to start back in order to reach that rendezvous position by 1900.

The answer was startling. Two hours from now, was all

you had. It would mean nine hours' steaming, at fourteen knots, to get you there actually at about 1830. It would be a mistake to cut it *too* fine. And best to reassess the 0930 deadline at, say, 0900, in the light of how much time had been spent on diversions or actually lying stopped.

Dixon on the monkey island pipe again: 'Ship's boats fine on the port bow about four miles, sir!'

Those weren't the ones the *Aurelia* was diverting to. She was stern-on now and diminishing; these of Dixon's would have been too far ahead of her when she'd spotted the others and turned south. He was back in the forefront now, with his glasses searching for Dixon's. The Old Man meanwhile had adjusted the course to 235, which should have put them nearer dead ahead. Four miles, 8,000 yards: at twelve knots, twenty minutes – which *sounded* as if they ought to be easily in sight. But Dixon with that extra height-of-eye had only just spotted them: and it wasn't at all that easy, boats being extremely low in the water and the surface as broken-up as it was now. If they had sails hoisted, it would help: they should have, and red ones at that, red being a lot easier to see than white, in all the surrounding whiteness. In the *PollyAnna*, they'd been issued with them in Halifax, he remembered, and Julia, seeing the boats being rerigged with them, had girlishly given tongue to 'Red Sails in the Sunset'.

He could as good as hear her. That sweet, clear voice. That had been the time when he'd first intimated to her that he found her attractive: and then more or less apologised for having done so – as he remembered it. A matter of a few minutes – moments one might remember all one's life. Just sort of coming out with it, quite unintentionally – and continuing thereafter to take care not to intrude between her and young Mark Finney.

If one docked in Glasgow pm 8th, might be with her in Newcastle by pm 10th or 11th, say?

But speak to her on the phone before that. Evening of the 8th, surely. Day after tomorrow, for Pete's sake!

Believe that?

He'd spotted the boats: had been looking right at them and not seeing them.

'Half a point to port, sir. Two of 'em – about three thousand yards . . .'

Fifteen minutes' steaming. During which time the Old Man sent Merriman down to inform the mate and bosun, stand by scrambling nets port side, probably the after one. Port side would be the lee side.

Thinking again, while watching the distance lessen, *Day after tomorrow, for Christ's sake: actually hear her voice!*

No red sails. Dirty-grey ones, and crowded boats. Harve now making himself heard in the wheelhouse behind him, reporting to the Old Man – reception party standing by, etc . . .

'Slow ahead.'

Andy being the closest to the telegraph, jerked it over and back to 'Slow', waited for 'Stop' or 'Dead Slow', and after a minute got 'Stop'. Old Man telling Samways, who'd taken over from Freeman, to bring her a couple of degrees to starboard: 'Want 'em inside heaving-line distance, don't we?' Some of those people were working to get the sails down. The typically cheerful, scruffy-looking, beat-up crowd, in shirts, sweaters, singlets. A dozen in one boat, rather more than that in the other – including one officer – at any rate one uniform jacket and peaked cap, and a third mate's single stripe on the sleeves. Harve had started down, Old Man telling Andy, 'Best lend a hand down there, Holt.' Because of his star performance with the *Sarawak* children, he supposed. Waller moving to take his place beside the telegraph, he went rattling down, catching up with Harve Brown as they reached main deck level.

'Should be easy enough, this lot.'

'Twenty-six, I counted.'

'Only one officer.'

'Drill is not to show rank – uh?'

'Ah . . .'

Because U-boats at the scenes of their crimes had been known to seek out the more senior men, especially masters and chief engineers, in order to take them prisoner. Captains of merchantmen had been warned of this.

Bosun McGrath was down there, with stalwarts including Patterson, Selby, Pettigrew and O'Donnell. Heaving-lines soared, fell across both boats, were caught and turned-up and the boats hauled in alongside. It wasn't necessary for *Quilla* men to go far down on the nets: seven of the twenty-six were injured in some way, but their mates brought them up and they only needed helping over the rail. Dutchmen, all of them: didn't understand when the Old Man shouted down to remove the boats' plugs and puncture buoyancy tanks if any, but had it repeated by one of their number already on board who had some English. That was done, and the lines cast off by the last ones out, *Quilla* by that time getting under way again, steering west-southwest. Lessons had been learnt when getting the *Sarawak* crowd on board, but it had been a lot rougher then, and dark – *this* had been easy. There were three officers: a bald, fat man in a pink-striped sweater introducing himself as the master – Captain Jan Stikker – of the SS *Mallemock*; she'd been torpedoed in her engine room at about 0430, and only an hour ago had rolled over and sunk, he thought when the bulkhead of number three had gone. None of her black gang or engineers had survived. She'd been carrying a mixed cargo of machinery, bulk wheat, bagged barley, sugar, canned goods and dried fruit.

There had now to be a reshuffling of berths and cabins, including Waller moving to share Andy's and the cadets clearing out of theirs again. Harve muttered to Andy, 'Where we put the next lot if there is one – don't ask me . . .'

'Bound to be *some* more.'

'Want to help with the First Aid now?'

'Oh, Christ.' Then saw Harve's expression, and

241

shrugged. Harve looking fairly haggard in any case. 'All right. If the Old Man doesn't want me up top.'

'No reason he should, he's got Waller.'

'One thing I do need to tell him, though. Where'll you set up shop?'

'Down aft, where the patients will be anyway. Issue of tea and a meal of sorts first, any road.'

'I'll be there.'

He needed to talk with the Old Man about the 0930 deadline for starting back. It was close on 0800 now, didn't give one all that long.

He wasn't keen on the patching-up business, First Aid, but had felt he had to support old Harve, who was looking as if he could have used a bit of patching-up himself. In some ships the medicine-chest and rough-and-ready doctoring was down to the second mate, and he'd been glad to find it wasn't so in *Quilla*. Hadn't been in the old *PollyAnna*, either; he'd had his own neck wound sewn-up in heavy-handed fashion by the *Anna*'s mate, who'd later gone over the side in heavy seas. Anyway, these injuries were all within the scope of the *Ship's Captain's Medical Guide*, and he and Harve were assisted by the Dutch third officer, whose English wasn't bad. It was mostly a matter of splints and binding-up, and a couple of them needed morphine; all the injuries had been sustained at the time of the torpedoing – men being flung around, one down a ladder from top to bottom, and so forth. The *Mallemock*'s mate, bosun and two ABs had been killed – drowned, whatever – when soon after she'd been hit they'd tried to get down a fiddley into her machinery spaces in search of trapped black gang survivors; there'd been a secondary upheaval – bulkhead going, it had sounded like – and Captain Stikker had barred further efforts of that kind.

Harve had his hands full with what he called hotel management – accommodation and catering – after the doctoring, and Andy returned to the bridge. It was half eight: low sun still only a brightness filtering through cloud, but it might clear by mid-forenoon, allowing a sunsight – on their way east by then, of course. A good noon position would be reassuring.

Quilla was on 260, he saw, steering a straight course, zigzag clock switched off. Old Man wanting to cover as much ground as possible with so little time left. When Andy had broached the subject of the deadline he'd shown surprise, then gone to the chart to check it out: was absorbed in calculations for several minutes, and on his way back to the forefront gave Andy a hard look, growled, 'Need to check your figures, Second.'

It was pretty obvious, when you put your mind to it. *Shockingly* bloody obvious. Convoy heading east, *Quilla* west, distance between them opening at the sum of their respective speeds: fourteen plus eleven – twenty-five. Three and a half hours' steaming, by 0930, or not much less, making the distance apart close on ninety miles; and the rate of overhauling could only be the difference between their speeds, say three and a half knots.

No question of making any 1900 rendezvous. Nothing *like*. Catching up was going to take about twenty-six hours. Rejoin tomorrow around mid-forenoon, maybe.

Certainly no sooner . . . He put a new DR on the chart and went to apologise to the Old Man.

'Should've seen it hours ago, sir, I'm sorry.'

A nod. 'You should, I should.' Putting his glasses up. 'Commodore should've, maybe.' A shrug. 'Say our prayers an' get on with it, is all.'

Cool customer, Nat Beale. Truly was. Hadn't maybe seen him all that clearly, until now.

At 0840 Dixon reported a raft three points on the starboard bow, distance about two cables. *Quilla*'s course being 260, the Old Man told Samways to bring her to starboard to 295. Then asked Andy, 'How long's Dixon been on the island?'

'About two hours, sir.'

243

'Have one of the others relieve him.'

'Aye, sir.' He looked at Elliot. 'Up you go.'

Quilla swinging to her new course, putting herself bow-on to wind and sea. Wind force three rising four, sea a little steeper than it had been but still classifiable as moderate. The next category up from 'moderate' was 'rough', and you couldn't call it that. Not yet, anyway.

Old Man glancing at Waller: 'Ring down Slow Ahead.'

Andy had the raft in his glasses now. It was just about right ahead, and he was making out – just – a slumped figure in it.

A heap of something, anyway.

The Old Man had his glasses on it too. As did Waller. Dixon at this moment lurching in from the starboard wing, looking cold. 'Looks like one man in it, sir. Or body.'

'Go on down, tell Mr Brown and the bosun to stand by port side.'

'Aye, sir.' He went down. Andy wiping the front lenses of his glasses with his thumbs, then putting them up again. It was very hard to make out. But if you were looking at a man and confusing it with a heap of something, the odds had to be that you were looking at a corpse.

Might simply be unconscious, though.

'Holt – tell Mr Brown if the feller's dead we'll leave him. Third – telegraph to Stop.'

McGrath had sent one of them to get an oar out of one of the boats, with an idea of climbing down on the net and using it as a boathook somehow to get the raft in alongside. Andy gave Harve the Old Man's message, and he grimaced. Andy then offered, not having given it a moment's prior thought, 'I'll go down and fish it in.'

Having to do *some* damn thing, not just stand and watch people poking around with oars. That really didn't seem a very practical suggestion. Surprising, from McGrath. *Quilla* with the moderate sea thrashing along

244

her sides, the raft coming closer all right but not close enough: although the Old Man had stopped her now – engine vibration had ceased – with port rudder turning her across the direction of the wind. He thought that in the Old Man's shoes he'd have brought her up to leeward of it, since having no keel it would be more susceptible to wind, would be blown down on *her*. But maybe not, having no upperworks either. In any case, he didn't think much of this business with the oar. He was on the outside of the rail by this time, getting down on to the net, the raft washing in really close – might even be scraping alongside if things continued as they were. *Quilla* still with some forward way on, though, as well as the turning motion: in fact – OK, truth was it couldn't have been done better. But you couldn't leave a man for dead when there might be life in him, you had to be sure of it one way or the other. And he didn't want the oar McGrath was offering, yelled instead, 'Line! Heaving-line!'

They'd swung the business end of one down to him, the weighted end, which he caught one-handed about a second before he jumped. Less scary than it might have been, the raft being right under his trajectory, actually washing in still closer. He landed in it on his hands and knees, partly on the occupant's soaked bulk, but stable enough then to be able to use both hands, taking a round turn with a long bight of the line around an edging timber and putting two half-hitches in it. In one's own interests entirely. Shoving the man's head over with the heel of one hand: big head, thick neck. He was dead, all right. In a dark singlet and fearnaught trousers: a trimmer or a fireman, he'd have guessed. Solidly built, thick-armed, eyes wide open and mouth slack in the heavy, unshaven jaw. He wasn't sure he'd have the strength to get him over the raft's side, but in fact did manage it, taking advantage of its tipping away from *Quilla*'s side as she rolled and a wave mounted: heaving him up and over. The Old Man up there in the bridge-wing, watching – to see him

245

back on the net no doubt, so he could get her on the move again. McGrath and others were hauling the raft in, and he was poised for the next bit – *now* – grabbing the net above him, clambering up, yelling at them to cut the line.

Nine o'clock. He was in the wheelhouse, in dry clothes, the Old Man telling him, 'Get yourself a job at Bertram Mills, you could, Second.'

Bertram Mills' circus.

'Well, sir.' Grinning, appreciating the tone of voice. 'Might be better paid. *And* lady trapeze artists to practise with.'

Chief Verity – up here for a look-see, evidently – chipped in with, 'No job for a married man, then. What's it like in, Holt?'

'Cool enough to be worth staying out of, sir.' He told Waller, 'You can do the next one, Gus.'

Samways chuckling to himself. Ship's head 260 again, Andy saw, and revs for twelve knots, by the look of things. He went to the chart but there was really no change to the situation; she'd been stopped for about ten minutes, but that didn't change anything, the deadline was still 0930.

If the Old Man was hell-bent on continuing west until there wasn't another boat or raft in sight, though – which by and large did seem to be the case – then deadlines were irrelevant. Once you did turn back – well, you'd be a straggler, nothing else. The rest of the day, and tonight, and at least the *first* half of tomorrow.

As the man had said – saying your prayers and getting on with it.

The *Aurelia*, he guessed, would have turned back a couple of hours ago.

'Bridge!'

Monkey island voice-pipe: Elliot. Waller had jumped to it. 'Bridge?'

'Ship's boat five points to starboard, about three miles!'

'Starboard fifteen.'

Old Man not bothering to think twice. Well, he'd *found* them, at last, was finally in the right place, where the lives were that he'd been sent to save.

Samways acknowledging, 'Starboard fifteen, sir.'

'Steer 310 degrees.'

Andy asked Waller, 'You want this one?'

He didn't look all that keen. Anyway – nine-five now. Andy noted the time of altering course and the log reading against a new diary note: *Sighted ship's boat.*

Banal as that looked – and was, when you thought of lives being saved or at least extended, and the risks involved. But what else – when they were *there*, staring you in the face?

Dixon went down again to alert Harve, and at 0922 they had the boat alongside: seven men in it, all suffering from severe burns and one with a strip of shirt round his head, covering his eyes. Blinded, according to the others. McGrath and his team helped them as much as was possible, but it wasn't easy, the state some of them were in. It took at least ten minutes before they were all on board and the boat was filling, its plug removed. Andy noticed about then that the gunwale and rubbing-strake on the outboard side had charred away. The rescued men were Norwegians from the tanker *Norsk Bensin*, and were emphatic that they were the only survivors. None of them was in anything like good shape, but remembering how that ship had looked when she'd been dropping astern – a floating fireball – you could only think what a miracle it was that they'd come out of it at all. No officers had survived. The *Norsk Bensin*'s navigation bridge structure had been amidships, and these men had mostly been gun's crew, right aft, abaft the funnel and aftercastle. There'd been four boats on that structure, and this had been the aftermost on the windward side.

It was 0935 by the time the Norwegians were inboard and *Quilla* under way again. Old Man conning her back

247

on to 260 degrees at revs for twelve knots, telling Andy when she was settled on that course, 'We'll start back around ten, Second.'

In the owners' suite, out of which Harve's and Chief Verity's gear was being moved, Harve had told the Norwegians that *Quilla* would be rejoining the convoy at 1900, and that by then they'd have an escort of a sloop and some corvettes. The sloop would almost certainly have a doctor, and with any luck they'd be able to arrange for him to transfer by boat soon after daylight and give them his skilled attention. Measures being taken now would, he hoped, provide temporary alleviation of pain and general discomfort. He had morphine, and ointment for smearing on burns, but nothing for that poor fellow's eyes except boracic in which to bathe them – if that would help, and he was scared it might be the wrong thing entirely.

Andy had gone along to see if he could help, but wasn't needed. Harve had Merriman with him, and the steward, Hastings, had been there at the time, having brought up a couple of gallons of hot soup, and bread and cheese. RO/3 Ted Shaw had also, surprisingly, offered his services: his mother was Norwegian, apparently, and he could get along in it.

'Leave you to it then, Harve.'

A nod. 'Get us back where we belong. Turned yet, have we?'

'Starting back around ten.'

Harve looked rotten, he thought. Greyer and older. Last night had done him no good at all.

Returning to the wheelhouse, he found *Quilla* under helm, altering to 245, Elliot having spotted a boat on that bearing at about 5,000 yards – two and a half miles. It had a red sail on it, Waller mentioned. The wind was up a bit now, much more like force four than three, sea verging on rough; *Quilla* being deep-laden was paying only small attention to it, but there was a lot more surface turbulence than there had been earlier, and if the boat's sail had been white it might well not have been visible.

The Old Man was on to it now. 'There. Come five degrees to starboard, Selby.'

To 250 degrees. Rolling quite a bit, with the weather on her beam. Selby would have taken over from Samways at a quarter to the hour, when Andy had been visiting the owners' suite; it was 0950 now. Two miles to that boat, say – ten minutes to get there, plus however long was necessary for the embarkation. Clearly you wouldn't be on your way by ten. By a quarter-past, at best. But one thing at least, this did have to be the last.

At 0953 there was another shout from the island, Elliot reporting a second boat also under a red sail a thousand yards beyond the one they were heading for, about a point on the bow to port. Andy, in the forefront, starboard side, had this one in his glasses too – a small splodge of red, was all, while the boat they were making for – well, you'd be there in five minutes. He told the Old Man, who was still searching for the new one, 'Thousand yards between 'em's about right, sir.'

A grunt, as he settled on it. Shifting back to the first one, growling, 'Bloody regatta, could be . . .'

Snorts from Selby and Dixon. Andy recognising that they'd undoubtedly be going for that boat too. Old Man telling Dixon, 'If Mr Brown's got his hands full, find McGrath. Port side again. Let Mr Brown know, any road.'

'Aye, sir!'

He'd be quoted from Glasgow to Shanghai and back on that regatta comment, Andy thought. And no-one could blame him for going to pick up the second lot either. In fact he couldn't possibly *not* do so. Even knowing it would result in missing the 1900 rendezvous with the convoy.

But the hell: you'd *make* it, that was the thing. Samantha's voice in memory, *You'll come through it, Andy.*

And thanks to *Quilla*, so would a good few others who otherwise might not have.

The first of the two boats had nineteen men in it, including some Lascars and two officers, mate and third mate of the SS *Garthsnaid*, which had been torpedoed in the light from a burning tanker and taken a few hours to sink. The other boat, the mate told Harve, had fewer in it, but one of them was the ship's master. She'd been Birkenhead registered, 5,400 GRT, and he – this mate – was a Liverpudlian. The master's name was Grogan. Injuries among these nineteen consisted of no more than a broken wrist and sundry cuts and bruises. The torpedo had hit right aft and nine men had been killed in its explosion, including the crew of the twelve-pounder.

Time now, 1016. Andy had been down there in case Harve was too busy with the Norwegians to take charge of this, but Merriman and the RO/3 had been coping well apparently, and Harve had left them to get on with it. The embarkation had gone smoothly enough, although it had taken a little time – on account of the numbers involved and scrambling nets being only twelve feet wide. In the course of it he'd noticed that the cloud-cover was at last breaking up, at least to some extent, and decided that if he watched for a break and was quick in taking advantage of it when it came, now might be as good a time as he'd get. It was fast-moving cloud, and in half an hour's time chances mightn't be as good as they looked now.

When he got back up to the wheelhouse, *Quilla* was on course at slow speed for the second boat, with a couple of hundred yards to go, Waller was standing by the engine room telegraph, and the Old Man was telling Selby to bring her three degrees to port. Andy told Dixon to be ready to note down the chronometer time of this sunsight, and took his sextant out into the starboard wing. Checking that Dixon was watching him, and seeing Elliot up on the island searching all round for yet more ships' boats.

He heard the clang of Waller ringing down 'Stop'. Time now 1027, and there it was: a sizeable clear patch shifting in the right direction. More or less right direction anyway, and *at this moment* clear, might not be by the time the sun was in it. Dummy-run first anyway, while waiting for it: bringing the centre of what at this moment was only a diffuse brightness down to the horizon – which was a good one, sharp and clear. Quickly back up to the approaching blue, thinking *come on, come on* . . .

But Elliot was on his feet up there – one hand on the rail and the other pointing – a high-pitched shriek of 'Torpedo –' and the day exploded. Actually number three hold, the high-octane in it, a solid *thump* and standard-sized eruption before the truly *colossal* one: sound and flame, huge upshoot of flame, sky and surroundings black, fire-streaked, hatch-covers and pit-props in an upward avalanche, the other bridge-wing and forepart of the wheelhouse shattered and on fire. Andy – well, God knew what, *he* didn't.

15

Finally: and thank God weeks ahead of the best he'd been able to promise her at the outset. He'd said – could hear it like an echo in his skull – 'Back in ten weeks, maybe, I'll call as soon as we get in.' Over the phone, that had been, before she'd implored him to rush over there. But in the first days of August – when ten weeks would have taken you to the end of September, or even the start of October, for Pete's sake: and here you were now, 8th September, not even *six* weeks later. Cutting out Cuba had been the big thing, of course. Actually, he *thought* he'd told her he might be away ten or *twelve* weeks; might have when he'd been in Newcastle. But at the beginning of August she'd been two months gone, she'd said. *Would* have been, the timing of it, the previous visit, and adding twelve weeks, three months, to that – well, crikey, wouldn't have been much of a secret by *that* time. OK, she'd have known for some while now that she wasn't going to have to sit it out quite that long – she'd have had his letters from New York – but to start with, hadn't she been damn brave?

And must have been worrying about it for at least a month before she'd mentioned it. As she'd explained it, not being absolutely certain at that stage and not wanting to distract him from his studies.

Well, she *was* brave. Brave as a little brown-eyed lioness. One had known that from the start, from that bad time in the *PollyAnna* – on top of all she'd been through in the *Glauchau* and the sinking of her uncle's *Cheviot Hills*. Which had been something else, of course, a more overt, semi-public kind of bravery. This kind now – alone, all of it locked up inside her, no-one she could even whisper to about it, relying totally on *him*, and at such a distance and isolation relying not only on the promise of ten weeks or twelve but on *Quilla* making it back at all, when so many hadn't and still weren't, as every Tynesider as well as Clydesider or Merseysider knew damn well. And OK, it would be bad enough for her in the future too, for as long as this business lasted, but it would never be as bad as these past weeks must have been. She'd never forget it, and you'd better not either.

Cold . . .

Having told Chief Verity, 'It's cold, all right.' Or some such snappy answer. Bumpy as well as cold. Still wet through, despite having shifted into dry clothes. Soaked, and crashing around. Time to try again now, though – put another shilling in. All right, all right. Hands frozen, was the trouble now, more thumbs than fingers. But hearing it now as well as feeling it, the jolting around. Not unlike it had been earlier, on the raft with the dead trimmer, if that was what he'd been. Might not: a lot of trimmers were scrawny bastards, not man-mountains, despite the work they did. Could have been a greaser, or even AB, and whatever he was, he'd have gone down as soon as his lungs had filled, come back up when the gas expanded and forced the water out, sunk again for good a day or two later. It had certainly been better than leaving him in the raft to rot. Like that crowd in the boat they'd come across on the way from Cape Town to Monte Video in the old *PollyAnna*, vicinity of Tristan de Cunha, when the Old Man had sent him in the jolly-boat to see whether any of the people in it were alive, or if there were any clues to their origins – which there had not been, only men who'd been dead a long time, bled as long as there'd been blood still in them – in that heat, and having attracted the attentions of gulls, putrefying.

One's introduction to war, you might call it. Or as that bastard Halloran had put it afterwards, 'Another memory to treasure.'

'Seems he's breathing proper now. Must 'a done it right, Stoney.'

Distractions one *didn't* want, or for that matter understand. All that mattered was getting through to Julia, whose line seemed permanently engaged. He had enough shilling pieces in his pocket for a good long talk, had made sure of that, told himself back in Halifax when daydreaming of this moment to be sure of having plenty.

But Christ *almighty* –

'He's comin' round. Alleluia, fellers, he *is*, he's bloody comin' round!'

'Mind my fuckin' arm!'

More a whine than a voice, that one, but something familiar about it. Andy got his tongue and lips to move, respond, react to something that couldn't be real, must have been part of some other dream – asking, although in doubt there'd be anyone to hear him, '*Who's* coming round?'

A laugh – somewhat nasal, *not* familiar. But from the first one, 'By the sound of it, *you* are, sir. We pumped you out – me an' Stone 'ere –'

'Who's Stone?'

Behind the question, a flash of memory – image of that *giant* flash, like a vision of lightning and thunder at its very source and a volcano spewing timber. But for real ... Hearing now – echo of it, of what *had been* said – 'Loader, sir – gun's crew, Stone, OS? I'm Fellaby, sir – carpenter.'

'Fellaby. Well ...' Then the sounds and motion, and a further leap of consciousness: 'On some raft?'

In sunshine, at that.

No call to Julia, then. No reality in *that*. Would be, but not yet. Please, bloody have to be ...

'How'd this come about?'

'Well – U-boat, likely –'

'I meant how come we're on this raft?'

'See, when she split open –'

U-boat might still be hanging round. Except no reason it should be, really. Even to have been there in the first place: but *now* – no, couldn't be.

Julia'd have to hold on a little longer. Thank God, had never told her 8th September or any other actual date: and not knowing anything about *this*, obviously – well, few days, or even a week, she'd be OK. Might have told her middle of the month, something of that sort, but –

'Sorry, Fellaby, missed that.'

'Sir?'

'Didn't hear what you were telling me. How many of us on this?'

'Ah. Five. You, me, Stone, RO/2 Newton and Bayliss 'ere. His arm's broke – Bayliss's that is, but –'

'Goes on about it like he 'as been, I'll break the other for 'im.'

Stone had said that. Fellaby adding, 'But Mr Newton's worse off than what Bayliss is. That arm looks bad enough, but . . .'

But Newton was – something or other . . .

He hadn't caught it. There was a lot of noise and rocking around. Getting himself up – or half up – telling himself to stop asking questions, look and bloody see. Sitting now, looking around at them all, hanging on as the thing bucked and tipped, throwing itself about. Fellaby and Stone both grasping paddles as if they might be weapons, not doing any paddling. Well, paddle *where*, except round in circles? Plenty of the wet, cold stuff coming over: he thought he remembered the wind had been rising. Mightn't be all that much stronger now, though the difference was that you were *in* the bloody stuff, and rafts weren't built for comfort. He knew Fellaby well enough – one of *Quilla*'s personalities, a Mancunian, thirty-ish, had a wife and child – but Stone less well, except

255

as the gun loader, a smallish man, mid-twenties, with flat
eyes and a set of jaw, slit of a mouth that gave him the
look of a bull-terrier. Someone had said he had a tempera-
ment to match, a tendency to lash out when provoked.
He'd nodded to both of them, was looking now at the
Marconi man, Newton, with his pale eyes – shut now –
and white face, ginger sideboards. In fact more than sideboards, he might have decided to grow a beard.

'He asleep?'

'Conscious a while back, gone off again. Got a knock
on the head, he said, that and couldn't move his neck.'

'Got knocked on mine too, I think. Hurts, anyway. I
was dreaming – until you spoke, thought we'd got back
– Clyde . . . Bayliss, which arm is it?'

Stirring enough to point at the left one, its elbow.
'Here. It's no joke, no matter what Stone reckons. Pit-
prop, I reckon – when I went in, landed on it like, less
broke than smashed I'd say, bloody agony and that's the
truth!'

Fellaby said, 'Pit-props did for them as was in the boat.
Bloody wonder *we* come through, raining great lumps of
timber!'

'D'you mean the second boat from the *Garthsnaid*?'

'One we was makin' for when she went up, yeah.'

'Pit-props smashed down on them?'

'Smashed-up the boat an' all. Never seen nothin' like
it. Me an' Stone got to what was left of it – an' them. We
got this raft away port side aft, see. Bayliss wasn't stayin',
he went in over the stern – landed on whatever it might've
been, screaming like a stuck pig when we got to him.
Then we was paddling around when we found – well, Mr
Newton there first, then you, sir. You was face-down in it
– could've been dead, but –'

'Thanks to you I'm not.'

He decided not to say anything about damage to his
head, something or other having belted him quite hard
on the back of it – back and top. Blame *that* on a pit-
prop, maybe? Putting a hand up gingerly: finding no

wound, only extreme sensitivity, leaving it. Thinking of the Norwegians – who'd have been better left in their boat, as would the Dutch and the *Garthsnaids*. Realising then that both Fellaby and Stone were watching the sea all the time, presumably for bodies – swimmers, floaters: *could* still be swimmers, he thought, the water was cold but not Arctic cold. Depending on how long they'd been in it, and their state when they went in. In fact, coming out of that holocaust, as far as one remembered it, as well as what Fellaby had said about a rain of pit-props, you'd guess nobody'd have lived even minutes. Miracle that as many as five had.

The blow he'd taken to the back of his head couldn't have been a falling pit-prop. Wouldn't have *had* a head.

And as for a whole shower of them: bloody terrifying . . .

The mind drifted, went off at tangents. Thinking of the convoy and that escorts were supposed to be joining it tonight, and what might be the Commodore's likely reaction to *Quilla*'s non-appearance. In practical terms, he thought, there'd be none at all. He still had two-thirds of a convoy on his hands and the duty of getting as much of it as possible into UK ports. He'd be sorry, that was all, anxious for them. What more could you expect?

Change of subject: the U-boat that had done it *might* have been using the two boats with their easily-spotted red sails as stalking-horses, on the off-chance of a rescue attempt? In which case, would by now have gone on its way? Or might have been on passage, purely by chance happened on *Quilla*?

That was the more likely answer, he thought. No reason they'd have expected a rescue ship. Who'd even *heard* of rescue ships?

Or coming up the convoy's track to become a shadower or take over from a shadower already there?

Fellaby said, 'They was a fine lot, was the *Quillas*.'

'Certainly were.'

'Good a crowd as ever I sailed with.'

257

'Yeah.' Stone nodding, flat eyes scanning the sea around them. 'Yeah.' A scowl. 'Don't make no fucking sense.'

'Doesn't, does it.' Pushing himself up for a longer view of empty, tumbling ocean, he amended that. 'Except we were getting a lot of blokes inboard, you know, *they* weren't complaining.'

'And likely ain't now.'

Ignoring that. But make a list of the Quillas, he thought, remember them. All your damn life, remember them. Remember all of this, every detail that isn't actually sickening, to tell Julia. And tell *all* of it to the old man, let him know how right he was a couple of years ago.

His watch had stopped at 1029. When he'd gone into the sea, he supposed. Maybe half a minute after that, when its works had flooded. But how long ago all of that might have been . . .

Noon now?

Sun in and out of cloud, which was sparser now than it had been then. *Could* be noon, or thereabouts. They hadn't said how long after the torpedoing they'd found him and fished him out, but it couldn't have been long or he'd have drowned. Had been face-down, Fellaby had said, presumably more or less submerged, wouldn't have been long before he'd have filled up and gone down. But then again, how long he'd lain unconscious since they'd pulled him out . . .

He asked Fellaby, 'How long would you say since she blew up?'

'Might be – hour?'

'What I guessed. Hour, hour and a half.' He tapped his wristwatch. 'Stopped, of course.' It had cost him five bob in Marks and Spencer's in Glasgow and had a luminous dial – black dial, green figures. If you called it noon now, anyway – well, if they'd turned back at 0930, as had been his advice to the Old Man, at fourteen and three-quarter knots they'd have been nearly forty miles east of here by now. And a lot of men who were now dead would be alive. Not that you'd blame the Old Man for that: his reasons for holding on had been to save as many lives as possible. Having got into the thick of it, what you might call the rich pickings, and wanting to justify the risk he'd accepted back in Halifax.

But old Harve, for one. And young Waller. Who would *not* be sending Samantha any Christmas cards. No more than one would oneself, come to that, since her aunt's name and address had been in his panic-bag.

Maybe just as well.

Address was Exeter, anyway. Name, no recollection whatever. Might come back, of course, at some later stage.

Newton's eyes were still shut but his mouth had dropped open.

Leaning forward to look more closely: Fellaby seeing him do it, and grimacing. 'Not too good, sir.'

'No.'

'Looks dead, from 'ere.' Stone had said that. He'd been on his feet, balancing against the raft's erratic motion while gazing round: from time to time you did need the longer view, not only for the obvious practical purposes, but as if it offered some kind of escape. Crouching again now though, staring at Bayliss, who'd groaned and said, 'Wish *I* was.' Fellaby shouting at him, 'No you don't, boy! Bloody daft, that kind o' talk!' Newton did seem not to be breathing, though. Andy crawled to him and squatted, felt for a heartbeat and couldn't find one. Wrist, then, for a pulse.

No pulse.

'Not a spark.'

'You sure, sir?'

'Afraid so.'

'Put him over then, should we?'

'Well . . .'

Bayliss had his head back and his eyes shut, face running with sweat. They were all soaking wet, naturally, but that was sweat, not least from the way it shone. Like glycerine, welling from the narrow forehead and around the eyes. The question in Andy's mind meanwhile, relating to Fellaby's proposal, wasn't why, what for, so much as *why not*. It wasn't doing Newton any good to keep him with them: his body took up space, and mightn't be the best thing for morale. Especially in the case of Bayliss, whose morale wasn't all that outstanding anyway. All right, so he was in pain – with a smashed elbow and constant, quite violent movement, maybe excruciating pain. If so, one had to admit he wasn't doing at all badly. Wasn't for instance screaming, as he might have been. Scared of Stone, who obviously had it in for him? If he did break down, lose control, Stone wasn't likely to give him much rope, you could have *real* trouble on your hands.

As distinct from what? A small spot of it?

Not, in any case, that ditching Newton's body was going to stop any of that happening. Hadn't even had two hours of it, as yet.

Fellaby suggested, 'After dark, maybe?'

Thinking about *that* now. The man was dead, burial at sea nothing out of the ordinary for seamen, so why funk it?

Hadn't earlier on. Hadn't hesitated for one second with that stranger. Maybe that was the difference, that this one had been a shipmate? But also the thought of doing it under the eyes of this close group, whose own lives were clearly on the line?

That was unquestionable. No prospect whatsoever of rescue, no fresh water, no food, and sea conditions more likely to worsen than to improve. One's brain might be working erratically, in a somehow damaged head – skull, maybe? – and other shock effects, but one might say with some reason that apart from being alive *at this moment*, one wasn't that much better off than all the rest of them.

Poor girl. Didn't bear thinking about. Poor *darling* girl.

So don't give up. No bloody *right* to give up or even think of giving up.

He'd begun – to Fellaby – 'I don't know . . .' and Bayliss cut in – surprisingly in touch with what they'd been contemplating – 'I'll go over with him. I will. Fucking mean it, I –'

'*Hell* you will. Listen, Bayliss – you may not realise it, but you're doing well. Just stick to it, man. They'll be coming for us, don't think they won't, Commodore'll send the sloop, I'd guess, when we don't rejoin as he's expecting. He knows within a mile or two where we'd be, and two things a sloop has which a corvette may not – I'm not certain of that, but a corvette's smaller – one's the range she'd need, and the other's a doctor. I'd guess soon after first light tomorrow – or early forenoon maybe. All right, means sticking it through the night, but you can do it, you're showing us right now you've the guts –'

'Fuckin' *agony*'s all I got. You don't know the *half* –'

'We do, lad. Even Stone 'ere –'

'Fuck 'im. *Fuck* 'im.'

Eyes wide open for a second, then he slumped. Head back, and breathing in short gasps through his open mouth. The three of them watching him but seeing no further change, only the fact he'd passed out – and for the time being, some relief in that. Fellaby meeting Andy's eyes then, nodding towards Newton, and a gesture miming the act of putting him over. Andy nodded. Stone moved as if to help but they didn't need him, did it between the two of them.

Given pen and paper, tell her something like *With you in a matter of days, my darling. I swear it. Only a matter of sitting it out, we* will *be picked up – not necessarily by any sloop, that was only the first thing came into my head, giving the lad here something to hold on to. Right away what he needs is morphine. But the last thing the Commodore'd think of would be to deprive himself of any part of the escort he should have had days ago. In any case, he'd have no authority to detach any one of them, his job's to run the convoy in collaboration with the escort force commander. Sure, he was an admiral in the Royal Navy, but he's a commodore in the RNR now, can't order White Ensign ships around. There'll be other escorts though, other convoys, even long-range patrols by Sunderland aircraft – rare enough, but one's heard they come out this sort of distance, twenty degrees west or thereabouts, survivors in boats and rafts do get spotted and ships sent to pick them up. OK, after a while maybe, might get worse before we're out of it. Well, it* will. *Could even be a week or more. Just hope to God it won't come to the worst with Bayliss. Imagine it, an elbow actually crushed – who wouldn't moan? All I've got's a pain in my head, which isn't helped by the way the raft's throwing itself around. Bayliss's problem too, poor devil, and his is a lot worse than mine. The fact is I was very, very lucky, could have had my face burnt off, been blinded too. When number three went up I was trying to get a sunsight, had the sextant up in both hands in front of my face, must anyway have been facing away from that great rush of flame. Although it's a fact I saw it. Anyway, that's how I recall it, all I know. One thing, my darling, is although I've got off lightly, when we're home I may need attention to the old nut – unless it's mended itself by then, which it may well have done. After all, this only happened a couple of hours ago. And a great thing – ill-wind thing, you might call it – is I'll be entitled to survivors' leave, ought to be around long enough to see out the period of reading banns, getting spliced and even – dare I say it – having a bit of a honeymoon somewhere or other. Oh, I do love you so . . .*

'Mr Holt, sir!'

'Uh?'

'You're not goin' to credit this, sir!'

'What? Oh – Fellaby –'

'Mr Holt – long as they *see* us – and she's bearing down on us all right –'

'Long as who *what?*'

'The other one on the rescue lark, sir – name like *Orlia*, or –'

'*Aurelia*. Sixty miles east by now.'

'Where you're wrong, sir. She's – mile, maybe two mile –'

Dizzy again – although a better word might be 'bleary' – and with it, this weird feeling of none of it being real. He'd joined Fellaby and Stone waving and shouting – not easy, keeping your balance upright on the raft with so much movement on it, but scared stiff you'd not be seen – *obviously* wouldn't be heard, but still yelling – *expecting* her to turn away, the rather squat, squarish bow-on view of her at any moment begin to broaden as she swung, zigzagging or simply altering away. Knowing how tricky spotting boats even with sails on them could be, let alone this thing, and only too well aware that if you missed this chance, mightn't get another.

Not for a week, someone had said. And not a hope in hell you'd survive a week. So Julia, then –

He'd sat down. Head pain really quite bad at that stage. Was sitting, following events only through Fellaby's excited commentary as the *Aurelia* cut her speed and gave them a toot on her Willet-Bruce.

If that was what she had. Steam-whistle, or siren. Stopping anyway, turning across the weather to provide a lee, Fellaby and Stone by this time busy with the paddles.

Happening?

OK, now – get yourself together . . .

It was the *Aurelia*, all right. Men all over her decks and bridge-wings, and a bunch waving from her main deck starboard-side rail where there'd be scrambling nets. All still quite hard to believe in. Distinct possibility you'd wake and find it was some kind of mirage – a scene you might have dreamed-up, given half a chance – at least until a heaving-line came arcing across the gap of partly sheltered but still lively sea and fell close enough for him, Andy, to grab, the other two dropping their paddles, chuckling like maniacs, taking the line over from him, and Bayliss saying weakly, 'You was right then. Can't believe it, 'ardly.'

What he'd said about rescue by a sloop: referring to that, presumably. He nodded to him, told him, 'See, you did stick it out. Well done.' A mental note to suggest they gave him morphine double-quick. His own head seemed to have cleared again, and he could see it wasn't going to be easy for Bayliss on the net. Looked like they'd lashed a second net to the bottom of the top one, the *Aurelia* having about twice the freeboard old *Quilla*'d had. Wasn't going to be *at all* easy for young Bayliss, no matter how many were on the net to help. Half a dozen were clambering down it, others watching from the rail, calling jocular things like get a move on, boys, put some bloody muscle in it! And Fellaby yelling back at them, 'Begun to think you was never coming!' Getting in close now, though, close enough to recognise the master watching from the bridge-wing – big man with a beard whom they'd met at the conference. He himself hauling Bayliss up by his good arm: 'Let's start you over first', Bayliss doubled over, whimpering, and Fellaby shouting to the reception party, 'Smashed elbow on this one, go careful with 'im!' Stone helped with getting Bayliss over – hurting him, obviously, but no other way to do it – Fellaby then offering, 'Give you a hand, sir?' but he waved him on: 'Go on. And you, Stone.'

Thinking, what if you find you can't? More or less daring himself to try . . . Then somehow he was on the thing and climbing.

The mate, name of Bennett, thin-faced and hard-eyed, cap aslant on the back of his head, stared at him unbelievingly. Andy had introduced himself, Bennett had asked how did they happen to be on their own, where *Quilla*'s boats might be, and he'd told him, 'We're all there is.'

'No boats?'

'No. She blew up. With a whole crowd on board we'd rescued.'

'Christ. *Christ.*' He looked at the man beside him:

second officer, who'd been at the conference in Halifax but seemed not to know *him*. Thickset, with a wide, strong-boned face. Bennett telling him – Brice, his name was – 'Tell the Old Man, no other survivors. I'll be up there in a minute.' To Andy then: 'Hell, U-boat obviously –'

'Right. We were stopping for another boat-load –'

'You said *blew up?*'

'We had high-octane petrol in drums in three lower holds with ammo on it. Took it on in New York, no option – the Ministry, and the STO. Old Man didn't like it – who would – but –'

'And you were hit in one of those lower holds?'

'In number three. I was in a bridge-wing getting a shot at the sun, and she just – exploded. Oh, a cadet on monkey island spotted the track a second before the thing hit. I heard him yell, he was pointing, but – all just in seconds. Torpedoes run some distance ahead of their tracks, don't they . . . Anyway, I must've been blown overboard: the guys on the raft found me floating face-down and hauled me out. Look, one thing – young assistant cook name of Bayliss, smashed his elbow, thinks he landed on a pit-prop. Anyway he's really suffering. If you had morphine to spare –'

'Sawyer – hear that? See to it, I'll be down in a jiffy.' Turning back: 'Are the rest of you all right? I can only offer you a cot in the saloon, cabins are all full, including deck-space.'

'A cot in your saloon'd be fine.'

'And sustenance, of course. Soup to start with. And – yeah, medication. Mind coming up top a minute first, brief word with the Old Man?'

'I'd like to. I met him in Halifax, at the conference. How come you aren't halfway back to the convoy? I mean, thank God you aren't, but –'

'We kept seeing more boats. One hundred and thirty survivors on board, would you believe it? Then we did start back, heard this *fucking* great bang – which you've now explained – hour and a half ago, maybe –'

'Taking a heck of a chance. Won't come anywhere near making the 1900 rendezvous.'

'The Old Man guessed it could only be your *Barranquilla*. Felt he'd no choice.'

'God bless him.'

'Between you and me, Holt, he's a rumbustious old sod, but bloody marvellous in his way. Not all that amenable to – you know, orders and procedures. Except his own, of course.'

'Far as *I'm* concerned –'

'Come on.'

The *Aurelia* was turning east, he noticed, would no doubt be working up to – whatever, fourteen knots or probably more. Following Bennett in through a weather door and up by a dual ladderway on the centre-line: less ladderway in fact than staircase – carpet on its treads, for Pete's sake. Giddiness returning now in waves . . . Three decks in all, to reach bridge level, and entering it from the rear, passing the entrance to a proper chartroom. Wide bridge with a modern layout, and in its forefront several men with glasses up, the heavily-built master lowering his as Bennett called to him, 'Second officer Holt, sir. *Barranquilla.*'

'Poor damn *Barranquilla.*' A hand out to him: Andy remembering at that moment that his name was Coverdale. 'Damn sorry, Holt. That captain of yours, very decent feller. Name Beale?'

'Yessir.' He'd shaken the hand. 'Nat Beale. And – well, all but four of us. Want to thank you, sir – owe you *our* lives, for sure.'

'Owe damn-all.' Peering at him. 'You said you blew up – carrying explosives, that it?'

'High-octane petrol in drums in lower holds with ammo on it. I was telling Mr Bennett –'

'All right, he can tell me. You'd best go down, get out of that wet gear, so forth.'

'Aye, sir. Thank you. Thank you *very* much.'

'One question, if you've an answer to it. With that cargo, why'd your captain say yes to the rescue job?'

266

'He didn't think it made any odds what we were carrying. Also – he told our mate this – believed in taking things as they come. Not ducking and weaving, was how he put it.'

'Suppose he'd have known what he meant by that?'

'Well.' A shrug. Remembering old Harve's grey face and tired eyes, telling it and clearly *not* understanding it or in agreement with it. Andy's own short answer to it being that the Old Man had counted on his chances of bringing her through, and what else mattered?

He'd nodded. 'I think I get it, sir.'

'Good for you, then. Explain it to me some other time.' A nod to Bennett. 'See he has what he needs.'

Hadn't asked him about prospects of rejoining the convoy, but guessed he'd make his best speed to rejoin, might hope to come up with them around first light tomorrow. With of course the possibility of further U-boat activity during the dark hours: and touch wood staying clear of that, despite being to all intents and purposes a straggler, with all the attendant hazards.

He asked the cadet who'd shown him to his cot and blankets and was going to take his wet clothes to dry in the engine room, 'What's this steamer's best speed, flat out?'

'Close on fifteen, sir. Fourteen point eight five, something like.'

'Spitting distance of being routed independently, then?'

'Suppose so . . . Get you some soup, shall I?'

'If that's what I can smell – yes, please.'

This end of the saloon had been curtained-off with a tarpaulin slung from the deckhead: there were other bodies humped on cots or donkeys' breakfasts, and a lot of coming and going on the tarpaulin's other side. The cadet told him, 'It's got kidney in it. Don't know what else.'

'Smells marvellous. What's the time now?'

'About three, sir.' A pause while checking, then, 'Three-ten. Is soup in a mug all right?'

'Perfect.' They had what Harve had called the 'hotel management' well organised. Bayliss had been given morphine and passed out again, so Brice – second mate – had told him. His own priorities now were (a) to get some of that good-smelling soup inside him, and (b) sleep, rest his head.

Ten past three, the lad had said. Quarter-past now, maybe. Three and a quarter hours since *Quilla* had blown up. So much having happened in that space of time that it could have been a month. One of the images in mind as he started on his soup – wrapped in a blanket – was of the shattered forefront of *Quilla*'s wheelhouse and the other bridge-wing starting into flame, and inside there the Old Man, Selby, Waller, Dixon. Images in one's brain like charred snapshots, vestiges of friends who only a month ago had been strangers. Stone had been right, none of it made sense.

Sounds of knives and forks at work, and men's voices. Behind that, the humming of the ship's diesels, regular slamming of her pitching. Memory kicking in then: she'd be heading east or as near east as made no difference, and unless the weather had changed dramatically she'd have it all astern. Getting the feel of it now: weather hadn't changed, not in that respect. The lighting was dim on this side of the tarpaulin, brighter the other side where they were eating. Turning his head with difficulty – stiff neck – he saw that two of the other four cots were empty, and that on one of the others a man was sitting, bald head resting on forearms on raised knees.

Andy raised a hand in greeting. 'Hello there.'

'Ach. You wake.' Pointing. 'Some boy is bringing you your clothes.'

It had sounded like 'clothses'. Foreign accent, maybe Dutch. There'd been several Dutch ships in the convoy, although for the moment he didn't remember any of their names. But someone had indeed brought his clothes – at least, some of them: shirt, trousers, sweater, underpants and socks; no reefer jacket and no shoes. Items presumably not dry yet. And 'some boy' he guessed meaning a junior steward, galley-boy, whatever.

'You a Dutchman?'

'Belge. Motor vessel *Saint Luc*. I was her mate.'

'Many of you saved?'

'Sadly, not so many.'

'Nor of mine. I was second of the *Barranquilla*. Me and three others – and we had a lot of survivors on board. Maybe not as many as in this ship, but –'

'I think is your name Holt?'

'How'd you know that?'

'Was here also a person who look for you. You sleeping, he say coming back ozzer time.'

Bennett, he thought, or Brice. Or even Fellaby. Could have been something about Bayliss. Might well have been Fellaby, he thought. He struggled up, reached for his clothes, thinking he'd maybe get something to eat. The soup *had* been good, but he'd suddenly felt too tired to finish, put it down on the deck before he dropped it.

Gone now. That cadet would probably have taken it. Or whoever had brought his clothes. Head still bloody hurting. Dressing, he asked the Belgian, 'D'you know what time it is?'

'I think per'aps nine o'clock. I was having to eat at eight-thirty. Baked beans, was it.'

Nine. So he'd got his head down six hours ago. Baked beans would be fine, and tea. They'd have tea all right. But pee first. If I can remember where the washplace is. On his feet, he tried, '*Au revoir, Monsieur.*'

A smile: 'So long. I mention, however, I am Flemish, French my second language. I am from Antwerp, it so 'appens.'

'Family?'

'Wife and little boy – *still* in Antwerp.'

'Where Germans are now.'

'Exactly.'

'Must be tough.'

'That is one way to say it. You too young to be married yet, I think?'

'I have a girl I'm *going* to marry.'

'And where she?'

'Newcastle. Tyneside.'

'I am there many times!'

'Well. Talk again later, eh?'

He found the washplace easily enough. Rather more sumptuous than *Quilla*'s. Washing his hands and face, unwisely allowing a vision of her interior as it might be now into his throbbing head. Twelve hundred fathoms down, ruptured, filled, bodies you'd have recognised and a lot you wouldn't. The mind shut down, shut it out, seeing himself in the mirror above the steel basin and recoiling from that too: bruised, dirty, crazy-looking, needing a shave, eyes like pink slits.

Then another moving into frame behind it.

'Andy Holt . . .'

Dick Carr: also unshaven but otherwise much as always. You'd never have thought he could have been any close relation of Julia's.

'Well, Dick.'

Remembering having seen the *Blackheddon Hills* hit, and having wondered whether she might float on the buoyancy of her timber. He showed him his wet hands, as a reason not to shake. 'Glad you made it.' Actually *was*, for Julia's sake. 'I saw you hit and go on fire.'

'Fire didn't last, and we got three of the four boats away. Very sorry for you and your *Barranquilla*. Brice, second mate, told me. I says not a man by name of Holt by any chance, and –'

'All a toss-up, isn't it. But Julia'll still have a husband.' He noticed a flinch, and went on, 'Where've they put you?'

Blank look: thinking about what Andy had just said,

no doubt – said purposefully, the message being take it or bloody leave it. He prompted, 'Cabin, or what?'

'Cabin, one deck up – on a donkey's breakfast. Come looking for you, Brice told me where, and that frog –'

'Belgian. Most of your people got away, eh?'

'Only lost seven. She was a good while settling . . . Want to talk to you, Andy.'

'About me and Julia?'

'Well – about her, yes. Last time –'

'In St John you weren't keen to.'

'Plain truth is I couldn't, and – Christ, wish I didn't have to now. Then – that *fucking* awful morning – look, I'm *sorry*, how it must have seemed to you –'

'Didn't much matter. I was simply *telling* you, not asking your damn blessing.'

'Not the right place for this, is it.' Looking around: basins, urinals, lavatories, and open to interruption at any time. Andy suggested, 'Try in the saloon, if you like. Where I was bound, in search of food. *Why* couldn't you talk at St John?'

'Couldn't have – found the words, like. I'd only heard that morning. A Friday – right, twenty-third?'

'Heard *what?*'

But seeing it then. Sudden glimpse of the unthinkable.

'She was killed, Andy. She and her Mum. August fifteenth, Gerries hit Tyneside, more than a hundred bombers with a big screen of fighters. Got this from my brother Garry, he'd docked the day before in his old *Redheugh*. Two letters in one mail, t'other from our ma. Well – one stick of bombs went miles off-target – docks, of course – hit their road, and a direct one on the house, and – finish, no more 'n a heap of rubble. See, we got into St John from Sydney Cape Breton two days before you came. Twenty-first, you got in twenty-third. No mail at Sydney, but they'd written – oh, sixteenth, air-letters, in a mail as come that Friday. Ma's was saying – well, they'd gone – plain and simple, not much else, but Garry's

271

with stuff in it from the paper or maybe the BBC, how the RAF was waiting for 'em, shot down thirty at hardly no cost at all –'

'Can't see that as having much to do with it, tell you the truth.'

'*Part* of the story as it come though, see –'

'Damn-all to do with Julia or me.' Why wasn't he on his knees, why just semi-collapsed against a steam-wet bulkhead? 'Christ all bloody mighty . . .'

He'd got into the saloon at some time after ten pm – alone, thank God, having requested Dick not to hang around and go on and bloody on about it – and had not only baked beans on toast but soya links as well. A link being a sort of skinless sausage which he happened to like, although a lot of people didn't. He also drank two mugs of strong, dark tea, and managed not to weep again.

No-one had seen that anyway.

Had told Dick, when he'd apologised again for that extraordinary carry-on in St John, that he understood, didn't blame him. It was a lie, he'd only said it – well, for *her* sake, putting the thing to rest between him and Dick, whom one saw now as a peculiar, mixed-up character with child-like weaknesses behind a rough-neck front.

A thought that strangely enough was helping a little was that it would have been worse for her if it had been him who'd died – if she'd been alive, and he'd drowned before they got him in the raft for instance, leaving her on her own to face all *that* discordant music. For all her guts, it would have been truly hellish for her, a long-lasting hell. The thing he'd had in mind throughout recent weeks, an *imperative* to survive.

Which no longer applied. Wouldn't pretend disinterest in survival, but didn't need to be as fixated on it as one had been.

Had been dozing, and now woken or half-woken to a chorus of snores from the tarpaulin's other side. Had dreamt of her, also of his parents. Awake now, thinking of his sister Annabel, the desirability of contacting her as soon as possible, asking her to destroy his letter and forget it all. See Dick's mother too – in case there'd been suspicions or Julia had told them, make certain the old woman knew they'd intended marrying. Otherwise – well, having taken soundings, would have called to express – what did they call it – sympathy.

Sympathy, God's sake . . .

Let her have died without knowing a thing about it, believing I'd be back next week?

Brice woke him. Having come to the saloon for coffee before going up to take over the middle watch. Time by the clock on the bulkhead – eleven-forty. He was getting his coffee from the pantry, called to Andy, 'Bring you one, shall I?'

'Well – thanks. Hell, I'll –'

'No, stay where you are. Take sugar?'

'Please. One spoon.' Condensed milk, of course. Brice said when joining him with the mugs, 'Must be horrible, losing all your mates. I'm sorry, very sorry.'

He nodded. 'It's not – good . . . But thanks, this'll do me a power of good.'

'Interferes with sleep, though – which could be what you need most?'

'Been doing nothing else. Half the day, and on and off all evening. Had about enough of it. Cheers. How long since you took your mate's ticket?'

'So long that I'm now due to take my master's. After this trip, I'm booked in to the Nautical College for it. How about you?'

'Only took my mate's this summer.'

'Yeah. Course. You were third in your *PollyAnna* when you got that bunch out of the German prison-ship – correct?'

'You know about *that*?'

'Your Old Man in the *Barranquilla* reminded ours of it

273

on their way back from the conference. The famous Andy Holt, eh?'

'Sooner forget it, tell you the truth. I was there, did what I was told, that's all.'

'Made headlines, didn't it. I'd better swallow this down and get along. Going to turn in when you've drunk yours?'

Gulping his own down, hot as it was. Andy moved his head; it was better than it had been, but he knew better than to shake it. Telling Brice, 'No point. Wouldn't sleep.'

'Want something to read, then?'

'Uh-huh. Tell you what, though – as you're going up, might I tag along, have a decko at the chart?'

'Well, if you feel up to it –'

'Captain won't object?'

'Hell, no, he'll be glad to see you on your feet.'

The mate, Bennett, had taken a set of stars at about 1900, since when they'd been steering east with wind and sea astern, now at midnight had covered seventy-four miles by log since that fix, in other words were making-good as near as damnit fifteen knots.

'Convoy should be – here.' Brice, with a pencil-tip. 'So another hour like this, then we reduce to twelve knots, to stay this distance astern of 'em. First light, all things being equal, crack on speed again to close up.'

'And come up with 'em by eight, nine, thereabouts.'

'As you say. Have to leave you now, though – having a watch to keep. Unless you'd like a spell in the wheelhouse with us?'

'Well – might lend a hand as lookout?'

'Come on, then. Here –'

Spare pair of binoculars.

'Fine. Thanks.'

'Glutton for punishment, eh?'

'It's no punishment.'

Never would be, either. In fact compared to sitting down there doing bugger-all except thinking and trying

274

not to think: well, your life, what you were *for* – serving at least *some* purpose. Dark, wide bridge – wider than *Quilla*'s, though not as deep, on account of the chartroom taking up as much space as it did – the ship juddering as she pitched, thrum of her machinery, creaking of steel and timber and wire stays. Quartermaster a stooped, thin figure at the wheel dead-centre, a cadet lowering his glasses to look round at them, captain a dark bulk in the port fore corner. Brice calling to him, 'Brought Holt up with me, sir, extra lookout, says he's had as much shuteye as he can stand.'

'Good man. Good man.'

The starboard for'ard corner had no occupant, so he put himself there, put the glasses up: vision in mind of the convoy making its eleven knots at that distance ahead, quite possibly with U-boats stalking or shadowing, so if you saw one it would be surfaced and stern-to, doubtless making *more* than eleven knots. Black, white-streaked sea, dark overhead with a patch or two of stars. *Aurelia*'s beam and forepart down there was noticeably broader than *Quilla*'s, blunter for'ard and the foremast shorter, sturdier. Andy reflecting, as he lowered the borrowed glasses to polish their front lenses, that he now lacked glasses of his own, lacked also a sextant, as well as uniform and other gear, all of which would have to be replaced. Some way to start married life, this would have been. Saving all one's pennies, and having to borrow more – advance of pay from owners, probably – in order to acquire such basic necessities. Let alone a ring and whatever else, and the cost of even a few days' stingy honeymoon. All that other stuff you'd need before you could sign on as second mate wherever a job might be offering.

There'd be one going here in the *Aurelia*, for instance, with Brice going back to school. Unless her captain had someone else in mind, which he might well have. The timing mightn't work out too well either. But there'd be berths on offer, all right. Might be in one's best interests to stay with the same owners – especially needing an advance.

Don't think about it now, though. For the time being just keep your bloody eyes peeled, help to get this one home.

Postscript

The *Aurelia* would have got back all right. She'd have had to, if only because we haven't finished yet with Andy Holt. Either in convoy or solo she'd have made it into the Clyde in late afternoon on 8th September.

Evacuation of children from Britain to North America was stopped after the sinking of the SS *City of Benares* on 17th September. Only thirteen of the ninety children on board were saved, six of them after spending a week in a lifeboat in the care of a Miss Cornish. The boat was eventually spotted by a Sunderland of the RAF's Coastal Command, which guided a destroyer to it, and the *City of Benares*'s fourth officer, Mr Cooper, who was in charge of the boat, stated in his report that all the children were in good form, having looked on the whole thing as a picnic.

Good for them. Less so for the other seventy-seven. The torpedo had hit at about ten pm, when they'd have been in their bunks.

The extraordinary practice of loading leaky drums of aviation spirit into ships' lower holds, with ammunition stowed on top of it and an improvised system of 'steam-ejection', is described by Captain R.F. McBrearty in his memoir *Seafaring '39–'45*. It was resorted to in certain North African ports, where it was applied to ships supporting the post-Alamein advance of the British 8th Army.

Once again I'd like to thank Captain I.D. Irving, FNI for his kindness in vetting the script of this novel for me, as he did with its predecessor *Westbound, Warbound.*